*   *   *

She rolled her eyes heavenward. S.   "Look at that."

"What?" Tommy turned. "Is someone wa   g us?" He checked the fraternity house windows.

"No, the moon. I read about this in the Trib. Se ' It's a crescent moon and that star hanging off the very bottom tip is Venus. They call it the Christmas Star. It's a celestial event. Some say it's the real star of Bethlehem. Venus being that huge in the western sky happens only once in thirty years. Do you realize we'll probably only see it twice in our lifetime? It's a sign."

"Of what?"

"Of how special this night is. This time is. How special we are. You and me. Together forever."

Hugging her, they gazed at the star together. "It's our star."

Tommy smiled and kissed her neck. "I can feel it blessing us. Nothing bad will ever happen to us."

Susie kissed him. "Nothing. Not ever."

Other Books by Catherine Lanigan

Dangerous Love
Elusive Love
Romancing the Stone
The Jewel of the Nile
Bound By Love
Admit Desire
Sins of Omission
Web of Deceit
A Promise Made
All or Nothing
The Way of the Wicked
At Long Last Love
Seduced
Becoming
In Love's Shadow
The Texan
Montana Bride
Tender Malice
California Moon
The Legend Makers
The Evolving Woman: Intimate Confessions
of Surviving Mr. Wrong

CATHERINE LANIGAN

THE CHRISTMAS ★ STAR

Banbury Publishing, Inc.
Chicago, IL

Printed in U.S.A.

THE CHRISTMAS STAR

Copyright© 2002 by Catherine Lanigan
Copyright© 2002 by Banbury Publishing, Inc.
Cover art copyright© 2002 by Catherine Lanigan
and Banbury Publishing, Inc.
Cover design by Paramark Inc.

ISBN: 0-9706007-2-0
Library of Congress Catalog Card Number: 2002109640

Banbury Publishing, Inc.
Chicago, Illinois

Printed in the U.S.A.

Dedication

This book is dedicated to the thousands of American souls who were lost on September 11, 2001 due to the terrorist attacks at the World Trade Center in New York and at The Pentagon. Your tragic deaths have left us sorrowful yet inexplicably aware that we are all one holy family.

And to my father, Frank J. Lanigan, World War II hero and attorney, who died on Valentine's Day, 1992 , and to my mother, Dorothy Lanigan, who together created a loving, American family.

God Bless Us, Every One.
Dickens—"The Christmas Carol"

Chapter One

July, 1965

Plunk. Thud. Plunk.

Tommy felt numb as pellets of earth fell through his fingers and clattered against his mother's sleek wood casket. His hearing muffled every sound and the people around him appeared to move in slow motion. He could see the priest's lips moving in prayer, but in Tommy's world, sound was a distant rumbling like a radio transmission from another galaxy. He didn't hear the priest's urging.

"Your turn," Father Antonio said.

Tommy stared at the priest who had baptized him, administered his first communion and confirmed him. Father Antonio had sat at their family dinner table at Easter and Christmas saying the blessing and joining in the rounds of Italian toasts that seemed to go on forever keeping hungry children from plowing into mounds of homemade pasta. Tommy knew Father Antonio as closely as his many uncles, aunts and cousins, but today, he looked at Father Antonio as if he were a stranger. Today, Tommy felt like young Ebeneezer Scrooge when his mother had died, Tommy had cut himself off from the world to protect his heart.

The entire scene was strange. It was unreal. He shouldn't be here and neither should Father Antonio. Tommy's mother was too full of life to be dead. He could not fathom where or how he would find joy again. For the twenty years of his life, Joyce Magli had been the light in Tommy's eyes and those of his father's.

To the Magli men, Joyce was the reason they got up in the morning. She made their ordinary existence an adventure of the heart.

Was it possible that it had been a year since his mother surprised him with a graduation party in the backyard with

Japanese lanterns strung through the maple trees and played Rachmaninoff's *Rhapsody on a Theme by Paganini* on the family piano? Aunt Loretta, his father's older sister, blasted Joyce for being anti-Italian.

"A Russian composer? Why not an actual Paganini? Or a Pagliacci? Everyone knows that only Italian composers have soul," Loretta questioned with obvious derision.

Joyce had ignored her. "This is my favorite. Tommy's, too." She continued playing like the concert pianist she had the talent to be, just not the education, nor the inclination.

It seemed like only last week, not last fall, that his mother had requested Father Antonio to say a High Mass to bless Tommy's initiation into the Sigma Chi fraternity. It had been a first for the priest. For Joyce Magli, it was standard operating procedure. There was nothing on this earth she wouldn't do for her son or her husband including moving heaven to make their dreams come true.

Tommy looked back at the casket.

You shouldn't be dead.

"Tommy. The rosary? You were going to put your mother's rosary on the casket," Father Antonio whispered.

Tommy blinked. He forced himself to come back to reality. He glanced at his father.

Jed turned his head slowly and stared blankly at his son. A tear fell from his eye, missed his handsome cheek and fell straight to his lapel. Tommy watched as the lone tear seeped into the polyester fabric, staining it.

Pulling the crystal beads from his pocket, Tommy kissed the crucifix and leaned over the casket. He placed the rosary on top of the two dozen pink roses his father had ordered. The aurora borealis beads glistened in the sunlight, looking like dew drops on the rose petals.

"Bye, Mom. I miss you already. So much," Tommy whispered.

The ice that had encased Tommy's exterior and had caused his senses to numb, shattered in an instant. His heart flooded with pain and longing. He'd never felt this kind of emotion that was at once piercing and sharp yet enveloped in a heavy iron-like pressure that took his breath away and promised never to ease. His future yawned before him, black, empty, eternal and devoid of joy.

All his life he'd met each day with eagerness to explore simple pleasures and gain seemingly impossible victories because he knew his mother was there to watch him grow. He won his third grade spelling bee just to see the smile on her face. He pushed himself in little league because his mother was a baseball fanatic and dreamed of his someday pitching for the Cubs. She taught him to ride his bike without training wheels. She was his Cub Scout Den Mother because if she had not volunteered, he, his neighborhood friends and two cousins had no troop with room for them. When he sat down to her piano and played with a perfect ear, she immediately found an ex-Chicago Symphony pianist who was willing to teach Tommy to play for half price as long as Joyce agreed to get Tommy to classes on time. She rode the bus with Tommy into the city on the days when Jed took the only family car to work. Tommy didn't know until years later the sacrifices Joyce had made to keep him in piano lessons. There was a reason she didn't have a new winter coat or a special Easter dress. She spent the money on Tommy.

For Tommy, his father and most of his school friends, Joyce Magli had been the center of their universe.

Now the sun was gone.

Tommy's world would never be the same.

"Amen," Tommy said with the rest of the crowd as the priest ended the last of the ritual prayers.

"The family of Joyce Magli invites you all to join them at the family home for brunch," Father Antonio said.

"Come on, son," Jed said putting his hand on Tommy's shoulder. "Your Aunt Loretta said she'd go on to the house from the church to make sure everything was ready. But you know how lost she gets in Joyce's kitchen." Jed pursed his lips together to keep them from quivering.

"Yeah, Dad. I never understood that about Aunt Loretta," Tommy said, grateful to think of something besides the emptiness inside him. "Our kitchen is so small compared to what Aunt Loretta has."

They moved carefully around the casket.

"Why is that, Dad?"

"I don't know, son. Loretta doesn't like anything she can't understand. She never understood your mother."

"Just what is her beef about Mom?"

"Nothin'. Far as I could see."

"Well, it's gotta be something," Tommy reasoned. Jed stopped when they reached the limousine. "That's the thing about family. You gotta take the good with the bad."

Tommy shook his head as his father climbed into the black limousine. "Family or no. It still all has to make sense, doesn't it?" He asked leaning inside.

Jed shrugged his shoulders. "Who ever told you that?"

Tommy smiled. "Mom."

Jed nodded thoughtfully. "She would." He glanced at the back of the driver's head. "Get in. I'll explain the meaning of jealousy to you on the way to the house."

Tommy rolled his eyes. "Now, that makes sense."

It had been ten years since Tommy had been to a Magli family funeral and at the time of his Uncle Carmine's death, Tommy had only been ten years old. He did not understand that the manner of the death itself mattered to Italians. His Uncle Carmine had died in a barroom brawl over a woman who was not his Aunt Loretta. Loretta was humiliated more than she was bereft. Her pain came not from her husband's death, but from the fact that he'd died in another woman's arms.

Because cancer had taken Joyce, Tommy expected his father's family to react with sadness and grief as most other families do when a loved one passes away. Tommy had been to other funerals. Irish ones. Greek ones. Polish ones. Protestant ones. People spoke in comforting tones to each other. Even when the moments were awkward, he noticed sincerity. In the Magli family, every funeral, every wedding and holy communion seemed to be an excuse for his Aunt Loretta to sound off against someone. Usually, she chose Joyce because she was the only "outsider".

Tommy's mother was English by heritage and Protestant when she fell in love with Guillermo Magli in high school during the war. When Tommy's father was drafted into the army, they ran away and got married. When Tommy's father returned from Normandy, a decorated war-hero, he changed his name to Jed. Aunt Loretta, Aunt Gina and Grandma Maria along with Grandpa Luigi exploded. They took his decision as a slam against the family name. They threatened disinheritance. They threatened to never speak to him again. They ranted, raved and fumed.

Jed was stoic during the onslaught. He'd been to war and back. Their tirades disintegrated into vapors when he announced simply, "Joyce is converting."

Luigi, Maria and Gina dropped their opposition, but their acceptance of Joyce was always guarded. It was Loretta who harbored bitterness like an internal warship, which she let sail at every family gathering. At the few occasions when she was exposed to Joyce's parents, Helen and Bob and Joyce's sister, Jerri, such as Tommy's baptism, his birthday parties and his graduation, Loretta ignored them all. It never occurred to her that she was missing out or that getting to know them could enhance her life.

Jed and Joyce were committed to being Americans in the new post-war world they had helped to create. They wanted their little family to be more loving, more tolerant and generally happier than the families from which they came. To that end, they did not participate in every Italian family gathering the Magli's thrust upon them.

The rest of the Magli family believed Joyce was the wedge that kept Guillermo from them.

5

The limousine pulled up in front of the little bungalow Jed had built only a few years after World War II.

Tommy peered out of the window at the crowd on the front lawn. "Who are all these people, Dad?"

Jed leaned over his son. "Some I recognize from church, but honestly, I've never seen half of them in my life."

"What can they possibly be doing here? It's a funeral for pete's sake," Tommy said getting out of the car.

A chubby woman in her mid-sixties dressed in a blue cotton summer dress rushed up to Tommy. "You must be Tommy," she gushed. "I swear I would know you anywhere. Joyce went on and on about you so," the woman sniffed and dabbed her eyes with a lace crocheted handkerchief. "I'm Sophia Kowalski," she said as if Tommy should know the woman's name.

"I'm sorry," he shook his head in bewilderment.

"Sophia . . . Kowalski? Your mother saved my life."

"Excuse me?"

"I was in the hospital last year...dying. Your mother volunteers on Thursdays on my floor. I was there for three months. I'm sure she told you about me. About the miracle?"

"No, I don't know anything about it." Tommy was stunned.

"I should be dead. Brain tumor. But your mother came to see me every day for three weeks. Right after she went to morning Mass. She brought me holy water everyday and told me that if I believed I was healthy I would be. She told me that she believed the tumor was a mistake and that it had never been there in the first place. 'Forget what the doctors tell you,' she said. So, I did. She said a prayer with me everyday until one day, they took X-rays and it was gone! Poof!" Sophia smiled widely.

Tommy could hardly believe his ears. "It just went away," he replied with disbelief.

Sophia dropped her smile. "Kowalski. She never told you?"

"No."

"That's strange," she said and walked away.

A man in his early thirties carrying a two year old boy moved behind Sophia to give his condolences. "Hi, I'm Adam Weissman. This is my son Ben. I'm a friend of your mother's. She was a saint, I can tell you. A saint. She changed my life, you know. Getting me that job at the hospital like she did."

"Job?"

"She didn't tell you?" Adam asked.

"No."

Adam fought a trembling lip as his emotions overwhelmed him. "I can't imagine what it must be like for you," he said looking over at Jed. "And your father. To lose a woman like that. I don't think I will ever find a friend that loyal. Joyce was," Adam choked back a suffocating sob, "one in a million."

Tommy felt as if his heart had been pulled from his chest one more time. It was amazing that somehow it kept finding its way back after each pummeling. He put his hand on Adam's shoulder to steady himself as much as to give strength. "Thank you for coming," he said.

"It was the least I could do."

As Adam and his son walked away, Tommy overheard other strangers relating similar stories to Jed. Trios of people walked up the sidewalk and entered the yard. More strangers. More people who had known the joy of his mother and the sight touched Tommy deeply. He wanted to hug them all and thank them for seeing the purity of spirit his mother had been.

Tommy edged his way toward the house, still shaking hands with people he recognized from church and close neighbors. He hugged his mother's sister, Jerri.

"Aunt Jerri. When did you get here?"

"Just before you did. Time enough to engage in the first Magli battle of the day."

Tommy rolled his eyes. "Aunt Loretta's at it already?"

"I'm afraid so. I thought I'd set up the bar out here under the maple trees. Maybe you could bring me some ice from the kitchen."

"Is that where *she* is?"

Tommy had no more than spoken the words when his Aunt Loretta's screech climbed over the voices of everyone else in the house.

"Tanta idiots!" Loretta bellowed.

Jed grabbed Tommy's arm. "Come on. Damage control."

"Yes, sir," Tommy replied shouldering his way into the house behind his father.

"Please, Maria, out of my way! I'm working at a disadvantage here!"

"I was only trying to help, Loretta," Jed's elderly mother, Maria, replied.

"It's bad enough," Loretta shouted, "that there's no equipment in this house. I can't find the pastry cloth. God only knows where the rolling pin is and what kind of house has no Parmesan? No Romano? And did anybody ever find the basil? God! How Guillermo functions in here I don't know!" Loretta ranted.

"Luciana," Loretta shouted to her second cousin, "Check on the lasagna, like I told you! It's burning."

"It's not burning and I'm making insalada!" Luciana barked back.

Jed looked at Tommy. "I think we're just in time." He rushed to the kitchen. "Mama? Loretta? Is there a problem?"

Loretta snarled. "I told them. Sauté the garlic first. Then sauté the tomato paste."

Luciana groaned and rolled her eyes as she looked at Jed. "I told her how you make it and you do it best. First the paste. Then the garlic."

"No!" Loretta yelled. "I know what I'm doing."

Jed wiped his hand over his face. "This has nothing to do with recipes. Loretta, please stop making a scene. Joyce's family is coming up the walk."

"I should be someone different for them? Who are they? They don't make my life!"

"They are part of mine," Jed replied.

"Not anymore," Loretta shot back.

Jed's jaw dropped.

Tommy's face went red as if she'd physically slapped them both. "I could almost hate you for that, Aunt Loretta."

"Better learn some manners, boyo," she shook a spatula at him.

"Leave my son out of this, Loretta," Jed warned.

They squared off. Heat matching heat. Anger assailing anger.

The tension in the room was enough to make the walls groan.

It was Tommy's grandmother Maria who stepped between her two children. As she smiled at Jed, her wrinkles spread across her cheeks like fine webbing. "No problemo, my son. Loretta, she is like the general. Forgetdaboudit."

Jed motioned to his mother. "Come, we'll sit outside. Under the maple trees where it's cool."

As Jed started to turn away from his sister, Loretta flung her fists to her hips. "That's another thing. If you'd get some air conditioners in here, Mama could work on the ravioli with me!"

Jed glared at his sister. "Lighten up, Loretta." He put his arm around his mother's shoulder and pulled her through the doorway.

Loretta had worked herself into such a state that a hunk of perfectly teased beehive hairdo had fallen over her forehead and threatened to obscure her vision. She blew at it, momentarily lifting it off her face.

"Maybe now you'll make some improvements around here, Guillermo!"

The barb stuck on everyone who heard it, especially Tommy.

"It's Jed," Jed shot back.

"She made you change your name. It wasn't good enough for her that you are Italian!" Loretta spat.

"Joyce had nothing to do with it!" Jed replied. "Unlike you, I am not an Italian living in America. I am an American with Italian heritage. Too bad you don't see the difference."

"You turned your back on us!" Loretta's eyes filled with burning, angry tears. "Just like Carmine did."

Tommy stepped around his father and loomed over Loretta. She glared at him, too embarrassed to back down.

"Tommy, don't," Jed pleaded.

"You get this straight, Aunt Loretta. My mother was a saint. Canonization is imminent in my book. You're still working your way up from hell. You got that?"

Loretta shoved a spatula between them, shaking it. "You are a child. You got that? You pay respect to your elders."

"Respect? Who are you kidding? And by the way. I'm nearly twenty-one. I'm just as much an adult as you. For years I've listened to you criticize my Mom. Maybe you are jealous of her like Dad says. Maybe you wanted to be in love with your husband like they were. Me. I don't think so. I think you are a mean, vicious person without a life of your own and so you try to destroy everyone else's." Tommy sucked in his breath as he looked at a stunned Loretta.

The pain of his mother's death hammered into him like nails of crucifixion. He remembered the days of watching her suffer silently and the nights of helping his dad carry her into the bathroom as she vomited from the chemotherapy that never worked. He felt the ache in his father's heart for the only woman he'd ever loved with empathetic acuteness.

Anger boiled up in him like lava in a volcano. It needed release. He needed to vent. Loretta was just in the way. "My mother is dead. You got that? Dead! Too bad it wasn't you."

"Tommy!" Jed shouted. "That's enough!"

Tommy spun around to face his father. "She insulted my mother. I'd think you'd stand up for Mom. She's not here to defend herself... in case you forgot!"

Jed felt as if someone had knocked the wind out of him. "But we're family."

"You call this being family? Where's Loretta's love?" Tommy instantly regretted his words. "I'm sorry..." The hole inside him yawned again. He didn't understand why he was hurting other people. He didn't understand why he couldn't stop the flow of venom from his own mouth. He was as guilty as Loretta for blowing things out of proportion. In that moment, he didn't like himself very much. The future got darker.

"Oh, Tommy..." Maria said stretching her hand out to her grandson. "Loretta didn't mean it."

"I gotta get out of here," Tommy mumbled, avoiding his father's eyes as he rushed to the door.

"I think that would be best," Jed said regrettably.

Tommy shouldered his way past the oncoming stream of cousins and aunts and uncles. He didn't stop to shake hands with Father Antonio. He didn't see the faces filled with empathy. He didn't see the outpouring of love any longer.

All he knew was that he needed to walk. He would have walked off the edge of the earth if he could. He would walk all the way from Calumet City to Oak Street Beach where he often went to collect his thoughts.

Get yourself together, Tommy.

Tommy walked several miles before stopping at the bus stop. Looking back toward the direction of his house, he started to return. Then the bus pulled up, brakes squealing as it belched.

Flight.

He jumped onto the bus and dropped a coin in the slot. At that moment he would have gone to Alaska, where his emotions were bound to freeze. Instead, he rode north into the city on the same bus he rode every day during the school year to Northwestern's campus. It was a familiar ride. It almost felt comfortable, but this time he wasn't going to school. He was running away and he'd never run away from anything or anyone in his life.

"What am I doing?"

Tomorrow, Mom will still be dead.

Tomorrow his father would still need him and he would need his father. Aunt Loretta would still be bitter and his grandmother would grow a day closer to death herself. Tommy had come face to face with his grief and the pain it inflicted defied measure. But he could not allow pain of any kind to rattle his sense of honor.

The bus had gone only a half mile to the next stop. The brakes squealed once again. Tommy rose calmly and got off the bus.

"Hey, you paid full fare," the driver said.

"I know," he nodded. "I have to go back home. I'm needed there."

"Have it your way," the driver said, pulling the lever that shut the doors.

Tommy raised his face to the summer wind and inhaled deeply to steel his resolve. Home meant family to most people. For Tommy, both meant heartache.

Chapter Two

October, 1965.

The fall semester at Northwestern began methodically for Tommy. With his freshman year behind him, the thrill of newness was gone and his required courses were boring and unchallenging. He had little to look forward to either on campus or at home where his father continued to retreat within himself nightly.

"Like father, like son," Tommy muttered to himself, heels crushing gold autumn leaves as he trudged across the quad. Jed protected his aching heart with Jack Daniels and a television set while Tommy over-scheduled his days with extra classes, free lectures and fraternity committees. *Stay busy enough, there's no time to think or feel.*

Tommy volunteered as the Sigma Chi's social director telling himself he needed to beef up his "extra curriculum" column when he applied for law school. Truthfully, his heart was not in helping to organize "rush week", nor in ordering decorations for homecoming, or booking bands.

As much as he loved music, dancing and someone to dance with were the last things on his mind.

Ben Breedlow, Tommy's unofficial roommate, sprawled across a navy corduroy covered club chair his parents had expressly shipped to Chicago for their son. It was the only chair large enough to hold the six foot seven inch defensive tackle. Ben was New York born and raised and though his family had made a fortune in European antiques, Ben was the family black sheep. His sister, Karen, had breezed into Vassar, but Ben had wanted to put as much distance from his society parents as possible. He wanted to play football for a big Midwestern college and he did. Ben was built like a brick wall and no one crossed him. Ever.

He was the only junior with a room of his own and why he took an instant liking to Tommy, no one understood. It was just one of those mysterious connections that happen in life. Much like the connection between the mystery meat on Tuesday nights and the stack of empty plates in the frat house kitchen sink afterward.

Tommy walked into Ben's room with a handful of mail he'd pulled from the mailboxes in the basement.

"This one's for you," he tossed him a letter. "Some fan mail from a flounder?" Ben caught the envelope midair. "Thanks, Rocky."

Tommy shuffled through a handful of promotional postcards from local music talent agents. "Who comes up with these names? Listen to this, Aggravated Assault. Juniper and the Berries. Ugh! Man, I should never have signed on for this gig."

"You didn't," Ben said opening the letter. "I'm the one who put your name on the list. The vote was unanimous."

"Mine was the only name. They had no choice."

"True, but you're the only one in the house who knows the difference between a cleft note and a cleft palate." Ben replied absentmindedly as he read the letter. "Aw, man! My sister's roommate is going to be here for homecoming and she promised her I'd show her a good time." Ben threw his head back feigning agony. "I bet she's a dog."

"What's her name?"

"Who cares?" Reluctantly, Ben glanced at the letter again. "Joannie Howard."

"Well, since you're spoken for, I guess the choice of band isn't so critical any more."

Ben shook his head. "Blasphemer! Homecoming is the most important night of the year to this fraternity, Tommy," Ben said poking the air with his Parker pen for emphasis. "It's more important than Christmas. Even New Year's. We have to make an impact."

"Precisely. That's why I don't want some 'do wop' group."

"But I like 'do wop.' The Platters. The Stylistics. It's better than that classical crap you play on my hi-fi. Reminds me of my father." Ben began humming *Harbor Lights*. Placing his hand over his heart, Ben swayed to imaginary music. "You think this Joannie will like me?"

"I thought you said you wanted the Homecoming Queen to show up for our mixer."

"We all do!"

"Then remember," Tommy grabbed Ben's pen playfully and used it to circle an announcement in the Sun Times Entertainment section, "Chicks like Brits."

"Huh?"

"Keep sayin' it over and over. Like a litany."

Ben rolled his eyes as he slapped his hand against his chemistry textbook. "The Beatles are out of our league and I don't think the Phi Delts grabbed the Stones, either."

Grinning, Tommy said, "Ye of little faith. Leave it to the master."

Ben looked down at the newspaper announcement Tommy had circled. "The Yardbirds are touring the Great Lakes. Look at this schedule. They're playing every Podunk town from Racine to South Bend."

"Right. My guess is that we could get them for under five hundred."

"Our budget is three fifty."

"So, we cut back on the kegs."

"Blasphemer! We gotta have kegs."

Tommy was firm. "Not for homecoming. We're making a statement. You said so yourself. Beer is banal. It's every weekend. It's not special enough."

Ben pondered Tommy's words. "Right. Better go with zombies instead. Everyone will chip in."

"Glad you see it my way," Tommy smiled and started to leave.

"Hey, Master Blaster, who are you bringing to the dance?"

Tommy froze. "Bring?"

"Yeah, a chick, you know?"

Hesitantly, he said, "I haven't gotten that far."

15

"That Alpha Phi in my chemistry class likes you."

"Who was that again?"

"Amy Anderson. Blonde. Gorgeous. A little dumb like I like them."

Nodding, Tommy said, "I remember. You take her out. She's not my type."

"What the hell is your type, man, other than one that's breathing."

Tommy looked away. "I gotta go."

Ben swung his huge legs to the floor, then leaned his elbows on his knees and peered at Tommy. "Hey, man. I never lost anybody. Okay? I didn't mean anything by it. I just was hoping you'd...I dunno. Start livin'. You know?"

Tommy swallowed hard. "Yeah. I know." With a light slap he hit the doorjamb. "Later. Okay?"

"Yeah," Ben exhaled heavily as Tommy walked down the hall and out of sight.

*   *   *   *   *

Music poured out of the Sigma Chi house on Homecoming night as Joannie Howard yanked on her younger cousin's arm.

"Come on, Susie. You can do this."

"I've never been to a party uninvited in my life! I don't have a good feeling about this at all," Susie said, prying Joannie's fingers off the sleeve of her new pink angora sweater.

A handsomely dressed couple walked up behind them. The man was tall with thick wavy hair and a strongly chiseled face. The girl was strikingly beautiful, nearly as tall as Susie but with a perfect blonde teased flip that screamed hours of work to achieve. She clung to the man's arm, paying no attention to Susie and Joannie as they breezed past.

"Everyone on campus is talking about the Yardbirds being here. This will be the best mixer in decades," she said.

"Tommy Magli is a magician," the man said.

Joannie continued following the couple up the walk. Susie yanked on her cousin's arm. "Did you see that guy? His five o'clock shadow is as thick as my father's!"

"Your point?" Joannie frowned.

"He's not a boy.... he's a man!" she said, her eyes as big around as saucers.

"That was the general idea they had behind universities and fraternities when they invented them, you know. You can only come here when you're grown up. Look, Susie, you keep acting like this and everyone is going to figure out you're still in high school. I have to meet with Ben just for a little bit, then we can leave. Karen's mother is my mother's best friend. They talk about stupid stuff like this. Something about keeping the families connected through the generations and all that. All I care about is getting back to your house so I can call Bob. So, grow up a little bit, okay?"

"Geez. Is that what it's like to grow up? You miss out on a real live Mercy Beat band so you can call your boyfriend back home?"

"I'd rather be with Bob than meet Ringo."

Susie shook her head. "Good thing you guys are getting married at Thanksgiving."

"Jealous?" Joannie teased.

Susie smiled. "A little. But I'm happy for you." She looked up at the open door. Two more couples were coming down the walk eager to make their way inside. "I'll be mature. Don't worry. Everyone will think I'm thirty before the night's over."

Joannie rolled her eyes. "I have no doubt."

A red-haired freshman pledge acted as doorman and greeter. He wore a name tag that said "Doug Watson. Pledge".

"Hi," Joannie shouted over the loud music. "I'm here to see Ben Breedlow. He's expecting me. I'm Joannie Howard. This is my cousin, Susie. She's with me. Where would I find Ben?"

"Brother Breedlow is bartender tonight. In the basement."

"The basement?"

"Through this door to the staircase on the left. The stairs are marked, 'This way to the bar'."

"Thanks," Joannie said.

Once inside, the main living area had been cleared of furniture and a stage installed for the Yardbirds. Nearly fifty couples were dancing, clapping their hands to the music and singing along.

Susie was awestricken. "Groovy!" Slapping her hands on her cheeks she turned to Joannie . "I can't believe it! It's really them!"

"You aren't going to faint like some love-sick fan are you?"

Susie dropped her hands, straightened her back and lifted her chin haughtily. In seconds, she had transformed her expression into one of disdain and snobbery. "God, no."

"I've never understood how you can do that. Look like a kid one second and my mother the next."

"Talent," Susie droned deeply. "Sheer God-given talent. All actresses have it."

Joannie looked around. "Great. Use it tonight. I don't want you getting the boot before I schmooze with Ben."

As Joannie headed for the stairs, Susie looked around the room at the well-dressed crowd and expelled a sigh. It didn't matter if she was at a high school dance or a college mixer. Chicago fashion just didn't have any imagination to it. All the girls dressed in the same Pendelton wool jumpers over cashmere turtlenecks, pastel wool skirts and co-ordinating sweater sets with matching cappezio flats. They were conservative and classic. Which, in Susie's book, equaled boring.

"Flair, people. Ever hear of it?" she mumbled to herself.

Not a single soul was dressed anything like Susie.

Her tight black wool skirt was three inches shorter than anyone else's. Susie had read in *Women's Wear Daily* that the miniskirt had taken London by storm, though it was not expected to convert the puritanical United States fashion industry. With the skirt, she wore a frilly white Edwardian styled silk blouse with extra long sleeves and double lace ruffles at the cuff. She wore thick black tights and black pumps on which she'd glued black lace. Around her waist she strung her grandfather's pocket watch and chain. She thought she looked daring and lot more interesting than anyone else at the mixer.

Craning her neck to scrutinize everyone's fashions, Susie spotted a tall, dark haired man working his way through the crowd.

"Dreamboat," she mumbled to herself.

She expected him to have a girl in tow, but he didn't.

He doesn't have a date.

Susie smiled to herself. "Can I be this lucky?"

She watched him, his easy smile and his flashing blue eyes as he joked with friends, complimented their dates and eased over to the door where Doug Watson received some kind instructions from him.

Susie turned to a nearby dancing couple.

"Could you help me?" She asked the blond man.

"Sure."

"That guy over there by the door with Doug Watson. Who is he?"

"Tommy Magli. He's the man! This is his gig, man!" he answered, twisting his body to the music.

"They call him the magician. Right?" she replied.

"You got it!"

"Thanks," she said and watched as Tommy went up to the stage and spoke to one of the band members, then announced their break.

She liked the sound of his voice. She liked the way he held himself. She liked what she saw.

The famous Yardbirds left the stage, but Susie didn't even notice. Her eyes saw only Tommy Magli.

But how? You're only eighteen, Susie. And he's definitely a man.

Tommy stood on the back porch of the fraternity house gazing up at the moon while The Yardbirds sang their hit, "I'm A Man" to an enthusiastic crowd. It was meant to be the highlight of the night, but the body heat from the dancing couples drove Tommy to the cool night air.

Staring up at the full moon, his thoughts strayed to his mother. He couldn't help wondering if she was actually in heaven looking down on him, or if life after death was a myth conjured up by religious fanatics whose purpose was to rule the masses like Hegel, Kant and Marx believed. Was it just as simple as dust to dust. Or was it more?

"Are we stardust?" Tommy asked himself aloud.

"I don't know," a girl's voice answered from the shadows. "You got a light?"

"Sorry. Don't smoke," he replied, peering deeper into the darkness. "Cigarettes can kill."

"Says who?"

He heard the sound of her footsteps as she moved closer.

"My mother's doctor."

"I've heard talk about it," she replied with a husky seductiveness. "Smoking causes cancer."

"It did," he said, squinting at the darkness.

She moved into the moonlight. She was tall and slender as a reed with very long dark hair that shimmered like satin in the silvery moonglow. Her oval face was perfectly proportioned with a finely chiseled nose and lips that made him think of kissing and little else. Her skin was clear and smooth but it was the compelling gaze she fastened on him that rocked him to his core. There were lots of pretty girls on campus, but this girl exuded a strong sense of confidence. He'd never met anyone quite so beautiful up close.

Smiling at him with a look meant to beguile, she raised the cigarette to her face. Abruptly, she broke the cigarette in half. "Actually, I've never smoked," she chuckled lightly dropping her seductive voice.

"Then why did you . . ."

Crossing the distance between them in two steps, she was almost nose to nose with him when she cut him off saying, "I was hoping to pick up a guy."

"You what?"

"Not just any guy. You, to be honest."

"Me?"

Her lips curled mischievously. "I've been watching you ever since I got here."

"I'm flattered."

Tilting her head so that the moonlight fell on her long dark lashes, casting what appeared to be very practiced shadows, she said, "Is that all? You're not shocked? Surprised, then?"

"At what?"

"My behavior," she replied with a playful laugh.

"Should I be?" He could see now that the rim of the hair around her face was wet with sweat from dancing, no doubt. She probably had half of his fraternity brothers drooling over her by now.

"I don't know you. So, how would I know if this is out of character for you?"

"Good point," she replied feeling her nervousness ratchet up the longer she stood next to him.

I'm actually sweating! He's so intense! So much for being an actress. I think I just flunked the class on hiding emotions.

"I think we should change that. My not knowing you, I mean," he said.

"Oh, me too!" she said gleefully. "I'm Susie Howard," she replied, offering her hand to him.

"Tommy Magli."

"I know. I asked around. Which was easier than I'd thought, since I'm crashing here tonight."

"You're going to sleep in the Sigma Chi house?"

Susie burst into laughter. "You should see your face! You really are shocked! This is great!"

He laughed with her. "I am, aren't I?"

"You're funny, too. I like that. But no, I'm not sleeping here. I meant I'm crashing the party. I'm here with my cousin, Joannie, she's from . . ."

"Vassar."

It was Susie's turn to be shocked. "Yeah. But how could you know that?"

"My sometimes roommate is Ben Breedlow. His sister is your cousin's roommate."

"Well, that's serendipitous, isn't it?" Susie smiled with delight bursting across her face like fireworks.

"Fate. Kismet," he replied, gazing at her mouth as she talked.

"And I thought I was controlling this meeting. I saw you with the band when I first got here. I decided I'd maneuver things so that we'd get time alone. But all night, it never happened. You're a busy guy. Checking on the kegs. Getting the chips and dips. Talking to everyone. But you never danced with a girl. Ever."

"Observant, aren't you?"

"I think that's an important quality in an actress."

His eyebrow shot up. "You're an actress?"

"Well, not yet. But I will be someday. Either that or a model in New York, of course."

"Of course."

"I have to be somebody famous. I want to really make something special out of my life. I want people to know who I am."

"Why?"

"Because my father is famous. He's a hard act to follow, I can tell you that."

"Howard." Tommy threw his head back as it hit him. "Not Braxton Howard, the millionaire? The real estate developer who's behind Marina Towers? And the move to rebuild upper Michigan Avenue?"

"That and fifteen other companies. Daddy says cable television is going to be really hot in the future."

"Cable television? What's that?"

"TV you pay for."

Tommy guffawed. "It'll never happen."

"If Daddy says it will, it will. See? That's why I have to be somebody famous."

"As opposed to?"

"The housewife thing. You know?"

"Ah," he said. "No babies and diapers for you?"

"Nah, just the sex."

"What?" he snorted.

Susie laughed so hard she rocked back on her heels. "I was just kidding. I wanted to see what you'd say." She hugged herself.

Shoving his hands in his pockets he leaned against the porch post. "I can see your game now. You're like one of those crazed stalkers. You crash my party in my frat house, I might add. You single me out as your prey. You watch stealthily as I go about my business, all the while pretending to be dancing and having a good time. Then somehow, which I haven't quite figured out this part yet, you see me coming out here and you get here before I do and wait for me in the shadows. Then you spring yourself on me all for the purpose of seeing how many times you can shock me with outrageous statements. Is that pretty much about it?"

Flashing him a smile meant to melt icebergs, she said, "Not all of it, no."

"Then what's the rest? Dare I ask?"

"You want to kiss me, don't you?"

"I get it. You're the kissing bandit. Sorry, the famous kissing bandit. How does this figure into your plan to become an international celebrity?" he teased.

"It doesn't," she said dropping her banter. "I just thought since I want to kiss you..."

Tommy's smile vanished. "Susie Howard wants to kiss Tommy Magli?"

23

She swallowed hard for courage. "I know you won't believe this, but tonight, here with you, is just about the most outrageous thing I've ever done. But when I first saw you, something happened inside me. I can't explain. It was like a movie. Across a crowded room and all that."

Tommy put his hands on her shoulders and pulled her close. "This isn't a movie."

He'd meant for the kiss to be quick and impulsive much like the motivation behind the beautiful, but quirky girl who was doing the asking. He knew that after this moment, she would walk away, go on to kiss another guy in New York, or hundreds of guys if she were to become an actress. He would never see her again. She would never think of him again. And life would go on.

The explosion occurred somewhere between the pit of his stomach and the heart of his soul. It rumbled through his body like an underwater earthquake that snakes along its subterranean trench and dislodges all that was before and creates a new terrain.

"What was that?" he asked sliding his lips to her cheek.

"I don't know," she said placing her hands on either side of his face and pulling his mouth over hers. "Come back where you belong."

Their lips consumed each other with abandon but with a familiarity that neither understood.

Susie felt lightheaded as if she was spinning through space, yet her toes tingled inside her shoes which were planted firmly on earth. Slipping her arms around his neck, she held Tommy's nape with tender possession. Her passion had never been awakened until this moment. She felt its startling presence like a spring flower pushing itself up through the earth after a long winter's nap. She was eighteen and though she'd been kissed before, she'd never felt as if someone was making love with her. Kisses had been experimental things like educational toys. She'd never thought much about them except that on most of her high school dates they were obligatory, for the most part, at

24

her parents' front door before going inside. She'd meted them out carefully since the age of fourteen when she'd first been kissed. Tonight, she realized that she'd never been actually attracted to anyone special. Attending an all girls' school kept dating to a much narrower field than if she'd gone to public school. Most of her dates she'd met through her parents' friends or they were the sons of her parents' yacht club friends. Susie had never actually bumped into a boy she'd wanted to kiss until tonight.

She came to this dance on a lark and Joannie had not wanted to come either, since her fiancé, Bob, was back in New York. However, Joannie had promised Karen Breedlow, she would meet Ben and give Karen a full status report. Because Susie was still in high school, the idea of crashing a real Northwestern fraternity party was just the kind of juicy fodder she needed for the school lunch table on Monday. Her friends would think she was courageous and she would credit the evening as preparation for her acting career.

She had not been lying when she told Tommy she was intrigued by him from the moment she saw him. Although he was tall, dark and handsome, it wasn't his looks that compelled her to follow his every move. Tommy possessed a surety about himself that reminded her of her father. He was at ease when speaking with the famous band members and yet extended the same courteous behavior to the delivery boy from the delicatessen who had mixed up the order.

She watched how Tommy never stopped moving, greeting fraternity brothers and the girls. He introduced people to each other and made certain everyone was smiling.

She was intrigued that such an outwardly generous person did not have a date of his own.

She had watched him wipe sweat from his forehead and the back of his neck with a handkerchief. The room had been suffocating and she guessed rightly he wanted to cool off. When he headed for the back hall, she slipped out the front door, raced around the yard to the back porch steps and hid in the corner in the shadows. She even liked how he stared longingly up at the stars as if he was seeing someone in them.

She was breathless when he tore his mouth from hers.

"My God," he whispered, pulling her into his chest, her head resting on his shoulder. "You'll definitely win an Oscar with that performance."

The folly of her earlier behavior zeroed in on Susie like a bomb drop. She wished to heaven now she'd just been herself. But she'd been afraid. Afraid that a "real" man, an older man like Tommy, was used to sophisticated college women, who knew every trick in the book to land a guy. Surely, as good looking as he was, he had his pick. Sure, she could be flippant and cool. She could pretend this kiss was nothing, but the problem was, it was everything. It was the kind of kiss that wakes sleeping princesses from the dead. It was the kind of kiss that soldiers went to war over. It was the kind she would never forget. And would always regret if there weren't a whole lot more of them in her future.

The only thing she could do now was be herself.

"I wasn't acting," she said bravely.

He took her hand and placed it on his chest. "You feel that?"

"Your heart . . . it's racing."

"I wasn't acting, either," he said as she turned her face up to him. He searched the depths of her eyes, "So what's it to be, Susie Howard? Do you want to go on kissing poor defenseless guys for the rest of your life, or do you want to see me again? Because I sure want to see you."

"I want to see you," she replied.

"Good decision. I like a girl with brains. Sexy as hell, those brains."

Then he kissed her again knowing the stars were his witnesses.

Chapter Three

Chicago, Illinois.
Christmas Eve, 1965.

Susie ejected Bing Crosby off her hi-fidelity and closed her eyes as strains of Handel's Messiah filled her blue and white French Provincial styled bedroom. She inhaled deeply in order to feel the music rather than simply hear it, like Tommy had instructed.

Goosebumps riddled her body. "He was right. This is the music of the soul."

Opening her eyes, she focused on scads of Seventeen and Mademoiselle magazine covers which were plastered on her bulletin boards, along with tear outs of nearly every photo shoot Jean Shrimpton had published. There were Yardley ads, Pendleton and Bobbie Brooks layouts and interviews with Twiggy, Penelope Tree and of course, her heroine, Jean.

Only a few months ago, Susie had dreamed of becoming a model, then later, she wanted to go into acting. She lived and breathed movies and photo shoots. She talked of little else. She thought of little else. But life was different now.

"Childish fantasies," she said to herself, glancing at Tommy's photograph in a silver frame on her nightstand. "You've changed everything, Tommy Magli."

She glanced at the clock next to the photo. "Is that the time?"

Springing across the room, she knocked over her vanity chair.

"Hurry!" She rummaged in her closet for a pair of chunky heeled black dress shoes with massive square buckles at the toe.

Wiggling into a Puchi slip, she pushed back the closet door and looked at her reflection. The full-length mirror had cost her fifty dollars, nearly an entire paycheck she'd earned working after school at an upscale small women's boutique on North Michigan Avenue. It didn't matter to Susie that her mother's best friend, Colleen Cole, owned the shop and that she'd gotten the job by virtue of family connections. It mattered only that she'd kept the job now for these last two years of high school.

"I'm good at sales," she said proudly to herself. "After all, I have excellent fashion sense and people recognize that." She nodded firmly to herself.

"Now, where is that dress?" She rushed back into the closet.

Stepping into her black velvet Edwardian mid thigh length dress with white lace collar and cuffs, she struggled with the back zipper.

Suddenly, the closet door shut as if by its own volition.

"Eeeek!" Susie screamed.

"It's too short," Mary Elizabeth Howard said, her lower lip jutting her disapproval. "I thought you were going to let it out."

"I did."

"What? A half-inch? And since when do you listen to classical music? Though I have to admit if I hear, 'She loves you, yeah, yeah, yeah' one more time, I truly will lose my mind."

Susie exhaled, slumped her shoulders and rolled her eyes, matching her mother's disapproval measure for measure. "I've told you a hundred times that Tommy likes classical music. So does Daddy."

"Your attitude is surly," Mary Elizabeth snipped. "I won't have it!"

Susie walked to her vanity table, picked up a tube of Yardley's new Slicker lipstick in frosted yellow and swiped her full lips. "Admit it. It's not the dress or the music that disturbs you. It's the fact that I'm going out with Tommy."

"You can't bring him to the Foxes' Christmas Party. How many times do I have to tell you that? He wasn't invited."

"And I've told you I'm not going to the Foxes' party this year."

Mary Elizabeth flushed as she always did when anger challenged her impeccable manners. She patted her forehead with her fingertips. "You have been to every party of theirs for eighteen years." For emphasis, Mary Elizabeth slapped her white opera length gloves against her thigh.

"That's right. Surely they must be bored with me by now."

"They're our closest friends!"

"And that's why we only go to their house once a year at Christmas along with two hundred of the rest of their 'closest friends'?"

Mary Elizabeth glared as Susie heated her electric rollers and stuck them in a topknot of long dark hair. Susie watched her mother's reaction in the reflection of her lighted makeup mirror.

Mary Elizabeth Howard was the epitome of Chicago society. She was well educated, having earned a master's degree in French and she spent two summers at the Sorbonne in France. Her family's friends carried names worthy of historical markers, McCormick, Wrigley and Field. In the summer of 1945, her wedding was the most elaborate and expensive wedding the residents of Chicago's Gold Coast had ever seen. The *Chicago Tribune* and *The Chicago Daily News* sent a plethora of photographers. A journalist from *Town and Country* got wind of the story that Braxton Howard III, Normandy Beach war hero and bronze star recipient, equestrian, yachtsman and the guardian of the Howard millions had returned from France only four days before the wedding. It had taken the political pull of two Congressmen and an influential White House personal friend of General Eisenhower's to get him there, but he'd made it to the church on time.

Their wedding portraits plastered the walls of the main hall in their Sheridan Road mansion. Oils of Mary Elizabeth hung over every fireplace and alongside those of Braxton's mother, Grace. Where other families revered art and artists, the

Howards exalted bloodlines. Family was all. Family was God in Susie's house.

All things considered, Susie guessed this conversation could have been much worse, given her mother's indoctrination from her mother and her mother before her. After all, Mary Elizabeth could just as easily have handcuffed Susie to the bedpost and locked her in her room until she turned thirty-five.

Susie purposefully had not told her mother that she was in love with Tommy Magli. She'd only stated that she was dating him. She'd allowed Mary Elizabeth to believe there still remained a glimmer of hope that she would or could someday break up with Tommy and become the cellular link to the next round of sterling DNA her mother sought.

"That's decidedly not true, Susan. We see the Foxes at the yacht club all summer long."

"Mother, admit it. Father tells James Fox how to invest his millions and they both make money together. They have to invite you. They won't even know I'm not there."

"That's not the point."

Suzie ratted another mass of hair, building a beehive another inch. She hit it hard with Aquanet. "I know what the point is. Tommy. You've made that clear."

"Good Lord, Susie. His father is a steel worker! He's on scholarship to Northwestern because they can't afford the tuition. He's just . . . he's just not suitable!"

Susie spun around, waving her rat-tail comb at her mother. "I may dress like I just walked out of one of your Jane Austin novels, Mother, but this is not the nineteenth century. All people are 'suitable' in this century. Or maybe you've missed the news lately. They march in the streets over just this sort of thinking. Tommy is number one in his class. He's going to be a lawyer. A brilliant lawyer. That ought to be suitable enough for you."

"And what about you? You talk about going to New York, trying your wings as a model. Last year it was the Peace Corps.

The year before you wanted to be an actress. Before that, it was a ballerina."

"I hung up my toe shoes when I went through puberty. Don't worry, I'm not going to New York. I'm going to St. Mary's just like you and Daddy want me to."

"You've only decided on South Bend because it keeps you close to home. Close to that boy. You don't give a whit about a liberal arts degree. All you care about is how many weekends you can see...*him.*"

"I don't deny that Tommy has a great deal to do with my decision. I only wanted to be a model so I could travel. See the world." She looked down and lifted her toes off the floor. "I wish I had the courage to join the Peace Corps, but I don't. I'd like to think that I was brave enough to help people that much."

"The real truth, Susan, is that you don't know what you want. Ever since you met this boy at that Halloween party at Northwestern when, I might add, you disobeyed your Father and me and attended without our permission, you've neglected your studies, your clubs, and you've even missed your last homecoming dance."

"It was Tommy's homecoming the same week-end!"

"His wishes were more important than your own?"

"Yes!"

"All these years I've allowed, even pressed, you to think for yourself. To be your own person. When you wanted violin lessons, I drove you. When you dreamed of dancing with Nureyev, I hired the best seamstress for your costumes. I've sent you to art tutors, acting classes, even modeling school and now you throw it all away as if none of it meant anything to you."

"You never wanted me to be a model."

"It was a phase. You got over it," Mary Elizabeth looked up at Jean Shrimpton's face staring down at her from a poster. "New York is no place for a young girl of breeding."

"Or a breeding young girl," Suzie quipped unable to miss the chance at a stab. She was having too much fun at her mother's expense.

"Susan!" Mary Elizabeth gasped.

"Don't worry, Mother, I know what I'm doing," Susie replied adamantly.

"God! You're as bullheaded as your father."

"As you, you mean."

Mary Elizabeth threw her arms up in the air. "Thank God I was only given one child! You'll be the reason for my commitment to an insane asylum!"

"Think of it this way. I graduate in May. I'll be off to St. Mary's in September. I won't be in this house any more and you'll have your life with Daddy back. It'll be over soon."

Mary Elizabeth threw her daughter a stabbing look. "He's from a different world, Susan. It's a match that can't last. I've spoken to your father about it and we agree. If you pursue this nonsense, we'll…"

"What? Disinherit me?" Susie laughed.

"If necessary."

Stunned, Susie snapped her mouth shut. "You wouldn't."

"Don't push us."

"You would do that to your only child?" Susie felt her knees weaken, but she stood firm against Mary Elizabeth. She sensed if she wavered, she would lose the battle. And that's what this was. War. She hadn't wanted it this way. She'd wanted a Christmas to remember. She'd wanted her parents to accept Tommy. To come to love him and cherish him just as she had. Susie didn't care that she'd only known Tommy less than two months. She'd read stories about "soul mates". She believed that when her heart beat, she was feeling Tommy's heart. They had known from the instant they'd laid eyes on each other that the sparks between them were more than fire. They were shooting stars. It was as if he'd walked out of another lifetime to be with her. The sound of his voice was like an ancient echo she'd heard coaxing her from her own mother's womb the day she was born.

As pretty as others told her she was, despite the May Queen crown, the Homecoming Court Princess banner and the statuettes attesting to her popularity, Susie had dated only sporadically in high school. The boys she knew were her friends, her buddies, but none had come close to stealing her heart. She'd known to save it. She'd known to hold it dear until she gave it to her Prince.

Mary Elizabeth let her words sink into her daughter. Methodically, she slipped her hands into her opera gloves, taking her time to adjust them. Keeping her silence, she tromped toward the door.

"Mother."

Mary Elizabeth halted at the door. Her better judgment told her not to turn around. But she had hope they could still make peace. "You've changed your mind?"

"Never." Susie turned to face her. A wan smile crested her face. "I just wanted to say you look, well, very Jackie tonight."

Mary Elizabeth smoothed the ice blue Oleg Cassini satin sheath and pulled her evening gloves over her elbow. It was small consolation. She took it. "Thank you."

She shut the door behind her.

Frowning, Susie went to the hi-fidelity and pressed the eject button.

"Ugh. Mothers."

Then she sang along to Gene Pitney, suddenly understanding the words to "A Town Without Pity".

The Christmas Star

Chapter Four

Snow capped the shoulders of The Water Tower, the Tribune Building and the Drake Hotel like lacy epaulettes. The skyscrapers and hotels of North Lake Shore Drive gazed out on the frozen waters of Lake Michigan like grand ladies of a bygone era adorned in glittering tiaras and necklaces of twinkling lights. The shoppers had gone home to Christmas Eve dinners, parties and wrapping of last minute gifts. A recorded carol played on a passing yacht whose mast was lit with colored lights. Yet as the bewitching hour of midnight approached, snow fell in giant hunks dressing the earth in a pristine white satin tuxedo.

It took one hour for Susie to drive from her parents' house just north of the Sheridan Shore Yacht Club to Tommy's house on the very far South Side of the city. Following the directions Tommy had given her, she exited the Dan Ryan. Usually, she and Tommy met on his campus after her school let out for the afternoon. Tommy didn't have a car and she'd gotten her Mustang on her sixteenth birthday like most of her friends at St. Mary's.

Tommy rode the train from home to campus every day or bummed a ride from a classmate when he finished up classes. Sometimes, he bunked in with Ben Breedlow when he studied late or if he wanted to meet Susie in the city on weekends where they would walk for hours, go to the museums or grab a burger at the Wimpy's off State Street.

Susie calculated it would take her another hour for them to drive back up north to Holy Name Cathedral where Susie had wanted to attend night services.

Susie had been raised Catholic just like Tommy, but she realized not long after they met that Tommy and Jed had stopped going to Mass altogether.

"Dad is mad at God for giving Mom the cancer. I keep trying to tell him it was the cigarettes, not God," Tommy had said to her.

"That's his excuse for not going to church," she'd replied. "What's yours?"

"I miss her."

"I'm here now. I can never fill her shoes or be her. But I can fill the void," she'd said.

"And I thank God for you."

Susie pulled her red Mustang to a stop at the curb in front of Tommy's house. The rest of the post-war one story ranch homes were outlined in multi-colored lights. Painted plywood Santas, reindeer and Nativity scenes were scattered down the block and lit with floodlights. But at the Magli house the only glow was from the television set she could see through the picture window.

Taking a deep breath for courage, Susie walked up the sidewalk to meet the father of the man she loved. She rang the doorbell, hoping Tommy would greet her.

A tall figure approached the door.

"Rats," she mumbled to herself.

He unlocked the wood door and stood behind the winter frosted storm door. His breath hung on the air as he slowly opened the door.

"Merry Christmas, Mr. Magli," Susie greeted him cheerfully.

Jed stood ramrod straight, dressed in an undershirt and black chinos. He was a tall man, though not quite Tommy's six foot two inches. He had black hair like his son's and blisteringly blue eyes with long lashes. Susie could see that at one time he must have been quite handsome. In fact, he was still a good-looking man for someone nearing forty.

It was his expression that marred his face. His lips were pursed tight together as if he was biting his lip so as not to talk or cry.

"Oh, yeah. Merry. Merry."

She glanced down at his hand.

He held a glass filled with ice and a caramel colored liquid.

He watched her gaze. "It's Jack. You want some?"

"I'm not legal, Mr. Magli. Besides, Jack Daniels is a bit strong..."

"For a girl, yeah. You're right."

She stood there under the tiny porch light wondering if the day would come that he might be happy to see her...his future daughter-in-law.

Susie hoped for a lot of things.

She smiled, clapped her wool-gloved hands together. She peered over his shoulder.

Jed drew in a breath. "He didn't tell me you were comin'."

"Oh," she looked down feeling acutely unwanted. "We're going to church tonight."

"Christmas Eve."

"Yes." Susie was growing more uncomfortable by the second. Why wasn't he asking her to come in? Did he dislike her on sight without knowing her? Susie had not prepared herself for his resistance. For some naïve reason she'd thought resistance to her growing up and falling in love was territory reserved for her parents.

No wonder Tommy had not invited her to meet his family until now.

"Hey!" Tommy's voice broke her thoughts. "You're here!" He eyed his father suspiciously and reached around the older man, opening the storm door. "What's the matter with you, Dad? You gonna let her freeze out there?"

"Awww...." Jed walked away.

Susie realized at that moment that Jed was angry with Susie for coming into Tommy's life. Suddenly, her problems with her parents paled in comparison. She and Tommy walked the same street. She just hadn't seen the potholes.

"Thanks," she said and stepped inside.

Tommy kissed her cheek. Susie beamed up at him. Just the touch of his lips against her skin sent goose bumps down her back. She nearly lost her breath.

Tommy looked over at his father who flopped down in his Lazy Boy. The room was dark except for the light from the television set. A scrawny, four foot tree stood unlit in a corner.

"Are you going to decorate your tree tonight, Mr. Magli?" Susie asked hoping to break the ice.

He raised his glass to his lips and drank deeply. "Not anymore."

Susie winced at the sting.

"Guilt trip," Tommy whispered. "I'll get my coat," he said quite loud as he walked past his father. Taking his corduroy hooded parka off the coat hook in the miniscule hallway between the living room and the kitchen, Tommy paused behind his father. "Try plugging in the lights, Dad. They work. I tested them myself."

"You do it if you want the damn thing on so much."

Tommy went to the corner, bent over and plugged in the single string of lights.

The tree was a pathetic testimony to Christmas.

"Dandy," Jed grunted.

"I couldn't find any of Mom's decorations."

"I gave them to the church drive. We have no use for them."

"But I made some of those things!" Tommy assailed his father.

Jed glared at him. "When? In kindergarten? They looked rotted to me." He faced the television. "Get on with you. Your little honey is getting impatient."

"No, I'm not, Mr. Magli," Susie said defensively.

Jed grunted again.

"Come on, Susie. We better go before this gets worse." He glanced at his father. "By the looks of it, it will."

"I heard that!" Jed retorted.

"I meant for you to," Tommy said, putting his hand on Susie's back and pushing her toward the door.

"Merry Christmas," Susie said just under her breath as they nearly raced down the icy concrete steps to the mercy of the Mustang.

"You drive," she said handing him the keys.

"As you wish, My Lady." He opened the door for her. She got in. Tommy bent down and stole a kiss.

His face was more radiant than hers.

"How can you be happy after..."

"I'm with you," he interrupted. "How could I not be?"

Tommy climbed in the car and pulled the Mustang away from the curb. Away from his father's house. Away from his heartache.

For a long time they drove in silence, each absorbing the night. Each thinking about their parents.

"I'm sorry about that back there," Tommy said. "He hasn't always been like this. We used to be very supportive of each other."

"He misses her," Susie said. "It's understandable."

"So do I."

"It's different for him."

"I know," he replied thoughtfully.

Determined to turn the evening around she said, "You look quite handsome tonight, Mr. Magli."

"What ho? Mr. Magli? Now, I'm my father?"

"I'm trying to compliment you."

He took her hand and kissed it. "I bet you say that to all the dopey eyed guys who wanna hold your hand," he chuckled, turning the Beatles ballad off which had been playing on the radio.

"And are you dopey-eyed over me, Mr. Magli?"

"The dopiest."

She leaned over from the passenger's side, placing her head on his shoulder. He kissed the top of her head. In silence she watched the snow coming at them through the windshield.

"What would your dad say if he knew I was driving your car?"

"Off with his head," she joked.

"I was afraid of that," Tommy replied dourly.

"I was kidding."

Tommy put his arm around her shoulder and pulled Susie a bit closer. "There's some truth there, I think."

"Okay. So, I haven't won them over yet. But that's because they haven't met you."

"That's because they haven't asked. Have they?"

Susie expelled a heavy sigh and sat up. "Do we have to talk about this tonight of all nights?"

Tommy's blue eyes beamed just looking at Susie. "Of all nights? What's so special about tonight?"

Gesturing with her hand she said, "Just look. It's magic out there. It's nights like this that make you believe those snowflakes are fairies. That there's truly a Santa Claus. That the world is not at war. That all people are good and that someday we really will have peace on earth."

Flashing a grin, he said, "Sweetie, you really are meant for the Peace Corps."

She cuddled up to him, linking her arms through his. "That would take me away from you." Tears misted her eyes. "I don't think I could bear it."

"I know what you mean," he replied drawing her even closer. "It's going to be hard enough when you go to South Bend next fall."

"No it won't!" she protested. "You can come for the weekend and my parents will never have to know."

"There is that!"

"And we could even go away. To another city. Like...New York!"

"What?"

"I've always wanted to go to New York at Christmas time. Actually, I don't like New York all that well. You can't see the sky there. You can't see the stars like you can in Chicago. But the Plaza is wonderful. The Plaza is the best. We can stay there and take a carriage ride through Central Park and go to Rockefeller Center and ice skate and dinner at the Four Seasons...all my favorites."

Tommy frowned.

"What?"

"Susie, I can't afford the Plaza. I don't even own a car!"

"Well, I do. Besides, I'm rich!"

They laughed at their joke and then fell peacefully silent, happy to be in the moment together.

Majestically reflecting its heavenly counterpart, Holy Name Cathedral rested imperiously on North State Street at Superior. Tommy had to park four blocks away.

"Man! I never knew there were this many Catholics in Chicago!" he said watching throngs of people huddled together shuffling down snow slick sidewalks toward the Cathedral.

"I love this Cathedral. It's the closest thing to heaven on earth," Susie replied getting out of the car.

The night air cut like glass and she wrapped her arms around herself. Her eyes traveled to the highest turret. "It was rebuilt in 1872 after the Great Chicago Fire, but all these flying buttresses and the towers and Gothic arches look just like the medieval cathedrals I saw in France and Germany. Just looking at the stained glass and the statuary makes me think of the hours the artisans loved over this church. To create something so beautiful; to leave a mark like this on the world. What must that be like?"

"You amaze me, Susie Howard."

"What?" She smiled at him.

Leaning down he rubbed his nose against hers. "You feel everything, don't you? Like the stars in the sky . . . you don't just see them, you feel them. I've watched you. It's like you can touch and smell and see every living thing. What must that be like, to live life like you do?"

"You mean you don't?"

"For a long time after Mom . . . " he glanced away and then back to her thinking the mist over his eyes was just because of the cold. "I'm alive when I'm with you."

Light puddled from the windows onto the snow at their feet creating colorful tapestries. The strains of a choir singing Christmas carols moved toward them from inside the building like a magnet drawing their minds and hearts to the magic of the night.

Susie held on to Tommy's arm as they joined the congregation and passed through the massive woodcarved doors.

Being over six foot, Tommy quickly spied the last remaining seats in the middle of the enormous church. "Hurry. I see a place for us."

He took her hand and gently pulled her down the marble floor to the pew. They crawled over a little girl and her father who seemed quite perturbed that anyone discovered the vacancy.

"Merry Christmas," Susie leaned down to whisper to the little girl wearing a red coat and carrying a brand new muff. "That's a very pretty coat you're wearing."

She looked the girl directly in the eye and smiled.

Still scowling, the little girl stared at Susie.

"Leave her be," the father whispered. "The procession is about to start."

Susie glanced at him and chose to ignore him. "You're very lucky to have such a beautiful outfit." She kept looking in the little girl's eyes.

Suddenly, the scowl melted off the little girl's face like a late winter snowman in spring.

Susie reached in her pocket. "I have something for you. I was keeping it for myself but I think you should have it." She pulled out a candy cane. "I swiped it from a bowl full of them at home."

"Oh, thank you," the little girl replied, eagerly clutching the candy cane.

Trumpets blasted. The organ swelled and the midnight bells clanged and chimed. The choir sang "Adeste Fidelis" in Latin and Susie felt goosebumps blanket her skin.

"Strange. After five weeks of carols at the store, suddenly, they aren't so boring," she whispered to Tommy.

"It's because we're together," he said confidently and took her hand.

Susie felt her heart swell with the music. Something was happening to her. She was seeing everything differently. A heightened sense of awareness caused her to take in every poinsettia on the altar, the statues of the saints and the Holy Family standing guard around the church. The windows glowed brighter. The choir sounded more angelic and the words to every prayer and song reverberated through her cells.

This is what it means to be in love.

The procession moved down the main aisle. Priests, bishops, altar boys and finally the school children costumed as shepherds, townspeople and Joseph and Mary walked down the aisle to the crèche. Susie and Tommy watched as the young girl acting as Mary placed a life size doll wrapped in swaddling clothes in the manger.

Tommy squeezed Susie's hand, raised it to his lips and kissed it. Susie's heart pounded, then soared as the choir's voices rose past the Gothic arches twenty five feet overhead, through the domed roof and straight on to heaven.

"I love you," Tommy said for the first time.

"I love you back," Susie replied, her eyes unable to hold the well of tears.

Wiping Susie's tears with his fingers, the Mass began and everyone knelt. The hour passed in a flash. Susie couldn't remember a thing the priest said during the sermon. All she heard over and over was Tommy saying "I love you."

Throughout the Mass, Tommy kept Susie's arm linked through his, his finger intertwined with his own. As they knelt, Susie couldn't help thinking how similar their positions were to those of a bride and groom on their wedding day.

She envisioned the day when she would marry Tommy. They would promise themselves to each other for eternity even when they went to heaven they would always be one.

For the first time in her life, Susie knew exactly what she wanted. She wanted to love Tommy all the days of her life.

When it came time for the processional, Susie was stunned the time was gone. So immersed in her visions of her future wedding, she felt as if she had to "wish" herself back to the present.

How odd. Perhaps this is what "time out of time" means.

The choir sang "Hark the Herald Angels Sing" and the entire congregation joined in for the next chorus. Susie had never sung so loudly in her life. Tommy had to stretch his vocal chords to outdo her, but he couldn't help himself. He felt like racing up the choir loft staircase to the roof and shouting to the world that he had never been this happy.

When it was their turn to exit their pew, the little girl next to Susie and who had watched her throughout the Mass, tapped Susie on the arm. "Thank you for the candy," she said.

"You're most welcome. You deserve it."

The little girl blushed. "I hope when I grow up I'm as beautiful as you."

"What a lovely thing to say to me," Susie said with a radiant smile.

"I hope I'm as happy as you are, too," she smiled toothlessly. Then she motioned for Susie to lean down for a secret. She covered Susie's ear with her hand while she whispered. "My Daddy and I are very sad because my mother died last year on Christmas. I was so sad last year I didn't even open my rabbit muff my mother bought for me. I kept it until tonight. But then you came and gave me this candy. I almost didn't believe in angels or Santa or anything anymore. I just wanted you to know that."

Susie's struggle to contain her tears was a lost battle. The muscles in her chest constricted, she ached with her exploding emotions. She hugged the girl and kissed her cheek. "What's your name?"

"Bridget."

"You've made my Christmas everything it should be, Bridget. Don't ever forget that."

"I'll never forget. I promise."

Susie watched as the little girl and her melancholy father left the church. Turning to Tommy she said, "I never thought about what my life would be like if one of my parents died until I met you. Then that sad little girl. I guess I didn't realize how lucky I am to have both my parents still alive all this time. They give me a lot of grief, but..."

"You are lucky. Trying to be happy at Christmas is rough when you are missing someone you love."

"Then I'm glad you have me this Christmas so you don't have to be alone."

"Me, too," he said planting a playful kiss on her nose. "C'mon. Let's go."

"Just a minute, Tommy. Can we stay? There's something I always do after Christmas Mass."

"Sure," he said and waited until the crowd had moved away from their pew.

Taking his hand, Susie walked to the front of the church, genuflected at the altar and then walked over to the far right side where the crèche was set up that year. There were two bronze kneelers in front of the crèche with plush burgundy velvet pads. "I want to light a candle," she said, taking a taper and lighting the wick of one of twenty multicolored votives.

"What color?" Tommy asked slipping a dollar bill into the collection slot.

"Blue. Always blue," she answered. "It's the color of Mary's robes."

"How do you know? Just because artists always depict her that way doesn't mean..."

Susie shook her head interrupting him. "Silly. Don't you think somewhere along the line even one of those artists was inspired to tell the truth the way it really was?"

"I hadn't thought of it like that."

Susie said her prayer and then gazed at the chipped statues inside the crèche. "She was so young, you know? I can't imagine what that must have been like for her. Her friends thought she was pregnant by another man. They forced Joseph to marry her. Then she goes to Bethlehem, in pain, and has to give birth to her baby all by herself, in a barn," Susie's voice fell to a painful whisper. "How lonely she must have been. Not to have her mother with her. And what if she wasn't in love with Joseph? He would be like a stranger to her."

A sharp pang of compassion caused her to wince. "I hope I never know what that is like."

Tommy placed his hand on the small of her back. "I think you already do."

She gazed up at him. "No I don't." Her lower lip trembled. "I have you."

A searing lump in Tommy's throat kept him from responding. He rose, crossed himself and held out his hand to her.

Once out of the cathedral, Tommy and Susie tromped through a thick blanket of new fallen snow to her car.

"I don't want this night to ever end," Susie said.

"Then I won't let it. I'll make it last forever for you," he said, leaning her against the car and pulling her into him.

"Tommy Magli, are you going to kiss me right here in front of God?"

"Uh, huh. And all these people."

When he kissed her, it was if she could feel her heart open its chamber doors to a sun that had never shone its light on her. A song burst inside her unlike anything they'd sung that night.

"I love you, Susie," he said.

"This," she replied, touching his lips with her fingertips and peering into his eyes, "is Christmas."

Chapter Five

"This isn't the way back to your house. Where are we going?" Susie asked.

"I have something I want to give you," Tommy said, "but I didn't want to give it to you at my house."

"I thought we were going to my house."

"Not there, either." He drove onto the Northwestern campus. "Look, Susie. You don't have to pretend with me. I know your parents don't like me."

"They don't know you!"

"They didn't want me to be at that party tonight even though we'd already made plans of our own."

"Hey, you're the one who doesn't want to come to my house for Christmas dinner tomorrow."

"Susie, you understand so many things. Why can't you understand that my Dad . . . well . . ."

She put her hand on his arm. "I do understand. He does need you more than I do. Especially tomorrow. I want you more than he does, but he needs you."

"That's my girl," Tommy breathed with relief.

"Ah, here we are."

Susie looked up. "The Sigma Chi house? What are we doing here? The place is practically abandoned."

He opened his door. "There are a couple guys still here. They live too far to go home for Christmas. Costs too much, too."

Susie waited until he opened her door for her. "I can't imagine not having enough money to get on a bus to be with your family."

"Well, it happens," Tommy replied, leading her up the steps to the old house. "And for your information, I do have a 'sort of' room here. I crash here sometimes with Ben Breedlow when I have to cram for a test or something."

They entered the old house with its wood floors and large wood staircase. The Sigma Chi coat of arms with its blue

47

shield and centered Medieval Cross hung over the fireplace in the main drawing room.

"It looks like a Crusader's sword more than a cross, doesn't it?" she mused.

"It does," he said as he shucked his parka and she took off her coat. "Come on. My room is on the second floor."

She followed him up the staircase and down a hall to the third door. He unlocked the door with a key and let her in. Rolling Stones posters plastered the walls. A brown Philco radio turned low played Elvis Presley's "Blue Christmas". A set of bunk beds sat against the wall, covered in black watchplaid blankets. A battered oak desk sat under an undraped wide double hung window and to the right was a hand-me-down club chair covered in navy corduroy, the room's only attempt at interior design. A two-foot pine tree was propped up in a bucket of sand glowing with all blue lights. The tree was decorated with candy canes, strings of popcorn and cranberries and colored paper chains. "I made it myself," he said proudly.

"Dad didn't want a tree at home, but Mom and I . . ." he paused for a moment then continued. "We always did the popcorn and berries. One kernel. One berry. One kernel. One berry. It's prettier that way, don't you think?"

"I do."

Susie crossed to the tree touching the berries. "I like having just the blue lights."

"When I was little, Mom told me a tree looked more like the North Pole that way, all icy and blue."

"She was right," Susie agreed assessing the look. "It's . . . heavenly."

"Yeah. Like stars," he said standing behind her and slipping his arms around her. He nuzzled her neck.

"My mother does everything in white and gold. White flocked tree. Gold balls. Her decorator does it, actually," Susie said softly, mesmerized by the little tree.

"Mom always made cut-out cookies and we iced them and strung a ribbon through a hole in the top and put them on the tree. It would look better with the cookies."

"It's just beautiful. Thank you for making it for us."

"Okay. Now sit down."

"Why?"

He groaned. "Will you just do it?"

"Okay." She started to go to the bed, but he redirected her to the club chair.

"No. Over here."

"Okay . . ." She sat.

Tommy knelt on the floor in front of her. He reached in his slacks pocket.

Susie's hands flew to her mouth. "Oh, my God!"

"It's not what you think!" he said quickly.

"It's not?"

"Well, sort of . . ." He looked in her eyes. "I can't afford a ring. You have to know that."

"I . . ."

Putting his fingers on her lips, he said, "Shhh. I would give anything to have a gold band in my pocket right now. I want you so badly I wish we could run away to Kentucky and get married tonight."

Her eyes flew open. "Tommy . . ."

"But we can't. I have to finish school. Heck! I have law school to think about. And that . . ."

"Doesn't leave time for a wife," she interjected.

"Would you be quiet?" he laughed and fumbled with her sweater. "Would you promise to be my girl and wear my pin?"

"What?" She glanced down as he finished placing his Sigma Chi pin on her lapel.

"Marry me . . . someday?"

"Oh, yes! Yes! Yes!"

She threw her arms around him and kissed him happily. He held her face in his hands, kissing her tenderly.

"This way, you'll always be my own personal Sweetheart of Sigma Chi."

"Tommy, I love you."

He kissed her with more passion than he knew his heart contained. She leaned back in the chair, pulling him with her.

He couldn't hold her close enough. Couldn't kiss her long enough. "I knew the first night we met you were the one for me."

Tears sprung into Susie's eyes she was so moved. "I had hoped so. I hoped. And prayed, but I didn't know . . ."

She kissed him deeply, her passion matching his. Her heart opened and swelled to such proportions her soul shone brightly around her.

"Make love to me, Tommy," she said.

"We shouldn't," he replied breathlessly, not believing his own refusal.

Gently, she pushed him away and rose out of the chair. She kicked off her Capezzios and taking his hand, she pulled him with her to the lower bunk. "It has to be tonight of all nights. Christmas."

"Susie . . ." he shook his head. "I . . . I don't have anything . . . I didn't think. I mean, I didn't prepare for this."

"It's okay," tears streamed down her cheek. She lay down on the bed.

The blue light from the tree made her look ethereal, like the blue fairy in his mother's fairy tales. "You're the most beautiful thing I've ever seen in my life. I'm so lucky."

"We both are Tommy."

He stretched out alongside her. He swept the tears from her face with his fingertips. He kissed her again.

"I take you, Susie Howard, to be my wife."

"I take you, Tommy Magli, to be my husband."

Lacing their fingers and together without forethought they whispered, "God bless us always."

"And forever," Susie said, as Tommy moved over her.

It was two in the morning when Susie and Tommy walked out of the Sigma Chi house. Tommy held Susie close to his body against the night chill.

"I had no idea it was this late," Susie said. "And I still have to drive you home."

"When do your parents get in from their party?"

"Sometimes they go on till dawn. I can only hope. They'll sleep till ten, then we go to noon Mass and open our presents Christmas night."

"They made you wait until Christmas night to open presents?"

"Not when I was little. They still went to the party. They just got less sleep," she chuckled as they walked down the sidewalk to the curb. She noticed that Tommy's face was serious.

"What's wrong?" she asked.

"Promise me, you have no regrets," Tommy said.

She stopped under the street lamp. Golden light washed over her like a halo. Softly, she smiled, "No, I told you. It was my idea."

"I know but maybe . . . we should have waited."

"What? For five more years? Two of undergrad, three of law school?"

"I just want you to be sure."

She rolled her eyes heavenward. She stopped. "Look at that."

"What?" Tommy turned. "Is someone watching us?" He checked the fraternity house windows.

"No, the moon. I read about this in the Trib. See? It's a crescent moon and that star hanging off the very bottom tip is Venus. They call it the Christmas Star. It's a celestial event. Some say it's the real star of Bethlehem. Venus being that huge in the western sky happens only once in thirty years. Do you realize we'll probably only see it twice in our lifetime? It's a sign."

"Of what?"

"Of how special this night is. This time is. How special we are. You and me. Together forever."

Hugging her, they gazed at the star together. "It's our star."

Tommy smiled and kissed her neck. "I can feel it blessing us. Nothing bad will ever happen to us."

Susie kissed him. "Nothing. Not ever."

Chapter Six

New Years came and went and though both Susie and Tommy had mid term exams facing them, they both took every second in their afternoons and weekends to be together.

"You should be studying," Susie said cuddling next to him in her Mustang parked at Oak Street Beach.

"I have a 'B' average going into nearly every class. Except Biology. Good thing I'm going into law. This science and math makes me nuts. Requireds. Who ever came up with the idea we have to study subjects we are never going to use?"

"I don't know," she replied kissing him. "But I worry. You haven't cracked a cover since..."

"I'll do fine," he said, unbuttoning her cardigan.

Suddenly, she stopped him. "B average? I thought you were top of your class."

"I'll get it back."

"Now I'm feeling terribly guilty. You did have straight A's until I came along. Right?"

"Susie. You're the best thing that ever happened to me. What's a great grade point without a life?"

Tommy moved away from her and leaned back in his seat. "You sound like my Dad."

"Really?"

"He harps on it day and night. He's into scare tactics now."

"Explain," she said.

"That if I don't pull my grades up, I could be drafted. Go to Vietnam. Like I said, scare tactics."

"Tommy, he's right! You know how much I want to see you, but if you lost your scholarship . . . I'd never forgive myself. And the draft!" She shuddered and hugged herself as a foreboding swept over her like a glacier wind. "Okay, that's it. I'll take you home."

"What? Now?"

"Yes, now. You've only got a week until finals. So do I. But if I mess up, it's not the end of my life."

"It's not the end of mine, either," he said pulling her close and kissing her.

"Look. One of us has to be the responsible one. Tag. I'm it," she said with a smile. "So. You staying on campus or going home?"

"Campus. Less time wasted in traffic. I get more studying in that way."

"Good thinking," she said leaning over and turning on the ignition.

When Susie arrived home her parents were watching the nightly news. Walter Jacobson's face filled the new color television screen.

Hanging up her coat and scarf, Susie said, "When do you think they'll broadcast the news in color? Seems a waste of money for that TV . . ."

"Shhh!" her father warned leaning closer to the television rather than turning up the volume.

"Hello, dear," her mother said. "You're home early. Didn't you like the movie?"

"We didn't go. I have to study. Finals are next week," she replied walking into the den.

"Amazing. I didn't think anything could pry you away from . . . that boy."

"Mother."

Braxton waved an anxious hand at them. "Not now. I want to hear this."

They all focused on the television.

"American troops have launched their most aggressive offense of the war. Twenty miles north of Saigon, eight thousand American Army soldiers struck a Communist stronghold. The attack is being called Iron Triangle. Preceding this ground offensive, U.S. B-52's conducted the most intense bombing raids thus far. This new offensive was conducted independently of the South Vietnamese government signaling a turn in U.S. military politics and strategy. The Pentagon stated that Iron Triangle was kept secret for fear of infiltration of Viet Cong agents into the South Vietnamese army."

Susie stood ramrod straight as the impact of the newscaster's words sank in. For the second time that night, she felt her blood turn to ice water. Her mouth went dry.

Please, God. Don't let that be Tommy.

"Over one hundred and fifty-four thousand of our GI's are over there. Last month they moved into the Mekong Delta. Bombing raids. Artillery fire."

"What are you saying, Dad?" Susie asked.

"I'm saying that finally Johnson's got some balls and just may end this damn war and quickly." Braxton walked out of the room toward the kitchen.

Susie looked at her mother.

"Are you all right, Susie? You look pale. Like you've seen a ghost." Mary Elizabeth said.

"I'm fine. Just worried about my tests is all."

"You'll do fine, dear. You always do." She stopped, rubbed Susie's shoulder and then left her alone in the den.

Fine? Sure. But what about Tommy?

Looking around the room at the last of the Christmas clutter the maids had nearly finished packing away, Susie felt that feeling again.

Only this time she recognized it for what it was.

Fear.

* * * *

Susie stuck by her guns and didn't see Tommy during the week in order that they could both study. Stalwartness did not preclude him from telephoning her late at night while her parents were sleeping.

"Tommy, we have to get off this phone."

"Tell me you love me. Once more."

"I love you. Now will you study?" she laughed. "You know, you're incorrigible. That's what you are."

"I'm in love. That's all. Besides, I aced my Poli Sci final. I know it."

"You got the scores back already?"

"No, just intuition."

"Boys don't have intuition."

"Who said that? This is not a rule. Besides, I'll be finished on Friday."

"Just in time for our dinner with my parents on Saturday," she smiled.

"Oh, God. I forgot. Meet the parents," he groaned, wiping his hand over his face. "They won't like me."

Frowning, she said, "They already don't like you."

"What? Then why are we doing this?"

"It's your job to dazzle them," she grinned. "It's not you they don't like. They don't even know you. You're my pick and that's a problem."

"Love and trust go hand in hand. You're so easy to love. Why would you think they don't trust you?"

"To them, I'm still a child."

"That's natural. All we have to do is be patient with them. Time is on our side. They'll come around," he assured her.

"I hope so."

Tommy's finals were grueling two to four hour marathons as he filled up blue books with his essay answers. He went from one test to the next walking across the snowy quad, passing student anti-war protestors who were huddled together, their poster board signs arranged around them like shields against the blistering cold, their passions gone dim.

Tommy recognized one of them. "Mark! What's happening?"

Mark Conner broke rank and bounded over to Tommy. Both shoved their hands into their parka pockets. "Since when did you join the SDS?"

"I'm outta here, man," Mark said.

"What?"

"I screwed up. I bet I don't pull even a 65 on the first course. And I can't sit around here and wait to be drafted. My brother is already over there. It's hell, man."

"So what are you saying?"

"I'm driving to Toronto with Jesse there," Mark said sadly looking around him, drinking in the old buildings. "I love this place. My father went here. And his father." Mark pretended the tears in his eyes were from the cold. "Jesus. This can't be happening to me."

"It's not."

"What?" Mark cocked his head to the side.

"We make our own choices. Good or bad."

Their eyes met. Shame flooded Mark's face. Instantly, Tommy regretted his statement. "I'm sorry, man. I don't know what it's like to walk in your shoes. My Dad barely finished high school. He practically thinks I'm a god just for getting into Northwestern. It would kill him if I lost my scholarship." Tommy stomped his foot against the sidewalk knocking the falling snow off his Bass Weejuns. "Hey, I better get. I've got American Lit in five minutes."

"Sure, man. Good seeing ya'," Mark replied lowly. "You busy Saturday?"

"Yeah. I'm meeting my girlfriend's parents on Saturday."

Mark smiled coyly. "No kidding. That serious?"

Tommy smiled broadly. "The most."

"Good for you, man. Well, I'm heading out on Sunday. If I don't see you . . ." Mark's voice skipped over the lump in his throat.

Tommy grabbed him in a bear hug. "You take care, man."

"I'll write. Let you know where I land. Okay?"

"Deal." Tommy said walking backward and giving a short wave. "Stay in touch."

Tommy saw the handwriting on the wall before he finished his last final. He'd done well in American Literature but it wouldn't be enough to pull up his Latin, Math and Biology scores. The last of his required courses would kill him. By the weekend, his stomach was in knots. Ever since his conversation with Mark, he'd feared that he would be forced into the same decision.

Tommy's choice would be exactly the opposite. He'd enlist, try to get into the Marines with pilot training, maybe, then survive the war and use the GI bill to finish his education and go on to law school.

It wasn't the best plan. But it was a plan.

He told himself he was prepared.

That weekend, the frat house was full up over finals, but Tommy hung out only long enough to shower, change and catch a bus to Kenilworth. From the bus stop, he would walk the rest of the way to Susie's house. It was a matter of pride that he didn't want her parents to pay for a cab nor did he want Susie to drive to campus to pick him up.

The changes in his life echoed through the marrow in his bones. It was true that before Suzie he'd been near the top of his class. Since the day his mother had died, his father had retreated into alcohol and Tommy had retreated to his books. Each was a prison.

Susie had brought Tommy back to the living. He'd never felt this alive, this hopeful about himself and his life. Maybe he had screwed up. Maybe he should have kept his eye on the ball and listened to his dad's warnings about the draft. Foolishly, he'd thought he was invincible. He thought he could skip classes to see Susie. Skip reading his textbooks, compiling his term papers and research reports to spend half the night on the phone with her.

She was like a drug. The more he saw her the more he felt he couldn't breathe without her. He'd never smiled so much, felt so much, and wanted so much more for himself out of life.

There had never been anyone in his life who made him feel king of the world just by looking at him. He'd known it the second he laid eyes on her. He hadn't even been looking for a girlfriend. In fact, he'd purposefully kept himself and his emotions cut off from others. He was afraid to get close to anyone. Afraid of being abandoned again. Afraid of losing.

Death teaches that.

Maybe he had been a fool and a dangerous one at that. Still, as far as he was concerned, what difference would a war make when he was already dead inside?

Susie had changed everything.

Susie had made him want to live again. To live for her.

Tommy stopped in front of the Howard mansion and gasped. "Holy cow!"

The stone and brick French country manor looked like a chateau plucked straight out of the Loire Valley in France. Two huge Norman turrets soared three stories to the sky. Lamplight poured from a profusion of beveled glass windows casting glowing beams across the new fallen snow. A pair of heavily hewn curved dark wood doors sat majestically in the center of the structure, still bearing ornate pinecone wreaths. Two perfectly pruned conical evergreens shot up out of black wrought iron urns on either side of the doors.

Tommy rang the bell and stepped back as a butler wearing a formal black tuxedo opened the door.

I'm toast.

Tommy swallowed hard and stared at the man.

The butler stared back.

"Mr. Howard?"

"No, sir. I'm David."

Tommy gaped at the man, wracking his brain wondering if this was some relative he was supposed to have remembered.

"I'm the butler, sir," David smiled condescendingly.

"Of course. I knew that." Tommy stepped inside.

"Your coat, sir."

Tommy let the man take his corduroy parka. Though he wore his navy wool sport coat, gray pullover sweater with a white button down dress shirt beneath, charcoal gray wool slacks and his loafers, he'd never felt quite so inadequate.

"Tommy!" Susie nearly shouted from the top of the monstrously wide double staircase.

His eyes lit up at the sight of her.

Casually dressed in a Kelly green sweater and green and black watch plaid kilt, black tights and flats, she instantly put him at ease as she flew down the stairs to him.

"I thought you'd never get here!" she gushed, hugging him tightly not caring how much her love shone.

He kissed her quickly, watching as disapproval knit the butler's brows.

"You didn't tell me about the butler," Tommy said.

Rolling her eyes, she said, "David is part-time. Mother only employs him when she's trying to impress someone."

"And she's trying to impress me? That's a good sign," he said.

"Scare you off is more like it," Susie chuckled.

"That's what I love about you, Susie. You always tell it like it is."

"Hey, better to know thine enemies. First rule of guerrilla warfare," she said mirthfully, slipping her arm through his and leading him into the vast living room. "I think you're very brave to fight for me like this."

A fire roared in the marble fireplace. A long mushroom colored velvet sofa with gold bullion fringe sat facing the fire. Two antique Chippendale wing chairs flanked an eight-foot square marble and wood coffee table. The art on the walls were originals, Tommy could tell, though he knew little about the artists except that the paintings were not recognizable.

Mary Elizabeth and Braxton sat facing each other, each in a wing chair of their own. Silent. Watching. They turned when Susie and Tommy entered the room, their faces implacable. Stoic. Guarded.

They were prepared for battle.

Tommy leaned down to Susie's ear. "Remember, I would do anything for you. I would die for you."

Tommy smiled at them. "So wonderful to meet you Mrs. Howard. Mr. Howard."

They rose slowly, taking in every inch of his appearance.

Mary Elizabeth sniffed the air as if she'd smelled something foul.

Braxton clasped his hands in front of him and forced a smile. "Mr. Magli, is it?"

Tommy beamed a charismatic smile. "Thomas Magli. Yes, sir." Tommy dropped Susie's arm, walked around the sofa to Braxton and shook his hand. "This is good of you to invite me to your home, sir."

"Yes . . . well . . . ," Mary Elizabeth started to say.

"It's important," Tommy interrupted, "since we'll all be family." He turned to a stunned Susie. "You *are* going to marry me, aren't you?"

Mary Elizabeth's eyes rolled back in her head and she sank dead away into the wing chair.

The Christmas Star

Chapter Seven

"Why did you do that?" Susie asked, trying to stifle a giggle as she and Tommy walked out the front door into the cold night.

"You didn't tell me she was apoplectic."

"This was a first!" Susie said, walking him down the front steps of her house.

"Then she's not prone to fainting?" Tommy opened his jacket and pulled her close to his chest to keep her warm.

"Never! And the look on my father's face! I thought he was going to swallow his tongue. He actually turned blue!" Susie kept laughing. "It was a great joke. It really threw them off."

Tommy stopped dead in his tracks. "Joke? You know I want to marry you."

"But they don't."

"They do now. Besides, I thought everyone would be happy about it. Maybe they would like me, knowing I'm serious about us," he said looking at her droopy expression. "Where did I screw up?"

"That was my official proposal?"

"What? Not good enough?"

"I was expecting more . . . well, romance."

"Okay." He dropped to his knee still holding her hand. "Susie, will you marry me?"

Playfully, she considered his face for a very long beat. "No. Still not it. You'll have to do better."

He took both her hands, kissed them and said, "My darling, Susie, I beg of you to marry me."

"Better."

"But not there yet?" he asked.

"We have plenty of time for you to get it down right. Maybe you might want to brush up on your delivery. I was looking at second semester classes for you. Theatre arts. Shakespeare would help."

They were both laughing as Tommy rose and they walked toward the street.

"You better get inside," he said. "I wouldn't want you to catch cold."

"I'm fine . . . as long as I'm next to you." She looked up. "Moon's full tonight."

With his hands cradling her face, he kissed her. "Every time we look at the full moon, let's always think of us. I'm only half a moon without you, Susie."

"Now that was romantic," she said and kissed him back.

Every time Tommy held her, Susie felt the bond of their love grow stronger. Though they had only been dating for just a few months, she could not imagine herself ever kissing another man. Tommy was her prince, her savior and her partner for life. She didn't have to trap him into marriage. She didn't have to play games. She was already his for keeps.

Reluctantly, Tommy broke the kiss, snuggling his lips in the crook of her neck. "I hate leaving you. I really do. I wish I could stay with you all night. To hold you close to me until dawn is all I think about on that long, long bus ride home."

"Tommy Magli, I'm not going to sneak you up to my room."

"Damn," he chuckled, touching the tip of her nose with his fingertip. "That's not what I meant. I really do want us to be husband and wife. But I want to do it the right way."

"Me, too, and that means after law school, I know."

"But you're disappointed," he said. "So am I."

"Life isn't perfect, I'm discovering," she said hugging him close once again. "That said, you have to go."

"I'll call you when I get home."

"I'll be waiting," she said, hugging her arms around herself and skipping back up the walk to the front door. She turned just before going back inside. "I love you, Tommy. I'll wait forever."

Tommy blew her a kiss and dashed down the sidewalk to make the ten o'clock bus ride back to campus.

The following Saturday Tommy was one step ahead of the mailman who delivered his grade cards to his father's house. Tommy saw the mailman walking up the sidewalk and rushed out to the front porch.

"How's it going?" Tommy asked.

"Coldest winter I ever remember," the man replied.

"I don't know how you stand it," Tommy said, taking the stack of bills and the long envelope marked with Northwestern University's seal from the man.

"Silk long johns, that's how," the mailman answered Tommy's question. "My wife found them for me. They really do the trick. She said Olympic skiers use them. I'm as warm as toast in here. That and a big lunch of White Castle burgers and fries. I'm good to go."

Nodding absentmindedly as he stared at the envelope that carried his doom, Tommy said, "Silk. I'll remember that."

"Catch you later," the man waved as he left.

Jed was sitting at the Formica topped kitchen table eating cold pasta when Tommy walked back from the front porch. "I swear Loretta is never going to get the hang of marinara sauce. If I'm supposed to be her newest charity case, the least she could do is remember I like penne pasta and not linguine." He looked up. "What's that?"

"Bills." Tommy placed the stack on the table with the Northwestern envelope squarely on top.

Glancing down, Jed harrumphed. "More than that, I'll bet. From the look on your face I can tell what's in that envelope isn't good."

"It's not."

"Don't you want to open it?"

"Sure."

Tommy opened the envelope with the kind of care an archeologist employs to unearth centuries old secrets. He held the three-inch by three-inch squares of carbon-backed paper scribbled with letters that represented the biggest turn his future was ever to take.

"Dad. I'm going to enlist before they draft me."

Jed stopped grinding away on his pasta. He took his time rising and then shuffled across the linoleum to the cabinet, his slippers sliding across the floor echoing hopelessness. He pulled out a bottle of vodka. "Bloody Mary?"

"Why not." Tommy stared at the markings, then traced the four "D's" and one "F" with his fingertips. "Strange. A. D. C. They're only letters, aren't they?"

"Nope," Jed replied, dully choosing very long Tom Collins glasses. "They were chances."

"And you think I blew them?"

"Nope." Jed pressed a can opener into a large can of V-8 juice.

"You think I spent too much time with Susie. Now I have to make other choices with my life. I lost my scholarship," Tommy whispered, feeling pangs of pain in his eyes, but not tears.

"Yep. You lost your scholarship. But not because of Susie."

Tommy's head snapped up. "What?"

Jed stirred the drinks and placed one in front of Tommy. "You lost because you didn't believe in her love enough to trust her."

"Dad . . . "

"Yeah, you shoulda been studyin'. Yeah, you shoulda hung up the phone. But if you'd have really seen what I've seen when she looks at you, you would know. She loves you, Tommy. Any fool can see that. She's not gonna go away either. She's the kind of woman that stays. I've only seen that once before in my life."

"Mom."

"Yeah," Jed said, washing the fiery emotions in his throat down with the Bloody Mary. He stared blankly at his glass. "Your mom was eighteen when we got married. I couldn't wait to get out of high school just so's we could be on our own. All I wanted was to sleep with her every night and watch her face light up when I walked into a room. I never thought I could be that lucky. I never wanted anything else in my life either." He drank again. "'Cept you."

"I know just how you feel. Felt."

"I miss her so damn much I hurt inside." He turned toward the kitchen cabinets, not wanting Tommy to see him cry. He held onto the counter with both hands as if he'd sink to his knees without support. "It's all the time, you know? Some days I can't even breathe. I don't think it's ever going away."

Jed straightened and then drank again, draining his glass. "So. Here's the deal. You do what you have to."

"I'm not running, Dad. I'm not going to Canada or Brazil or anything like that."

"Geezus. A patriot."

"That's how you raised me." Tommy said slowly, then leveled his gaze on Jed. "Dad, I've always been proud that you fought for freedom. I still get goosebumps every time I hear *America the Beautiful*. I know this isn't a popular war and I know I could die, but damn it, I also believe that sometimes we have to fight for what we believe in and I'm not afraid to do that. How can I ask Susie to marry me when the freedoms of this country are in doubt? How can I bring a child into this world if I can't look him in the eye someday like you do and say, 'I did my best for my country and for my family'?"

"You've really thought about this."

"More than anything else in my life."

"More than Susie?"

"Perhaps. Or maybe she's the reason I feel so adamant about going over there. It's hard to explain. I came alive when I met her, yet I may lose my life because of her. Because of my wanting to keep this country safe for her."

Jed nodded. "Most wars are fought either because of a woman or for a woman. Keeping the homeland safe is what America is about."

Jed slapped Tommy on the back and smiled broadly for the first time in years. "I'm proud of you, son."

"Thanks, Dad." Tommy reached across the table and put his hand over those of his father.

It struck him for the first time in a long time, how similar they were.

Strong hands. Big hands. Hands that could tackle a great deal in life.

"You pick a branch yet?" Jed asked feeling uncomfortable with his emotions screaming through his insides like banshees.

"Marines. Get over there, get back quick. Get the GI Bill and get back into school."

"I hear ya. Good thinking."

"They told me that even law school wouldn't be a problem."

"Good plan. Don't worry about Susie, son. She's the waiting kind."

"I hope so."

"I know so."

January, 11, 1966

Susie met Tommy at a small café in Highland Park at 6:30 after her classes were out for the afternoon. It was bitter cold, with the wind slicing through her Yves St. Laurent wool pea coat like razors. When he kissed her hello, their lips were so cold they nearly stuck.

"I missed you," she said walking to the back of the café to a round table.

"I always miss you, Susie," he said, with more sadness in his voice than he'd known existed.

She looked out the window and clamped her hand over her mouth feeling dread wash over her. "This isn't going to be good. I can feel it."

"Feel what?"

She looked him in the eye. "Do you want to break up with me?"

"What? Where on earth did that come from?"

"Something is terribly wrong," she said excitedly. "I know it. I can feel every brain wave that shoots across your head, Tommy Magli. If you don't want to break up, what is it?"

"I'm going away."

"A . . way?"

"I enlisted."

Tears flooded her eyes. "Oh, God."

"I didn't want to wait to be drafted. I joined the Marines," he began quickly. "Even though my grades weren't all that good this past semester, the Marines seem to feel I'm top notch material. Officer's candidate and all that. I'm taking some extra tests. Maybe I can qualify to be a pilot or for the special forces."

Susie heard only every other word. The pressure of loss inside her made her feel as if she would erupt. Her heart was so heavy she actually thought it might fall straight out of her body.

This must be what it feels like to die. Surely I'm dying.

"You'll see, sweetheart, this is for the best. I can come back and go to law school on the GI bill. No loans to pay back . . . "

"Are you insane?" she finally interrupted. "How can it be good that you are going to war?"

She was crying hysterically now. She couldn't stop it. Sobs racked her body. Her chest heaved and all she could do was grab Tommy and hold on. She would never tell him not to go. She would never stop him. She loved that he was a patriot. She loved that he was proud of his country and his father and that he loved her enough to want to fight an evil, though distant, aggressor for her and for their future as a family. But at the same time, she hated him for making this choice. She hated all wars and anything evil or mundane that would keep her from being with Tommy.

She thought of a million things to say, a dozen arguments to present, but in the end, her mind quieted and she realized if she truly loved him, she would let him go.

"I love you, Tommy," she whispered between sobs.

"I love you so much, Susie, it hurts," he said cradling her face in his shoulder. "I didn't know how to tell you. I was afraid to tell you."

He reached across the table for a paper napkin from the steel dispenser and handed it to her. She blew her nose.

"When do you leave?"

"Saturday."

Tears began anew. "So soon?"

"The sooner I go, the sooner I get back."

"I hate when people use that logic. It's doesn't make sense."

He tried to smile. "It's the only logic I've got."

"Where do you go?"

"California. Most guys from east of the Mississippi go to South Carolina, but I've been taking these tests like I was telling you. Special Forces Training they call it."

"You mean dangerous forces," she said gulping hard.

"I figure, I'll be with the best guys the Marines have got. That's a plus."

Her eyes held his and she reached for his hand. "No, Tommy. You're the best the Marines have got. They just don't know it yet."

"Will you come to see me off?" he asked.

Touching his cheek, he took her hand and kissed the palm. "Tommy, I told you. I'll follow you wherever you want to go. And I'll wait for you forever."

March, 1966.

Mary Elizabeth sat at her antique white French desk paying bills and sorting through the day's mail. In a short period of time, she'd come to recognize the blue airmail letters Tommy Magli sent like clockwork to Susie.

It killed her not to open them and read them. She perceived that whatever lines were written there, would give her insight into her daughter's mind.

It was inconceivable to Mary Elizabeth that Susie was genuinely in love with Tommy. It was bad enough the boy had no family background to speak of, but for him to have flunked out of Northwestern and in the twinkling of an eye to enlist in the Marines, simply underscored the fact that he hadn't an ounce of foresight or breeding.

"Hi, Mom!" Susie called rushing in the front door tracking snow onto the parquet floor. Suddenly, she stopped and went back and wiped her feet, a habit she'd been taught. "Did I get any mail?"

"Yes," Mary Elizabeth did not turn or greet her daughter, but simply held two airmail letters over her shoulder. "Two letters today. I thought boot camp was grueling. This boy seems to have nothing but time on his hands."

Susie grabbed the letters and clutched them to her heart. "Two!"

She skipped up the stairs to her bedroom and turned on the hi-fi as Percy Sledge's *When a Man Loves a Woman* filled the room and her head. She felt an overwhelming desire to spend just five more minutes with Tommy. Every memory, every phone call from him, underscored her actions. Often, she would go back to the little café at precisely six-thirty and read his letters privately. Sometimes, like today, she would read them in her bedroom. Anxiously tearing them open, she read quickly at first, her eyes scanning past the passages about the dreary drilling exercises and study hours of his day to the all-important "I love you" at the end. Then she read the letter again drinking in every word. She kissed the letters, carefully folded them and replaced them in the envelopes.

There was so much about him she didn't want to share with her parents or girlfriends. Yet, she wanted to run out onto the middle of Lake Shore Drive and scream at the top of her lungs, "I'm in love with Tommy Magli!"

But she never did.

Instead, she kept his sweet yearnings written in his letters tied in a bundle and locked in her desk drawer along with pens and ink cartridges and high school memorabilia.

It never dawned on Susie that she was too young to be this intensely in love. She only knew that she was.

Braxton Howard arrived home early that afternoon, brushing the falling snow off his overcoat lapels, he called out to Mary Elizabeth. "Honey, I'm home."

Mary Elizabeth walked out of the living room. "Hello, dear," she said, offering her cheek for a kiss rather than giving one. "I heard you drive up," she said, her eyes glancing up the stairs.

Frowning, Braxton followed her gaze. "Susie's home?"

"Yes."

"What? No Art Club? No Glee Club? No sodas with Katie Roberts?"

"I haven't the slightest. She never talks about her school friends or their activities anymore. Not since this crush she's developed over that Magli boy."

Braxton put his felt hat on the top shelf of the closet and took off his coat and hung it up. "It's not a crush, Mary Elizabeth."

She brightened. "You don't think so? You think I'm making too much of this?"

He walked to the console and picked up the evening edition of the newspaper. "I'll make a fire. Then I'll explain it to you."

She followed him into the living room. "What do you know that I don't?"

He kept his back to her as he worked, taking a deep breath before pressing forward. "She's in love. I, for one, am a good judge of people and I can tell this isn't going to go away the way you'd like to think. Frankly, I'd just get used to the idea."

"It's worse than we thought," Mary Elizabeth groaned.

"Than you thought," he interjected.

"We have to do something to put an end to this. She can't marry a . . nobody. She doesn't realize what she's doing. She's young. There will be other boys. Other men. Men who have a standing in the community. Professions. Men who will make a difference in this world. Men like . . . well, you, Braxton."

He softened and faced her. "That's very sweet of you to say, dear. It's been a long time since you've been quite so flattering to me."

She was aghast. "Braxton, you know that I love you. I practically idolize you."

"Maybe we've been together for so long, I forgot how you felt."

"I can't be that remiss in not telling you," she went to him and hugged him. "You're my world, Braxton. I just wanted our daughter to find the same kind of love and friendship we have."

Braxton held her close and chuckled. "Well, you're not going about it the right way."

"You know, I thought that once Tommy was away at boot camp, she would start to forget about him, but it's only gotten worse."

"I'm not so sure about that. Sure, she waits for his letters, but it's a novelty right now. This being apart will either make them stronger or drive them apart. I have no idea if this is really love for her, but I do know that only time will tell. And whatever decision she makes, it has to be hers."

Mary Elizabeth broke away, nodding. "I suppose you're right. Still . . . "

He rubbed his arms, "It's getting cold now that the sun is down. Let me get this fire going. How about fixing us a couple old fashioneds?"

"All right," Mary Elizabeth said glancing back up the stairs. "I'll tell Susie you're home. Maybe she'd like a soda with us and some of those sausage balls I made for the party on Saturday."

"Good idea," he replied, stuffing pinecones under the logs on the grate.

Mary Elizabeth mounted the stairs.

Still acutely aware of the tension between herself and Susie, she thought twice about moving forward with her scheme to break up Susie and Tommy. It was possible Braxton was right in just letting time take its course. But Mary Elizabeth's womanly instincts told her that time was not on her side. She didn't know exactly why she felt pressed to plot against her own flesh and blood, but she did.

She told herself she was doing it for Susie's own good.

Resolve, Mary Elizabeth. You can do this.

She knocked tentatively on the door. "Susie, can I come in?"

73

"Sure."

I hate walking on eggshells. If only Susie weren't so stubborn!

"I got a call from your cousin Joannie today," Mary Elizabeth said walking into the room.

"Really? How's everything in New York?"

"Fine, I suppose. You can ask her for yourself. She's coming to visit."

Susie rolled over on the bed and sat up. "Why?"

"It seems her husband has been in training at Great Lakes Naval Base. He's being shipped out in a week and she wants to visit him before he goes overseas."

"Husband? I thought they called off the Thanksgiving wedding. Why didn't you tell me?"

"I did tell you about it, Susan, but as usual you weren't listening. They eloped the weekend after she left here in October. He was drafted. You weren't listening. I guess you were too busy back then to pay attention to others."

Susie glanced away refusing to rise to the bait. "When will she be here?"

"Tomorrow. I'll pick her up at Midway at four."

"I could make that from school by four. I know how you hate the Dan Ryan. I'll pick her up."

"Would you, dear? That would save me so much time. I thought we'd have a nice dinner here. I'll have Annie put in a prime rib."

"Joannie likes pineapple upside down cake."

Mary Elizabeth smiled genuinely. "How sweet you remembered that. Thank you." Pausing, she asked, "Do you have a great deal of homework tonight?"

"Not too much. Plenty of time to write to Tommy. Don't worry." Susie didn't hide the defiance in her eyes. If she could will her mother to love Tommy some day, she would.

But Mary Elizabeth didn't flinch. She knew exactly the game her daughter was playing and she knew that when it came to stubbornness, she was older, more practiced and she could outlast anyone. Even Susie.

"Oh, I wasn't worried, dear." Mary Elizabeth said "but your father is home and he wondered if you'd join us for a soda while we have cocktails. He's making a fire in the fireplace."

"Sure. Let me finish this and I'll be right down."

Mary Elizabeth walked to the door. "It must be really hard on Joannie to know her husband is going to war. To know he might come back maimed for life. Blind. A cripple. She might never be able to live a normal life being tied to a man like that. And what if he doesn't come back at all? I can't imagine how awful it would be to be a widow barely out of her teens."

Susie stared at her mother as she voiced aloud the black thoughts that haunted her nightmares. "Joannie's very brave to love someone that much."

"Yes. I suppose you could say that."

"What else would you say?"

Mary Elizabeth felt every fear a mother feels for her child explode inside her heart. Battling tears she replied, "That she chose poorly."

Susie swallowed hard as her mother quietly closed the door to her room.

* * * * *

Susie was at the gate in time to see the passengers climbing down the metal roll-up steps. From the window, she saw Joannie and waved.

Joannie saw Susie and rushed past the others to meet her cousin.

They clung to each other in a bear hug, laughing and jumping up and down. "I can't believe you're here!" Susie squealed.

"Me either! I haven't seen Bob for twelve weeks. It feels like a million years."

"I know exactly how you feel," Susie said. "I haven't seen Tommy for ten weeks."

"Who's Tommy?" Joannie asked, pulling to a halt in the middle of the concourse.

"Mother didn't tell you?"

"No."

"Figures."

They started walking again. "Remember the guy I saw at the Sigma Chi house?"

"Susie Howard, are you kidding me?"

Susie beamed. "Nope. Tommy called me the next day."

"But you didn't write to tell me."

"Look who's talking," Susie laughed. "Guess we've both been busy. Anyway, we're pinned. Engaged really. I don't have a diamond so Mother doesn't consider it serious."

Joannie saw the light in Susie's eyes. It was the same love she saw in her own reflection when she thought about Bob. Susie was genuinely in love. "Oh, it's serious all right."

"Thanks for saying that," Susie said.

The March wind blasted their faces as they walked outside.

"This all you got? Just carry-ons?" Susie asked, watching Joannie watch her, then scrutinize her.

"Yep." Joannie replied, taking her eyes from Susie's face and looking across to the parking lot. "Where's your car?"

"Over there."

They walked in silence to the car. After Susie put Joannie's bags in the trunk and closed it, she unlocked the door.

Joannie was still looking at Susie with an unusual intensity.

"What?" Susie asked.

Joannie leaned over the ragtop. "So, do your parents know you're pregnant?"

Chapter Eight

Shaking her head, Susie replied, "They haven't got a clue. How could you tell? I mean I barely show. I haven't had one minute of nausea like a lot of girls do. I don't get it. I'm even still taking PE and no one knows."

"You're scared. I can see it in your face. Besides, we're like sisters, you and I. I know you better than anyone. You haven't been afraid of anything in your entire life. So, I see you and I think to myself, Susie afraid? Impossible. Then you tell me about this fiancé. You haven't seen him for ten weeks. I put two and two together. I have an older sorority sister who has a one year old and she didn't show until her eighth month. I hope I'm that lucky when the times comes."

"Yeah. Lucky."

They drove down Garfield Avenue. Though spring was struggling to come in, huge mounds of ice and slush rippled up against the curbs. Chicago was a hotbed of anti-war demonstrations, anti-racism, anti-pacifists and anti-draft dodgers. Gangs and militants roamed the neighborhoods along Garfield Avenue and further east along Stoney Island Drive. It was no place for two young women to have a flat tire or linger too long at a traffic light.

Susie's red Mustang stuck out like an alien ship as she waited for the light to turn green. Though she'd been through rough neighborhoods from time to time in the past, she'd never paid attention to her surroundings. But now that she had life growing inside her, she was afraid of everything. Just like Joannie had said.

Checking both ways, the second the light turned green she hit the gas.

"Hey, take it easy!" Joannie said. "You want to live through all this don't you?"

"Sure. That's why I'm speeding."

"Good thing you cleared that up," Joannie said.

"I see the Dan Ryan!" Susie said taking her exit and driving North.

"Listen, Susie, this is none of my business and Lord knows I have a hundred things going on in my life, too, but don't you think you ought to start breaking the news? Or are you not going to keep the baby?"

"Not keep it?"

Joannie looked out the window. "You heard me."

"I'm Catholic."

"So am I."

Susie glanced at Joannie who was now looking at her dead square on. "I would never. This is Tommy's baby. Besides, Tommy will marry me . . . once I tell him."

"Damn. He doesn't know either? What did you think? This was going to go away?"

"No! No. I was waiting for the right time. Tommy's life right now is basic training. He marks off the days. Twelve weeks of hell but he said he's learned more in the Marines than he ever dreamed."

"Yeah. I'll bet he's really paying attention. Now his life depends on it!"

"I wanted him to concentrate on what was important."

"And you and this baby aren't?" Joannie slapped her forehead.

"Look. I'm going to see him in a little over a week. He finishes basic and then he's supposed to get a break. He'll come home . . ."

"Don't count on it."

"What?"

"Don't count on his coming home. They're shipping these guys out the second they think they can handle it. Bob is leaving in five days for Southeast Asia. I hate that. Why don't they just say 'war' and be done with it? Why don't they say 'Vietnam'? Instead of making it sound like he's got some pick of countries like the choices at the root beer stand? I'll have Laos with fries, please." She paused. She looked away and whisked a tear from her cheek. "Why don't they just say it?"

"Because it makes it too real. I won't even do it. I keep pretending all of this is just some news program."

"That's it, isn't it?" Joannie tried to smile. She failed as they both fell into thoughtful silence.

"Tommy has to come home. He has to marry me. I never thought that he wouldn't. Mother will kill me."

Joannie's eyebrow hitched up. "Yeah, your mother is a pill."

Susie exchanged a look with Joannie and was suddenly reminded of the dozens of times as children they had tried to sneak out of the house at night, or swiped Braxton's favorite box of cookies from the pantry or eavesdropped on her parents when they were having intimate conversations, or at gossip at parties. Parents were always the "enemy" to children. But now they were both making women's choices with their lives.

Smiles were more difficult to come by but they managed.

"God. My mother is like an acid trip and I've never done the first drug," Susie said glumly.

Joannie tried to lighten the moment and said, "I smoked dope once at fraternity party. I got sick as a dog. I'll never do it again." She paused and glanced at the exit sign as they turned off to Lakeshore Drive. "Yeah, your mother is not going to be easy. Even after you do marry this guy."

"It's worse than you know. Mother already doesn't like him because he isn't from Kenilworth. Isn't rich. Isn't going to Harvard or Yale. Isn't anything like she pictured."

"Oh, this is going to get rough," Joannie groaned.

"She's been off my case once Tommy enlisted."

"You're kidding. Why?"

"Because she really thinks that out of sight, out of mind. She figures I'll forget him. I'll find someone else."

Joannie watched Susie grind her jaw then stick her chin out ever so slightly but firmly. "But you wouldn't."

Susie's face softened. It glowed when she smiled. "Never."

Joannie nodded. "Yep. You love him all right."

"How is it that you've only been here fifteen minutes and you can see it and mother has had months and she is still blind as a bat?"

"Practice."

"Huh?"

"Takes years of tuning out your kids to get as good as she is. You might get lucky, tell her you're pregnant and she still won't hear you."

"I won't bet on it. Still, a gold band will help her cool off."

"What about your father? My Dad wouldn't even know if I dyed my hair orange. He's too wrapped up in his PHd. How can anyone think life is Columbia University is beyond me."

"I dunno. I think he'd be disappointed. He still thinks I want to be a model and I gave up that idea last summer."

"Yeah," Joannie nodded. "He should know by now to check with you every Friday about what you want to do with your life."

Susie laughed. "Okay. So I tend to be scattered. Okay."

Joannie raised her palms upward. "Look at this way. This baby has given your life focus!"

Susie considered this. "You think he'll buy that?"

They stared at each other. Years of shared memories. Family reunions. Vacations in each other's homes and whispered secrets in the dark skittered across their minds.

They burst into laughter as they pulled into Susie's driveway.

"Never!" they declared in unison.

Joannie spent little time with Susie, Aunt Mary Elizabeth and her Uncle Braxton. She went to Navy Pier with Bob, shopped along Michigan Avenue and one glorious night she and Bob went to the Pump Room for an extravagant dinner. They stayed at the Drake Hotel and made love endlessly, both acutely aware of the strong possibility that Bob would never return. Joannie's five days of reunion and romance were far too short.

In the blink of an eye, Susie was saying goodbye to Joannie at the airport.

"It seems like you just got here," Susie said.

"That's because I did just get here. Five days just isn't enough to be with the man you love and then not to see him again for fourteen months."

Joannie was in tears. Her hands shook as she wiped her eyes with a tissue. "I tried to be strong for Bob, but I think I cried more than I smiled. I just wanted to hold him. Make sure he was safe. I feel as if someone has ripped my heart out. I don't know how I can go back to school and act like everything is normal."

"But you will."

Joannie blew her nose.

"We're Howards, Joannie. We're strong somehow. I don't know really what that means but I feel it. Do you remember Grandmother Howard?"

"Not really. We moved to New York when I was ten. You got to see her more than I did."

"She was so tiny. I always kept thinking how lucky I was to be tall so I could be a model or an actress. Or something. Grandmother Howard didn't have all the options I've had for my life. But she never seemed to mind. She said life has a way of working itself out.

"I never really knew what she meant by that. But I'm starting to understand. Anyway, she went through all those years of World War I, with grandpa over in France. Then she had to live through World War II watching my father and yours enlist and survive. And then Aunt Sheilagh dying of cancer. That must have been awful to watch your own child die. I think about how she didn't lose her mind. She didn't unleash her pain on anyone. She was always a happy person. Even until the end. She was dying and still making jokes about it."

Joannie peered into Susie's eyes. "I wish I had known her then."

"Her genes run in both of us, Joannie. We can do this. We can make it through this war. However long it lasts. Wherever it takes us."

"Susie, you're going to need every bit of her strength to help you these next months. I can't imagine what it must be like to be you right now. Maybe your parents will understand. I hope so. But just knowing soon you have to drop out of school. Catholic schools don't like their girls to 'show'.   Then, knowing you can't go to your high school graduation with all your girlfriends. I know you don't want to admit it to yourself, but what if he doesn't marry you? What if he's not the man you think he is? I mean, it's horrible getting married to a man whom you know is going right off to war like I did, but your options all seem to lead to doom."

Joannie threw her arms around Susie, "I know I couldn't be that strong. You make my situation seem nearly blissful," she blew her nose still sobbing. "And it's hell!"

Susie nodded her head. "I know. I know. But once I see Tommy again, things will be different."

Joannie blew her nose once again. "For your sake, I hope so."

They hugged tightly.

"I'll write. I'm getting good at it," Susie said waving as Joannie charged up the steps, nearly the last to board the plane.

"I'm always here for you! I love you!" Joannie shouted, waved exuberantly one last time and then she was gone.

Susie was riveted to the moment as Joannie's every movement, the closing of the airplane door, and the sound of the engines, burrowed into her mind. She got the distinct impression that her life as she had always known it had altered drastically in this space and in this time. She had never felt this cosmic sense of awareness before. Not when she'd met Tommy. Not when she'd made love with him for the first time. Not even when he left for boot camp.

A loud "click" sounded in her brain and from the well of her soul, she knew that hers and Joannie's fates had been sealed that day.

This is the day my adult life begins.

It was nothing they'd done. Nothing they had omitted.

But Susie knew the words they'd spoken were prophetic ones.

In the days and years to come, they would find out exactly what it meant to have Howard strength in their genes.

None of it was going to be easy.

The Christmas Star

Chapter Nine

March, 1966

Dressed in full uniform, Tommy stood ramrod straight in the sunshine drenched office of Lieutenant Colonel Hugh Kipling who sat behind an austerely appointed desk. He was flanked by Gunnery Sergeant Steve Waters and Drill Sergeant Bud Mathers. Two stoic faced men in civilian clothes leaned against the window sill. Their arms crossed defensively over their chests, they surveyed the scene with detached robotic eyes.

"You sent for me, sir?" Tommy asked, saluting his superior.

"I did," Lt.Col Kipling replied closing a file folder in front of him. "Your six weeks review is very impressive, Magli. Where did you learn to shoot?"

"Wisconsin, sir. Mostly geese."

"From whom?"

"My father. He was . . ."

"Army issue," Kipling finished for him.

Tommy's eyebrow raised but only slightly. "You checked."

"Indeed. Sergents Mathers and Walters both agree your skills are top notch. In addition, your records show you've signed on for extra duties. Extra target practice. Extra courses. You appear to be energized by the Marines."

"Yes, sir."

Kipling looked down at the file. "It also appears that your college records and intelligence tests are far, far superior to any enlisted man on base."

"Sir?"

Kipling rose and folded his hands behind his back. "I have just one question, Magli. Your intelligence, your aptitude to learn just about anything we throw at you, suggests a man who could have gone a long way in the civilian world. Yet you flunked out of Northwestern University."

"Yes, sir. I did."

"What was it? A girl?"

"No, sir. It's love. Real love," Tommy replied earnestly.

"That's too bad," Kipling frowned.

"Sir?" Tommy was baffled.

"What I would like to suggest, Magli, is to put you in an accelerated program." He walked over to the two civilian men. "Since the day you arrived on base, we've been watching you, Magli. You keep your mouth shut and your mind on your duty. The men in your company look up to you. They respect you. They know by instinct you're a leader. We're looking for leaders, Magli."

"Yes, sir."

Kipling continued. "If we give you private instructions similar to what the Green Berets and special forces receive, would you be interested?"

"I stated as much to my recruiter, sir."

"Yes, I know."

Tommy's eyebrow inched up. "You asked, of course."

"It will be intense. We'll shove as much at you as you can take. But the decision is yours."

Tommy glanced at the two robots. "You're CIA, right?"

The taller of the two men in his mid thirties nodded. "I'm Hawkins. This is Special Operative Clark."

"You're spies," Tommy said flatly.

"So are you . . . now," Hawkins replied.

Tommy didn't miss a beat. "When do I start, sir?"

Lieutenant Colonel Kipling smiled broadly. "Immediately." He saluted Tommy.

Tommy returned the salute. "I'm honored, sir."

"Your father will be proud, son," Kipling said.

"As I am of him," Tommy replied, then turned sharply on his heel and left the room.

March, 1966. Chicago

"Come go to movies with us on Saturday, Susie," Katie said. Katie Roberts was Susie's best friend. She was petite, blonde and had a twenty-inch waist just like Sandra Dee. She was sweet, vibrant and acquiesced to her parents' every dream for her. There wasn't a single thought in Katie's head that wasn't put there by her parents, the Church or society. Katie always did the right thing for all the right people at the right time.

"Sherry, Carla, Meghan...all the girls are saying you're a recluse lately. You don't go to the Loyola games anymore. Or shopping. Or even to Wimpy's for a burger. Say you'll come with us. We could go see *Dr. Zhivago*, your favorite. *Alfie* is playing on State Street."

"I've seen it. Besides, I'm waiting for Tommy to call on Saturday," Susie said, hugging a stack of books to her chest as they walked to Biology lab. Susie couldn't imagine what it would be like for her cousin, Joannie, not being able to talk to Bob on the telephone. The phone was Susie's link to life these days. Even though Tommy could not get to a phone during the week, they always had their Saturday night "date" call.

Katie sighed. "It must be wonderful to be loved by a college man," she gushed.

"Marine," Susie corrected.

"That, too. But first he was a college man. Does he have a really thick beard?"

"Katie, you ask the weirdest questions."

"All the boys I've dated don't. But then mother won't let me date anyone who's older. Not even a few months!"

"Sounds boring."

"But you! You're my heroine! Not only is Tommy older and in college, but you picked him out all by yourself and your mother doesn't approve." Katie said. "I don't know anyone as brave as you. None of us do."

Finally reaching the lab, Susie held the door for Katie. "Maybe you should give independence a shot, Katie."

"I wouldn't dare!" Katie's blue eyes flew wide open.

"Why not?"

"I'd just get in trouble, that's why."

Susie shook her head. "That's the general idea when you exert your own opinions over those of your parents."

"So if you're in trouble with your parents all the time, why do you do it?"

"Because I love him," Susie replied confidently.

Katie stared at Susie thoughtfully. "Then I hope I never fall in love."

Susie marked boot camp days off on her calendar just as Tommy did. The anticipation of seeing him again left Susie breathless. She didn't know if she wanted to run and hide or rush into his arms. It was a strange elixir of wanting and restraint; joy and fear.

"I can't get a flight out of here," Tommy said five days before his leave. "Every 'boot' is trying to go home. And I've heard the standby lines are atrocious."

"Then I'll just have to come out there."

"San Diego is packed to the gills, sweetheart. There's not a hotel room to be had. I've checked. I don't know what to do."

"I *have* to see you, Tommy!" Susie felt hysteria coming on but tried to check it.

"It's okay, honey. I'm going to Camp Pendleton after this. I'm still in California, so maybe we can still work something out later."

"No later stuff, okay? I've waited twelve weeks. Then if you have twelve more weeks of training, God only knows when they'll give you a weekend pass."

"Ugh . . ."

"What? What's wrong?"

Tommy hesitated for a moment. "Susie, there's something you should know. We're hearing rumors that the gig at Camp Pendleton may only be ten weeks. Some are saying nine."

"My God, it's true what Joannie said."

"Joannie? Your cousin?"

"Yeah. She said all the branches were cutting the training short to send you guys over to Vietnam faster."

Tommy swallowed. "That's what you heard?" He had to be careful not to mention his special training. The less Susie knew about his life at base, the better. "It's true."

"Okay. That's it. If you can't come to me, I'm coming out there." She tapped her fingernail against her teeth.

"Susie, you can't come here," he said wondering how he would keep his commander and his girlfriend both happy when he needed every second to study and train.

"Sure I can, silly."

"Susie, you know I want to see you, but . . ."

"Tommy, I'm coming and that's that. Now, can you get a bus to San Francisco?"

"I suppose so," he said reluctantly.

"Tommy, what's wrong? Don't you want to see me? Don't you love me anymore?"

"You know I love you."

"But you act like you don't want me to come out there. And the only reason you'd act like that is if you had another girlfriend."

Or I had something to hide, he thought to himself. He realized he would have to explain the circumstances to his commander. He needed to see Susie before he shipped out. If he didn't see her, she would be suspicious about too many things and she was just stubborn enough to fly out whether he would allow it or not.

"Tommy, if you can get to 'Frisco, I can get a flight there and meet you there for the weekend. It's not New York. It's not the Plaza, but it will have to do."

"Plaza? New York? What are you talking about?"

She paused, thinking of the wedding she'd planned. A whirlwind New York weekend. She found a beautiful off white light wool coatdress. Very Jacqueline Kennedy with a pillbox hat and tiny detachable veil to match. She'd told her mother it was for Easter Sunday. Her mother had approved of her stylish and understated choice .

"My God, I've raised you well," Mary Elizabeth said when Susie had pulled the ensemble from the Marshall Field's box.

"Of course you did, Mother," Susie had agreed.

They would be married at New York's City Hall. Susie didn't think it would be all that difficult to get a license. She'd even had a blood test. And Tommy had one when he was inducted. She had the money to cover the costs. Then after the ceremony, they could walk down Fifth Avenue and have a passerby take their photograph as they kissed in front of St. Patrick's Cathedral. They could pretend it was a church wedding. Still, it would be the most beautiful wedding ever because she and Tommy were in it.

The only flaw in the plan was that the groom still didn't know he was to be the groom.

A minor detail.

"Oh, nothing. Just something I'd wanted to do for us. Remember I always said, 'New York is the best'."

"The Plaza is the best. That's what you said."

"Okay, so we'll stay at the Sir Francis Drake in San Francisco."

"And how am I going to pay for this?" Tommy reasoned.

"I'll get my travel agent on it. Don't worry. I have my own money."

"I can't let you do that."

"You can and you will. All's fair in love and war. And this is both."

Expelling a deep sigh, Tommy said, "I know when not to argue with you."

"Tommy, I just want this weekend to be special. The most special for you and I ever."

"How are you squaring this with your folks?"

"I was wondering when you were going to ask me that."

"In other words, they don't know," he said, regret clinging to his words.

"They don't."

"God, Susie. I'd give anything for you to tell me that somehow, somewhere they were proud of you. Proud of what

I'm doing. I'm proud of it, you know. You may not believe it, but honestly, I think becoming a Marine is one of the best things I've ever done in my life."

"I'm proud of you, Tommy. Proud enough for all the Howards in your life," she said, placing her hand on her stomach.

"Thanks, sweetheart. Listen, can you wire me the details? Hotel? Time? I'll find a bus. Or hitch hike. But I will meet you in San Francisco on Friday. You can count on me."

"I do count on you, Tommy. Always."

"I love you, Susie. More than life itself."

"I love you, Tommy. I always will," she said, and gently hung up the phone.

"A divine invention . . . travel agents," Susie said to Katie as they walked out of school the following Thursday afternoon.

"Wow! I'm so impressed. My parents would never give me permission to go all the way to California for a weekend with my boyfriend. At a hotel, no less!"

"Oh, my parents don't know," Susie replied as Katie stopped dead in her tracks.

"What? Have you totally lost it?" Katie nearly screamed at her friend.

"Not exactly."

Katie followed Susie like a puppy. "What are you going to tell them? How can you just disappear for three days and not tell them? And what about skipping out of school tomorrow afternoon to make your plane flight? How will you manage that?"

"Managed and done," Susie smiled covertly. "I wrote a note to my counselor saying I had a doctor's appointment and then shoved it in front of my mother while she was on the phone to one of her charity boards. I had her sign several things, she didn't know which was my bank deposit, which was my note and which was another college application. Then I told them I had to go with Darla Wick's parents to see St. Mary's campus this Saturday and that from there we were driving down to Terre Haute to see St. Mary's of the Woods and we wouldn't be back until Sunday night."

"You idiot! Darla's parents are in France!"

Susie smiled smugly. "I know. That way my parents can't call to check on anything. Plus, my parents are going on some sailing regatta thing this weekend from Racine to Chicago. They'll be so busy with their friends they won't know anything until I get back."

"Maybe they'll never know about it," Katie replied, her hero worship visibly dribbling off the edges of her lips. "I really wish I could be more like you."

As if her balloon had been spiked with a lance, Susie's face fell. "No you don't, Katie. You don't want to be anything like me."

Susie turned and walked away from her friend, for the first time feeling an unsettling shame she'd never experienced before.

"What are you talking about? You're Susie Howard. The incredible. Susie the invincible! Everyone wants to be you."

Her eyes on the sidewalk in front of her, Susie's feet couldn't move fast enough. In a matter of weeks, days, perhaps, her pregnancy would no longer be hidden. Someone was going to see the changes in her.

She would be no one's hero then.

In just the past week, she'd felt the ticking of the study hall clock like a gong banging out the reality of her life.

She was, as yet, not married. She was pregnant. She was about to be an outcast.

Once she told her parents, all hell would break loose. The sky would fall and Susie would be standing under it. Crushed.

Chapter Ten

The winding Pacific Coast Highway was dotted with uniformed men, some headed north to San Francisco, some going south to San Diego, flagging down trucks and cars, each hoping for a ride. Tommy figured he saved over twenty dollars of his Private First Class pay when the lime green Volkswagen bus stopped to pick him up.

The hippie with the leather thong strung across his forehead asked, "I'm going to Frisco. Haight Ashbury. Where you headed?"

"The same," Tommy smiled, not missing the irony of the moment.

"Not the same," the hippie said. "I'm into peace."

"So am I," Tommy replied gritting his teeth. "I'm just going about it differently."

"Yeah, that's what makes this country great," the hippie replied and pulled back into traffic. "Everybody's doin' their own thing."

"So, if you're a dove, why'd you stop?"

"Didn't say I was a dove, now did I?"

Tommy thought. "You've got a peace symbol painted on your grill."

"Van belongs to my sister. I'm going to 'Frisco to bring her home. She's shacking up with some bum. Me? I own a bar on the Venice beach. I'm 4-F. Otherwise, I'd go."

"Looks can be deceiving," Tommy replied.

"If you learned that much, you know a lot. My name is John Cleary."

They shook hands.

John looked at him. "Going to see your girlfriend?"

"How did you know?"

"Seems every week this war escalates, President Johnson keeps raising that bar on the number of servicemen he intends to send to 'Nam. I guess we've all gotten used to giving you Marines a lift. I bet I've met a hundred Marines in the past four months. All I gotta say is you are one love-sick bunch," he laughed.

Tommy chuckled and looked out the window. "Can you go any faster?"

Susie couldn't stand the wait in the hotel room. She went downstairs to the lobby, but the hours passed agonizingly slow. By late afternoon, she'd taken to pacing. Then she walked out onto the street watching each car that pulled up.

"Susie!"

She heard his voice calling her name from a block away. Tommy jumped over the heads of the pedestrians thronged in front of him as they spilled out of the retail stores and office buildings.

"Susie!" he shouted, laughing and waving his arms. "Over here! Can't you see me?"

"Tommy! Where are you?" She stood on tiptoes as a man brushed her shoulder, pushing her up against a trash barrel. She started walking toward the sound of his voice.

"Susie!" Tommy pushed his way past a man carrying a briefcase and sidestepped around a mother pushing a baby stroller. "Sweetheart of Sigma Chi!"

Then she saw him.

Tommy in his Marine uniform was a stunning sight. Chills spiraled down her back. Tears filled her eyes and her heart burst open.

"Tommy! Darling!" She ran toward him.

He bolted across the street in the face of oncoming traffic.

A cabbie screeched to a halt. "Hey! Asshole!" Then the cabbie stopped as he saw Susie fling herself into Tommy's arms and spin her around.

The cabbie sat back and smiled. "Atta boy!"

The man in the backseat grumbled, "Hey! What gives? Get a move on!"

"Getta life, fella!" the cabbie said.

Tommy whisked Susie away from the traffic and onto the curb where he kissed her deeply.

The crowd brushed past them. Two bleary-eyed teenaged girls dressed in granny dresses with daisies stuck in their hair and smelling of pot took a flower each and dropped them at Susie's feet. A fat middle-aged woman with heavily rouged cheeks and ruby lips snarled at them. A little boy giggled and covered his mouth then ran to catch up with his mother. A pimply-faced Marine gave them the peace sign, but the majority of the throng was unaffected.

Love and war were mixing in San Francisco.

"Come on," Tommy said putting his arm around Susie. "Let's see this room you've got for us. I can't wait to really hold you in my arms."

Leaning her head into the crook of his neck, Susie wondered if at any time any woman in the world could smile as brightly as she at that moment.

"It's just a double," she said apologetically as they entered the lushly carpeted room with fourteen-foot ceilings, elaborate crown molding and heavy brocade drapes.

"It's like a dream!" he said. "You forget. I've been sleeping on a bunk for twelve weeks. This is paradise. Sheer heaven," he replied locking the door behind them. "And I have my baby all to myself for three days."

"Yes, you do," she replied hugging him tightly. She buried her face in his shoulder. "I never thought I could miss anyone so much. I never thought I could feel like I feel when I'm with you."

This time when Tommy kissed her, Susie's heart and mind were transported to a place she'd never been. Suddenly, she understood every melancholy love song ever sung. She felt as if she was inside the splitting soul of every poet who'd ever roamed the face of the earth from the ancients to the contemporaries. She knew the agony of painters who struggled with the incomprehensible task of using human limitation to reconstruct the colors of heaven on mortal canvas.

There were no words to define the emotion inside her. There was no time. There was no space.

This was what was meant by "being".

They fell on the bed, kicking off shoes and unbuttoning buttons and peeling layers of clothing from bodies that sheathed their souls.

Kisses fell like rain from Tommy's lips onto Susie's satiny skin. With his fingertips he memorized every inch of her body. He buried his face in her long hair, inhaling the Shalimar perfume she always wore.

"When I'm over there, I want to remember every facet of you," he said moving himself over her. "I want you to never, ever doubt how much I love you. There will be so many days, weeks when you don't hear from me. Maybe the letters won't be written, but the words are in my mind, Susie. I want you to never forget that."

"I won't," she replied over the flaming ache in her throat. Tears streamed in rivulets down her cheeks and fell onto the pillow under her head.

He peered deeply into her eyes. "You of all people will know when I'm thinking about you. You are in my heart. You're a part of my soul. I think you've known that since the first time..."

"I saw you. Since I first saw you, Tommy. Not just since we made love. I've known it longer than you have."

"That's not possible," his eyes swimming in tears. "I'm so afraid," he said pulling her naked body to him.

"Me, too," she said. "I hate this war."

"Oh, Susie," he pulled back, forcing a smile as he looked at her. "It's not the war that frightens me."

"Then what?"

"I'm afraid you'll forget me."

She burst into sobs and flung her arms around him. "I can't...I won't. I could never...not now..."

"Now?"

"Uh-huh," she replied meekly as she released her hold on him. "I waited until we were together to tell you."

"Tell me what?"

"That I'm going to have our baby."

"A baby?" Tommy's face burst into joy. It radiated around him as if she'd just given him the sun.

It was a stunning sight and one that Susie knew she'd never forget.

"How I prayed this would be your reaction. I wanted you to be happy about it."

"Why didn't you tell me before?" He said sitting up and looking at her stomach.

"I had to know how you really felt. What if other guys talked you out of wanting it? Wanting me? What if..."

He stared at her stomach. "That's silly. Does it hurt?"

Susie burst into laughter. "Of course not. I hardly feel a thing. I think I must be cut out for making babies."

"One at a time, please," he joked reaching toward her belly. "Can I touch it?"

"You were about to make love to me. Of course, you can touch it. You won't feel much, though."

He put his hand on her flesh. "I thought you were supposed to be fat."

"Me, too. But luckily I'm not. It's just been the past few weeks where it felt hard. It hasn't moved yet."

"You think it's okay? What does the doctor say?"

Susie hung her head.

"What?" he asked.

"I haven't seen a doctor."

Tommy sat back. "What? Isn't that a bad thing?"

"I'll go. Soon as I get back."

In that instant, Tommy sobered. He felt as if he'd just walked through a tunnel and now had been vacuumed back out by some powerful reality force. "What else haven't you done?"

Susie pulled the rumpled bedspread up around her. "No one knows. You're the first." She paused. "Actually, that's not true. Joannie knows. She guessed. I didn't have to tell her."

"Oh, boy." Tommy rubbed his arms.

"That's why I needed to come out here and see you. We have to get married this weekend."

For a full ten seconds he stared wild-eyed at her as a thousand thoughts riddled his brain. He looked at his watch. "Get dressed."

"What? Now?"

"We have to get a license. How far is it to City Hall?"

"I dunno."

"I bet they close at five," he stood and began pulling his slacks on. "Shoot."

"Aren't they open on Saturdays?"

"Not government offices."

"Oh, no! I hadn't thought of that."

He pulled on his socks. Rammed his feet into his shoes. "Blood tests. Gees."

"I brought mine."

"I don't have mine!"

"I figure, this kind of thing happens all the time. You got into the Marines didn't you? So you can't have syphilis, which is the reason they make you get the darn test anyway. I've got the eight dollars for the license. Social security numbers. Driver's license."

"I even went to Peacocks and got us some rings. Just plain gold."

Tommy stood and grinned. "Pretty sure of me, weren't you?"

"Just hoping."

His eyes gleamed. "Nah. You got me wrapped."

She smiled back. "Ditto."

Sticking his arms through his shirt he said, "Let's go!" He grabbed her hand and together they raced out of the room.

The doorman hailed them a cab.

"The marriage license bureau," Tommy said to the driver.

"You'll never make it," the cabbie said, putting the flag down on the rate box.

"There's an extra ten in it for you if we do," Susie said.

"You'll make it," the cabbie said and peeled away from the curb.

Tommy and Susie walked out of the City Hall building along with two dozen other couples who, as a group, had forced the municipal workers to put in twenty seven and a half minutes of overtime to process all the marriage licenses necessary.

Susie had discovered while standing in line that a county judge was performing weddings on Saturday morning on a first come first serve basis for three hours starting at nine o'clock. While Tommy stood in the line for the license, Susie signed them up for a nine-thirty wedding ceremony.

By the time they got back to the hotel, they were exhausted.

They ordered room service rather than eat in the hotel dining room, preferring to be alone. Sleep came in shadowy flutters between planning their wedding vows, toasts of champagne and making love.

When morning came, Susie wore her white coatdress of which her mother had so proudly approved and Tommy wore his starched and pressed Marine uniform. When they got to the Court House, the line had already formed.

Tommy smiled at the other couples and nodded to a fellow Marine. Curiously, he noted that the grooms were beaming and most of the brides appeared concerned. Some were crying, though they clung to their men like lichen on rocks. Then he heard the young blonde girl in front of them say, "Less than eighteen hours is all we have left."

"I promise, baby, when I come back I'll take you on a month long honeymoon. Nothin's too good for my baby."

All night, Tommy had refused to think about time. Enduring the past twelve weeks without Susie had been agony, but looking at her now with so much love in her eyes, he realized there was a very good chance this moment would have to sustain him for months.

Maybe longer.

Suddenly, he pulled her close. "Susie, I'm sorry I can't give you a big church wedding. I'm sorry you don't have your parents here . . . or my dad. Why, I didn't even get you flowers."

Hugging him back she said, "I brought my Misselette. Bring me flowers when you come home."

"That's a promise," he said kissing her.

Just then an attendant opened the door to the courtroom. "Magli?"

"Here! Present, sir!" Tommy said.

"Front and center," the attendant instructed sourly.

The judge wore traditional robes and an anxious demeanor as she rattled off vows that meant the world to Susie and Tommy.

"I do," Tommy said.

"I do," Susie replied with a thrill in her heart.

They slipped rings onto each other's fingers, each lost in thoughts of the precariousness of their future. It was not a mistake that they grabbed each other's hands and held tight. Neither heard the judge's voice until she said, "I now pronounce you man and wife."

Tommy beamed when he pulled Susie into his arms for what he thought should be the kiss of a lifetime.

"No time for that here," the attendant said, breaking them apart. "We've got seven more ceremonies before lunch. You have papers to sign."

Disappointed, Tommy didn't argue with the man.

They followed the attendant to an anteroom where the judge had pre-signed a stack of marriage certificates.

Susie signed first with her new married name. Then Tommy signed his name.

"We're legal?" Susie asked the attendant.

For the first time, the man cracked a smile Susie couldn't help thinking it was an entirely new experience for the man. "As legal as they get," he said.

"How about breakfast, Mrs. Magli?" Tommy put his arm out for Susie.

"I'd love it," she replied.

Once outside the courthouse, they paid six fifty for a wedding portrait by an untrusting sidewalk hippie who carefully handed over the Polaroid at precisely the same second that Susie held out the cash.

They strolled to a café for strong coffee and sourdough toast. They sat by a window but never looked out.

Susie rested her face in her hand, stirring cream into her coffee. "I feel so strange," she said. "I don't feel married."

"Gee. Thanks a lot."

"You know what I mean," she shot him a smile. "It's not that I'm disappointed.

"Sure you are. I am."

"What? No."

"Guys can want a special wedding as much as girls. Don't you think I wanted a fancy tux and a limo and more flowers than the law allows? Don't think for a minute that I wasn't capable of putting together an incredible repertoire of classical music. Incredible as it sounds, I'm a very classical guy. Mom said musical talent was biological," he rambled as Susie listened patiently, absorbing every anecdote. "Anyway, I wanted trumpets, you know," he sat back smugly nodding his head.

"Trumpets."

"No banjos or guitars. None of that Vatican II crap. Violins. Trumpets. Very Mendelssohn."

"And the reception?" She looked around the quaint café with its French lace curtains, dark wood chairs and French bronze chandeliers. "I think this is nice."

"Actually, this is exactly what I would have ordered for a wedding breakfast. Just the two of us. Nope I would have blown the bankroll on the church part. Skip the reception. My frat brothers are deadbeats anyway. They wouldn't have appreciated it."

"Tommy. That is not true!"

He laughed and abruptly stopped. "The guys in my company. They're aces. Got their heads screwed on straight." He sighed pensively, his thoughts going to dark regions. "They know some of us won't be coming back."

"Tommy, we promised not to talk about it. Not today." She looked out the window. Across the street a small group of students carried protest signs down at their sides as if headed somewhere for a rally. It was a scene she was witnessing more each week. The news was filled with stories of student protestors chaining themselves to pillars in the student unions and administration buildings. They thought they could fight President Johnson. They thought they were strong enough to be heard all the way to Hanoi and Saigon.

They think they can save their own asses.

"I'm proud of you, Tommy. I think it's the bravest thing I've ever witnessed in my life."

"Lots of guys are going to war."

"I meant marrying me."

"Oh, that." He chuckled then reached for her hand. "Yep. Takes real guts. But I think I'm up to it."

Drawing his hand to her lips, she kissed his fingers. "Maybe right now it doesn't seem like so much. A ceremony. Signing papers. But in the years to come. In our life to come, you'll see what I see. This was a very brave deed."

"You have it all wrong, Susie. This isn't the test. Courage is the ability to stay the course. And we will."

"We will," she whispered and realized at that second she'd made the vow that had truly bonded herself to Tommy for eternity.

Chapter Eleven

It was pouring rain as Susie fumbled in her purse for her house keys. Her flight was two hours late landing due to the weather. The line for cabs was worthy of a world-class convention weekend. She was over four hours late arriving home. Noticing the lights in the house were on, she instantly knew her parents had returned from their weekend trip as well. She would have to come up with a good story about why she was carrying her suitcase.

I could just tell the truth.

Susie paid the taxi driver and dashed through the rain to the front door. Just as she reached for the handle, the door was flung open.

"Where the hell have you been?" Braxton demanded.

Mary Elizabeth glared at her daughter with arms akimbo.

Rain slicked Susie's cheeks. "Can I come in before this interrogation starts?"

"Fine." Braxton stood aside.

Susie hauled her American Tourister suitcase into the house noting that neither of her parents made a move to assist her.

Carefully she shucked off her London Fog coat so as not to damage the marble floor. Oddly, Susie felt a sensation of moving in slow motion. It was as if she'd entered some kind of void or time warp. Nothing was quite real to her.

A myriad of thoughts rattled through her brain, but nothing gelled. Seldom had she seen her father quite so angry. Memories transported her back to when she was a small child running in the rain to this door and opening it. She remembered clearly how painstaking Mary Elizabeth was when it came to the care of the parquetry and marble of the reception area.

"Susie, wipe your feet outside. Water spots are impossible to get out of marble."

"Susie, water warps wood. Remember that always."

"Susie, must you plunk your feet like that? You'll mar the wood."

"Susie, don't bring your wagon across that good wood floor!"

Susie's eyes went to the floor.

My life can be measured in the grains of this wood and these marble squares. The care and protection of this floor has meant more to my mother than my feelings. More to her than me.

Susie raised her eyes. She blinked.

They came into focus again. She could see their mouths moving. She saw the pinch in the bridge of her mother's nose. She saw the disdain in her father's eyes. He was shaking a finger at her. He was demanding answers from her.

"Did you happen to hear a word I said?" he bellowed.

"No," she replied flatly.

"What?" Mary Elizabeth's voice shot to that crescendo she used when she was truly incensed. "You answer your father this instant!"

Susie felt incredibly heavy, as if the world had just been hoisted onto her shoulders. She was overburdened, but she didn't know of any course of action other than to bear up under it.

"I didn't exactly hear the question, but rather than have you repeat it I'll tell you that I was in San Francisco."

"That I know!" Braxton said.

"*How* could you know?"

"Seems the Sir Francis Drake Hotel makes it a policy to double check when an underage person uses a parent's American Express card."

"Oh. I hadn't thought of that." Susie felt her feet pushing heavily into the floor, as if the floor were melting or decomposing under the strain of her enormous weight. She felt smaller, as if she were shrinking like Alice in Wonderland. The only thing was, Susie didn't have a rabbit to follow. No hole to which she could escape.

She had to stay the course. She had to be brave.

"And just why were you in San Francisco? Is this some new manifestation of 'senioritis'? Some high school prank? You couldn't go to Fort Lauderdale with your friends for spring break so this is how you pay us back? You never asked us about going. You just went. When did you start behaving like this, young lady? Well, I'll tell you when. When you took up with that . . . that steel worker!" Mary Elizabeth didn't realize she was spitting again.

"Don't get in a tizzy, Mother. It makes you spit."

"I'm not spitting. I never spit."

"You do," Susie replied, wondering where she was getting this courage to stand up to her parents as an equal. What had come over her?

"Don't take that tone with me!"

"I'm married." Susie said it dully. And for that she was not proud. She'd wanted to shout it triumphantly. She'd wanted to say it proudly. Instead, it had come out with precisely the thud she'd expected of a somewhat lesser person. She was Susie Howard Magli. She could do better than this.

"Married?!" Braxton gasped.

"Married?!" Mary Elizabeth slammed her palm against her cheek.

"Susie Howard Magli. That's my name now."

There, that's more like it!

Still, she wasn't feeling any lighter for having said it. The weight of her problems was leaden. Her feet sunk a few more inches into the decomposing wood. Her world was falling apart.

"Where? How?" Mary Elizabeth demanded.

"A justice of the peace. I guess. She was nice."

"A woman judge?" Braxton asked. "It figures. Probably some liberal Democrat."

"Sorry, I didn't ask. It was a long line."

"Then you didn't get married in a church?" Mary Elizabeth asked suddenly finding her rational tone.

"No."

"Thank God," Mary Elizabeth sighed.

"We'll get it annulled."

"Annulled? You can't do that!"

"Look, young lady, I don't want any gory details of your, er, honeymoon night. I can get this thing annulled by Friday. I'll talk to the Bishop myself if I have to."

Susie shook her head as she backed away from them. "You won't be talking to anyone, Dad. I wasn't married in the church because there wasn't time. I still plan to get married in the church someday. Tommy wants a really big church wedding. Violins and trumpets. And more flowers than the law allows."

Tears filled Susie's eyes as she moved away from them.

They loomed over her like a judgment board about to pass sentence. They had tried her in their heads. They were not interested in her side of the story. They didn't want to hear how much she loved Tommy. Her mother didn't want to know any details. Not even about the dress that made her look so Jackiesque. They wanted to negate her first real decision as an adult.

They wanted her to remain their child.

And Susie wanted desperately to grow up.

"You can't have my marriage to Tommy annulled because he's the father of my baby. I'm pregnant. That's why I got married now. This weekend in San Francisco."

Silence hung in the air like the echo of heaven's gong. Reverberating. Ricocheting off their nerve endings.

"Oh, that's just great! I need a drink," Braxton walked away and into the living room where a long French console held heavy lead crystal glasses and Waterford decanters filled with Scotch, Bourbon and Vodka. He poured a Scotch neat. He stared at the liquor glowing golden in his glass. Then he belted it back, not tasting a drop.

"Pregnant?" Mary Elizabeth said the word aloud to give it validity.

"Yes." Susie was wise enough to give them time for the truth to shock and then for reality to graze their minds. Mary Elizabeth's eyes darted to Susie's belly and then back to her face. "Impossible. I would have known the signs."

"I didn't get any morning sickness. I've only gained two pounds. I still don't show. At least what little I do, I've been able to cover it up."

"Actually, I can see it now."

"Yeah." Susie bit her lip self-consciously. "It just happened. Like overnight. Weird."

"It happens like that."

"Oh."

"Your friends at school. Do. . .do they know?" Mary Elizabeth's words came in starts and sputters.

"No. No one knows."

"Thank God.

"But they will and soon."

"They most certainly will not, because you're not going to tell them anything!" Mary Elizabeth turned on her heel and went to the living room. "I'll have a Tom Collins," she instructed Braxton.

"Of course I am!" Susie followed her mother into the lushly appointed living room. "Once I tell them I'm married . . . "

"You'll say nothing of the kind," Mary Elizabeth glared.

"We can thank our lucky stars she doesn't show," Braxton said to his wife.

"Precisely what I was thinking."

"We pull her out of school immediately," he said.

"We can say she's landed a huge modeling contract. Something believable. Hair spray. Revlon maybe. She has to go to New York. I'll call Joannie. Maybe she knows of some homes . . . "

"Homes?" Fear shot up Susie's spine.

"Yes," Braxton replied benignly.

"What kind of homes?"

"Why, for unwed mothers, of course. You have to put the baby up for adoption."

Braxton nodded. "Then once it's all over, you come back home, I'll arrange for you to finish out your courses by correspondence. You can't graduate with your class, of course, that's the price you pay. But you'll get your degree. Then you go off to college in the fall."

Suddenly, he glanced at Susie as if realizing for the first time that she was in the same room. "When exactly is the baby due?"

"I don't know."

"Need to check that out," he said, pouring another Scotch.

"Surely, you have *some* idea," Mary Elizabeth growled.

"September twenty-fourth. Twenty-fifth."

The room went dead silent. Ice clinked in Mary Elizabeth glass. "It was Christmas eve!"

"Yes."

Instantly, Susie felt what they must be feeling as shame pushed her neck down and forced her to look at the floor again.

What have I done? How would I feel if my daughter came to me with news like this? How hurt they must be. How disappointed they are.

Tears filled her eyes and fell straight to the Persian rug. The teardrop soaked into the wool.

Another flooring damaged . . . because of me.

Protectively, her hand went to her belly. For the first time she sensed a presence inside her that she'd not known before.

I'm so sorry, baby. I'm so sorry. I didn't want any of this life to be like this. Not like this. You deserve so much more. So much, much more.

She raised her face to her parents.

They were both staring at her stomach.

"I'm not giving my baby away. I would never give Tommy's child to someone else to raise. I love him. I will never ever love anyone else. I love this baby. So, you just forget all these plans you're making."

Mary Elizabeth gasped. "You can't stay here!"

"Pardon me?"

"Here. In this house."

Braxton stepped forward. "You thought that?"

"Well, yes. Where else would I go?"

"Seems you should have thought of that. Guess you weren't thinking all the way around were you?" he grumbled.

"Susie, we have a sacred trust in this family to protect each other. To act in respectful, honest ways and to never bring ridicule or scorn down upon us. Your father's repu-tation and mine were hard won. We were and are good parents to you. I'm not some floozy alcoholic woman who beats you or neglects you. I know I have faults. We all do. I'm only human. But I have conducted myself in such a manner that you and your father never have to question my actions. I would never dream of bringing scandal on the Howard family. Neither would your father. We've worked all our lives to give you what we felt was the best start in life possible. And this is how you repay those dreams we had for you."

"But I love Tommy! Can't you see?"

"I do see! Very clearly. Perhaps more clearly than you. You are spoiled and that's my fault. You are selfish. And that's your fault," Mary Elizabeth paused briefly. "No. You cannot stay in this house and have a baby out of wedlock."

"I *am* married, Mother."

"You *had* to get married. In my crowd, it carries the same stigma."

"So my being married makes no difference to you?"

"None," Braxton said.

"In fact," Mary Elizabeth interjected, "I would have preferred you weren't. I have been perfectly clear about my feelings in regard to that boy and that I did and do still believe he's unsuitable."

"Unsuitable. Just what in the hell does that mean, Mother?"

"He has no money, Susie. It takes money to support a wife and now . . . a child in today's world. I didn't struggle all these years making society connections, which have furthered Braxton's business, by the way, for nothing! My intent was to use my friends' influence to get you into the best college. Possibly an Ivy League school. To get you into the best sororities. Or land that modeling career. Or help you with a career after college. You get ahead in this world not by what you know but who you know."

"Getting ahead. I forgot."

"Damn straight you did," Braxton said, walking toward the extension phone in the alcove between the living room and the family den.

"What are you doing?" Susie asked.

"Calling Joannie. Isn't that what we decided?"

Susie's breath caught in her lungs. "Haven't you heard one word I've said?"

"Haven't you heard one word *I've* said?" he asked in mid-motion picking up the receiver. "You can't stay here. In a few weeks you'll be . . . popping out all over the place and every one of our friends, my clients and associates . . . they will all know. My daughter got herself knocked up."

They glared at her. Demanding.

She stared at them. By some twist of an invisible hand their faces had been transformed into grotesque masks. She didn't know who these people were. The love they'd claimed they'd had for her vanished. The caring she expected was non-existent.

They weren't parents.

They were aliens.

She had to run from them as fast as she could.

"I'll pack immediately. I can leave in the morning." She walked away from them, took her American Tourister suitcase from near the front door and mounted the staircase placing one shaking foot on a step at a time.

Braxton nodded and stuck his finger in the rotary dial. "Maybe she can stay with Joannie for a day or two till we find a home."

Chapter Twelve

Hearing the knock on the door, Jed Magli hauled himself out of his Lazy Boy and turned off the television. "I'm coming."

He opened the door.

Standing on the steps on the other side of the storm door was Susie.

He noticed the two suitcases before he saw the tears in her eyes.

"Susie."

"There's no room at the inn."

"Come again?"

"I think I should tell you everything first. You may not want to open that door to me, either."

"I don't understand."

"I know you don't. And that's my fault. I should have told you before this. I married your son. And I'm going to have your grandchild."

"And that's why you are here?"

"No. I'm here because I got pregnant first. Then I married your son." She looked down when the tears got to be too much for her. "And I love them both. So much."

Jed froze. He watched her struggle with emotions he'd forgotten existed. He wanted to warn her.

Don't fall in love. They'll only leave you in the end. The pain is unbearable. It's more than I can stand.

She was so young. Standing there in her light blue spring coat, dark hair spilling over her shoulders, he wondered if the Blessed Virgin had felt any different than Susie at this moment. She, too, had brought scandal. She too, had no place to go.

But she had what Susie had.

She had faith. And love. And trust.

Jed couldn't remember what it was like to feel any of those things.

His heart burned with a flame of injustice. He wanted to scold his son for not telling him about the marriage. Or the baby. He'd always dreamed of the day when his son would get married. He'd made those plans a long time ago when he was a newlywed and a new father and such musings were only just that. They weren't reality.

But then death had come to knock on his door and his life and his dreams had changed. He'd put hope in a box and left it there.

He allowed himself not to feel joy or love. Sorrow or pain. He'd kept his life shut off from Tommy.

He had only himself to blame for not having an invitation to Tommy and Susie's wedding. He was to blame for this self-inflicted amputation.

No one else.

And least of all, this girl who was now his family.
She was bringing him all the facets of life he'd struggled to ignore. For so very long no one had needed Jed. Not even Tommy.

Her tears pried open his heart.

Placing his hand on the metal handle, he turned the knob.
"Welcome home."

Joy sprung from Susie's soul. "Thanks."

She walked inside.

Chapter Thirteen

Gossip spread to the North Side like the infamous Chicago fire. The flames of the scandal were fanned by the betrayal from Susie's closest friends.

Katie Roberts was the first to announce her heroine's feet of clay.

"Susie Howard isn't in class because she ran away."

Meghan, Carla and Sherry gasped.

"She did not," Meghan MacDowell said.

"Did so. Her parents called my house looking for her three days ago. I didn't think anything of it except that now it's Wednesday, and she still isn't back in school."

"It could be a lot of things." Sherry reasoned.

"I'm telling you she ran away. Take my word for it," Katie said haughtily.

Carla's eagle green eyes scoured Katie's face. "You know more. Fess up."

Katie examined her pink pearl nail polish. "I helped Susie pack for a three day weekend with her boyfriend."

"No!" Sherry gasped.

"Yes," Katie said excitedly spilling the beans. "She went to San Francisco to see Tommy Magli. In a hotel."

Eyes flew open. Mouths gaped. Smiles came with delicious wicked curves.

"Tommy is so dreamy," Carla cooed.

"And older."

"He's a Marine," Sherry said with disdain.

"He's a man!" Carla said. "Not a boy. He should be a marine."

"Can you imagine being in a strange city? With a *man*? In a hotel?" Meghan gushed sensually.

"Uh, huh." They all nodded.

Katie enjoyed center stage. It was a heady trip.

The girls huddled around her.

"Susie went to San Francisco, she slept with Tommy and the sex was so incredible, she must have phoned her parents and said she was never coming home."

"That makes no sense. Then why did they call you asking if she was with you? Obviously, they don't know where she is, Katie," Sherry offered.

"Okay. Then she didn't tell them. But she's probably having the time of her life right about now. I know I would if I were with Tommy," Katie sighed.

Sherry was unconvinced. "She better be damn careful otherwise she's going to get pregnant and where does that get you? Nowhere. Shit and diapers and no more sex. Who wants that?"

The girls stared with distracted confusion as if their thoughts were slow to derail.

Sherry continued. "I say there's something else going on. Personally, I would never fly off to a strange city only weeks away from Prom, finals and graduation. Think about it. She's missed three days of school now. We don't know when she's coming back. If she's coming back."

"What are you saying?" Katie asked.

"Susie Howard went to San Francisco alright. But she went to get an abortion."

Carla nearly fainted. Meghan let out a tiny scream.

"Not the A-word! She would never! She's Catholic!"

"Who gives a damn?" Sherry countered. "You wait and see."

Sherry turned on her heel and walked off as the others stared after her, raising her to heroine status.

Sherry Wilson had been the only one in Susie's crowd to be accepted at Vassar. While everyone else chose top Catholic women's colleges, Sherry couldn't wait to plunge herself into the culture, the lifestyle, the mien of the East Coast.

But first, she had to get a complete physical exam.

Fate is a cruel comedian when it pits a jealous but aspiring apprentice against an unsuspecting heroine.

Dr. Adam Klinger's obstetrical and gynecological practice was situated just north of the Northwestern Campus in Evanston.

Though the five-story building was old, utilitarian and boring Dr. Klinger's wife, Bonnie, had re-decorated the offices to reflect her garish femininity. The walls were bubble gum pink; the slick white pearlized Naugahyde chairs sat on modern chrome legs, which tended to trip clumsy, overweight and pregnant women. Plastic palm trees decorated with Styrofoam coconuts brushed up against hideous cheap modern art framed in chrome metal. Stacks of high-fashion magazines littered the chrome and smoked glass tables reminding every pregnant woman of what she never actually looked like prior to her pregnancy and now had no hope of ever attaining.

The only aspect of this office that brought patients by the droves was Dr. Adam himself.

Tall, broad shouldered and narrow hipped, his prematurely gray, full head of hair and soulful dark eyes, gave women the scintillating combination of medical experience and sexual tease that kept them faithful to their monthly appointments.

Susie Howard had never been to a gynecologist in her life. In fact, when she'd entered high school and received the last of her inoculations, it had been from Dr. Browne, the pediatrician she'd seen since she was in diapers. Susie had no earthly idea which gynecologist to choose, but she remembered hearing Dr. Adam Klinger's name at the Sheridan Shore Yacht Club. As far as she was concerned, it was a place to start.

Her face stuck behind the pages of the latest Vogue Magazine, Susie didn't look up when the door opened and a new patient walked in and went to the frosted glass window where the receptionist sat.

Susie turned the page.

The girl rang the bell.

The receptionist opened the window.

"Sherry Wilson to see Dr. Klinger."

"Would you fill out these papers Miss Wilson? And you're here for . . . ?"

"I'm going to Vassar and . . . "

The nurse cut her off. "Ah, yes. College physical."

Susie felt her cheeks flame. Of all the people in the world, she did not want to see today, Sherry Wilson was it. Sherry was as smart as Susie, as pretty and as ambitious. For four years, Sherry had pitted herself against Susie in some phantom contest the rules to which Susie never understood. Susie didn't believe that Sherry was jealous of her because they both came from the same kind of family background. They had not tried to steal each others' boyfriends, still, for some unknown reason Sherry wanted to be better than Susie.

Now she's going to get her chance.

Susie sank back in the chair but the naugahyde was so slick she slipped down nearly falling off.

"You all right, honey?" the older woman sitting next to her asked.

"Yes, I'm fine," Susie tried to whisper, but instead drew the attention of the room.

Sherry turned around from the reception desk and faced Susie. Their eyes locked.

Susie knew in an instant the word about her weekend with Tommy was all over school. Being in a gynecologist's office was all the confirmation Sherry would need.

Sherry smiled.

Susie gulped. "Hi."

Triumph kept Sherry's feet from even hitting the floor. She practically floated toward Susie. "I heard you were in San Francisco."

"Katie told?"

"Not all of it." Sherry sat in the empty seat to Susie's left.

"I'm back. It was great."

"You saw Tommy?"

"Oh, yeah. Sure. Sure." Susie suddenly didn't know what to say. She wasn't planning on another interrogation. She instantly realized that the choices she'd made out of love, were choices most of society and especially her friends did not and would never understand. And what of her parents' fears?

Everything they'd said to her was the truth. They had spent their lives building good reputations for themselves. They would never forgive her now if she betrayed them.

No one, not her parents or Sherry or Katie knew what it was like to live in her shoes. How could they? She had just begun to try them on herself.

She had to think fast because Sherry's impact on her life had suddenly become critical.

"How is he?" Sherry asked.

"He's fine. Fine." Susie smiled broadly. Too broadly.

"When did you get back?"

"Sunday. Afternoon."

"I'm only asking because I missed seeing you in school this week."

"Oh, I took some time off."

"Time off?"

"Yeah," Susie smiled. "Actually, it was raining buckets when I got back. I had the sniffles."

"Sniffles?"

"Yes, so I thought I'd see the doctor."

"A gynecologist for sniffles."

"Actually, I'm killing two birds with one stone. I have to get that exam just like you. You ever had a pelvic before? I haven't. And I don't mind saying, it gives me the willies."

"After a weekend with Tommy Magli, a pelvic would give you the willies?" Sherry laughed pointedly.

Sherry was too smart for Susie's evasions. She took the offensive, but only for protection. "Look whose talking, Sherry Wilson."

Sherry leaned closer. "Don't give me some shit, Susie Howard. I don't know whom you think you're kidding, but your parents have called half of Cook County trying to find your ass and you act like you're in some Annette Funicello movie. Stuff it."

Susie ground her jaw. "My communication gap with my parents is my business. Not yours. I'm dealing with them in my own way. Let's not pretend we don't know what happened between you and John Reynolds junior year. Just exactly where did **you** go over Christmas vacation? Huh?"

Sherry stiffened.

"Just so you know, I never said anything to anybody about you and John. I saw what I saw. I can't help it you guys chose the Art Club room to do it in and it was my afternoon to deliver the paint for the play props. And I never told anyone that your mother called my mother for a doctor's name all the way in New York. So don't go throwing that finger at me. Look at yourself first."

"Mrs. Magli," the nurse announced.

Without thinking, Susie stood instantly.

And she blew it.

Sherry's face lit with triumph and just as quickly, sadness set into furrows where youth should yet dwell. "He married you?"

"Yes."

"Lucky," Sherry said painfully as their eyes locked again.

It was the first time Susie ever realized that Sherry deeply loved John Reynolds and he was already off to another girl. Her parents had gotten to her. They had made her have an abortion. Catholicism or no. Sherry had given up a great deal. In that moment, her heart broke for Sherry.

Susie leaned down and touched Sherry's hand. "Thanks for saying that, Sherry."

Sherry bit her lip to hold back the emotion in her throat. "You're welcome."

Susie started to go.

Sherry pulled her back and whispered, "Good for you, Susie. You take care."

"You, too."

Susie walked away marveling over the miracle that had just taken place. An enemy had become a friend.

Chapter Fourteen

Susie set the kitchen table for dinner while Jed hung his corduroy jacket on the wall peg in the hallway. "Did you see the doctor today?"

"Yes, I did."

He walked into the kitchen and took out his usual old fashioned glass. "Everything okay? I mean you look healthy as a horse to me."

"It depends upon how you feel about twins."

"Twins?"

Susie looked at Jed as he pulled his bottle of whiskey out of the kitchen cabinet. For a long pause he studied the bottle. "Twins."

"Yes. He's not positive. It's too soon, he said. But in another four to six weeks when he can hear the heartbeat more clearly, then he'll know if he hears one or two."

Jed put the bottle back in the cabinet and closed it soundly. Suddenly, his life looked different to him. "Twins. That's going to make a real change around here."

When he looked at her, he was smiling. Genuinely. "You want some tea?" he asked.

Susie smiled back knowing he had made a conscious choice at that very second.

Miracle number two.

"Tea would be nice."

"You can have that, right? Tea?"

"It's not on the list of foods to avoid. I had no idea there was so much to this," she said, looking at the stack of information the doctor had given her. "Some of it is common sense. No smoking. No alcohol. No raw meat."

"Raw meat?" he asked.

"Yeah. It can cause blindness in the baby. No steak tartare. Darn. And I love that stuff."

"Yeah, me, too." He looked up. "What is it?"

"It's yummy. Raw ground sirloin, minced garlic and onion. I like it with really skinny crisp French fries like we had in Paris once."

"Paris." He filled the battered teapot with tap water. "You been to Paris?"

"With my parents. When I was fifteen."

"I never took Tommy anywhere. Wisconsin Dells once. When his mother . . . was alive."

"I'd love to see the Dells. Is it wonderful?"

He watched her as she turned in the plastic covered aluminum chair, her eyes eager and sincerely wanting to know his answer.

No wonder he fell in love with her.

"It was okay, I guess. Tommy liked it."

"What about it did he like?"

"The cliff walls with waterfalls and pine trees growing right out of the rock. He liked the Indian dances there. They put on a show at night near the lodge where we stayed. There was this one Indian who jumped from a cliff right onto this giant Tom Tom. Probably just a trampoline."

He put tea bags in two mugs. "You want sugar or something?"

"I usually take lemon and honey."

He looked around sheepishly. "I don't . . . "

"I'll get some at the store tomorrow," she offered. "Sugar is fine for now."

Jed poured the boiling water over the tea bags and placed her mug in front of her with the sugar. Then he sat. "Are you scared?"

"Yes." She reached for her cup with trembling hands. "Oh, not about the baby. Babies. I can feel them or it, you know. It's like having Tommy with me all the time. But I'm scared because I have to tell my parents."

"They'll come around. You call them. You'll see. It was just the shock of it all. The wedding. The baby. Now the babies. They'll come around. They love you."

"But you don't know them. They aren't like you."

"Yeah, they're rich."

She paused watching his overburdened face drop.

"Jed. Don't worry about the cost of the birth and hospital. I saved quite a bit of money for college. I'll use that for the delivery. Plus Tommy is going to be sending his monthly check back here. He said he wouldn't need much in a foreign country. I argued with him. Told him not to send any. But he wouldn't listen."

"Yeah. That's my boy. Always thinking of others."

Susie swallowed hard. "Do you . . . think I'm a burden to him?

His head shot up. His eyes bored into her. "Not for a minute. Not ever. I'm sorry if it sounded that way. I think you're the best thing that ever happened to him. Look, Susie, I don't have much around here. Not even a damn lemon for your tea. Not that I can't afford it, I just don't think of those things anymore."

"Anymore?"

"She . . . Tommy's mother . . . she took lemon and honey in her tea."

Susie caught her sob mid-throat. "Oh, Jed. I'm so sorry." She spilled out of her chair onto the floor next to him and flung her arms around him. "I wish I had known her. She must have been the most wonderful woman ever to have lived."

"She was. But how . . . could you know?" He asked, wiping a lone tear from his eye.

"You and Tommy miss her so much."

"We do."

He swiped his face with his palm and forced a smile. "We were a family then."

Susie smiled softly. "Now we're going to be a family again." She put her hand on her stomach. "A blessed family."

Jed's tears washed anew.

He couldn't believe this girl with her bright beaming face could open her heart so wide as to let not only his son move in, but there was obviously room for him as well.

At that moment, Jed realized that the Philco radio had been playing for hours. Maybe even for days or months but he hadn't heard it for years. It had been a long time since he was aware of background music. As if the dial had been turned by an angel's hand, he heard the words his heart could not form.

I bless the day I found you,
Wrap my loving arms around you,
Now and forever,
Let it be me.

Susie counted the rings before her mother answered the phone. Five. Six. Seven.

"She's not home."

Eight. Nine.

"Mother."

"Susan," Mary Elizabeth said it like she was announcing what she was serving for dinner. "Steak au poivre. Avec pommes frittes."

"Mother, I wanted to call and tell you that . . . "

"What, Susan? That you didn't go to New York as we expected? That you turned your plane ticket in for cash and you abandoned us without a word and are living God only knows where? Tell me, what, Susan?"

"Gee, and I thought you'd be glad to hear from me. That I was alive and okay."

"Oh, for God's sake, Susan. Don't be so melodramatic."

"Well, Mother, this is melodramatic. You're making it be that way."

"I am. I am?"

"You want me to give my babies up for adoption? I'd rather die! That's pretty dramatic."

"What would you have me do? Throw a party? Tell all our friends you've lost your mind? Have you really thought about what you're doing with your life? Throwing away this chance at college."

"I can go to college later."

"And who is going to pay for that? Not us I can assure you."

Default two.

Stupid. Stupid. Fool. Susie, what were you thinking?

The incredible thought that her parents would not want the best for her had never entered Susie's mind. She had actually believed in her naiveté, obviously, that her mother and father may not approve of her choice of husband, may not condone her pre-marital sex and her unwanted pregnancy, but never in a billion years had she thought they would refuse to help her out when it came to her education.

"I am your child after all, Mother. Isn't it a parent's duty to see to a child's education?"

"Hell no!" Mary Elizabeth scoffed. "Not when it costs them tens of thousands of dollars. Why not explain what you've done to deserve such magnanimity on our part? Is it true you dropped out of high school? And you didn't even bother to tell us that. High school, Susan! My God! That's like finishing kindergarten in my book! I had hoped you'd get a masters. I can deal with you chucking college to be a model before I can deal with this . . . this . . . "

"I'm not going to be a model."

"Really." Suddenly, Mary Elizabeth stopped. "Did you say 'babies'?"

"I did."

"Babies. Plural."

"Yes. We're not absolutely sure. Dr. Klinger says it will be another six weeks then he should know."

"Dr. Klinger. Evanston's Dr. Klinger?"

"Yes."

Mary Elizabeth clicked her tongue against her teeth. "The one whose wife, Bonnie, is the biggest gossip on the lakefront."

"I didn't know about that."

"Obviously."

"Look, Mother. You can't hide me forever. I am married. I'm going to have a baby. Twins, possibly. This is my life and I'm part of your life. I am sorry you think I have ruined your reputation. I didn't do this on purpose. I didn't do this to inflict pain on you."

"Then why did you do it?"

"Because I love him."

"Fine."

"Mother, you can't shut me out of your life forever. You're my family. I'm a part of this family."

"Is that so? Well, consider yourself shut out. Your father is seeing the attorney to have his Will changed. As for me, no daughter of mine would do this to me. No daughter of mine would be so inconsiderate not to think of the repercussions of her actions. So, I guess I don't have a daughter anymore, now do I?"

Odd, how emotional pain strikes. It's different from physical pain. A lance to the heart would be stabbing and sticky as blood oozes out onto the skin.

But at that moment, Susie felt numb. Everything seemed empty and cold. She was taken back to a time when she was a little girl and she'd been playing on the playground at school. She'd fallen off the swings and scraped her knee on the pavement. One of the nuns had come to help her up, but she'd been screaming so loudly, she suddenly couldn't hear anything.

In her deafness, she didn't understand what the nun was saying; all she felt was the pressure on her arm as the woman guided her to the nurse's office. The nun had been very gentle as she applied Mercurochrome to the scrape and then pressed a bandaid in place. Susie had instantly stopped crying.

The nun had told her that her mother would be proud of her for not crying.

"Oh, no. My mother will be angry with me."

"But why? You were so brave."

"She'll be angry because I tore my socks and ripped my skirt. These bandages are ugly. Now, I'm unsightly."

Instantly, Susie was back in the present. "I just realized. This pregnancy makes me unsightly."

"As unsightly as one can get," Mary Elizabeth replied.

"I've dropped out of school. I won't come around. No one will see me or be embarrassed by me anymore."

"Good."

"Can I ask you a question?"

"No. Yes."

"Don't you even want to know where I am?"

"You're at that boy's house. I assume his family took you in."

"How did you know?"

"Think about it, Susan. No one in our family is very pleased with you right now."

"I'm not pleased with them, either. I think I'm right where I should be."

"Ducky. And while you're at it, find yourself another doctor. I'll instruct Dr. Klinger not to take you on as a patient. He's too visible at the club. There are other doctors for you to see."

Susie's head pounded as her blood rushed through her veins in an attempt to stifle her anger. "What else would you like me to do, Mother? Vanish?"

"That's the idea. Susan, I'm going to say it one more time. Go to New York. Put this child or whatever up for adoption. We can cover our rears with stories. In time, people will forget. But they can't forget what you've done with a baby strapped around your waist."

"Will you never stop?" Susie screamed at her mother while holding the receiver at half an arm's length.

"Will you?" Mary Elizabeth banged down the receiver.

Susie slammed the phone down. When she looked up, Jed was standing in the doorway. "Didn't go well?"

Susie's face started to crumble. "They hate me."

Jed was non-plussed. "Hate you? No way."

Stunned, Susie replied, "What? You're on their side?"

"I'm on yours. They're still in shock. I bet your father drinks twice what I do these days. But you're young. You have to learn how to fight dirty," a slow smile crept over his lips.

"Fight dirty." She responded to his smile.

"Yep."

"What's the first rule?"

"Hard core training is necessary," he said taking his sweater off the hallway coat peg.

"And where do we start?"

"At the Dairy Queen," he laughed tossing her a jacket. "Come on. I'm buying."

Chapter Fifteen

The dichotomy of the mid sixties was that although everyone talked about the gaps, the communication gap, the gender gap, the generation gap, no author, no media guru came up with wartime romance rules.

But they were there.

The rules were hard and fast and consisted of more don'ts than do's.

Don't talk about the headlines. Don't talk about body counts. Don't ask about specific missions or points of deployment or embarkation. Never openly admit fears of death. Never cry on the phone. Never mention loneliness.

Never *ever* talk about anti-war protestors.

When the phone rang, Susie jumped on it. "Tommy?"

"How's my Saturday night girl?"

"I'm fine. Just fine. Missing you as always, but we're great here."

"God, I live to hear your voice. How's my dad?"

"He's great. He wants to talk to you after we finish."

"Sure, great. Is everything okay with him?"

She knew just what he meant. "You'd be really proud of him, Tommy. He hasn't had a drink since I moved in. He's fixing dinner now. Ravioli."

"He's cooking."

"He's really, really good at it."

"He always was. It drives my Aunt Loretta crazy."

"I met her a couple weeks ago. She came over after Mass on Sunday lugging huge pans of the worst lasagna I've ever tasted. Jed had a refrigerator full of food and she acted like she didn't know he ever cooked."

"For awhile after Mom died, Loretta did do all the cooking."

"He's made a lot of changes since I moved in."

"You see? Susie girl, you're the miracle he needed."

"I wouldn't go that far," she said. "Tell me about you. What are you up to?"

"Studying like crazy. There aren't enough hours in the day *or* night. Seems I'm number one in all my classes."

"Why won't you tell me about these things you're studying?"

"Classified."

She laughed. "Very funny. What are you studying?"

"I'm serious. I can't tell you."

Silence hung like death.

"You're not kidding."

"No," he said solemnly.

"But you're the best, right?"

"I'm the best, baby."

Putting her hand on her swollen belly she said, "I have something to tell you. I didn't want to say anything until I was sure."

"Sure? There's nothing wrong is there?" His voice rose with alarm.

"What's your position about twins."

"Is this a rhetorical question?"

"No," she chewed her bottom lip nervously. "It's official. We're having twins."

"Holy Mother of God!" He slapped his hand against his forehead. "I can't believe this!"

"Are you happy or upset?"

"I'm . . . speechless. Happy! Yes! Wow!"

He was genuinely happy. She could hear his heart smiling over the phone. "I'm so glad you're happy about it."

Not like my family.

"How does Dad feel about this? I mean . . ."

"He says he's always wanted to add onto the house."

"You're kidding. He said that?"

"Yes, why? I mean there are only two bedrooms here. I mean, I love it, living in your room with your things around me. It even smells like you."

"It's English Leather, sweetie. Don't romanticize it."

128

"I love English Leather," she laughed.

"So, Dad would really do that?"

"He wants to talk to you about it."

Trepidation entered Tommy's voice like an unwanted bastard. "Adding on. That's a pretty permanent situation. What happened with your folks? Did you tell them about the twins?"

"Yes. Weeks ago. I let it slip. I haven't confirmed it to them. Not that it would matter."

Susie knew she was bending the wartime romance rules. She shouldn't get so heavy with the conversation. She should keep it light. In a few weeks, Tommy would be shipped out. He'd be gone for over a year. She'd never get to talk to him.

Tommy was insistent. "Susie, what the hell is going on?"

"My parents have disowned me."

"Because of me." His words dropped like lead weights.

"Because of me. They're mad at me. Don't take on a bunch of stupid guilt. They have a problem, okay?"

"I can't believe this. I can't imagine turning my back on my own child. Hell, my kids aren't even born yet and I would never abandon them. Never! You tell them that, Susie. I would never leave you. Never leave them. I don't want them to think everyone is like your parents." He paused. "What's wrong with them?"

"Selfish."

He was stunned. "As always, you can nail anything right to the wall."

"Have to. Look who I've been living with all these years. Being here with your Dad, it's like a breath of fresh air. It's so strange. I feel as if I'm learning to live for the first time."

"Because you are. So am I."

"Tommy, you really feel that way? You don't feel like you're tied down?"

"Honey, I want to be tied down. I want to know there's someone out there waiting for me. Doesn't everybody?"

"I never thought about it like that."

"Look, my turn at the phone is getting short. I love you, Susie. Always remember that. And I'm coming home to you. Now put Dad on."

"I love you, Tommy. And I miss you so much."

She laid the receiver down and opened the bedroom door. Jed was standing just outside.

She smiled. "Your turn."

Jed let her pass as he reached for the phone. "Tommy, how are you, son?"

"Doing great, Dad. You wouldn't believe it. These guys think I hung the moon around here. My test scores and grades are off the charts. They put me in some special intelligence classes and I just have this knack for it. I'm learning more about myself, about my endurance, loyalty. It's incredible."

"I'm proud of you, son."

"Now you know how I've felt being the son of a soldier. I've always been proud of you, but . . ." he choked back his emotion. Suddenly, he was tremendously homesick. The days of karate and akido lessons, stealth maneuvers, special weapons, explosives' training and the night classes of encryption, Vietnamese language skills and the new forms of disguise with latex masks and makeup that had been filling his head vanished. All he wanted was to hug his dad and kiss his wife.

"Dad, Susie told me about the . . . the, uh, addition."

"I know what you mean. I haven't touched the stuff and don't intend to. But listen, what do you think about the addition to the place?"

"Can you afford it? I mean Susie's a financial burden already and my pay . . ."

"Is just the extra we need. Besides, I'm getting a second mortgage from the bank to cover it. I'll do most of the work and Susie, she's a trooper. She used her college money to buy a sewing machine. She took some classes over at the Singer place. She'll get the hang of it in no time. She said she wants to make the baby clothes and her own stuff. Said she'd make the curtains and things for the babies' room, too. I thought I'd go all the way. A nursery, bathroom and a playroom."

"Dad, are you really sure? I mean after I get back we'll be needing a place of our own."

"I need this, son. Can you understand that?"

"Yes, I can."

Jed sighed. "Besides, once you get back we'll still need the space here for when you come to visit. Who's gonna baby-sit? Old Grandpa, that's who!" Jed laughed.

Tommy held his breath. "It's been a long time since I heard you laugh, Dad."

"Long time since I did. But things are different now."

"Yeah, they are. Look, I gotta give up the phone to another guy. Take care of my babies . . . all of them."

"You do the same, son."

"I will."

"Tommy, I know I haven't been much good since your Mom . . . well, I just . . . I love you, son."

Not knowing if he heard correctly, Tommy said, "Thanks." And hung up.

Another enlisted man anxiously took over the phone, pulling two rolls of quarters out of his pants pocket. "C'mon, man. Give it up."

Tommy scratched his head. "Sure. Here."

"What's up with you?" The man asked looking at Tommy's baffled expression.

"I think my dad just said he loved me."

"Groovy."

Smiling, Tommy nodded. "Real groovy."

Susie made perfect scores on all her final exams. Her book reports and term papers were the best she'd ever written.

"This is scary," she said to Jed as he threw a sledgehammer through the back wall of the house.

"No, it's not. It's liberating."

"Not the house. My grades. Straight 'A's on everything. 'A' pluses on my reports. And I didn't go to class. What does this say about the American Education system?"

131

He held the sledgehammer mid-motion. "Skipping classes is good?"

"That's it!"

He threw the hammer through the wall knocking out studs.

"I'm going to get the mail. See if there's a letter from Tommy."

Susie walked out into the hot July sunshine. Chicago was sweltering and she was swollen. For all her bragging about not showing in the beginning of her pregnancy, she made up for lost time. There was no question she was carrying twins. Most days she felt as if she were going to have a litter of twelve. Holding her hand on the small of her back, she walked onto the porch and opened the box.

"Hey! There's two letters!" she shouted into the house through the screen door.

"Great!" Jed replied ripping the hammer through more plaster.

Sweat trickled down Susie's temple as she gazed up into the silver maple tree. A hot breeze moved the branches and danced across the tops of black-eyed Susans she'd planted two months ago.

"Hello, Susie."

The hairs on the back of Susie's neck stood on end. She turned and saw the parked car at the curb.

"Hello, Father."

Chapter Sixteen

"I missed you," he said, closing the door and walking to the front of the Lincoln Town Car.

Suddenly, she was stingingly aware of her size, the blatant blossom of her pregnancy and all the nuances that went with it.

She wore a bright orange, brown and rust print cotton granny dress she'd made herself. It was about as crude a job of dressmaking possible, but it only cost her three dollars to make. The elastic in the rounded neckline had never been right and dipped lower than she'd originally intended, but due to the over one hundred degree heat, it was cool. But it also revealed her engorged breasts. Breasts she still was not comfortable owning. Breasts her father had never seen.

She watched his eyes as they traveled the length of her, taking in her belly and breasts. The cheap dress. The sweaty tangle of hair she'd pulled up in a ponytail.

"You're really different," he said.

"Nothing like your daughter?"

She watched as he glanced at the sidewalk, its cracks filled with a profusion of summer weeds she'd been too busy and tired to pull.

"I don't really know her, either." He paused to gather his words. "At least, not since she was very small."

"You came a long way," she said, not moving an inch.

"There's not much traffic along Lake Shore on a Saturday."

"I should try it sometime."

He brightened but only slightly. "I wish you had."

She stiffened. "Had."

He opened his mouth to speak, but words failed him. He stood there feeling dumb and useless and he had never felt this way. He was Braxton Howard. The man with the answers. The man who forged new businesses. Made history. Changed lives.

"I just came from the club. I wanted to hear it from you."

"Hear what?"

"Sherry Wilson told her parents she saw you before school let out at Dr. Klinger's office."

"Sherry." Susie closed her eyes to ward off tears. She realized at that moment that hope had sprung alive inside her. Her heart had actually stopped beating in the anticipation that her father had come to be with her. She realized she'd wanted him to beg her for forgiveness.

One of these days I'm going to learn not to play the fool.

"I guess you knew she'd told everyone you got married."

"I didn't know. But I assumed she would."

"She went back to the office last week to get her paperwork for college. She's going to Vassar."

"I know."

"She asked the nurse how you were. She told her you were best friends. The nurse informed her that you were just fine. You and the twins."

"We are."

"Then it's true." He swallowed hard and clasped his hands in front of him to keep them from shaking. "You're having twins."

"Yes. I told Mother. She didn't tell you?"

"No."

"I wouldn't think so. It's too real to her. But don't worry, I won't be using Dr. Klinger or going to his office anymore."

"Oh, no. It's fine. Cat's out of the bag."

"Oh, I wasn't going somewhere else because of the gossip mill he runs there."

"Then why not?"

"He's too expensive." Susie didn't want him to know about her mother's threats. She wanted to protect him from the truth.

"I heard he's the best," Braxton said.

"You heard. Why on earth would you ask around about a gynecologist?" She scoffed.

"I want my daughter to have the best. I'll pay for the doctor."

"Why would you do that when you disowned me?"

"I never did anything of the kind! Where would you get an idea like that?" he asked, sincerely shocked.

She took a deep breath, feeling stronger and more loved than she had in a long time. Obviously, it was her mother who was orchestrating the barrage against Susie. The more Mary Elizabeth stirred the pot, the more Susie realized how devastated her mother must be. She was reacting out of pain and anger. What Susie didn't know was how long Mary Elizabeth would feel like this. Surely, she wouldn't keep them estranged for the rest of her life. Would she?

She looked at Braxton. It was interesting even to herself how far away the world of the North Shore and the yacht club suddenly seemed.

"Don't worry about the money, Daddy. Tommy took care of it. He sends nearly his whole paycheck home."

"What, all eighty dollars of it?"

"Seventy. I get seventy a month."

Braxton took three long strides and stood at the bottom of the steps looking up at her. "Geezus, Susie, why does it have to be this way? Can't you see what torture you've brought on yourself? Living like this. On this side of town. It's not safe here. The gangs. The Black Panthers. The demonstrators are all so near here. I can't sleep at night for worrying about you." He paused. "Please tell me you don't go out at night."

"Go where?"

"I don't know? Movies. For a root beer. You know what I mean."

"No, I'm afraid I don't," she said feeling inexplicably proud of Jed's house suddenly. Proud of the shabby dress she'd made. Proud of the healthy babies growing inside her. Proud that somewhere inside her was some quality, some trait that drew this man, her father, away from the Gold Coast to the South Side to confront her.

She was only eighteen, but in that instant she knew what many people didn't know their whole lives through. She had worth.

She had changed Jed's life by the simple fact of her presence. Because she was pregnant with Jed's grandchildren, he had rediscovered his own dreams. He'd wanted to be a chef. And now he was inventing dishes again. He'd prided himself on being a good provider for Tommy and now he was building a bigger house. A better house.

And her father.

He'd never kow-towed to a human in his life. He'd been too self-centered. Too sure that his beliefs were the right ones; the only ones all of society should follow.

Now he was here.

She'd found the chink in his armor.

She had caused him to think for himself.

"Why are you here?" she asked.

"Two children is a lot to hide, Susie."

She lifted her chin defiantly. "Are you worried that I can't hide them or that you can't hide from them?"

He dropped his jaw. "I . . . both," he admitted. "Look, Susie, I came here because . . . honestly, I couldn't believe it. I wanted to know the truth. We've never had twins in the family."

"You're kidding, right?" She rolled her eyes.

"What? Is there something I missed?"

Shaking her head she asked, "Is there anything in your life you're connected to?"

"What are you talking about?"

"Grandma Howard. She was a twin, Dad."

"She was not!"

"She was. She told me so herself. Her sister died at birth. She said there were times when she thought her sister came to her in dreams like an angel. Sometimes she would hear her talking to her."

"That's preposterous . . ." His voice trailed off. He peered at her thoughtfully. Illumination struck. "That would explain the extra plaque in the family mausoleum. The one with no name."

"She had a name. It was Faith."

"Grace and Faith? Why didn't they put it on the plaque?"

"I don't know. Maybe it was just the name Grandma Howard gave her. I don't know."

"How is it you know all this?" he asked.

"I asked. I talked. I communicated with your mother. Obviously, more than you ever did."

"Well, it just wasn't *done*. Boys didn't talk to their mothers about such things."

"Sorta like fathers don't talk to their daughters about such things. These things." She put her hand on her stomach.

"I'm trying, Susie."

Looking intensely at him, she said, "Yes. You are."

"Your Mother is devastated by all this . . ."

"So am I!" she interrupted.

"I mean the gossip and all."

"Who gives a flip about the gossip? Obviously, that gossip is more important than I am."

"Now you're the one who doesn't understand. This has hurt us deeply."

"I know that," she said sadly. "But you hurt me, too."

Her words hit him like a punch to the belly. He was guilty as charged. He had spent his life building his career and spending his time in the business world instead of at home. He thought of the vacations they should have taken. The picnics they could have had. The Christmases when he flew to London to close just one more "deal". He could have spent his time on his wife and his daughter, but he hadn't. He'd thought about Braxton and Braxton alone.

Tears filled his eyes. "I never wanted it to be like this. And I don't know what to do."

Susie's defenses fell like the walls of Jericho. Tears flooded her eyes. Her heart burst open. "Oh, Daddy!"

She waddled down the steps and put her arms around him. "You can be such an idiot sometimes. But I love you."

They clung to each other, chuckling through tears. Braxton was not familiar with such displays of emotions and he felt awkward holding his only child.

Finally, he composed himself. "I don't understand half of what is happening to our family. You won't listen to reason. Your mother is intractable. And I feel caught in the middle."

"You don't have to be."

"Of course I do. I agree with both of you. You have brought shame on the family. I've even been to confession about it. I would be lying if I didn't say that I still want you to give these babies up for adoption and then move back home and make things like they used to be. Go to college. Marry some nice young man."

"But I did marry a nice young man."

Braxton gazed into her eyes. "You know what I mean."

"But do *you* know what you mean?" she asked.

The silence reverberated as revelations about each other ram-rodded themselves into existence. For the first time, they saw each other as adults.

She continued. "What you meant to say is marry a man like me."

"What's wrong with that?" he forced a smile.

Susie touched his cheek. She no longer felt like the fool. She realized that perhaps all her life she'd been sent to earth to be the parent to Braxton and Mary Elizabeth. In their bias and intolerance, they were such children. They had tiny selfish childrens' hearts, which were more needy than they were giving.

Perhaps it was her job to be even more giving than she'd thought possible. Perhaps it was her job to move them along to adulthood.

Slipping her arm through his, she began to lead him back toward the car. "There's nothing wrong with you, Daddy. In your world, you're a hero. People look up to you and you need them to do that. It gives you validation."

They walked to the driver's side of the car.

"I'll miss you," she said and kissed his cheek.

"Miss me? When will I see you again? Can't I come here to see you?" he asked with a child's terror in his voice.

"Yes, Daddy. You can come here any time. But remember, there are a lot of heroes here. Jed. Tommy. And there is so much room for you."

"Do you really believe that? That I'm a hero?"

"You are the man by which I measure all men."

Braxton closed his misty eyes. "I was so wrong," he said looking at her again. "I should have honored your choice in Tommy."

She kissed his cheek. "That's all I wanted to hear," she said and then turned and walked back up the walk.

Braxton stood for a moment, got in the car and started the engine. Before driving away, he looked at the door to see if Susie was there to wave at him like she always had when she was small.

Susie waved.

He waved back knowing his world had been glued back together again.

The Christmas Star

Chapter Seventeen

July 27, 1966

In the summer of 1966 the world split apart. The brunt of the focus for the rupture was in Vietnam and Chicago. In Chicago, the grizzliest and ghastliest mass slaying in history learned the name of the killer, Richard F. Speck, when the sole survivor of the murder identified him at Cook County Jail. The same week, Chicago police quelled race riots in which two people died and fifty-seven were injured. By the 31st, over four thousand National Guardsmen were sent to Chicago to halt the ongoing war between police and black snipers. Firebomb attacks made the South Side into a war zone. Black and white gangs clashed in broad daylight. Residents were warned that venturing out at night was dangerous, if not deadly.

In Vietnam, Ho Chi Minh ordered partial mobilization of his troops. North Vietnam announced they would try captured U.S. pilots for war crimes. United States planes bombed the demilitarized zone between North and South Vietnam for the first time and American deaths and casualties outweighed those of the Vietnamese.

Susie was unaware of the history being made around her. All she knew was that Tommy was being shipped overseas and she was too pregnant to fly in a plane to see him.

"You're going two weeks early," she said on the phone.

"I told you, baby. I'm top of my class. They think I'm good at what I do."

"And what is it that you do?"

"Look, honey. You know I can't say. But don't worry. I'm a crack shot with a gun. Any kind of gun. Even the big ones."

"This is supposed to make me feel safe?"

"The way things are going in Chicago, I'm more worried about you than I am about myself. You stay put. In the house with Dad, okay?"

"I will."

"How's the house coming? I saw the photographs of the tear out..."

"I love you, Tommy," she interjected. "I miss you so much, sometimes I don't think I can stand another day of waiting. If I weren't so . . . fat . . ."

"Honey, you're pregnant, not fat."

"You haven't seen me since the beginning when I didn't even show. Now I can't even take a bath anymore, only showers. Your Dad has to help me out of the Lazy Boy."

"Susie Howard Magli, you got my father to give up his Lazy Boy? Now, that's a miracle."

"Tommy, promise me you'll come home alive. In one piece?"

"We promised not to talk about this, okay? But yes, I'll be home before you know it. You got the calendar I sent you? I marked the days I land and the day I come back. You just take care of yourself and be strong. You have a lot to go through in the next two months."

"I'll think of you every night. Dream of you. I promise."

"And I'll do the same. I love you, Susie. Send me lots of pictures of you now and some every week. Okay? And I got the tape player so you can record messages for me. You and Dad. And when the babies are old enough, they can cry onto the tape okay? You send me their voices."

"I will. And I'll bake cookies and send those and anything else you want from home."

"Send me love, Susie. Just send me love."

"Always, Tommy. Forever."

Southeast Asia. September, 1966.

The air was sweltering with more moisture than heat as Tommy stood inside Captain Ralph Arnold's tent staring at aerial photographs and maps. The meeting was private and of the highest security. Tommy had been to the "hot zone" on four previous missions and proved he could handle 35 mm guns as well as fire rockets and hit the targets dead on. He was more than capable of instant critical decisions which saved himself and the eight men in his squad. Whether flying two-pilot attack Huey's under the canopy of trees and following enemy trails into the jungle, or the task of keeping the nose of his Cobra down until he pulled out away from the trees, berries and vines dangling from the landing gear all the while knowing that the trajectory of the Cong fire kept his odds of dying at ten to one, Tommy proved himself to his superiors.

Counting out the fatal ten seconds once he landed his chopper on the ground had been drilled into his brain.

Ten... "You're a number, boy!"

Nine... "Your ass is gone, boy!"

Eight... seven... six... "Let's move it, boy!"

Five... "We've been hit!"

Four... "Let's go, let's go, let's go!"

Three... "Rev."

Two... "Man down! Man down!"

One... "Lift off!"

Numbers to Tommy from this time on would never be math again. They were death tolls. Men he used to know.

"Magli," Captain Arnold addressed him.

"Sir," Tommy replied, eyes staring past the Captain's head and as he looked, he realized that not even First Lieutenant Jameson, Captain Arnold's right hand man, was allowed in on the proceedings. The seriousness of this secret mission hung in the air like daggers.

"I've been informed you're the cream of my crop, Magli," Captain Arnold said. "There's talk around base you'll be leaving here with a chest full of medals."

"I do my best, sir."

The middle aged raven haired man leveled ice blue eyes on him. "If you want to come back from this mission alive, you'll have to do better than that."

"Yes, sir," Tommy replied still standing at attention. "Not a problem, sir."

"You'll leave tonight for Saigon just like the other men on weekend passes. You'll disappear into the city. Your commander will meet you at the Paradise Club."

"That would be Lieutenant Brookings."

"Yes. Fine officer."

"I agree, sir. I've conducted several missions under his command since I arrived."

"This mission is highly classified. I can't stress that enough. You won't know where you are going until you get there. Only Lieutenant Brookings knows the details of this mission. He has personally hand-picked this team."

"I consider that an honor, sir," Tommy replied.

"As well you should. Brookings is the best son of a soldier I've ever known."

"I concur."

"Excellent. You have your orders."

"Sir, thank you." Tommy shook the man's hand.

Tommy walked out of the tent and sucked in a deep breath. He'd taken to combat like a born soldier. But this was different. Captain Arnold had dismissed him with finality in his eyes.

Captain Arnold did not expect to see Tommy again.

"Only a miracle is going to get me home again alive."

Chicago.

Susie never wrote the truth to Tommy.

Sitting in Doctor Klinger's office after her tests and exam, she watched his handsome face tense as he flipped through the reports.

"I have some disturbing news, Susie," he said.

"Such as?" She braced.

"You have pre-eclampsia," he replied looking at her with concern.

"I don't know what that means."

"It means the water in the uterus around the baby and inside the sac is toxic. You've gained fourteen pounds in your total

144

pregnancy thus far, which is good. However, in the past week you've gained nine pounds."

"I can't even see my feet anymore, but I thought it was normal to feel like I'm walking around on sponges filled with water."

"That's exactly what you're doing. Walking on water. Too much of it."

"Also, you have very rare blood. B negative. Tommy is A positive. The babies may be what we call a 'blue baby' and they may need a transfusion right after birth. You'll need a Rhogam injection after delivery."

"Why?"

"When and if you get pregnant again, this will prevent that child from needing a blood transfusion as well." He folded his hands. "Though I don't expect it, you might need to have surgery. A Cesarean section."

"Oh, God," she said feeling suddenly vulnerable and helpless. "That will cost a lot of money."

"At least three thousand more."

"It might as well be three million."

Doctor Klinger smiled. "Your father will gladly pay it."

"I know. But that's not the point. I have to rely on him so much already."

"Believe me, he can handle it. Your life is more important than money, Susie."

She looked down. She thought of Jed slaving away at the mill and spending his weekends building the room for his grandchildren. Every dime meant the world to them right now. Jed had spent more money on the house extension than he'd planned and he'd dipped into his savings as well to pay for cribs, mattresses, diapers and even a new washing machine as the twenty-two year old Speed Queen had conked out last week.

She'd done her part as well to save money. She made yellow gingham café curtains for the nursery herself. She'd altered baby clothes patterns and adjusted to make winter buntings, hats and even blankets for the twins. She painted whimsical designs on the walls of the nursery instead of using costly wallpaper.

Yet for her parents, money was abundant and seemingly easy to come by. She knew her father had always worked hard for his money. But so had Jed.

She was proud of both of them for all they were doing for her and for her unborn babies.

"I wanted to have a natural birth. I'm even going to Lamaze classes."

"Keep it up. You'll still need it, but I want you to be aware of the dangers. I mean, the situation," he corrected himself. "I'll see you next week. No more painting on ladders or hanging mobiles from the ceiling, you got that? You rest. And stay positive."

"Positive."

"Yes."

"Doctor the only thing positive in my life is the cross I make through each day on my calendar knowing it is one less day I have to live through until Tommy comes home."

He nodded. "Then keep making those crosses."

Southeast Asia.

The night was pitch as Tommy huddled inside the helicopter as they lifted off the ground from a secret base camp he'd been spirited to out of Saigon. It was only an hour till dawn. They needed the cover of night to cover as much ground as necessary.

Tommy wore a black tee shirt, civilian black slacks, a baseball cap and civilian hiking boots. Nothing on his body was military regulation. Not even his underwear.

His CO tossed him a tin. "Magli. Paint up."

"Yes, sir," Tommy said watching Lieutenant A.A. Brookings toss each man a different color camouflage paint.

Upon opening the tin, Tommy smeared his face with the dark greasy paste. His mind wandered thinking of Susie and his soon-to-be-born children. He wondered if they would both be boys. His guts or his male pride told him to expect boys. Susie was convinced they were girls.

He painted dark stripes under his eyes then down the center of his nose. The action felt ceremonious in a way and he couldn't help thinking this act was probably the most ancient tradition of man. Since the earliest tribal hunters, man had been disguising his skin to protect himself from his enemies to render himself the hunter and not the prey.

From the American Indians who decorated their faces in war paint, to the Celtic and Scots tribesmen who wore garish blue paint into battle, millions of men before him had engaged in this same ritual.

Those men died defending their land and families. Those men held strong to their faith that what they were doing was right. Slicking the camouflage paint into the creases of his face, bonded Tommy to those ancient ones. He felt a part of the world like he'd never felt before. Only by the grace of God would his blood not be spilled in a foreign country. In Washington, politicians and generals played dice with his life and those of all the men on this mission. Yet Tommy sensed their orders, their strategies and their agendas had nothing to do with the outcome of this mission.

Somewhere out there, Tommy believed, his fate had been assigned before he was born. What was meant to be would be. He was just going through the motions.

It's all in God's hands.

"Hell, man," Jack Bruce said, "I didn't think we'd be going back to Cambodia."

"Laos, too," Mel Prandel grumbled in a low voice as he stuck a piece of Doublemint in his mouth.

"How do you know that?" Tommy asked.

"Been there. We're heading north west, right?" Jack said.

"You don't know that," Mel threw the gum wrapper at Jack. "The entire war is north west of us."

"What? I'm not supposed to know what's going on?

Lieutenant Brookings turned toward the opening and looked

out at the dense jungle below them. "You'll learn, Magli, the less you know the better."

"I've already learned that much."

Lieutenant Brookings looked back at Tommy and smiled. "Then you know everything."

Tommy stared at him. He knew a great deal about this man he admired so much and with whom he'd flown into the face of death.

Brookings was a legend at base camp. Tommy knew that his idol's full name was Albert Aloysius Brookings, the Third. Some said he was the Fourth generation of Boston Brookings family whose law firm had been in existence since before the Civil War. The family was one of the first families of Boston and had a lineage that would have brought tears to the likes of Mary Elizabeth Howard. Still, every Brookings went into the military and left with Medals of Honor and stars of bronze and gold. Then they all went into the Law. Tommy liked to think of himself as having a similar brain structure as A.A. Brookings. Both men had a talent for war; and a talent for the law. The difference was that A.A., three or four, whichever he was, had no intention of going back to Boston, it's ivy or his family. A.A. liked the wilds of the jungle. He liked this war and he was good at it.

A.A. Brookings was the kind of man you wanted on your side. He was the kind of man who would save your rear and never abandon you.

There was much to admire about A.A. Brookings.

"I've meant to ask you before, sir. How long have you been over here?" Tommy asked the Lieutenant.

"Two years. No leave."

"None at all?"

"No," Brookings replied looking down at the jungle beneath them. "The men need me more than I need a break, you know?"

Tommy was surprised at the man's openness. He'd always been closed-off to the men. A loner. But then a lot things about war and this war in particular had shocked him. "You gave up the law to serve, isn't that right, sir?"

"Yes," he replied sharply.

Tommy glanced away. "I wasn't prying. Just curious. I sorta did the same thing. Gave up my studies, I mean. I was planning to go to law school."

"Really? Where?"

"I hadn't decided. Notre Dame if I could afford it."

"I went to Harvard."

"That's what I heard," Tommy said.

"I saw your record," Brookings said. "You could get into Harvard even without my recommendation."

"Sir, I wasn't sucking up."

"I know you weren't." Brookings' smile was fleeting. There was no time for smiles or the thoughts that brought them. "When we get out of here and if you're still interested, I'd put in a good word for you."

"That's awfully generous of you, sir."

"You only have to do one thing for me."

Tommy stared at his superior. "Live through this mission?"

"Yes."

Chapter Eighteen

At dawn Susie discovered she'd started bleeding, but because her water didn't break, she dismissed the situation. It was a cumbersome task doing the week's laundry, but she was so proud of the new washing machine she and Jed had chosen together that she didn't pay attention to the pain in her back. She determined it was due to the bending and stooping to withdraw the clothes from the dryer.

All morning she went about her daily household chores ignoring the pain in her back. At ten, when Jed had a break, he telephoned her.

"How are you doing?" he asked.

"I'm making a big pot of chili for tonight."

"Your water didn't break yet?"

"No, not yet," she replied.

"Well, I've got your suitcase in the car and the doctor's number is on the pad by the phone," he said, reminding her for the twentieth time that week.

"Jed. I know the babies are due in a day or two, but I just saw the doctor three days ago and nothing had happened. First time deliveries can be very late. Besides, the carpet for the nursery is being laid tomorrow and I want to be here! I'm so excited! Actually, I can't believe I'm this excited about a silly thing like carpeting. I never thought much about things like that before. It was always something the decorator took care of."

"Things are different now," Jed reminded her.

"Yeah. Better," she smiled. "Had I known it was this much fun to change a house and build something new, I would have listened more intensely to mother's decorator. Think of what I could have learned. The wasted knowledge!"

"Let that be a lesson to you," Jed laughed. "Any mail from Tommy today?"

"Not yet. The mailman is late. Call me at lunchtime."

"You got it," Jed said and hung up.

Cambodia. Dawn.

The helicopter moved toward the clearing.

Brookings held out his hand toward the men. "Dog tags."

The crew took off their dog tags. Brookings stuck them in his pocket. Then he turned back to his civilian clothed troop. "Here are new passports and papers. Some of the names are fake and some are those of deceased fellow Marines. The backgrounds are fact and fiction. Basically, you don't exist. If you get captured, you have only a name and social security number to remember. Remember, we are here to retrieve four members of "Red Call" team. The village we are nearing is friendly. The villagers have kept our men hidden for the past week and we've radioed them. Everything is a go."

Tommy took the false visa and passport. His new name was Michael Kelly of New York City. "From a wop to a Mick," Tommy laughed to himself. He looked up at Mel.

"Sven Swanson? From Minneapolis? I'm not even blond. Who comes up with this crap?"

"Who cares? It's only for a day. If that," Jack Bruce said.

"A day? That's all?" Tommy asked.

"A few hours. We'll be back in time for that rot gut they call food at the base," Jack assured him.

"How many of these kinds of missions have you been on?" Tommy asked.

"Dozens. Just move fast. Get the guys out. Get back to the pickup point. Simple. Clean. Neat. We're Marines, right?"

Tommy nodded.

"Magli. Man your gun!" Brookings ordered. "Get ready for the drop, men. Magli, cover us. Then you bring up the rear."

"Yes, sir," Tommy replied, situating himself behind the mounted machine gun.

Peering through the sight, Tommy viewed the thatched huts below. "That's a village? There can't be more than four or five huts down there."

The village is friendly.

Brookings' voice reverberated in Tommy's head at the same moment that the first ray of dawn leaped from the East. A glint off steel shot Tommy in the eye.

The hairs on the back of his neck stood on end.

His belly turned over. His blood turned cold and his mind raced to make sense of the unthinkable.

The village is friendly.

Tommy opened his mouth. "Ambush!"

Shots from the earth rang out.

"Jump!" Tommy screamed. Inside the chopper there was silence.

Time slowed. The world stopped. Tommy slipped into a time warp. He fired his gun but it was not enough to fend off the round of fire already heading at them.

He saw it coming. Every bullet. Death.

And then the helicopter blew up.

Susie stood motionless at the kitchen sink. The plastic dishpan held her lunch plate, ice tea glass and a fork. Instead of soapsuds skimming the surface, her imagination played tricks on her. Staring into the water, she thought she saw smoke.

Smoke? How ridiculous!

She realized her sleepless night last night had made her more tired than she'd thought.

"How could there be smoke in a dishpan? And smoke from what?"

In that instant, an unfamiliar chill climbed up her spine. She held her breath.

"Tommy?"

Dread filled her mind. Sweat broke out on her forehead. She stared back at the water. The vision before her had not disappeared. In the hazy, sudsy water she conjured Tommy's face. He was crying out for her. It was nearly as if she could hear the sound of his voice.

"Susie!"

Then it was gone.

"Oh, God!" She clamped her shaking hands on her cheeks. Tears filled her eyes. Her stomach twitched.

A stabbing pain across the expanse of her abdomen sent her to her knees.

"Oh my God! What is this?"

Clinging to the rounded porcelain edge of the sink, she tried to steady herself, but her body was too cumbersome, the memory of the pain too intense.

Breathing deeply, she dismissed the vision.

"What am I thinking? There's nothing wrong with Tommy. I'm . . . my God!" She smiled broadly. "This is it!"

She crawled on all fours across the kitchen floor to the side of the counter where the black telephone sat. She pushed herself up off the floor.

"Slowly. Easy. Take it easy," she ordered herself.

Excitedly, she placed a shaking finger in the rotary dial and dialed Jed's number at work.

Speaking with the operator, she left a message for Jed, which would be delivered, to him by his supervisor. The operator stated that Jed would return the call within the half hour.

"That will be fine. I'm not going anywhere," Susie said and hung up.

She checked the clock on the wall above the sink. It was nearly one-thirty. "The doctor said when my pains were ten minutes apart to call him."

Within five minutes, Susie experienced another tightening of the muscles across her belly. "That can't be right. It's not ten minutes yet," she said to herself, breathing out with long pants. "I'd better get these dishes cleaned."

Susie had just put away the last dish when the phone rang. "Hi, Jed."

"How are you doing? Did your water break yet?"

"Actually, no. I just had some pains."

"Do you think this is it? Or is it false labor?"

"The pains aren't ten minutes apart yet," she said.

"Okay. Well, if they get to ten minutes, then you call me. Everyone here knows I could be leaving at a moment's notice. So, it's not a problem."

"I'll call you if my water breaks."

"Okay," he said and hung up.

Why didn't I ask him about Tommy?

Rolling her eyes, she mumbled, "What's the matter with you, Susie? What could he possibly know about Tommy? Brother. The onset of labor can make you really goofy!"

Holding her hand on the back of her waist she waddled into the bathroom.

*   *   *   *   *

Tommy's mind swam in a sea of confusion. Discerning little about his circumstances, he struggled for clarity.

Smoke.

He could see white smoke. Black smoke. Mingling, then rising to the sky.

The smell of burning flesh enveloped him. He grimaced but the tiny movement in his face caused excruciating pain.

An explosion rang out.

A man screamed. Then his voice was gone.

It hurt to open his eyes. It hurt more to close them.

He didn't know where he was.

A car crash. I've wrecked my car. But what kind of car? And where was I going?

He felt none of his body. He didn't know if he could lift an arm or leg because his head hurt so much, he could not lift it off the ground.

Grass. I'm lying in tall grass. Unusual grass.

I must have been thrown from the car.

The light was dim as if the sun had not yet set. Or risen. He was unsure which.

From out of nowhere a tiny dirty hand appeared in his field of vision.

Squinting, he saw an Asian child of no more than ten years old, he guessed.

The boy put his finger to his lips. "Shh."

Then the boy shook his head.

The boy tied a rope around his chest and suddenly, Tommy was being pulled away from the burning flesh smell.

Then everything went black.

"Jed! Something's wrong. I don't understand," Susie said anxiously three hours later.

"What do you mean?"

"My pains never got to ten minutes apart."

"What are they?"

"Five minutes."

"Since when?"

"Since I called you."

Jed gasped. "Call the doctor!"

"But my water didn't break. This can't be it. But, Jed. I'm bleeding a lot."

"Calm down, Susie. What else did they not teach you in Lamaze class?"

"I guess I didn't pay enough attention. I only went three times you know. It was such a long way and the cost of the gasoline . . . and . . ." She started to cry.

"Look, I'm on my way. Okay? You call the doctor's office and the hospital. I'll get you there as fast as possible."

"Okay," she said licking her dry lips. "You really think this is it?"

"Yes, I do."

"I better put on my makeup," she chuckled. "I wouldn't want anyone to see me looking like this!"

Jed groaned. "Just call the doctor."

"Okay," she said and hung up.

The child pulled Tommy to a clump of trees and underbrush where a low, long trench had been dug. Unceremoniously, he shoved and pushed Tommy into the ditch.

Pain shot through Tommy as if he'd been struck by lightening. No cell in his body was unaffected by the torment. He slipped into merciful darkness.

In a matter of seconds, a minute at the most, the boy covered Tommy completely with palm fronds, dirt and grasses. Tommy came around just as his face was being covered. "Who . . . ?"

"Shhh." The boy reiterated.

Through a cloud of pain, Tommy forced himself to remember the child.

The angel. The Asian angel sent to save me. Now I remember.

Tommy nodded. Only once.

The boy slithered on his belly back to his aunt's hut on the far edge of the 'village'.

The sound of gunfire filled the air off to the distance.

Guns? Automatic rifles? What are they doing at a car crash?

Staring up at the palm frond over his face, Tommy realized he was mistaken.

Not a car crash. Something else. Someplace else. But where?

Voices shouted to each other in a strange language Tommy had never heard. At least he never remembered hearing.

Where am I?

More shots. More voices. Some were commanding. Some were answering as if one voice was that of a superior.

Footsteps. Some running. Some moving nearly silent through the grass toward him.

Tommy held his breath. With the strength of all his human will, Tommy blocked his pain. He commanded his throbbing head to desist.

A bayonet struck the ground next to his hand so closely, it nicked his skin. He remained silent. The man above him on the other side of the grasses and cover he lay beneath paused.

Tommy waited for him to remove the debris and find him.

The bayonet struck the ground a half dozen more times, but never came close to him.

The assailant moved away from Tommy's hiding place. He shouted something to the other men who were off in the distance.

Tommy remained awake for an hour or more listening to the strange chatter as the group of men gathered what sounded like hunks of metal. Drifting in and out of consciousness, Tommy lost track of time. The sun rose overhead and pierced the slits between palm fronds on his face. He watched the sun fall to the west and night descend.

Or perhaps he simply died.

Susie's labor intensified over the afternoon. She was informed her doctor was away for the weekend. A stranger dressed in a white lab coat came to the labor room.

"I'm Doctor Gillman. I'll be delivering your baby," he said.

"Babies," she corrected.

"You didn't know she's having twins?" Jed asked. "It's on her chart."

"I haven't read the chart," Dr. Gillman replied. "I just got here. Traffic was a b . . . was a bear." The young man took the chart off the end of the bed as Susie went into another contraction.

"Breathe with it," he said, not looking up from the chart.

"I *am* breathing," she said.

His head shot up. "Your contractions are every four minutes. Forget those deep breaths. It's too painful." He moved to the side of the bed and Jed stepped back. He placed his hand on her throat.

"Put your center of concentration in your throat. Don't pant until I tell you to. But put the breath here. Then keep it as shallow as possible. That way the contraction totally takes over and you'll have a quicker delivery."

Susie tried it. "Okay. So. Good. On a scale from torturous being the top to nirvana at the bottom, I'm down to just excruciating."

Dr. Gillman laughed.

Jed frowned. "How old are you, Doc?"

"Thirty. Why?"

"How many of these have you done? Babies, I mean?"

"Hundreds. But you're my first set of twins," he smiled at Susie.

She didn't smile back. "Is that a problem?"

"The twins no. But everything else in your chart doesn't help either of us and I think you should know that."

"I do," she replied, biting her lip nervously.

"Would you step out, Mr. Magli? I need to conduct my exam and break her water."

"Sure," Jed replied and left.

Dr. Gillman examined Susie. "You're over seven centimeters dilated. It will speed up from here on," he said, piercing the amnionic sac.

Susie felt an instant relief as if her belly had deflated by a foot. "How fast."

"My bet? You'll see your twins in less than two hours."

Tears sprung to her eyes as the doctor left the room.

"Did you hear that, Tommy?" she asked the ceiling tiles. "You'll be a father in less than two hours. And I'll be a mother."

The Christmas Star

Chapter Nineteen

Dr. Gillman raced down the hall to the family waiting room. "Mr. Magli," he said lowly so as not to disturb the young man staring at the linoleum and wringing his hands.
"I have some rather bad news."

"My God, what is it?"

"Your daughter-in-law has been in labor for fifteen hours now and after four hours in delivery she should have had these babies hours ago. We need to X-ray. And I think we're going to have to operate."

"Operate?"

"That's my learned opinion, yes. A section."

"It's expensive?"

"Yes."

"I can get a loan from my credit union," he said straightening his back. "You do whatever you have to for her, you hear?"

"That's all I wanted to know."

Susie was wheeled from the delivery room down the hall where Jed was waiting. He rushed alongside the gurney with her.

"I'm so sorry, Jed. I thought I could do this on my own," she said.

He shook his head. "None of us are ever alone, Susie. You taught me that. I'm always here for you. Don't you worry about anything. You just think about yourself."

"And Tommy," she said.

"Not tonight. Not even Tommy."

"Oh, Jed," she expelled an emotional sigh. "I could never do that."

In an instant, the steel doors of X-ray swung closed behind the gurney and Jed was alone in the corridor.

Buried alive.

I'm not dead. I'm alive. But where?

Afraid to move, he felt the area around him with his fingertips.

Dirt. A hole. But not the same hole. This one is deeper. No palms. No sun.

Pain overcame panic. His entire body felt as if it was aflame.

Struggling, he managed to move his arm to his chest. Then raised it to touch the area above him. "Cloth. Stuffing?"

No, a mattress.

Muffled voices moved toward him. Then away from him. More movements. Light flooded the pit where he lay. He was blinded by the light.

He blinked, closed his eyes, and then forced himself to open them. Visions wafted in before him, fuzzy mirages they were.

An Asian crone crouched above him. She frowned and moved away from the opening.

The Asian boy smiled down at him.

Tommy could not smile back, his face was lacerated. His lip was torn and bleeding. For the first time he realized he could not talk. Perhaps they had cut out his tongue. But who were *they*? And why was he here?

The crone returned with hot liquid in a bowl. She used a porcelain flat spoon to feed him the salty concoction. Only three spoonfuls. He choked. Gagged.

The crone moved away. The boy winked before he, too, moved away from the opening. The mattress was placed over the pit.

Awareness of his bodily condition brought more pain. His head felt as if a tornado had been let loose inside him. Never had anyone experienced such a headache, he was certain.

Throbs graduated to torturous stabs. If he could have cut off his head and thrown it away, he would have.

Bolts of light ignited behind his eyelids. He had to think of something to help him forget the pain. Someone.

Then he saw her.

A face. A beautiful face. The sound of her voice. "The Plaza is the best, don't you think?"

Her voice sounded as if it was right next to him.

"I love you," she said.

He heard the memory of his own voice reply, "I love you back."

The only problem was that he didn't know who she was.

Then he realized he didn't know who he was.

And he blacked out.

"Susie," Dr. Gillman, said from behind his operating mask. "Stay with me, okay?"

She was hanging on. She had heard what the nurses had been saying about her when they thought she couldn't hear.

"She's not going to make it. Dr. Gillman is just trying to save those twins is all," one nurse said.

"Poor thing," another replied.

"She fought like a trooper."

Susie's mind seemed to float somewhere outside her. She didn't feel any pain now. They told her they had given her a spinal block and that it was the anesthetic that killed the pain.

She knew better.

She was dying.

"Susie, I'm making the incision. Oh, my God! Susie, can you hear that? Your baby is crying in your belly and he's not even out yet." Dr. Gillman grasped the baby's heels and pulled him into the world.

He.

"Susie! It's a boy. First born. Six fifty-three in the morning."

Dr. Gillman cut the umbilical cord and handed the baby to the nurse. "Susie, he's healthy. He's perfect. All ten fingers. All ten toes. Now, let's see who else is waiting to meet you," Dr. Gillman said, with a new father's excitement in his voice.

Susie was no longer in her body. She was above the operating table, hovering at the ceiling's edge, though already, the ceiling had melted away. There was nothing but heaven above her.

"Susie! This one is a girl! She's got hair! Lots of dark hair! Black as coal!" Dr. Gillman said even more excitedly.

She.

"Doctor," the anesthesiologist interrupted. "Her blood pressure is dropping. Breathing is faint. I'm losing her . . . Oh, Jesus!"

Susie moved beyond the stars feeling unattached to anything on earth. Her pain was gone. Her broken heart over her parents' disinheriting her mended.

She thought only of one thing. One person.

"Tommy?"

She came to rest on a grassy hill where plants grew without soil. The sky held a sun and moon and stars simultaneously as if night was day and day was night. Silver and gold light beams danced upon a river's surface as a cool wind kissed her cheek.

She leaned against the trunk of a willow tree next to the riverbank.

"Susie," Tommy said running toward her. "I knew I would find you here."

Without hesitating, he rushed up to her and scooped her into his arms, kissing her with the tender passion that was only Tommy. His hand grasped the small of her back crushing her to his chest and belly as if to show her that this was not a dream and was quite, quite real.

The taste of him. The feel of him. The smell of him.

They told her she was here and he was here and this was heaven.

"Tommy, I've missed you so."

"I've missed you," he said between kisses.

"Please don't ever leave me again."

"Oh, never, never," he said.

"But then, why are you here?" she said, pulling away and glancing around her. "Why am I here?"

"What's wrong?"

"This place," she said. "This isn't Earth."

"Sure it is," he said, holding his cheek against hers and then taking in his surroundings for the first time. He sucked in his breath. "Where are we?"

"Oh, Tommy. Did you die?"

"No. I couldn't do that. The babies."

"It's a boy and a girl. I came to tell you that."

"Then you didn't die either," he said gratefully.

"No, I have to go back and take care of them. They need me."

"Yes," he replied. "Just as I do," he kissed her again.

"And you're coming home?" she asked.

"We're a family now, Susie. A real family."

She smiled.

Her face radiated with the light of a thousand angels' hopes. The light circled her like a halo, then like a cocoon.

"Susie?" Tommy tried to pull her to him, but she vanished.

"Susie!" He yelled. "Susie! I'll be home . . . soon . . ."

The Christmas Star

Chapter Twenty

Jed raced around the car and opened the door as the orderly wheeled Susie out of the hospital in the wheelchair. Two nurses followed behind, each carrying one of his grandchildren.

Susie eased herself into the passenger's seat. "Here," she said to the nurse. "I'll take Noelle first. She'll ride in the carrier. Then I'll hold Chris."

"It's a long drive, Mrs. Magli," the orderly said.

Susie smiled. "It's not so bad, believe me. Driving here a week ago was much more difficult."

"Yeah," Jed laughed. "I was a wreck."

"Men," the nurse laughed. "Good thing women have the babies. Oh, and Mrs. Magli, here are the birth certificates."

"Thank you," Susie said, taking the envelope.

Jed got into the car and started the engine. Never in his life had he smiled so broadly. Never had he felt so proud.

As they drove, Susie opened the envelope. "Oh, no!"

"What's wrong?" Jed asked.

"They did it wrong! They misspelled Magli."

"How's that?" Jed asked taking one of the certificates and reading it when he came to a stop light. "Magi."

Smiling slowly, Susie said, "You think it's a sign?"

"Of what?"

"Magi. The three wisemen. Noelle and Chris? I came up with those names when I was half drugged. I kept thinking I'd get a letter from Tommy about what to name the children but he could never decide what he liked for a boy's name."

"But he picked Noelle, right?"

"Yes. I wanted Angela. Angel. Something like that."

Jed looked at the sleeping little girl. "Noelle fits her."

"It does, doesn't it?"

"My mother used to tell me that babies pick their own names and whisper it into the mother's ear before they are born."

"Hmmm. Guess I wasn't listening."

"I don't know. I think Chris is perfect. But is it for Christmas or Christopher?"

"Will the Church let me call him Christmas? Maybe that's too radical for them. Better stick with Christopher."

"Why not let Tommy decide?" Jed offered.

"That's what we'll do," she said. "I'll write to him tonight."

Tommy sat half in the hole and half out waiting for night to fall. The woman would bring him rice. It was good rice and there was plenty of it but little else. She brewed a bitter tasting hot tea, which he assumed was used in this part of the world as medicine. Once he'd downed it, she gave him a small cup of green tea so smooth it slid down his throat like satin.

After their meal, the boy would take him to the latrine in the trees surrounding the hut.   He kept close to the ground, avoiding detection. He knew as well as the boy that every tree, every leaf was a hiding place for the Viet Cong. As much as he yearned to stand tall, walk and run away, he knew his healing would never have progressed this far without the daring of the old woman and the boy. Thanks to them, his bruises were gone, the lacerations scabbed over, but his mind remained a blank.

The boy had shown him the American passport they'd found on him. Tommy stared at the name, Michael Kelly, of New York, New York, but nothing about his name sparked the first memory about his identity.

"Dreams. All I have is dreams."

He remembered sweet dreams of a beautiful girl in a heavenly place. But not her name.

He remembered nightmares of twisted steel, smoke, his fellow marines screaming. Dying. He knew he was in Cambodia somewhere near the border of Vietnam. He knew he was not supposed to be here. He knew he probably would not be rescued for some time to come. He knew he was on his own and it was his job to survive.

Chattering like magpies, the old woman and boy returned to the hut.

Upon hearing their voices, to be safe, Tommy slid down into the hole and covered it up with the mattress. Because he did not understand Vietnamese language, he never knew if they were alone or not. Despite hearing only their two voices, he always took precautions.

The boy moved the mattress and smiled down at him.

"G.I.," he said.

The scabs on his face did not allow Tommy to return the boy's smile. He nodded instead. "We go?"

"Go," the boy's head bobbed up and down. He grabbed Tommy's forearm pulling him upward.

As Tommy crawled out of the hole, his numb legs began to resurrect. Pain shot down his back, but he didn't mind the pain. It told him he was still alive.

The night was pitch, the flickering candles from inside the hut barely casting enough light to create shadows, the boy and Tommy went into the jungle undetected.

They remained silent as ghosts until their return.

The crone was nervous until Tommy slipped back into his hole. Only then did she breathe. She went about boiling the pot of rice on a small wood burning stove, her eyes forever darting to the door, then the window; her senses on alert for the presence of the Cong who would behead them for harboring the enemy.

Handing Tommy a wooden bowl of rice and a clay spoon, she warmed momentarily.

For some reason, his healing was important to her.

"Thank you," he whispered, making an even greater effort to smile.

She gazed into his eyes and seeing the gratitude there, she smiled.

"Why do you do this for me? I'm American. The enemy. It's dangerous for you to keep me here. I must leave."

The boy chomped away on his rice, shoveling it into his mouth faster than he could chew.

The old woman looked at the boy.

He avoided her gaze.

"Nguyen," she spoke the boy's name for the first time that Tommy could remember. Then she spoke forcefully to him, reprimanding him.

My God. It's as if she understands English!

Tommy looked at the boy. "Nguyen."

The boy nodded.

Tommy pointed to himself. "Michael." Then he pointed to the old woman.

"Thuy," he said the woman's name, which sounded like Twee.

"Thuy is your mother?"

Nguyen shook his head.

"What am I doing? Of course you can't understand English." Tommy dipped his spoon in the rice.

"Mother sister," Nguyen said, pointing to Thuy.

Tommy's head snapped up. "What? You understand me?"

"Okay, G.I.," Nguyen said with a sly smirk.

Dread shot down Tommy's back. Suddenly, he saw a million courses his fate could take. This boy could be a Cong. Perhaps he and the old woman were holding Tommy prisoner until the Cong came to take him away. Or execute him.

"How do you know English?"

"My mother. She go with G.I."

"And this is your aunt. Your mother's sister." Tommy had to know basics. "Are you Cong? Charlie?"

"No," Thuy said.

"No," Nguyen added.

Tommy exhaled with relief. "The Americans came to your village before?"

"Okay, G.I."

He realized that Nguyen's English was rudimentary and that he didn't understand as much as he hoped, but it was enough for now.

"That means if they were here before and your mother was able to run away with an American soldier then they know this place. They could come back . . . for me."

Nguyen and Thuy stared at him watching hope light his face.

The Christmas Star

Chapter Twenty-One

Susie placed a trio of pumpkins on the steps of Jed's house when the dark green Ford pulled up. Two men wearing Marine uniforms and somber expressions walked toward her.

"Go away!" She screamed dropping the armload of cornstalks. "I'm busy. I'm decorating for Halloween here."

They continued up the front walk.

"Mrs. Thomas Magli?"

Her mouth went dry and her blood turned to ice. It was all she could do not to urinate. She felt as if the world had just imploded. Her heart stopped. "I haven't checked the mail yet. It's late today. There will be a letter!"

Tears welled in her eyes. "You'll see! There will be a letter from Tommy today!"

Hands shaking, she covered her face.

"Mrs. Magli," the taller of the two men said. "I'm..."

"Shut up!" she glared at him. "Don't tell me your name. I don't ant to know your name. I don't want you to be here. Go away! Tommy is fine!"

"He's missing in action, m'am," the tall one said.

"Missing?" The word groaned out of her throat as if it knew it had no business being part of her psyche. "Not dead?"

"We can't know for certain, m'am."

"What the hell is that supposed to mean?" she demanded.

"His helicopter was shot down. Burned. We have not recovered his body, but we found his dog tags."

Her eyes pierced their faces. She knew she'd never remember what either of them looked like. All she could see was Tommy's face. It was as if she could reach out and touch him. And that was when she knew.

"He's alive."

"We hope so."

"No. I'm telling you. Tommy is alive. I know it! I can see him! I would know if he was dead."

The two men glanced at each other.

"I'm not crazy here!" Susie screamed at them. "A woman knows these things. A wife knows if her husband is dead or alive."

"Sure, m'am," the shorter one said taking an envelope out of his breast pocket. "These are the official documents, Mrs. Magli. There is a contact number in there for you to call for further information. However, the moment we receive any information about your husband's whereabouts you will be notified immediately."

She took the envelope.

"Rest assured the United States government is doing everything in its power to locate your husband."

"Sure they are," she scoffed glancing at the envelope.

The men turned to walk away.

"I want you to know…"

"M'am?" The tall one said.

"My husband was proud to be a Marine. He'll come home. You wait and see."

"Yes, m'am," he said. Their eyes connected. His breath caught in his chest. "I believe he will."

Tommy kept a record of the days he lived in the hut by drawing a calendar on rice paper, which Thuy had given him. Every day at sunset he marked two lines through the box. By recreating his recuperation time on paper he determined that he had now lived with Thuy and Nguyen for three months.

Halloween had come and gone. Thanksgiving had passed and to the best of his ability he knew that Christmas Eve was approaching. He struggled trying to learn the Vietnamese language and simultaneously teaching English to Thuy and Nguyen.

The boy was more open to learning than the old woman who clearly wanted nothing more in life than to work in the rice paddies and end her days peacefully. She didn't like to talk about the Cong or the movement of troops through the jungle.

She was a simple and giving woman yet she was more terrified about Tommy's presence in her hut than ever before.

Tommy's body was healthy again, his pain only a memory. He no longer spent his day in the hole. He built himself back up by doing hundreds of pushups and sit-ups daily. Thuy taught him yoga positions and stances in which he could now remain perched on one leg for ten minutes or longer, feeling his muscles tense, then quiver with exertion. He'd sharpened his hearing to a keenness that could hear a cricket's footfalls. His eyes were capable of picking out the slightest rustle of a palm frond even in the dense jungle darkness.

Yet, with all his physical rejuvenation, he still could not remember the life he had led before the helicopter crash.

Christmas, 1966.

"I want us to start our own family traditions this year, Jed," Susie said holding the pine tree steady as he screwed the trunk into place.

"That's fine with me. What did you have in mind?"

"Well, for one, I'd like the tree to only have blue lights. Tommy had blue lights on a little tree for us last Christmas at the fraternity house."

"Blue lights. Check."

"Then I want to take the babies to Holy Name Cathedral for Midnight Mass."

"Done. What else?" he asked, standing back and observing the full tree.

Touching his arm, she said, "I want us never, ever to give up hope. He will come home, you know."

He looked into her upturned face. "I'm certain of it."

Braxton Howard stuck his arms into the sleeves of a black cashmere coat. "Mary Elizabeth, come away from that window. She's not coming."

"It's Christmas Eve. She'll come."

"She won't. She has no reason to. After all, we didn't send her an engraved invitation. It's not like we called her, now is it?"

"This is her home. She can't stay out there in that hovel forever. Sooner or later, she is going to realize that she's made a wretched mistake and she'll come home. And then we can go back to being normal."

Braxton went to the gilded mirror in the hallway and checked his silk scarf. "She has twins now, Mary Elizabeth. I doubt she's going to give them up for adoption at this late date."

"But how can she feed them? She has no money, no job. I know my daughter. She's never had to want for anything in her life. Believe me, struggling through Christmas with no money will be impossible for her. The thought of it. Twins. It will cost a small fortune. Doctor bills. Diapers. Food. Clothes. Those are screws that pinch. She'll come back with her tail between her legs and then..."

"Then what? You'll gloat some more? Make her feel a bit more like crap?"

"Braxton! Whose side are you on?" she demanded.

"Frankly, I'm not quite sure anymore." He placed a charcoal gray hat on his head. "Are you coming? We don't want to be late for the party."

"God forbid," Mary Elizabeth said picking up her mink coat.

Susie held Noelle and Jed held Chris during the celebration of the Mass. Both babies slept soundly until the final processional when the organ blared "Hark! The Herald Angels" and the congregation sang at the top of their jubilant lungs.

Noelle's eyes burst open but rather than cry she smiled as if she knew the song and wanted to sing along.

Chris awoke, cried for a second then burped.

They remained behind in the pew until most of the crowd had left. Then Susie went down the aisle to the crèche and knelt down. Jed stood behind her.

"Dear Baby Jesus, this is Noelle and Christmas Magli. I wanted to introduce them to you because this is their first Christmas. I was hoping that you could do a favor for them. You see, unlike you, their father is not here with them this year. So, I was wondering if you could give them a Christmas present and find their father for them? I miss Tommy . . . very much. So much that sometimes I think my heart can't ache any more, but then I realize I am wrong and it can hurt so much more. So, could you ask your angels to find Tommy for us and send him home? He's all I ever wanted for Christmas."

Susie put a dollar in the collection box and lit four candles. "The red one is for Noelle. The yellow one for Chris, the green one for Jed and the blue one for me."

Jed put his hand on Susie's shoulder and squeezed it. "We'd better go."

Susie nodded.

As they walked out the side door, Susie turned back and looked at the crèche. "Thank you for answering my prayer," she whispered, and closed the door silently behind her.

Chapter Twenty-Two

January, 1967

Susie wheeled the twins into Colleen Cole's boutique during the after-Christmas sale. She was met with precisely the scene she was hoping to find. A bevy of customers stood in line to be checked out and the sparse staff appeared harried and overworked.

Maneuvering the double-seated stroller around the bargain tables, Susie went up to Colleen.

"Looks like you could use some help," Susie said.

Colleen who was folding a stack of sweaters looked at her and burst into a smile. "There is a God!" She threw her arms around Susie. "Where have you been and why haven't you called? And what has been going on?"

An obese, overdressed woman of fifty-five with frosted blonde hair thrust a dress in Colleen's face. "Can I get this in an eighteen?"

Susie brightened. Taking the dress she said, "Let me check the rack for you. We keep the eighteen's over here."

Susie stuck a pacifier in each of the babies' mouths and went to the rack of dresses against the far wall. "I think you'll find some wonderful bargains in this area. Just look for the green tags. Those are the sale items. And remember, if you buy three regularly priced dresses you get the fourth one at half off."

"Half off?" the woman shed her disapproving manner in a flash.

"That's been our policy for three years."

"I had no idea!" the woman went straight to combing through the rack.

Susie walked back to Colleen.

"Well, that was just about the most brilliant stroke I ever heard. Why didn't I think of that?"

"You need me, Colleen," Susie said glancing over at her slumbering children. "And I need a job. Today."

Colleen followed her eyes. "Your mother would crucify me."

"I'll carry the cross. Can I have the job or not?"

"Susie, you're the best sales woman I've ever hired. Of course you can have the job."

"Thanks. I was hoping I could count on you."

Placing her hand on Susie's shoulder, she said, "How are you managing this, this *thing* with your mother? She is positively outraged that you don't speak."

"She's not mad that I don't speak to her. She's mad that I'm living my life."

"Well put."

"Look, Colleen. My mother is my mother. Frankly, I don't have time to think about her. The babies take every second of my day."

"They're beautiful. I can't imagine not seeing my own grandchildren. I've always said I thought your mother had some screws loose. This proves it, if you ask me."

Several customers ogled the babies. Invariably, they all commented on the matching hats, coats and blankets the babies wore. Colleen watched their faces. Her ears picked up their compliments.

Susie and Colleen walked over to the stroller.

"Mother will come around in time," Susie said, feeling her own maternal pride explode as more customers hovered over her children.

"And if she doesn't?"

"That's her loss. Still, she can be pretty stubborn. I thought curiosity alone would have forced her to come see Noelle and Chris."

"Oh, God, what darling names!" Colleen gushed, touching Noelle's hand. Then she peered more closely at the sleeping infant. "Say, Susie, where did you get these outfits?" She peeled back the blanket. "I've never seen designs like this."

"I made them. These were their Christmas outfits."

"You? Sew?"

Shrugging her shoulders, Susie said, "I couldn't afford the real thing. I found upholstery fabric on sale. Fifty cents for each outfit. Not counting buttons and thread."

Colleen's eyes widened. "That accounts for the ice blue brocade and midnight velvet."

"I was listening to Bobby Vinton's *Blue Velvet* with a little Mercy sound thrown in. The Kinks. So, I did an Edwardian theme. It was tough with no patterns."

"My God, you're a natural then."

"It was weird. I took some classes at the Singer place. My first attempts were just awful, but I kept at it and then, I found a natural rhythm to it all. It was as if I understood the drape of fabric, the way it should fit the body. I remembered last Christmas I saw the most adorable little girl in a red coat. The muff she carried was a gift from her mother the year before, but now the mother was dead. I never forgot that little girl. I guess you could say she inspired me. Children should take pride in their appearance, but when I looked around at what there was to offer, I thought that maybe I could improve on things. At least for my own children. Once I made the decision, the designs just came to me. I couldn't sleep at night, worrying about Tommy. He's missing in action, you know."

"I'm sorry, I didn't," Colleen said.

"Anyway, I'd be almost asleep and then it would come to me how to make the little bonnet hat for Noelle. And the little cap for Chris."

"That's exactly how inspiration works," Colleen said.

Susie looked over at Noelle. "I made Noelle's coat in brocade with velvet collar and Chris' coat in velvet double breasted with a brocade collar. It was all the fabric I had. I lined them in white satin from an old high school formal."

"The Oleg Cassini? You cut up an Oleg Cassini you bought here two years ago for some lining for your children's Christmas outfits?" Colleen started laughing. Then she couldn't control herself. "I can't wait to see Mary Elizabeth's face when she hears of this one!"

"Better not tell her."

"My dear, there is no question. You *are* a natural born designer. You just didn't know it yet."

"You think?" Susie found the idea appealed to her.

Colleen grew serious. "You need a job, but where's your nanny? Or a sitter for them during the day when I need you here?"

Susie's eyebrow rose skeptically. "I haven't figured that out yet."

"That's a big hurtle.

"Saturday is no problem. Jed is home and can sit."

"Jed?"

"My father-in-law. I live with him. We live with him."

Colleen was silent for a minute. "Hear me out on this, Susie. Can you make more of these clothes? What I mean is, do you have other designs in that head of yours? Besides this? Valentine's Day is coming up. Then Easter, spring, summer wear? I'd need several sizes of each dress. Each boy's rompers."

"You would put my kids' wear in your store? This is a woman's boutique."

"We could carve out some area up stairs. Maybe open the ceiling, put in a circular staircase. One of the wrought-iron jobs."

"Colleen, have you lost it? You would renovate for me?"

"I'm staring at the undiscovered American Mary Quant and you ask if I'm nuts?"

"But I'd need fabrics and threads and . . ." Susie slapped her hands against her cheeks. "I don't think . . ."

"Don't think. Do it. I'll bankroll the fabric. I've got several Asian seamstresses who do alterations. They're always sewing on the side. I'll ask if they can do the sewing. You do the designing. Bring in the samples. We can produce this first line. See how it goes. If we sell, I'll make the floor space. You just create. In the meantime, I need to plan a trunk show. How much can you get ready in three weeks?"

"Three weeks?" Susie gulped. "Okay. Okay. Two dressy dresses, boy's matching outfits to pair with them for Easter. I can re-create what they have on, that would give us two more. Two play outfits for spring. With hats."

"Hats. Have to do the hats. Great. And bring the babies. They can be the models. The rest we'll hang on hangers. I'll call the printer and get some invitations. We'll mail them out next week. I want the trunk show on February 8. That way we can sell the samples for Valentine's Day and take orders for Easter." Colleen clocked off her ideas on her fingers. "Wait. What will you call yourself? Er, the clothes, I mean."

"Call them?" She paused for a moment racking her brain. Her eyes lit up. "Serendipity Sweets. I'll design a tag that looks like candy slices. They match the slices to put an outfit together."

Colleen rolled her eyes. "Thank God you didn't waste your time going to college. This kind of creativity can't be found in a classroom."

"No, but business courses can. I still want to go to college. The difference is that I think I just changed my major from English Lit to Business."

"Bravo, my dear. Your father would be proud."

Susie held her breath.

"I'm sorry. I didn't mean . . ."

"It's okay, Colleen. I know he's not proud of me now. I'm proud of myself. Suddenly, that's more important."

A customer came up to Colleen. "M'am. I need some help."

"Sure," Colleen said glancing back at Susie. "Call me the second you have the first sample ready."

"I'll do it," Susie said, kissing Colleen on the cheek before she walked away.

Susie turned the stroller around to face the door and was just about to exit when she heard a familiar voice shout her name.

"Susie!"

Her back stiffened. Susie turned slowly. "Hi, Sherry. You

183

still home? I thought you'd be back East by now."

Sherry came up to her, shaking her head, "We get a month off," she said sheepishly. "Susie, I couldn't help overhearing you back there with Colleen."

Susie glanced toward the door, thinking to make a run for it. It was one thing to go begging for a job. It was another to have one of her old crowd listen in. "She got pretty excited, I guess."

"No. I mean about Tommy. Being missing and all."

"Yeah."

"I know you may not really believe this, but I want you to know that if there's anything I can do for you, please call me." She dug in her black suede purse. "Here's my number at school," she scribbled a number on the back of a clothes' receipt. A receipt that showed over a thousand dollars Sherry had just spent in Colleen's store.

A thousand dollars. That would pay my tuition for an entire year as a day student. Or it would pay off the doctor bills. Or it would feed us for three months and then some. What I could do with a thousand dollars.

"Thanks," Susie said.

Sherry swallowed hard. "I want to tell you how sorry I am that my mother blabbed everything about you to the Yacht Club."

"Your mother did? I thought it was you."

"I was afraid of that," Sherry said apologetically. "The thing is I'm so proud of you for not giving in to your parents. I had a hell of a fight with my mother. All my regrets came out and in the middle of our argument, I told her how I thought you were the most courageous girl I knew."

"You said that?"

"I meant that! And I'm so sorry if I caused you any pain. I think the world of you."

"That clears up the mystery for me, because I didn't understand why you'd tell anyone especially after that day in the doctor's office. I felt we were friends. But in a strange way, Sherry, you gave me a miracle."

"I did? How?"

"Because of you and the gossip, Daddy heard it and came to me. He says he's working on Mother. Trying to get her to come around. She's pretty stubborn."

"Stubbornness comes in handy sometimes, I guess."

Susie laughed. "Yeah, I inherited it from her, that's for sure!"

"Listen, Susie Howard Magli, I really do want to be your friend. I won't always be away at school. Turns out I'm even smarter than I'd thought. I'm doubling up on my hours this coming semester. I think I can finish in three years. I've decided to go on to law school after that."

"Really?" *Bully for you. And your thousand-dollar wardrobe.*

"So, if there's ever anything I can do for you . . ."

"Tommy is missing in action. Nobody can help with that." Susie said.

Sherry pondered this. "You never know."

"Look, I write a letter every week to the Government. To the Pentagon. To the Pope."

"And?"

The weight of her frustration with the bureaucracy she'd encountered caused Susie to burst into tears. "They can't find him. He's missing. They found his dog tags. But that's all. Some body parts at the wreckage."

"Body parts." Sherry shuddered.

"He's not dead. I know it. I see his face everywhere. Sometimes I can hear him calling me in the middle of the night."

"Susie, grief is a difficult thing . . ."

"It's not grief!" Susie insisted. "It's flat out anger and I can't get any kind of cooperation from anyone. I just don't understand."

"Me, either," Sherry said caressing Susie's shoulder then looking down at the twins. "My God, Susie, just think, if I hadn't gone to New York, I'd be standing here with a child of my own."

Susie wiped her tears as she watched Sherry bend down and touch Noelle's cheek. "I'm sorry, Sherry. I didn't mean to lay all this on you. Maybe you're right. Maybe I am grieving. Just like you still do."

Sherry straightened and looked at her. "I don't have any real friends, Susie. I've been afraid to get close to anyone after John. Few people have ever walked in my shoes. You're the only one who has come close. And even at that, there is pain we both have endured and we're still just teenagers."

Sherry took a deep breath. "We have a strange bond you and I. I've thought about that and what that means to us. Who knows where it will take us in the future?"

"I hadn't thought of it that way."

"So, tell me, how is it that you can be so sure, so certain that Tommy isn't dead?"

"I have visions of Tommy. Not dreams. These are so real. I can feel the temperature, hear things. It's as clear as if I were living this with him. I saw him in a hole in the ground. He was okay. He was in pain, but then the pain went away. But for some reason he's wandering around. I don't think he's in a prison. It's as if I can be inside his body and look out at the world through his eyes. He's alive. And he's coming home." Susie smacked her fist against her palm.

"I believe you," Shelly said putting her hands on Susie's shoulders. "I want to help."

"There's only one way you can help me."

"How's that?"

"Pray."

"Okay. But give me your address. I can write to you, too."

"You'd do that?" Susie wiped her tears.

"Yeah."

"I'd like that," Susie replied taking out a piece of paper and writing Jed's address on it. "Here's my phone as well."

"Great." Sherry smiled at Susie.

Susie smiled back. "Take care at school."

They embraced.

Susie walked away pushing her children's stroller out the door, feeling ancient and remembering Sherry's words: *We're still just teenagers.*

The Christmas Star

Chapter Twenty-Three

Mary Elizabeth Howard opened *The Chicago Tribune* and found herself staring into her daughter's face.

Baby Boomer's Babies, the headline read.

"Good Lord! Braxton! Did you see this?" Mary Elizabeth bolted from her vanity table.

"What?" he asked, whisking an electric Norelco shaver over his graying stubble.

"Susie's in the paper."

He flicked off the shaver. "In the Trib? Why?"

Mary Elizabeth read the article. "She's designing baby clothes and sewing them. Sewing them, for god's sake."

Braxton smiled to himself. "Enterprising."

"Don't give me that 'chip off the old block' look. She's flaunting herself and these children in the newspaper!"

He paused. "How did she manage to do that?"

"Colleen Cole put her up to it. Says here she had a trunk show at Colleen's. Colleen's calling her the American Mary Quant for children's wear."

"Mary who?"

"Some young English designer apparently. Must be one of those Beatles things."

"Oh."

"Braxton, what are we going to do about this? Do you think we can get the story retracted?"

Braxton put on a heavily starched white shirt, monogrammed on the French cuff. "Hardly." He stuck his black stockinged feet into his alligator shoes. "Face it, Mary Elizabeth, our daughter is married. She is the mother of twins. She's entrepreneurial and she's successful. Today is her birthday. Or have you forgotten?"

"No, I haven't forgotten."

"Well, neither have I."

Mary Elizabeth dropped the newspaper. "Why do you bring that up?"

"Because I'm going to see my daughter today and take her to lunch. And I'm going to play with my grandchildren."

He grabbed his tie and walked to the Cheval mirror in the corner of the bedroom.

"You can't do that! Why, it's nearly time!"

"Time for what?" he asked flipping his tie into a perfect knot.

"Time for her to apologize and come home."

Braxton finished tying his tie and faced his wife. "You really believe that don't you?"

"Of course. It only stands to reason . . ."

"That you, my dear, are an idiot. And I'm an idiot for listening to you and to all our friends who appear to be horrified about our daughter because she got pregnant and got married."

"Appear to be?"

"Susie just made the front page of the Lifestyle section of one of our country's leading newspapers. Do you think the world is sitting in judgment of her? Look around. The only one riding high is you. And you're losing."

He glared at her so intensely, she fell backward onto the bed. She dropped her face into her hands. "She shamed us. I can't ever forgive that."

"I can."

"How is that possible?"

Braxton took his cashmere sports jacket off the brass valet and put it on. "Because yesterday I had some chest pains. I thought I was having a heart attack. I didn't say anything because by the time I saw the doctor, he told me it was gas. But it scared the bejesus out of me. And it taught me a lesson. All my life I've worried about our social connections. Our friends. I didn't do this or do that because of what others would say. Well, I could go to my grave and not see my grandchildren. They may be the only ones I'll ever have. I don't want to miss any more of their life." He paused for effect.

"Now are you going to get down off that high horse and get dressed and go with me or not?"

The gold antique clock ticked away minutes that seemed to hang on the edge of eternity. Mary Elizabeth considered her husband. She looked at the paper.

"She named them Noelle and Chris."

"I know."

"Then you did read the article."

"No, I called Jed the night they were born and I asked."

"You called him," she said matter-of-factly.

"I call every week."

"You talk to her?"

"And I've been to see her and the children. They are my family. You're the one who has been choosing not to be part of this family."

"I had no idea."

He put his hands on her shoulders. "You can change all of this, Mary Elizabeth. You know you can."

She looked at him, love shining in his eyes like she hadn't seen since they were young.

"You were so sure I would go to her?"

"I knew she was never coming here."

"What made you think that?"

"Tommy is missing in action, Mary Elizabeth."

Her hands flew to her face in shock. "You think she blames us?" Tears filled her eyes. "I never dreamed that . . . I never wanted anything bad to happen to him. I would never do that. You know that don't you?"

He took her hand. "We aren't bad people, Mary Elizabeth, we were just misguided. Let's not do it anymore."

She looked at her hand in his. For the first time in years she remembered what it was like being a young mother, being the emotional support when Braxton wanted to strike out on his own against his father's wishes. She'd forgotten all that.

She'd forgotten the courage it took to stay the course over the years and keep her family safe. She'd thought that was what she'd been doing. Protecting her family from themselves. She realized now that she'd been the wedge that had driven them apart. She was to blame.

And in every fiber of her being she was heartily sorrowful.

She squeezed his hand. "I want to go with you. I want us to be a family again."

It was dark and cold when Jed came home from work. Susie was sitting on the living room floor with the twins crawling over her patterns and pieces of fabric. She'd turned on the evening news watching horrific scenes of death and body counts on WBBM. He could hear the sound of gunfire nearly drowning out the announcer's voice.

Half mesmerized, she looked up at him. "He's not dead."

"I know, Susie-girl."

"He's alive," she recited her mantra. "He's alive."

Noelle looked up at her grandfather, sat up straight and lifted her arms. Jed picked her up. "Don't you worry, cupcake. Your daddy is coming home."

Just then the doorbell rang.

"Tommy!" Susie's heart leapt. Then it crashed. She looked at Jed. "Sorry."

"It's okay. You get the door. I'll change Noelle."

Susie stood, picked up Chris who was about to tear her pattern to shreds and went to the door.

She turned on the porch light and froze.

Not Tommy.

She didn't know what to expect. Their faces were tense. Mary Elizabeth looked down. Braxton ground his jaw.

"What are you doing here?" She asked.

"Your Mother and I were hoping, well, I thought . . .we thought that," he cleared his throat.

Mary Elizabeth looked up. "I came to apologize, Susan. I have been egotistical and I've never been egotistical. I have been mean. And I like to think there isn't a mean bone in my body. I was wrong. Very, very wrong."

Susie was speechless. "I was wrong, too."

"No you weren't, Susie," Braxton said. "We were. And it won't happen again.

"Welcome to our home," Susie said flinging the door open along with her heart.

"Happy Birthday, Sweetheart!" Braxton said scooping Susie and Chris into his enormous embrace.

"Oh, Daddy," Susie sobbed. "I missed you so much."

Chris began crying, the intensity of their emotions frightening him.

"Mother, I love you," Susie hugged her.

"I love you, too," Mary Elizabeth said looking at a smiling Braxton over Susie's shoulder.

Braxton wiped his eyes. "This is Chris," he said taking the baby's fingers and letting him pull his finger to his toothless mouth.

"Yes. Jed is changing Noelle," she said.

Jed came down the hallway with Noelle just as Braxton and Mary Elizabeth entered the house. "Look, Noelle, here's your other grandpa and your grandmother."

Noelle squealed with delight when she saw Braxton. She held out her arms to him.

Susie turned to Mary Elizabeth. "Would you like to hold Chris?"

Mary Elizabeth's eyes filled again. "More than anything else in this world."

Susie watched as her mother cooed over her son and her father held her daughter. The generations were united again. Their smiles warmed the room like no fire could and joy erased their sins toward each other. Peace settled into their souls and the world was a bit more right for her that night.

The only Valentine she wanted now was for God to answer her prayer.

Please God, send Tommy home to us.

The Christmas Star

Chapter Twenty-Four

Christmas, 1970

Tommy's stack of calendar pages resembled a book. Besides his passport, it was his only possession he shoved into his rotted shirt as they continued on the move.

In the years of his private captivity, Tommy had learned that Thuy and Nguyen were outcasts from their village because Thuy's sister, An, had run away with an American soldier. She had fallen in love with him and he with her. She knew that she could never support Nguyen once in Saigon where they were headed. She also knew that the village was pro-Viet Cong and they would have executed all three of them had the Cong known of An's American lover.

Because their hut was secluded even from the other four huts of other outcasts who were branded as everything from thieves to witches, no one knew about Tommy's presence. Thuy spoke to no one whether working or not. She wanted only to survive.

Once Tommy learned their story, he realized how monumental and dangerous that simple task was for his Asian angels. He did everything in his power to never reveal himself, no matter how tempting or deep his desire to bask in the sun, to go for a swim or just to walk free in the jungle.

He was living on borrowed time.

He still hoped for the day when the Marines would find him. Yet, even this simple wish was a double-edged razor.

Once he was rescued, they would ask questions and he did not have answers. He still remembered nothing prior to the crash.

Day after day he struggled to re-create his past in New York City but he couldn't remember a house, a family, a wife, a mother, father, a school or even a friend. He scoured his brain incessantly for threads of memory. Did he have a dog? Or perhaps a cat? Maybe he didn't like animals. What kind of music did he like? What did he study in school? Did he go to college at all? Which one?

Tommy figured there were easily over a hundred thousand questions about a person one could ask themselves if they didn't know who they were.

Oddly, from time to time, he would doze in the middle of the day and just as he was falling asleep, he would hear a girl's voice. He heard her laugh. And then it vanished like the vaporous morning mists that clung to the tall reeds in the rice paddies.

Once he had a dream about a red convertible. He heard a girl's voice say, "Mustang".

He believed he owned a Mustang, though he wasn't sure if that was a particular brand of car. He remembered airplanes and jets and helicopters. He remembered training as a soldier, but it was in a detached manner as if he'd watched it somehow.

Visions of being in a city slipped through his mind and then out again. He remembered an older man smiling at him.

My Father.

But he drew a blank for a name.

He remembered drive-in movies, hot dogs and hamburgers, swimming in an icy ocean, Ferris wheels, chewing gum, baseball games, riding a bike, drinking scotch, television sets, English Leather cologne, stacks of clean socks and underwear in a bureau drawer. He remembered picnic tables along the roadsides, hula hoops, the Beatles music, chocolate, blue Christmas lights, a funeral, roses, pasta, donuts and fresh asphalt paving.

But he didn't remember who he was.

The trio stayed still at night covering themselves with jungle sticks, greens and palm fronds they'd tied to their bodies with green vines. They looked like moving shrubbery as they worked their way south out of Cambodia and into Vietnam. They spoke very little to conserve energy and to avoid detection. They carried water in pigskin pouches, rice and nuts in sacks tied around their necks. They slept in shifts, no more than three hours at a time and only in the daytime. Nights were meant for movement. To stay stagnate was to die.

The Cong were all around them, though moving west to east with the influx of American troops pushing north.

Thuy had heard in the rice paddies that American Marines were scouring the countryside for Cong. The Cong were scouring the countryside and killing villagers at random. The Cong were taking no chances with a band of "outcasts" who were more likely to be sympathetic to the Americans than to the Cong.

Tommy convinced Thuy and Nguyen their only hope was to find the Americans before the Cong descended. The situation had become too dangerous for Thuy and Nguyen to stay in their safe little hut.

For ten days, the trio moved silently before they encountered American troops.

It was an hour before dawn when Tommy heard men marching up the riverbed. His heart stopped. He held his breath then signaled to Thuy and Nguyen to take cover in a naturally formed bunker under a gigantic tree.

The Cong and the Marines both traveled in water to avoid leaving tracks or scents that could be detected.

Which are these?

Tommy's eyesight was better than a pair of infrared binoculars when it came to night vision. Peering through the dark, he saw camouflage uniforms that were worn at times by both sides.

These men were tall.

Still, he took caution as he moved away from the tree. Too many good men had been killed in too many wars by friendly fire.

Then Thuy sneezed.

"Halt! Who goes there?" A soldier commanded pointing his rifle in Tommy's direction. He kept Thuy hidden behind him.

"Stop!" Tommy shouted. "I'm an American!"

A half dozen rifles focused on Tommy as he slowly stood. "Don't shoot. I'm a Marine."

"Rank and file."

"I . . . I don't remember," Tommy said taking off the sticks and leaves he'd secured to his head with vine. "My name is Michael Kelly of New York. I don't remember anything before the helicopter crash."

"When was that?"

"Four years ago as far as I can figure."

"Four years?"

"If today is Christmas Eve, then it's four years and three months."

"It's Christmas Eve," the soldier replied, stunned.
Tommy smiled widely, unaware that his shocking appearance in tattered civilian clothing rendered his story as unreliable. "Merry Christmas to me."

"We'll see about that."

Tommy motioned for Thuy and Nguyen to stand. "With me are a boy and his aunt. They saved me after the crash. They nursed me to health and have cared for me all these years. They need asylum. I told them I would take them to the states with me.

"We'll see about that as well."

Tommy glared at the man. "You bet your ass we will," he said. "They need asylum. I intend to get it for them."

"There will be paperwork and legal . . ."

A trigger went off in Tommy's head. "I'm a lawyer. I know what I can and cannot do," he said with such practiced authority, the soldier backed down.

Where did that come from? An attorney? Am I?

"Okay. Fine. Well, we need to get you all back to base."

"Yes," Tommy said peeling off the rest of his camouflage. "Let's get back."

Christmas Day, 1970. Chicago.

"Gwamma, Santa Cwaus is comin' and we get to open pwesents," Noelle said to Mary Elizabeth as she held up a red velvet coat with white rabbit fur collar and cuffs for Noelle to wear to Midnight Mass. The ensemble was one of the samples from Susie's winter collection that she always constructed in Noelle's appropriate size. Now that the twins were four, Susie did not dress them alike so much as "complimenting" each other.

"I know, darling. I sent a letter to Santa myself telling him not to come until after Church and to make sure you were sound asleep."

Noelle scrunched up her nose. "Gwamma. Why would you do that? I want to see him."

Mary Elizabeth held a white fur muff embroidered with green holly and red bugle beads. "Because it's the way it's done."

Chris came running into the second floor bedroom Mary Elizabeth had converted to a nursery for the twin's three years prior. She'd started the redecoration the day after the family's reunion. And she'd never looked back.

Those days of her estrangement from her daughter and grandchildren had been the bleakest in her life. She just hadn't known it at the time.

Now, she awoke everyday filled with a new sense of awe about her life. She had her daughter to thank for it.

"I hate this!" Chris said plopping down on a beanbag.

"I think you look good in green corduroy," Mary Elizabeth said.

He looked down at his bottle green slacks and matching bomber-style jacket. Shaking his head he said, "I mean I don't want to go to church. I want to stay home and wait for Santa."

"That bottom lip of yours is going to trip you," Jed said following Chris into the nursery carrying black shoes and socks his grandson had left behind.

Mary Elizabeth laughed. "Now, Chris. You had a nice nap after supper tonight. You know it's tradition for us to go to Midnight Mass. Maybe this year when we come home, Santa will surprise us and come early. Maybe your presents will be here tonight. Did you ever think of that?"

Noelle's eyes widened. "Do you think he could do that?"

Chris jumped up, his face glowing with excitement. "Then I really can't go to church. I have to see Santa tonight."

"Me, too!" Noelle chimed in and stood next to Chris.

Jed glanced at Mary Elizabeth then back at the children. Chris was always the instigator of mischief. Noelle was his backup team. Noelle was better at manipulating every adult in her life while Chris was not only the brain behind the scenes, he tried to bully his way through every situation.

Once they reached an agreement for a common goal, the two were intractable and stubborn.

"What's going on, you two?" Mary Elizabeth asked.

Putting his hands on his hips, Jed studied them. They were up to something. "So which is it? You just don't want to go to Church? Or that you want to talk to Santa?"

Noelle looked at Chris.

Jutting out his chin, Chris said, "Talk to Santa."

"About what?"

"It's a secret," Chris said.

"Oh," Mary Elizabeth nodded. "It's a special toy you didn't tell us about?"

"No," Chris replied.

Jed looked at Noelle. "You both agree on this secret that you want to discuss with Santa?"

"Yes," Noelle answered.

Chris gave her the "shut up" look.

"I didn't tell!" she glared back.

"But you want to!" he said. "We won't get our wish if we tell."

"Who told you that?" Mary Elizabeth asked.

"We saw it on TV," Noelle said. "On Garfield Goose. Special wishes are special secrets."

"Okay, I'll go along with that," Jed said. "But we are still going to Mass. You know what this means to your mother and you don't want to make her sad, do you?"

Chris and Noelle exchanged a glum look. "No," they said in unison.

"Then let's go to church and say our prayers and make our wishes and ask baby Jesus to help. Then maybe we'll come back at just the right time and if we are very lucky and you are very good, we might catch Santa after all!" Jed said.

Chris considered this for a long moment, his face scrunching with concern. His eyes cataloguing every morsel of information.

Noelle waited patiently while he made his decision.

"Okay," he said.

Noelle brightened. "That could weawy happen?"

"Sure."

Noelle skipped to Jed and took his hand. "Are you gonna stay overnight at Gwamma's with us?"

"Not this time, honey. I have to get home and see what Santa is leaving at our house."

"Did he weave pweasants at both houses wast yerah?"

"Yes, he did, as a matter fact," Jed replied.

"Noelle," Mary Elizabeth said, "Don't you remember how we do it? Christmas Eve at our house and then Papa and I will come to your house for Christmas dinner. After all, Jed is the best cook in Chicago." She winked at Jed.

Chris trounced to Jed's side and looked up at him. "He's the best in the whole wide world."

Jed looked down at Chris. "You don't fool me for a second. You're just saying that because you're hoping to get that new engine for your Lionel train this year."

"I saw you wooking in the gawage, Gwampa," Noelle said.

"I was fixing the lamp for your mother," Jed explained.

"She thinks she's getting a doll house," Chris said.

Noelle scrunched her face. "Gwampa isn't making it. Santa will bwing it. He can do anything. Even bwing Daddy home like you said."

Chris' eyes rounded. "Shut up!"

Horrified, Noelle clamped her hand over her mouth.

The hairs on the back of Jed's neck prickled. Mary Elizabeth stood frozen as her jaw dropped woodenly.

"I told you not to tell!" Chris said stomping out of the room and then running down the Persian carpeted hallway to the staircase.

"Chwis! Come back! I'm sowwy!" Noelle raced after him.

"Now it will never work!" Chris shouted, tears of anger and frustration filling his eyes and throat.

Hearing their shouts, Susie and her father rushed to the bottom of the staircase. "Chris? Noelle?"

"What's going on?" Braxton asked.

Chris held the banister as he quickly descended the stairs one foot, two feet per stair to keep his balance. "Mommie! She told! She told the secret and now she's ruined everything! Forever!"

"What are you talking about?"

"Chwis! I'm sowwy!" Noelle was sobbing as she followed her twin down the stairs to their mother.

Susie put out her arms to hold them both. They were inconsolable.

"Mommie! He's wight! Now we can never get our Daddy home!"

Susie smoothed Noelle's dark hair from her flaming cheeks and pulled Chris even closer. Her eyes flew up the stairs to her mother. "Mother, what's going on? What are they talking about?"

Rushing to help, Mary Elizabeth said, "I don't know where they got the idea, but I think they thought if they could catch Santa Claus tonight they could ask him to bring Tommy home and Santa could make it happen."

"He can!" Chris insisted. "Santa is magic. You said so, Mommie. You said he makes magic."

"Oh, God." Susie was lost in their pain and hopelessness and she could feel her own heart breaking all over again.

For four years Susie had taught herself to be a workaholic. She'd designed clothes, sewn them herself and pressed Colleen to expand the store. She immersed herself in college classes at night thanks to her parents' generosity of paying her tuition at Northwestern. She studied, she worked, she designed, and she cared for her children all in the pursuit of making time her ally not her enemy. And still, not a day went by that she didn't rush home to check the mail hoping, praying she would hear from Tommy or about him. Every day she was disappointed.

She thought she'd been a good mother telling them stories about Tommy and his kindness, humor and goodness. She thought she'd done the right thing to keep his memory alive for them. But holding them as she was, their tears wetting her neck and face, their sobs banging against her chest wall, she realized they didn't know him. They'd never met their father. He was a phantom to them, a magical ghost like Santa.

He was no more real to them than a myth.

"Noelle. Chris," she whispered sweetly hoping to calm their fears. "Neither of you did anything wrong. Sometimes secrets are best if we do share them."

"Nah uh," Chris said, swiping the back of his hand over his eyes.

"It's true. Just as long as you keep the secrets in the family, it's okay. We can still ask Santa to help us. But, I have to be honest with you. I don't think he can do it."

"Why not?" Noelle asked.

"Because Santa can only bring toys. You see it's not his job to put families back together. That's God's work. And sometimes God doesn't want families to be together."

"God wants us to be sad?" Chris asked.

"No, he wants us to be strong. Sometimes he does this so he can teach us to believe. To have faith. Sometimes, keeping our faith isn't even for us to learn a lesson. It's for other people to watch us and for them to learn to have faith by our example. So if one person believes with all his heart and someone else sees that, then maybe they'll believe and then another and another."

Chris smiled and nodded. "Then all the people in the world would believe."

A searing lump in her throat caused Susie's voice to crack when she said, "And when all the people believe, then we will have no more wars. And there will be peace on earth."

"That will be a good time." Chris smiled slowly and hugged his mother.

Braxton put his hand on Susie's back just as Mary Elizabeth and Jed came to stand next to him.

"Peace," they said together in the strongest prayer they'd ever spoken.

Chapter Twenty-Five

New York, 1971.

A flurry of gold leaves surrounded Tommy as he walked across Central Park. The late October sun warmed his face, despite the chill in the air. Nannies pushed infants in strollers and young mothers raced behind mischievous children dressed in Halloween costumes. He could hear the mothers shouting names, threatening bodily harm with love-filled voices with only a pretense at irritation. Old men sat on park benches ogling young co-eds and shop girls dressed in hip hugger pants and platform shoes. Along the walking path a quartet of anti-war protestors handed out leaflets to passersby while only fifty yards away a trio of Hari Krishnas dressed in flowing white robes chanted and sang. A pair of lovers kissed under a monstrous maple tree, the woman never closing her eyes, disclosing the fact that her affair was no doubt illicit.

The scenes recalled distant memories in Tommy's mind and though they appeared familiar, his recollections continued to attenuate and dissolve back into mental mists that defied clarity.

So little here is familiar. If I lived here all my life, as the doctors told me, then I would know this place. Wouldn't I?

After seven months in military hospitals in Saigon, then Honolulu, then Portland, Tommy's amnesia had never been cured. He'd endured an operation on his brain to remove a blood clot that, had he not been treated, could have killed him. Should have killed him. But he lived. He'd survived the days in the hole in Thuy's hut. Survived the trek through the jungle. Survived. But not thrived.

The military told him that Michael Kelly had been sent on a secret mission. He was on a "need to know basis" and he did not "need to know". Trying to pry information out of the military was exhausting and impossible. The fact of the matter was that he'd gone to a country where the military claimed it had never sent troops.

The only fact he unearthed was that Michael Kelly's destination near Thuy's hut was hundreds of miles from Michael Kelly's destination. No one knew how Tommy had gotten as far south in Cambodia as he had.

Tommy had no answers. The truth was that he probably would never know.

Now he was in New York. His home. Or so everyone thought.

Tommy returned to the address the military had given him, an apartment in Little Italy, just off Mulberry Street. He was expecting to find his mother, Mary Kelly, but the landlord explained that she had died in 1968. Tommy was suddenly without the one link who could have told him everything about his past he wanted to know.

The incident had been a blow to him. For months he'd based his future on the encounter with Mary Kelly. Initially, the shock sent him reeling. All this time he'd expected Mary Kelly to fill in the gaps of his life. Oddly, he felt no remorse, no grief over this woman's death.

If she was my mother, shouldn't I be moved by her passing? How can that be?

Now he was left with a stenciled blank canvas like a paint by number sketch.

Naively thinking he would live with Mary Kelly once they re-connected, now Tommy needed an apartment. That thought led to a domino effect of imminent realities.

A place to live. A bed. A phone. A day job. Enroll in college. Get a degree. Get a law degree. Find myself. Create a life.

In the process of enrolling in college at New York University, the military had supplied him with his enlistment information. He discovered that Michael Kelly was originally from up-state New York and had graduated from Bishop Ludden Catholic High School in Syracuse.

Being cast adrift in New York for anyone was daunting. To not know who you were was frightening. To have survived in the Asian jungles then to be in New York City without a past was terrifying.

Tommy booked a bus ticket to Syracuse and took a cab to the Fay Road location. The high school buildings, set in a cross-shape with the chapel at the center of the cross, failed to jar his memory. He stood on the campus ground watching the students. Girls and boys in segregated classrooms spilled into the circular corridor around the chapel. He felt more of an alien than he did in the jungle.

He inquired from a student where to find the principal's office. Just as he entered the office, he was met by a priest.

"Can I be of service to ye?"

"I certainly hope so, Father . . ."

"Father Shehan," the smiling Irishman replied with a brogue.

"I believe that I graduated from this school in 1963."

"Ye believe, but dun'ch ye know now?"

"No. I was in 'Nam. There was a helicopter crash. I don't remember anything before that."

"I see. And yer name would be bein'. . .?"

"Michael Kelly."

Father Sheehan turned white. "I taught Michael to be an altar boy. He was me fav'rite."

It was Tommy's turn to freeze. His face went ashen. "And. . .I'm not Michael?" He felt tears threaten his eyes. He felt as if his soul was being rent in half.

Father Sheehan put his hand on Tommy's shoulder. "Me son. . ."

"My God!" Tommy swallowed hard.

"Let us go into me office," Father Sheehan said.

Unable to speak, Tommy followed the man down the hall, watching the black fabric of his vestments swirl around black rubber soled shoes.

"Sit," Father Sheehan said kindly, staring intensely at Tommy.

Digging up his courage, Tommy blurted out, "I don't know who I am." Then he explained about Vietnam and the past he could remember.

"Perhaps ye know more than ye give yer mind credit fer," Father Sheehan said.

"I don't understand."

"How did ye come to be here?"

"I took the bus from New York."

"That's only half an answer. The truth is here," he said touching Tommy's chest. "Inside ye there is a voice struggling to get out. Something made ye realize ye, whoever ye be, is Cat'olic. Michael Kelly was Cat'olic. I am aware that his mother died three years ago. Lovely woman. When she was told Michael was missing in action, her weak heart jes shattered. Ye took the information given ye and accepted it. Take that belief and build on it."

"How?"

"If that one piece is there, surely there be others. Even if the mind can close down fer a time, the soul cannot. It will resurrect just as Our Lord did. Pay attention to yer dreams at night. I want ye to keep a journal by yer bedside fer times when ye be rememberin' fragments of t'oughts. Even the tiniest clue will lead to a revelation."

"You know, when I was in Vietnam, and I was wandering in the jungle, I finally met up with the Marines who sent me back. I blurted out that I knew the law. In my heart, I knew I wanted to be lawyer. I was hoping to get asylum for the boy and woman who saved me, but I failed. They returned to their jungle hut. You know, I don't even know how old I am. I could have already been a lawyer. The reason I'm here is because I know I have to get my degree. Then get into law school."

"Do ye not see? 'Dat is yer soul speaking! Ye already know this. Ye jes needed to hear it out loud."

Tommy looked at the kind man. "Thank you, Father."

"Yer welcome."

"Could I ask you another question?"

"Ah, sher,"

"May I call you from time to time?"

"I'll always be here, Michael."

Tommy smiled. "You don't feel strange that I have to use his name?"

"Me son, I t'ink Michael would be honored to have such a fine person carry his legacy. I will think of ye both as one. How many times has that ever happened?" Father Sheehan asked.

"Rarely."

Tommy stood and extended his hand. The priest engulfed him in a bear hug so filled with empathy and kindness, Tommy felt as if he'd come home at last.

In the weeks that followed, Tommy began his freshman course. By midterms in October, it was apparent to himself and several of his professors that his abilities were much advanced. He tested out of four freshman classes and moved up to sophomore status in over half his required subjects. Even though his personal life was a blank sheet, his academic memory bank had kicked in full throttle.

He got a job as a bus boy at *Tavern on the Green* which helped to pay his rent and food bills. He was working his way up to the wait staff in a few months. He found an apartment on the lower West Side of the Park in a building from the turn of the century and which had yet to undergo renovation. The walls were thick, the windows rattled and the radiators failed to warm him, but it was his and he loved it.

With his back pay from the Marines, he had enough money to buy a very good mattress and box springs, cheap sheets and towels, a second-hand all cherrywood kitchen table and two miss-matched chairs. He kept a tight fist on the rest of his bank account intending to use the funds for emergencies and his future.

He strolled up to a sidewalk magazine and newspaper vendor he'd come to know since moving to the neighborhood. Charlie Hobbs was the only person in New York who took time to talk to Tommy. In many ways, Charlie was the only relationship he had.

Glancing at a pumpkin Charlie had placed on the ground next to a stack of daily newspapers, Tommy said, "How's it going, Charlie?"

"Right as rain."

"Are you decorating for Halloween here?"

"It's for my grandson," Charlie smiled toothlessly. "He's going to carve it after school."

"Sounds like fun."

"So, what will it be today, Lieutenant?"

Tommy had told Charlie about Vietnam and the fact that he was a Marine. Charlie, a self-proclaimed *hawk*, admired Tommy for his bravery and developed the habit of elevating his rank every time he saw Tommy. By Christmas, Tommy figured he'd be up to a general.

"The Wall Street Journal, I think."

"They teachin' you that at NYU?"

"Nope. But I hear all kinds of conversations at the restaurant. You know stockbrokers eat a lot. Tip big, too. Not as much as the mergers and acquisitions guys, though."

Charlie nodded, "Nothin' like the 'swells for hot market tips. If you get a good one, let me know."

"I will." Tommy folded his paper and took out a dollar. "Keep the change."

"Don't mind if I do," Charlie said giving him a salute. "See ya, Captain."

Tommy saluted him back. "Tomorrow, Charlie," he answered with the same phrase he'd used every day since they first met.

It was routine.

It was a place to start.

Chapter Twenty-Six

Christmas Eve, 1972. Chicago.

Susie pulled her red Mustang up to the Sheridan Shores Yacht Club. She'd been running like crazy all day and was still behind schedule. This lunch with her father was important.

She glanced at herself in the rear-view mirror. "Aw, nuts!"

She'd been scrambling so fast to get Christmas orders out she'd forgotten she hadn't even put on her makeup or brushed her hair. It was freezing outside so she kept the engine running while she rolled on mascara and glossed her lips. On the radio, *Me and Mrs. Jones* was playing.

She stopped mid-motion as Billy Paul sang "we meet everyday at the same café at four-thirty". Memories of herself and Tommy meeting at a little café after he'd left Northwestern came spiraling back to her. In that unexpected instant, she was living the past all over again.

Staring at her reflection in the mirror, she could barely remember what it was like to be that young girl, holding hands with Tommy. Dreaming about a future she now sensed she would probably not have. She hadn't given up hope that he would come home someday, but every hour that ticked off with no word about him felt like shark's teeth snapping at her. Each moment that there was no proof of his life, moved her closer to a life without him.

The mournful, bittersweet words of the song hit her hard. She had indeed built her hopes up too high sometimes. She should have been "extra careful" about her life, but she hadn't. She'd plunged into her love with both feet. She was more practical now. More realistic.

She had two children to support and that meant money.

For that, she needed her father.

Susie shut off the radio and quelled the heart pangs she wished she had the luxury to succumb, but she didn't. Her mind was on survival.

Buttoning her black wool maxi-coat, she dashed into the club.

The second she was through the doors she was struck with the opulence of the decorations, the well-dressed patrons and the highly trained staff. She hadn't walked through this portal in five years. It was a world she had forgotten. But as one familiar face after another turned and spied her, she realized they had not forgotten her.

"Why Miss Howard!" The maitre d' chirped. "How absolutely marvelous to see you!" He walked over to her and shook her hand with both of his. "You're more beautiful than ever."

"Thank you, Charles. It's good to see you as well. I'm meeting my . . ."

"Yes, of course. We have a special table arranged for you. He's here waiting."

"Lord! I'm not that late, am I?

"I wouldn't know. He's been here for over an hour."

"Really?"

A striking blonde woman in her mid-fifties approached wearing a red cashmere cowl neck sweater and a long red and black plaid skirt and matching red fashion boots. "Susie!"

"Emily," Susie expelled surprise having nearly forgotten the woman along with most of her mother's gossipy friends. "Merry Christmas. You look stunning. And in the holiday spirit as you always do."

"You remembered. How sweet," Emily Waterson replied grabbing Susie's hands and planting kisses in the air on either side of Susie's face. "I saw your father. He said he was meeting you here. But I want the real story. Why have you abandoned all of us?"

I thought it was the other way around. I am the outcast. Or had you forgotten.

Susie thought of all kinds of things a younger version of herself would have replied. "I'm swamped with work."

Emily's mouth rounded in an O. Her eyes flew open with recognition. "Why, you're famous around town!"

"I wouldn't say that," Susie replied.

"You're definitely a chip off your father's block. You mark my words, Susie, you keep this up and you'll be world famous."

"I can only hope!"

"It was wonderful seeing you, dear. We would love to have you join in some of our activities. Think about it."

"It was good to see you, Emily." Susie said her farewells and, looking up, saw her father give her a raised arm.

As she made her way through the white linen draped tables filled with people who once represented her only world, she nodded and smiled to them, wishing a blanket Merry Christmas to whole tables at a time.

When she finally got to Braxton's table, she kissed his cheek as he rose to assist her with her chair and expelled a huge breath. "That was exhausting."

"But you maneuvered it like a champ."

"You think so?"

Braxton smiled. "You see? It wasn't what you'd thought it would be, was it?"

She glanced behind her. No one was watching her. She looked at her father. "I expected it to be like walking to the guillotine."

"I know." He leaned over to whisper to her, "You've always been too dramatic."

"I wanted to be an actress."

"I remember," he said.

The waiter came and asked for their drink order. "Two Old Fashioneds, Harold. Fix them the way I like them with the orange juice."

"Yes. Sir." Harold replied and left.

"An Old Fashioned for lunch? Daddy? Isn't that a bit strong?"

"It's Christmas Eve. We should celebrate."

"Well, I know, but . . ."

He took her hand. "I meant celebrate our business partnership."

213

"What?"

He leaned back and leveled serious eyes on her. "Susie, you haven't been to my club in five years. You're overworked. You have more orders than you can fill and you think I don't know what's going on?"

"What's going on?"

"Your company is too successful to stay small and not successful enough to be big. You need an infusion of cash. The way I see it, you need a manufacturing facility or at least a wider cottage industry of employees to do the sewing for you. You should buy larger lots of fabric and that takes money up front. You need machines. You need better distribution and you need legal work to set up the trade marks for a franchise."

Susie's eyes popped wide open. "No one said you were Braxton Howard the Magnificent for nothing. You took the words right out of my mouth. I guess I do need that Old Fashioned."

As if on cue, Harold delivered the drinks.

Braxton toasted her, they clinked glasses and then he smiled. "I want thirty percent of the company."

Susie registered none of the surprise she felt. "Ten."

"Twenty," he said.

"Fifteen," she replied with a sly grin.

"Fifteen, it is," he agreed.

She took a sip of her drink. "I think Emily was right."

"Emily Waterson? What did she say?"

"That I was a chip off the old block. I was prepared to give you twenty."

Braxton's eyebrow shot up. "I was prepared to take ten."

Susie laughed loudly and clinked glasses with her father again. "I'm going to make this company fly, Daddy."

"I know you will. You have passion and that's what it takes to succeed. Remember that."

She smiled. "I will. Merry Christmas."

Christmas Day, 1972. Chicago.

Chris stood at the bottom of the sweeping staircase at his grandmother and grandfather's house wearing a black cape and miniature top hat that Susie had made for him for the little Christmas play.

"Ladies and Gentlemen," he said with a sweeping bow to his audience of four. "My sister and I would like to present you with the story of the first Christmas."

Chris gestured toward the top of the stairs where Noelle, dressed as Mary and carrying one of her baby dolls to represent Jesus, walked solemnly down the steps.

"And so it was that Mary and Joseph went to Bethlehem to pay their income taxes," Chris said proudly.

Susie put her fingers to her mouth to stifle a laugh. Mary Elizabeth jabbed her playfully with her elbow. "Cute, huh?"

Their eyes went back to Chris who then turned to Noelle. "Mary. You have a baby now!"

"Yes," Noelle replied shyly without the innate kind of acting talent and self-assuredness of her brother.

"How did this happen?" Chris asked with mocked surprise.

Noelle shrugged her tiny shoulders. "I saw an angel."

"And what did the angel say?" Chris asked and then quickly dashed over to the entry to the dining room where he'd placed a portable record player and turned on the music.

"Do you believe in magic, in a young girl's heart," the song began.

Braxton burst into laughter as did Susie, Jed and Mary Elizabeth.

Chris raced back to Noelle, took her arm and they did an impromptu square dance of a type, Noelle dropped the doll twice and nearly tripping on her blue and white robe and shawl.

The entire family applauded the children as the pop song finished playing.

Susie rose from her chair and hugged Chris. "And you wrote this little play all by yourself?"

"I did!" he replied proudly.

"It was genius," Braxton announced.

"As I would expect of any Magli," Jed said hoisting Noelle into his arms.

"And Howard," Mary Elizabeth said kissing Chris on the head.

Braxton was so proud his face turned crimson red. "Chris, I think you should do this every year for us. Write us a Christmas play. What do you think?"

Susie looked at Chris. "It's a great idea. We'll start our own tradition. Every Christmas Eve we'll be right here for our special performance. Who knows, Chris? You could grow up to write plays someday."

"I want to write the songs," he said.

"You could do that, too," she agreed. "You certainly inherited musical talent from your daddy and grandmother Joyce. Isn't that right, Jed?"

Jed's eyes misted, but he didn't let anyone know. "Yes, he did. And they are both very proud of you."

"Just as we are," Mary Elizabeth gleamed, patting Jed approvingly on the shoulder.

Chris took Noelle's hand and they went to stand on the staircase. "You have to sit down for the finale."

"Oh! The finale!" Braxton said with a wink to Susie.

"How do you know what a finale is?" Susie asked.

"Grandpa Jed helped us," Noelle answered.

Chris frowned. "You weren't supposed to tell."

"It's okay," she smiled at her brother.

Chris squeezed her hand cuing her to bow very deeply. They straightened and in unison said, "God Bless us, every one!"

Susie applauded briskly thinking to herself, "I know you're out there somewhere, Tommy. Maybe by some miracle in your dreams you can see them sending you this prayer."

Chapter Twenty-Seven

Christmas, 1974. New York.

Tommy met his friend, Ted Schmidt, from NYU at Maxwell's Plum for a quick Christmas Eve toast.

"Hey, ya, Mike! Over here!" Ted yelled over the din waving him toward a table at which sat two blonde girls.

"Ted!" Tommy waved back, groaning to himself. *Not again.*

What is it about me that makes Ted feel he must incessantly comb New York for my perfect woman?

Tommy worked his way through the throng of couples and groups of on-the-make men and pretty young women.

Ted slapped Tommy on the back. "Jill. Heather. Meet Mike Kelly. The hottest Irish ticket in town."

Tommy shook his head. "I apologize right now for my friend. He knows," Tommy glared at Ted who was grinning from one overly large ear to the other, "that I hate this meat market."

"You think it's a meat market?" The blue-eyed blonde in the light blue and white Norwegian ski sweater and white ski pants asked coyly.

"Sweetie, where *are* you from?"

"Buffalo," she replied wide-eyed.

"Figures," Tommy replied.

She pouted, "I only moved here last month. I'll be a freshman at NYU in January. I had to go to a community college first. I didn't do so hot on my SAT's first time around."

"Is that so?" Tommy asked leaning over to Ted and whispering to him, "I'll kill you later."

Ted frowned. "Okay!" he clapped his hands together. "Heather, this is Mike Kelly. Mike, me boyo, Heather is a Psych major. She's a senior."

Heather's dark eyes scanned Tommy like security devices. "Ted says you went to Vietnam."

217

"That's right."

"Do you have those creepy nightmares like I've read about that you ex-G.I.'s have?"

Tommy opened his mouth to shoot back a flip retort and shocked himself by telling the truth. "Yeah, actually, I do."

"What?" Ted's jaw dropped. "You never said anything about 'Nam. Ever."

Tommy wiped his face with his hand. "I don't know why I said that."

Heather leaned forward on her elbows, genuinely interested in Tommy's plight. "I'm sorry to hear about that. I've decided to go to med school and become a psychiatrist and I'm fascinated with dream study."

"So, great!" Ted slapped Tommy's back again. "Mike here can be your guinea pig."

Shaking his head, Tommy said, "I don't think so."

"Aw, come on. It would help me a lot."

"No, I said," Tommy shouted with more anger than he'd anticipated. "I'm sorry. But, no."

Heather leaned back in her chair, never taking her steady-beamed eyes off him. "You really have a lot to hide, don't you, Michael Kelly?"

"Yeah. I do. So let's leave it at that," he replied with eyes just as stern.

Ted clapped his hands together and rubbed them. "Okay. So this is going just about as badly as it possibly could. I'll see about some beers."

Heather didn't take her eyes off Tommy. "I bet you'd like to take me home to bed though."

Tommy smiled. "You're gorgeous. I'm sure that's never been a problem for you. But sorry, I still won't answer your questions."

A wry smile curved her luscious lips. "Oh, honey. I wasn't planning on any talking at all."

"Here's one for your research books. I've tried that kind of fling thing you want and know what? I didn't like it. Didn't like it at all. Guess I'm just not that kind of guy."

"What kind of guy are you? The marrying kind?"

"Nope. Can't say that either," he replied honestly.

Jill clamped her hand over her mouth to stifle a gasp. "God! You're not gay are you?"

"No," he answered flatly.

"Then what else is there?"

Thoughtfully, he answered, "The eccentric kind."

Ted returned with a waitress who bore four tall glasses of beer. "Hey, truce, okay. Merry Christmas, everybody."

They raised their glasses and clinked. "Merry Christmas."

Tommy drank heartily, thinking how much he hated Christmas. It was a season fraught with traps for someone like him with no memory of his history. One question led to another and he didn't have enough energy to make up lie after lie about what were his family traditions. Where did his parents live? Did they have a tree? What was their favorite drink? Did they serve turkey or roast beef for dinner? Was dinner early or late?

Women were the worst culprits. They wanted to know everything about everything. And they never stopped. They wanted to know where he went to school, his favorite toy as a child. They all thought they could figure out who he was by asking the right questions over a long enough period of time and eventually they would find out if he was marrying material or not.

It was impossible for a woman to like him just the way he was. A figment of his imagination.

"I gotta go, guys," Tommy said, putting his empty glass on the table. "Ted," he shook his hand. "Say hi to your fiancée for me." Tommy grinned.

"What?" Jill glared at Ted who had his hand on her knee.

"Fiancée? I didn't know about this," Heather said haughtily.

"That's because I don't have one," Ted said, shooting a damning look at Tommy. "Mike, here likes to play jokes."

Tommy smiled to himself and tied his scarf around his neck. "See you kids later." He waved and walked out.

Snow was falling as he exited the restaurant. It was a long walk to his apartment. He would have taken a cab if he had any extra money, which he didn't. He'd spent it all on his tuition to Columbia Law School which started in January. He'd left Tavern On The Green last year and now worked part time as a paralegal in a law firm. The pay was better, but with tips at the holidays taken into consideration, there truly wasn't much difference. When he calculated the stock tips he used to get and make money on, he was definitely in a reduced financially rewarding position. Still, his stocks were holding steady and he loved his work at the law firm.

He supposed there was plenty to be thankful for this Christmas. His undergrad days would be over once he passed his finals, a minor step since he'd never gotten less than an 'A' on any final.

Tommy walked up to Charlie Hobbs' magazine stand. "How's it hangin', Charlie?"

"Merry Christmas, Michael!" Charlie said, giving Tommy a salute.

"How's the grandson?"

"Itchin' to open presents. I was just getting ready to close up for the night. You got any plans?"

"Oh, the usual. Read. Feed the cat. Water the African Violets. I got a new cassette of the London Symphony."

"Maybe once you get that law degree you can afford to hear the New York Philharmonic."

"That's the plan, Charlie. That's the plan."

"Yep. That would make everything right as rain," Charlie agreed.

"Right as rain," Tommy said with a smile and walked away.

Symphony tickets. Theatre tickets.

From the darkest, furthest regions of his mind, Tommy could hear the faint memory of a girl's voice.

We could go to New York. See a play. I want to be an actress someday.

Snow fell in fat flakes marring his vision. It rained down on him like heavy goose feathers. He felt as if he were walking in a tunnel. The sounds of the city became muffled, but the girl's voice became clearer.

"Who *are* you?" he asked aloud as he reached his apartment building.

He unlocked the door and turned on the light.

A calico cat stood on the back of the herculon plaid sofa and stretched.

"Hey, Jimmy Doolittle! I think we made a breakthrough tonight!" He picked up the cat and tucked him under his arm.

"She's an actress! I remember that. She said she wanted to be an actress. So, now all I have to do is search every city in this entire country for every girl who ever acted in a high school play, majored in theatre in college, every Hollywood actress. Every Broadway actress. Every off-Broadway and off-off Broadway actress and when I'm finished . . . I figure I should be celebrating my eighty-fifth birthday."

He stared out the window at the snow, stroking Jimmy Doolittle's head.

"But she's out there. Somewhere. And I swear to God, I will find her."

Jimmy Doolittle meowed.

He looked at the cat. "You're right. What if she doesn't want me when I find her?"

That's a question only God can answer.

The Christmas Star

Chapter Twenty-Eight

July, 1976. New York.

"My God!" Joannie giggled as she greeted Susie, Noelle, Chris, Mary Elizabeth and Braxton at La Guardia airport. "I didn't think I could ever get you pried out of Chicago." She hugged Susie extra hard.

"Hey, if I weren't matron of honor for Katie Roberts, we wouldn't be here. Thank God she believes in planning ahead."

Mary Elizabeth chuckled. "Thank you very much, but I was the one who told Katie's mother eighteen months ago to get the church first and the plane reservations second! I just knew this was going to be a fiasco wanting to be married on the Fourth of July for the bi-centennial. It's so . . . Hollywood. And so unlike Katie."

Susie leaned over to her mother's ear, "It's the day after, Mother. Besides, maybe Katie always wanted to be outrageous and never had a chance. Maybe this is who she really is deep down."

"Then why doesn't she be herself?" Mary Elizabeth asked with a shrug as she maneuvered her tote bag and over-large purse.

Susie rolled her eyes. "Her mother wouldn't approve."

"That never stopped you!" Mary Elizabeth replied.

Everyone held their breath.

Braxton burst into laughter. "That's the god's truth! Now let's get to the house. I'm famished! I was thinking New York style Reuben sandwiches with plenty of cheese."

"Daddy, do you always have to think about food?"

They walked to the baggage carousel with Noelle and Chris running ahead as they spied their luggage coming off the conveyor belt.

"Hurry, Noelle. Our stuff's here!" Chris shouted racing ahead.

Susie turned to Joannie. "I have to agree with Mother. The whole world is in New York this summer for the bicentennial."

Noelle chimed in, "You should see New York Harbor from the air! All those tall ships!"

"Yeah," Chris said, plopping his Cub's baseball cap on his head. "It was cool!"

"Well, there's plenty to do, but you are going to be busy enough with the wedding."

"Thank God, they are having the rehearsal dinner at Windows on the World. We will all get to see the fireworks."

"And the wedding is in Central Park the next day?" Joannie asked.

"But she's not a hippie," Chris said, not missing a single word the adults were saying despite the unusual number of bags he was pulling off the carousel.

Noelle nodded. "She's a lawyer. Just like Daddy wanted to be, right, Mom?"

Susie froze. It had been a long time since anyone had mentioned Tommy except for herself and Jed. Such questions and conversations always seemed to be relegated to winter holidays when the presence of him seemed near. But it told her that in Noelle's head, she made every day connections to the man she'd never met but whom Susie had successfully kept alive.

Susie smiled. "That's right. Just like Daddy," she said, touching her daughter's long dark hair.

Mary Elizabeth didn't miss the pain in Susie's eyes. Neither did Joannie. Braxton put his arm around his wife and hugged her slightly, letting her know that it was all right for Susie to handle the situation in the way she wanted.

Joannie felt every nuance of the pregnant moment. Not having been around her extended family in so long, she didn't know how to react. She took her cue from Mary Elizabeth and changed the subject.

"So, it's not a barefoot wedding then. No hippies. Where's the reception?"

"Oh, Tavern On The Green."

"That will be lovely," Joannie said. "I've been there so many times, Bob being a stockbroker now and all. He just loves it there for lunch. He says that by now he's spent enough on client lunches to have bought a private table," she laughed. "Service is good, too," she said non-chalantly.

Tommy shoved the brief into a manila folder and then deposited it in his battered, second-hand briefcase he'd bought from one of the elder law partners.

"I hate to make you work on this over the holiday, Mike," Peter said to Tommy. "But I have a wedding I have to make."

"And a honeymoon," Tommy teased.

"That, too," Peter replied in his starched, formal Eastern manner. "Why Katie wanted to get married during all this bi-centennial folderol is beyond me."

Peter stared at Tommy as if hoping for an answer to his puzzle.

"I wouldn't know, sir. I've never met your fiancée."

"True." Peter nodded. "She's young and impulsive," he said, glancing at Katie's photograph on his desk.

"And beautiful."

Smiling was an uncommon act for Peter. He never allowed his mouth to break into a full smile. But he was smart, thoughtful and honest. Tommy thought Katie was getting a good man in Peter Hatchings.

"Beautiful," Peter said allowing a slight muscular movement to crimp his lips. "She is that." His eyes widened as he glanced back at Tommy. "And damn smart, too. That's important in a woman, don't you think?"

"I absolutely do," Tommy agreed.

"Really?" Peter hoisted his chin higher, inspecting Tommy a bit closer. "Come to think of it, I've never heard you talk about a woman."

Shrugging Tommy replied, "Don't have one. I have to get my law degree. No time."

"Ah! Good decision. Good decision!"

The Christmas Star

"Glad you think so, sir."

Peter packed his things away, making certain his desk was whistle clean. He shook Tommy's hand. "Mike, have a great holiday. I'll see you in two weeks. Now you have the number of the hotel in Maui, correct?"

"Yes, sir," Tommy snapped.

Peter hoisted his chin again, observing. "One thing about a military man."

"What's that, sir?"

"Once it's drummed into them, you can't drum it out."

Tommy smiled.

Peter actually smiled back.

The bi-centennial was just about the best thing that ever happened in Tommy's recorded history. For months, he walked the streets of New York seeing the American flag waving from poles, buildings and house fronts feeling his heart pound.

Streetwalking trumpeters played the national anthem for coins and Tommy tossed in dollar bills to have them keep playing. He liked the sound of the church bells ringing out the spirit of freedom for which he'd fought and lost his memory.

These days leading up to the Fourth of July, gave him hope, but he didn't know why. It was simply something he felt inside. And he believed in that feeling.

Tommy wandered into his favorite deli where newspaper men and women gathered along with stockbrokers, lawyers and artists dressed in torn jeans and tie-dyed tee shirts.

Tommy ordered his favorite. "I'll have a Rueben on rye toast. Extra mayo. Extra cheese."

"For here or to go."

"To go. I'll eat it in the park."

"Nice day for it."

He dug in his pocket for a ten dollar bill and paid the cashier and left.

Braxton walked up to the counter, looking at the back of the man who'd been in line ahead of him. He took out the list of the sandwiches Joannie wanted him to bring back to her townhouse. He heard Tommy place his order.

"Reuben on rye toast. Extra mayo. Extra cheese."

Braxton smiled to himself. "Now there's a guy who knows what to order!" he mumbled to himself, but didn't pay attention to the man until he turned away from the counter and went to the register.

Braxton rubbed his chin. "Something about that guy looks awfully familiar."

"What'll you have, mister? We got a long line here, see?" the brusque man behind the counter said.

"Oh, so sorry," Braxton said. "I'll have the same thing as that young man. The Reuben on rye toast. And two turkey on white, no mustard. Three roast beef on wheat and one tuna on wheat."

"You want chips and pickles?"

"Yes," Braxton replied still thinking about the young man in front of him in line.

"For here or to go?"

"To go."

Chills shot down Braxton's spine. He snapped his fingers.

"Now I know why he seemed familiar! He looked a bit like Tommy!"

"'Scuze me, mister?"

Shaking his head, "But that's impossible. Tommy is surely dead."

"Come again, mister?" The man behind the counter growled.

"Nothing," he took the grocery sized bag from the man and went to the cashier. He tried to hurry his transaction so that he could try to find that young man again.

The weather was hot, but clear and dry. The city was crowded with tourists coming to see the parades the fireworks. Tommy walked out into the sunshine and was swept into the melee of people coming down the sidewalk. Everyone was headed either to the park or to the harbor. They were shopping for souvenirs, going to lunch or rushing to yet another party. It was the bicentennial and the people in New York were celebrating the loudest and happiest of all.

Braxton rushed out of the deli and scanned the crowd of pedestrians for any sign of the young man who resembled his son-in-law. The afternoon sun blazed above and blinded him momentarily. Holding his palm to shield his eyes, Braxton searched every face, but it was useless.

He knew too well he was looking for a dead man.

Susie gazed at Katie and Peter kissing after a round of toasts to their happiness at Tavern On The Green. Bob was kissing Joannie. Her father was kissing her mother. Chris pecked Noelle on the cheek, if only to get a rise out of her and to pick yet another fight.

There's no one for me to kiss.

I'm twenty-eight years old. Ten years since Tommy and I met.

The band started up for the couple to dance their first dance. The tent just outside the restaurant held a huge dance floor just for the wedding guests and the band was one of the best in New York, Joannie had said. Chris had even brought his trumpet hoping he could play a solo which Katie had promised she would negotiate with the band leader.

Couples filled the floor and the table at which Susie sat was suddenly empty.

Sherry Wilson walked up to Susie. "I should have known I'd find you sitting alone," she said.

Susie looked up. "Sherry!" Her face broke into joy as she shot out of her chair to hug her friend. "This is like old home week. Katie said you couldn't make the wedding because you were in London."

"I was. But there was a last minute first class cancellation and I took it. Cost me a month's salary but it was worth it."

"Tell me, what's been going on with you?" Susie asked. "Work is good, I can tell. You look fabulous. Is this Oleg Cassini?" Susie glanced at the lapel of Sherry's exquisite dinner suit.

"It is. But I didn't buy it. My new boyfriend did."

Susie's eyebrow racheted up. "New?"

"He's a London banker, if you can believe, but what hot sex!"

"Sherry!"

"Well, it is. He is!" She laughed.

"So, do you think this is it? Is he the one?"

"God no. I mean, I'm not looking for 'the one'."

"Oh," Susie answered sitting back down.

Sherry sat as well. "What about you? Any word about Tommy?"

"None. Though Daddy is pulling some strings in Washington for me again."

"And?"

"Zip."

Sherry's face fell, the earlier excitement over seeing each other again, fading. "I'm sorry. Then nothing has changed."

"No. Nothing."

Sherry peered into Susie's eyes. "How is that for you? I mean, and please, I don't mean to pry, but don't you want to get on with your life? Fall in love again? I mean you don't have to marry them, you know."

"Odd you would ask tonight. I was just thinking, all these people. They have each other to kiss on holidays and at weddings and parties. A decade has passed since I met Tommy and I've just realized I've been holding my breath. I kept thinking any minute he would show up. But it's been ten years," her voice cracked. "Between the kids and building my business, I'm always busy. Too busy."

"But you haven't been living your life," Sherry offered.

Susie glanced back at the dancing couples. "I thought I was. I'm twenty-eight years old. And in some ways, I feel one hundred and twenty-eight. Maybe I am missing out on life. Maybe I should think of being with someone else. And yet . . ."

"What?"

Susie looked back at Sherry, her eyes filled with torment and a strange kind of luminous hope. "I couldn't do that to a man. He'd be wanting a part of me I haven't got to give away anymore. I'd always be comparing him to Tommy."

Sherry inhaled solemnly. "And you'd both lose."

"Eventually, it would have to turn sour."

"It doesn't have to turn sour," Sherry said.

"I know myself. I know what it was like to be with Tommy. I still dream about him at night. I still believe I can will him to come home. He's just there inside me somehow. No, I could never be a good partner with someone else."

"How can you do that?"

"What?" Susie asked.

"Be so wise. You're not even thirty!" Sherry laughed.

Susie threw her head back and laughed with her. "Yeah, at this rate, I'll be levitating by the time I'm forty!"

"Himalayas here you come!"

Susie caught her breath and looked around the room. "You know. It's the strangest thing. It's been a decade since I was here in Central Park and at this restaurant."

"Strange, huh?"

"It wasn't like this back then."

"Yeah, you were a kid."

"No," Susie replied, her face searching the crowd. "I mean, it feels different now. You know that feeling when people say it's like someone walked over your grave."

"I hate that feeling."

"That's how it feels here for me. It's as if Tommy was here with me. Not like a ghost or something like that, but like he walked through this place a hundred times. I think I told you I did this kind of thing before when he was in Vietnam . . . during the war, I mean. It's like I'm inside his head, seeing the world through his eyes. If I didn't know better, I'd say Tommy worked here or came here a lot like Joannie's husband does."

"Tommy? Work here? Like a waiter? Don't be ridiculous. He's too intelligent to take a wait staff job."

Susie nodded. "I suppose you're right."

"Damn straight."

Susie hugged herself as eerie chills scrambled down her arms.

I know what I'm feeling. I don't care what anybody thinks. There is something about this place and Tommy. I'm as sure of it as I am about anything.

Chapter Twenty-Nine

Christmas, 1978. Chicago.

"Twelve year olds do not get pierced ears," Susie said, hustling down the front porch of Jed's house where she still lived with her children.

"But, Mom, how can I be in a rock band without an earring? It's required," Chris said, following her down the walk to her brand new white Cutlass Supreme. She still wasn't used to giving up her high school red Mustang. It had so many Tommy memories along with one hundred and fifty-seven thousand miles on the odometer. Her new car represented her vow to move on with her life. It was the only move she was emotionally prepared to take now that she had turned thirty.

Susie opened the trunk with the key and dropped a box full of new children and pre-teen designs on top of a pile of precisely cut squares of fabric to be used for a new line of luxury patchwork quilts she was introducing in Colleen's store.

Closing the lid, she said, "Chris," she glared, "I don't want to discuss this again. Your sister doesn't even want pierced ears and she's a girl."

"She also is not a musical genius."

"Don't start," she wagged her finger at him. "I have to go."

"You always have to go," he huffed.

Susie checked her watch. She didn't have to go. She had fifteen minutes, traffic being light this time of mid-afternoon; she'd be fine getting to the Loop. She clenched her jaw. "Grandpa will be home in two hours."

"He won't listen to me either."

"That's because your parents aren't about to let a child desecrate his body."

"He's not my parent," Chris tossed the barb.

Susie was used to it this year. Chris, at twelve, was the terrible twos, the fearful fours and God only knew what other stage of childhood misdevelopment rolled into one. She was certain she'd never survive till he turned thirteen.

"Don't make me consider murder, Chris."

"You can't murder me. You'd go to prison. There'd be Noelle left and she'd miss you."

"Don't be logical."

"Grandpa is always on your side."

"Thank God." She paused. "Okay. You want to discuss this? Let's discuss this. Besides the fact that pierced ears for boys and girls is not allowed at Loyola High School which you will be attending in less than two years, there is the fact that the Stones and the Beatles are on their way out."

"No way."

"How many times has Noelle been to see 'Saturday Night Fever'? Travolta is it, kid. He doesn't have an earring."

"So, if John Travolta gets an earring, then can I get one?"

She checked her watch again. "Yes. No!" She rolled her eyes. "Instead of arguing with me about the fashion statement you wish to make, why aren't you perfecting your craft? Is it the violin or the guitar today?"

"Mom, it's Tuesday. It's piano. Mrs. Levandowski will be here at four. She's got the hots for Grandpa, you know."

"Chris!"

"Well, she does!"

"How do you know this?"

Crossing his arms over his chest, the way he did when he was four, only reminded her how fast he was growing up. He was taller than any of the children in seventh grade. At five foot eight already, she was sure he'd hit six feet before he was fourteen. Jed said he was "just like Tommy". And it was true. He did everything like Tommy. He combed his hair like Tommy. He wore the same kind of conservative colors and clothes like Tommy and yet he had that adventurous streak that had pushed Tommy to enlist when he could have waited to be drafted. And Chris was headstrong like Tommy. When he wanted something, he never held back. He rushed into life before it had a chance to catch him.

"Mom, just because you never have a date, doesn't mean other people in this household aren't thinking about it."

"I'm married." She held up her palms. "Don't even go there, Chris."

Suddenly, the front door banged shut.

"Mom!" Noelle called, bounding down the steps dressed in her cheerleader's uniform and grey wool Eisenhower jacket which was part of Susie's new fall collection. "Can you drop me at Shelly's? We're going to practice."

"Football season is over!"

"Think basketball, Mom," Noelle rolled her eyes.

Susie grabbed her daughter's face by the chin. "What is this? Mascara?"

"I was practicing."

Chris snickered. "Liar. Shelly's older brother is home from school."

"Older? How much older?" Susie's heart nearly stopped as visions of Tommy in his fraternity sweatshirt flashed across her mind.

"He's a freshman in high school. I told you he goes to prep in Wisconsin."

"Yeah, he musta been some kinda delinquent," Chris teased.

Noelle hit him playfully on the shoulder feigning indignation. "Shut up!"

Laughing and ducking her pseudo blows, he said, "Yeah, his old man sent him out of state he was so bad."

Noelle stopped. "Mom, it's not true. He's a genius. Math, Shelly said." She stuck out her tongue at her brother.

"He's fifteen. You're twelve," Susie calculated.

Noelle stared at Susie like her mother was nuts. "So?"

Susie threw her head back far enough to see the sky. She took a deep breath. "Just remember what I told you about the birds and the bees."

"Mom, I'm not going to have pre-marital sex with him. I just wanted to look pretty. And by the way, if Chris gets a pierced ear, can I get gold studs for Christmas, too?"

"Arghhh! No one in this house is going to have any needles poking any holes in any place in their bodies. Only Gypsies have pierced ears."

"And rock stars," Chris corrected.

"Exactly! And you, my favorite son, are going to play with the Chicago Symphony not with Mick."

"Mom! I don't like that stuff."

"Liar," Noelle said. "I heard you playing Handel last night and no one was making you."

"It's a surprise for Grandma," Chris said sheepishly.

Susie dropped her jaw. "You can play *The Messiah?*"

"Nearly. I said I was a genius."

Stunned, Susie took a step back. Just at the moment when she was about to give in to exasperation and chalk up her parenting skills to an abysmal failure, Chris turned around and revealed his heart to her . . . one more time.

At times in his life, she sensed Chris' anger and hurt that he did not have a father like the other boys in his class. Boy scouts had been difficult for him, though Jed had done his best to be both father and grandfather. And Susie had done all she could to be two parents.

It was enough for Noelle. She was accepting of her fate. She had so much love to throw around to her mother and all her grandparents that she was looking for even more people to love. It wouldn't surprise Susie if Shelly's brother didn't fall in love with Noelle this very afternoon. What wasn't there to love about beautiful, intelligent, carefree and kind Noelle?

"Chris, if you keep this up you just might get a scholarship to Juilliard in New York."

"I know I can, Mom. The only horn I don't like is the tuba. Not because it's too big but because it's boring. The violin is my favorite, but I like the piano, too."

Noelle looked at Chris with pride in her eyes. "Playing is one thing. The real money is in writing the songs like Grandpa said."

"Jed said that?"

"No, Grandpa Howard," Noelle said. "He said since Chris is so good at writing the Christmas plays he should write the music, too."

"Yeah," Chris rocked back on his heels with just enough machismo, giving a preview of the teen he was about to become. "I've been working on a couple."

"You have?" Noelle asked. "Great. When you do, I want to be your manager."

"Manager?!" Susie raised her eyes heavenward as she sometimes did when tears threatened. "You are both growing up way too fast for me."

"Mom, are you crying?" Noelle asked.

"No."

"Good thing. It will run your mascara."

New York.

Tommy hung his framed Columbia University law degree on the wall of his freshly painted, windowless, claustrophobic cubicle of an office.

"Looks good," the young blonde woman with the "Farrah" hairstyle said, leaning against the doorjamb. She was dressed in a mushroom colored gathered velvet skirt, dark beige long sleeved satin blouse and matching velvet and satin vest. "Hi. I'm Amy Goodwin."

"Amy. The secretary."

"Legal assistant."

"Excuse me?" Tommy grabbed a paper clipped stack of orientation notes he'd received from Jake Sloan, the senior partner who had hired him. He didn't see any notation about legal assistants on his list.

Amy smiled. "I went to a meeting of NOW. National Organization for Women. We want to be called assistants. Not secretaries. It's a women's lib thing."

"Oh, yeah. Right. Right." He shook his head.

She straightened. "You have a problem with that?"

"No! No." He cleared his throat. "You'll have to forgive me. I'm kind of rattled by a whole lot just now."

"You should be. You're the first time Sloan, McHenry, Battle and Sloan has ever hired someone in their second year of law school." She eyed him from foot to head and back down again. "Guess you set them on their ear at Columbia, huh?"

"I don't know about that," he answered sheepishly. "Say, how did you know . . ."

She flashed him a coy smile. "It's my job to investigate everything."

"Really?" Jutting his chin outward. "What else do you know?"

"Michael Kelly. Graduated Bishop Ludden High School in Syracuse, 1963. Honor Roll. Marine. Vietnam hero. Bronze star. MIA for four years. Mother Mary deceased, 1968. Relocated to New York City. Finished pre-law NYU in three years. Dean's List every semester. Barnstormed his way through Columbia. Four O. They're still talking about your internship at Jacobson, Kettering and Hatchings. I heard it was your research for Peter Hatchings that turned the tide on the class action law suit against Con Ed. They bid for you and lost to us. Not enough money, huh?"

"Money? No."

"I'm sorry?" She turned her head as if she hadn't heard him correctly.

"I didn't take this job for the money," he said, taking another plaque out of the cardboard box on his desk.

"What else is there?" Amy asked.

Tommy's grin was wide and mischievous. "Why, the challenge, Miss Goodwin. The challenge."

"Fair enough." She smoothed her skirt. "Look, it's nearly five and the bosses are throwing a Christmas party in the conference room. I'm supposed to bring you."

He looked at her outfit again. "I was wondering . . ."

"You like it?" she smiled. "I splurged for Christmas. Makes me feel like a little girl. All velvet and satin."

Something inside Tommy rang like a reverberating church bell. Quickly, he opened a desk drawer and withdrew a leather journal. Using the red ribbon, he opened the book to his last notation.

He quickly wrote down the date.

Like a little girl. All velvet and satin. Amy Goodwin. Christmas Eve, 1978.

Do I have a little girl? Or do I remember a girl who seemed little girl-like?

Snapping the journal closed, he put it in the drawer and locked the drawer.

"What was that all about?"

"About?" he stuttered.

"You looked like you'd seen a ghost."

"A ghost?" He blinked at her. This was the familiar part. "Sort of."

"O . . kay . . " Amy glanced around uncomfortably.

Tommy didn't care. His journal had become a new game to him in the past year. In the past decade, he realized that his mind wasn't entirely shut down. Certain inflections, groups of words, emotions, particular time of the day and even the weather were keys to unlocking his past. If he could gather enough puzzle pieces, perhaps someday he could put it together and find the mysterious woman who haunted his memories. There was no telling what would be the magic that would give him back his life.

No incident was too trivial. No impression was wasted.

This was Tommy's life. For now.

"So, do you want to meet the rest of the staff?" Amy asked.

"Sure," he said.

"Good," she replied, and when he got to the door she put out her arm for him to take.

"I thought you were women's lib and all that."

Lowering her gaze beneath heavily mascara-ed lashes, she said, "Only when it suits me."

He took her arm and put it through his. He stopped. He sniffed. "What's that perfume you are wearing? It's familiar somehow."

"Shalimar. I've worn it since high school."

"Shalimar. I have to remember that," he said.

Amy smiled up at him wrongly believing he meant to think of her whenever he smelled it. She didn't know that the perfume reminded him of someone else. Another girl. In another world. Locked in an impenetrable mist that shrouded his past.

Chapter Thirty

June, 1984. Chicago

Susie sorted carefully through the mail as she always did, making certain a letter from Tommy was not stuck to a piece of junk mail, but there were only bills.

"Chris," Susie called out, walking down the hall and checking his bedroom. "Chris, are you ready yet?" she called again walking past Noelle's room. She knocked on the door.

"Come in," Noelle replied.

"Honey, have you seen Chris?" Susie asked and instantly stopped. Noelle was dressed in her graduation cap and gown. She turned around from her full length mirror and faced her mother.

"What do you think?" Noelle beamed.

"I've never seen a more beautiful valedictorian." Susie felt her heart pound in her chest. Wasn't it just yesterday she was coming home from the hospital with the twins? In her mind, she heard echoes of Noelle practicing her cheers. Then later, her speeches as President of the Student Council. Her elation over being named Homecoming Queen, Captain of the Pep Squad and just last week, Prom Queen. To know Noelle was to love her. Everyone did.

She was even more to her community. She was a Candy Striper at Northwestern Medical Center Hospital. She volunteered for the Holy Name clothing drive and served meals to the homeless on Thanksgiving and Christmas along with Susie and Mary Elizabeth. If there was a historical site, endangered whale, baby seal or rain forest to be saved, Noelle threw her passion into the cause. Her heart was as big as the world and was currently expanding to take in the universe.

At eighteen, she always had a date for parties, dances and movies but had not lost her heart to anyone. She was a friend to all, and astonishingly, the boys preferred it that way. She loved them all and they loved her back.

She had been accepted to St. Mary's in South Bend where Susie had once been accepted.

Susie, herself, had graduated from Northwestern in 1980 with honors in business the same year she broke from Colleen to open her own store.

Serendipity Sweets opened its doors on Rush Street and two years later, Susie was well into the black. She was proud of the fact that she wouldn't have to lean on her parents for help in sending the twins to college.

"I'm really nervous," Noelle said. "My speech isn't good enough. I should . . ."

"Sweetheart, it's a great speech," Susie assured her. "Keep it up and you could be a professional speech writer."

"I'd rather be in business like you."

Shaking her head, Susie said, "Amazing. How could I have produced two such level headed kids?"

"Mom, Chris is not level headed."

"He's an artist. He's moody," Susie justified Chris' intensity for music and composing. At times, Chris would shut himself away for an entire weekend in the music room Jed had built for him on the last remaining square of back yard. "You've always been the little 'manager'."

"Yeah, but he won that scholarship to Julliard. He really is a genius, isn't he?"

"Your father would be so proud of both of you," Susie replied wistfully.

Noelle smiled just as she always did when Susie referred to Tommy. Noelle was Susie's ally in keeping Tommy's memory alive. "I've always been proud of him." She walked to her mother and hugged her.

Susie reveled in the moment wondering what Tommy would say or do if he were to walk in on them at this minute.

"Hey, Mom, we have to get a move on. The ceremony starts in an hour."

"I'll find Chris."

Noelle, picked up her tassel. "Ten to one he hasn't even taken a shower yet."

Susie rushed out the back door and instantly heard the music coming from the miniscule studio.

Jed sat on the piano stool, his eyes closed, directing Chris playing the violin.

"Perfect!" Jed announced just as Susie opened the door.

"Hey, you two," she said looking at Chris who was dressed in a black tee shirt and black jeans. "We need to leave. Chris, you're not wearing that."

"Mom, I'll be wearing a cap and gown. This goes underneath.

"Oh, no. The party is at Grandma Howard's house and everyone will be wearing suits and ties. I laid your clothes out on your bed."

Jed shot Chris the "I told you so" look. "Better scramble, kid."

Chris packed up his violin. "I'm taking this to the party. I promised Grandpa Howard I'd play some of my new songs for him tonight. I've got a new one, it's called *Will Heaven Ever Find Me.*"

"Sounds lovely," Susie said approvingly.

"It is," Chris replied confidently. "Needs a bit of work on the bridge, but it's ready."

Jed rose. "I better scoot myself. See if I can rustle up my summer tie."

Susie chuckled. "It'll be the light yellow one hanging next to your winter tie in your closet."

"Right."

"I'll lock up," Susie said as they left.

She turned off the electronic amps and the lamp on the piano. Glancing around the room she thought of all the joy this tiny room had brought to both Chris and Jed. Jed had pounded every nail and attached every soundproofing tile. He'd put in a small window air conditioner and two space heaters for the cold Chicago winters. Chris had brought friends here after school and they had "jammed" during his early teens when he'd wanted to form a rock band. But once he turned fifteen, Mrs. Levandowski's influence along with an activation of Joyce's gene pool, had turned Chris to classical music and show tunes.

Many were the times when she'd referred to Chris as a one-man Rodgers and Hammerstein.

Who knew where his talent would take him, if anywhere? For now, he was happy and that's all that mattered to her.

Pelting rain melted the caps and tassels of the graduating class of Loyola High School, but Susie didn't mind. She sat in the bleachers under a golf umbrella next to her mother. Jed and Braxton sat under a similar umbrella next to them.

"For the first time, Mother, I think I truly understand why you were so disappointed in me."

"Susan! I have never been disappointed in you! You have given me more joy. . ."

"I meant when I was Noelle's age and was already pregnant. You were devastated."

"Oh," Mary Elizabeth sniffed. "That."

"What I'm trying to say is that I now know how it must have been for you, thinking I'd thrown my future away on Tommy. That I could have done so many things with my life. When you see this," she waved her hand over the spectacle below, "you realize that this is perhaps the one and only time in their lives when they really can have it all. They can do anything. And every single tiny move they make from this second onward starts defining them. Narrowing their options. Creating their path. Chiseling their future. When you're eighteen, it doesn't feel like anything but freedom from high school. Freedom from your parents' curfew. Getting your first real job. All you can think of are fraternity parties in college, football games. Summer trips. Spring break and sneaking a bikini your mother doesn't know you bought."

Mary Elizabeth clutched Susie's hand. "It's true."

"Oh, God. I want so much for them."

"I know," Mary Elizabeth said, holding her camera up to take Chris' picture as he took the diploma from the principal's hand. He glanced up to the bleachers and waved his arm over his head.

"Hi, Mom! Grandma! Grandpa! Papa!"

Braxton waved back, dropped his head to his chest and let a tear fall. "They grow up too fast," he whispered.

Jed reached over and clutched Braxton's forearm, giving him strength.

"I'm okay," Braxton nodded and looked up quickly so as not to miss Noelle.

"Miss Noelle Magli," the principal announced and the crowd whooped and hollered and applauded.

Mary Elizabeth clapped so hard she nearly bruised her wrists with her heavy bangle bracelets. "They love her so much!"

As Noelle walked off stage, Mary Elizabeth whispered to Susie, "I've become so used to having you and the twins in the house nearly every weekend, I just haven't prepared myself well at all for their leaving for school. For so long the house has been so full and now it will be so empty."

Susie put her arm around her. "I'll still be here and I'll still come on the weekends. I have the new store we're opening in Evanston and the one in Lake Forest. Why not help me?"

"Me? Go to work?"

"Why not? It's the only thing you haven't tried," Susie urged.

Mary Elizabeth peered lovingly into her daughter's eyes. "You know, you told the children when they were very small that your life was one of believing. All these years you still believe that Tommy would come back to you. And all these years people have been watching you. You've taught your clients and co-workers, friends, even my friends, to believe not just in themselves but that love transcends tragedy. Life is what you make of it. That's a very important lesson to learn."

She patted Susie's hand. "You've done a great job. A great job."

"Thanks, Mom," Susie replied sincerely.

The graduation announcements were over, the class tossed their caps and Susie stood clapping along with her mother, Jed and her father.

"Well, done!" Braxton said.

"Now, it's on to the party," Jed said. "I can't wait for you to try a new pasta I've made. I was able to import the flour from Italy."

"Jed," Mary Elizabeth said, "When are you going to take Braxton and me up on our offer to take you to Italy with us?"

Jed stopped at the end of the row, glanced down at the last of the processional of students. "You know, it's going to be an empty house this fall," he said with a catch in his throat. "Maybe we should discuss this."

"Thank God!" Braxton said, slapping Jed on the back. "You have a real talent for cooking. We would have so much fun in Tuscany. I can taste that clam sauce now."

"Braxton Howard, don't even think about it. You know what the doctor said about that cholesterol of yours. No gravy. No white sauce. No Italian sausage either!" Mary Elizabeth scolded.

"Oh, phooey! What does he know. We switched to that tasteless, no-cholesterol, pretend butter he wanted. Isn't that enough?"

"Mother is right, Daddy. You need to be careful."

"Jed doesn't seem to have a problem and he cooks this stuff."

"He also exercises and jogs with Chris."

"Jog. Who invented that word?" Braxton grumbled.

"I like it," Jed said. "I'm too old to run. And too young to merely walk. Jogging is just right."

"Fine. You do it, then. I'll watch the Cubbies. Okay?"

"Oh, Daddy. You're incorrigible."

New York City. June, 1984.

In the dream, Tommy saw himself at his graduation from college. He stood in the rain with a young boy on one side and a young girl on the other. They looked like younger versions of himself.

"Turn your tassel," the boy said.

"That's right. Move it over," the girl said.

"Have we graduated now?" Tommy asked them.

"Yes. We've moved to a new level," the boy said.

"And what level is that?"

"One very close to you," the boy said with a bright smile.

"And this makes you happy?" Tommy asked.

"No, the girl said. "It will make Mom happy, Dad."

Abruptly the dream ended as Tommy bolted wide awake.

"Oh my God!"

He shot out of bed, grabbing his silk summer robe and wrapping it around his naked body. His head was damp with sweat as if he had a fever.

"Except I'm not sick."

He turned on the lamp and sat on the edge of the bed staring at the dark blue wall-to-wall carpeting in his high rise apartment.

"Who are these symbols? They can't be real people because I don't have any children. Think, Mike, think."

A stack of psychology and philosophy books filled his night table. He remembered a particular volume written by Carl Jung. "Maybe this is some latent adolescent animas in conjuction with my animus."

Raking his hand through his thick hair, he plopped back on the bed. "Or maybe it's just a dream, man."

Sucking in a deep breath, he pulled the sheet over him. "It'll go away. They always do."

New York City. November, 1984.

Tommy stared out the spacious window of his corner office. Christmas lights twinkled along Fifth Avenue below. He could see the Christmas shoppers thronging their way across the intersections. Cabbies deposited and picked up fares in lightening speed.

What's it like to shop for aunts, uncles, and cousins? Is it any different than the monogrammed gifts I order for Hal, Bob and Samuel? I put a lot of thought into it. But what's it like to put emotion into it?

"Simply everyone will be there, Michael," Amy said. "Ferraro promised to show. Your friend, Mike Wallace. Word is he's going to get Westmoreland to drop that 120 million dollar lawsuit against CBS. Boy, I bet you wish you'd landed that case." She didn't pause for a reaction. She'd come to learn in six years that when Michael "spaced out" like he did staring out the window, he was absorbing information, just not inputting. "Then some of the usual crowd. Norman Mailer can't make it. The flu, I heard. So?"

"You know what it is? It's Christmas," he said.

"No, it's the day after Thanksgiving," she corrected. "It's the Wellman's party. We've been invited for the last four years."

It's the Christmas season I react to. That's when the dreams start. For the past six years, every Christmas season, my dreams kick into overdrive. I can fill an entire journal in four weeks. It takes eleven months during the rest of the year to fill one journal.

"Michael!"

He did not respond.

"Michael! Are you listening to me at all?"

It wasn't that he didn't hear her. He did. It was that for the first time he didn't recognize his name.

He turned his chair around and faced her. "Amy."

"Michael."

*That's not my name. I know it now. I really know it! It's . . .
T . . . Terry . . . Ted. Tom. No. Thomas. No.*

"Damn, I lost it!" He flattened his palms against his
temples. "I lost it!"

"Lost what?"

He stared at her. *Amy.* He'd dated her for six years. She
thought she knew him, but how could she, when he didn't
know himself. He never told her. He couldn't. For one thing, he
didn't want her to think he was a freak. Second, he had created
Michael Kelly, legal whiz. Not to mention financial success.
His Wall Street strategies were becoming more famous than the
cases he litigated. To this day, he still gave market tips to
Charlie in the Park. Charlie still worked his stand, but Tommy
knew the man was worth close to a million bucks. Charlie was
putting his money away for his grandson's education. Even
though Tommy didn't have a son or grandson, he still kept
squirreling his money away for the very odd reason that he *felt*
as if he had a family somewhere.

No, he couldn't tell Amy the truth. He couldn't destroy
something he'd built.

"Michael, are you going to the party with me or not?"

"I want to see *Amadeus.*"

"We can see it over the weekend," she said.

"I know this may sound strange, but it's important I go
tonight."

"Fine," she threw up her hands. "I'm going to the party. I'll
make your excuses."

Shaking his head, he said, "No excuses. I never accepted in
the first place. In fact, they don't send me an invitation. They
send it to you. You take whomever you like."

"But they assume you're coming with me. That's what
couples do, you know."

"We're not a 'couple'."

Amy stood stock still as if she'd been shot. "Then just what
the hell are we, Michael?"

He blinked. It was that one second too long that diverts the human path from one relationship to a secondary track.

Her bottom lip quivered. Her eyes registered every fraction of his hesitancy. "You're not going to do it, are you?"

"What?"

"Get me a ring for Christmas. Ask me to marry you. Get engaged!" Her voice rose an octave with each syllable.

"What gave you the idea I would?"

"Six years, Michael! For six years I have been patient. I have waited. I have never pushed. Never!"

"I . . . I can't marry you, Amy."

"You mean you don't want to marry me."

"I mean I can't."

She hesitated, her eyebrows scrunching as she observed him. "But you love me?"

"I care for you, yes, but I never said anything about marriage. I just feel that I shouldn't . . ." he looked down. "For some reason . . ."

My God! I'm married! I'm already married. That's it! There is a wife out there. I have a wife!

Showers of goosebumps littered his flesh. He shivered. He felt the truth ring throughout his soul. It was the biggest breakthrough he'd experience.

If I have a wife, then I could have kids. A kid. A child. Children? Boy? Girl? What?

But the moment passed. His soul went back to sleep.

"Michael, I love you. But, honestly. I can't do this. I can't fight you for you. I don't know what this thing is inside you that holds you back from having a life, but I hope you and it are very . . . happy." She turned on her heel and half ran and half walked out of the offices.

Tommy watched her leave.

He'd shared every holiday, every company party, client dinners, work, trials, and his bed with Amy and yet, as she walked out of his life, he felt nothing.

He hated being numb. He didn't want to live his life like this anymore.

He wanted to find his life.

He turned out the desk lamp, grabbed his tan cashmere overcoat and left.

Susie and Chris stood in line outside the box office. "This is the greatest movie, Mom. You're going to love it."

"You've seen it?"

"Twice."

"Then why are we seeing it again and not going to Radio City Music Hall? Or dinner at Tavern on the Green?"

"Because if you don't go with me, you won't see it. You'll get too busy with your clients and suppliers and . . ."

"Attorneys, Chris. I'm here to finalize these plans for the franchise of Serendipity Sweets."

"And I thought you came to spend Thanksgiving with me."

Noelle rushed up. "I got them!" She said, holding three tickets in the air. "Boy, this show is hot. There are hardly any tickets left. We better hurry if we want a good seat."

They rushed into the theatre.

Tommy waited patiently in line. When he got to the box office window, the attendant was about to turn the "sold out" sign around.

"Wait!" he said. "I have to see this movie tonight!"

"Are you just one?"

"Yes."

"Well, that's a first," the girl with acne said. "Here you go. Sorry."

"Oh, that's okay. As long as I got the ticket," he said.

"No, I meant that you're alone on Thanksgiving weekend. I thought everybody had somebody for Thanksgiving." She turned the sold out sign to face out.

Those in line groaned, then dispersed.

Tommy entered the theatre and found a seat in the front row. Just watching the opening credits, his neck was already hurting, but the music was haunting. He forgot his pain.

The movie lived up to its billing. It was as if Tommy had taken a trip back in history. He saw, felt, smelled and experienced Mozart's life along with the rest of the audience. Yet it was more. There was something about the music itself that jarred memories.

Midway through the film, the voice inside him grew louder. "The Plaza is the best." Only this time the voice was that of a woman.

He'd heard that voice before, right after the helicopter crash, but it had not returned for a very long time. This time, her voice was distinct.

"What did you say?" he whispered to himself and looked down at his hands.

"The Plaza is the best."

Not from New York!

The girl's voice did not have an East coast accent. It was like his!

How many times had people marveled over the fact that though he was from Syracuse and New York, his accent was Mid-western.

Mid-western. Mid West. And if I have a wife, this must be her voice!

Thrilled at his revelations, Tommy could not follow the movie any longer. He rose and walked out of the theatre.

He'd been right to come here. This was the best night of his life.

Chris watched the man in the front row rise and leave. Susie sat next to the aisle and glanced up as the man left.

"Mom, can you believe anyone could walk out of this movie? This . . . music. Mozart! This is what life is all about!"

The man brushed her arm with the tails of his coat as he passed. Susie's heart stopped. Chills blanketed her entire body. She hugged herself.

"What's wrong?" Noelle asked.

"I feel as if someone just walked over my grave," Susie said. "Or I saw a ghost."

She turned around peering at the curtained doorway. The man disappeared behind the velvet drapes.

She bolted upright. "Tommy!"

"What?"

Susie sprang out of her seat.

Noelle and Chris looked at each other, stunned. Then they raced behind her.

"What is it? What's going on?"

"I just saw your father." She kept walking.

Noelle froze in her tracks. Chris bumped into her. They shook their heads at each other.

Tommy left the theatre just as a cab pulled up.

"Taxi!" He rushed up to the cab and got in. Shutting the door quickly as he gave the driver his destination, he didn't see Susie, Chris and Noelle as they came running out of the theatre.

"He was here. I know it."

"What was he wearing?"

"A long tan coat." Susie looked across the street and spied a small Irish pub. A man dressed in a long tan overcoat was closing the door behind him.

"There he is!" Susie shouted. Her heart pounded in her chest as she rushed into the street not watching out for traffic.

"Mom!" Chris yelled and shot off after her.

A taxi screeched its tires as it swerved to avoid her.

Grabbing his mother, Chris pulled her back to the sidewalk. "Watch out, will you? You coulda been killed."

Noelle checked the traffic. When there was a break, she said, "All clear. Let's go."

Noelle was the first across the street and held the door for her mother and brother.

The pub was dark but neon-lighted beer signs and colored lights around the mirror behind the bar cast an eerie holiday glow.

Susie saw the man taking off his coat and hanging it on a rack at the end of two facing old leather booth benches.

Hands clammy, lips quivering, her nerves jangling, she walked up to him and tapped his shoulder. "Excuse me."

He faced her.

Not him.

He smiled. "Yes?"

"Sorry. I thought you were someone else."

Her heart plummeted. Her stomach re-tied it's knot.

Noelle's face crumbled and she turned away from Chris' scowl.

"Don't say it, Chris," Noelle said. "Have some compassion for once."

He looked at his sister and realized that the two most important women in his life had believed in fairy tales and Santa and Jesus long after he'd let his fantasies die.

All these years he'd thought they were giving "the belief" lip service. He thought it was something they did for Jed. Or for him.

Now he realized they truly believed.

There was nothing he could do for them until the truth about his father was revealed.

He put his arms around his mother. Then around his sister comforting them.

On that day, Chris realized he had become the man of the family.

Chapter Thirty-One

New York, Christmas Eve, 1985.

Tommy drummed his fingers on the arm of a leather camelback sofa in the psychiatrist's office. "You know, I've been coming here for six months and frankly, Dr. Kline, you haven't shed any light on a single matter for me. We've tried hypnosis, regression therapy, dream analysis. You've seen all my journals from day one, practically. So you tell me why I should keep coming to see you?"

Dr. Kline took off his reading glasses and twirled them in between his thumb and fingers. "If you want to remember, you will. But it's not that easy. Something in your past was so traumatic that you've erected this wall . . ."

"Tell me something I don't know."

"You shouldn't come back here."

Tommy's eyes widened. "That's honest."

"I hope so. I'm not here to take your money."

"Trust me, at one fifty an hour, you are here to take my money," Tommy chuckled cynically.

"I'm here to help, as well."

"But you aren't helping me. I'm in the same place I was." Tommy stood, shoving his hands in his pockets. He paced. He could think better on his feet and he'd developed the habit of pacing when he thought out loud. "I've banged my head against the US military for fifteen years trying to get some clue about who I am, but the files are top secret and classified. I can't go there. Hell, no one can! You were my last hope! If modern medicine and science can't help me remember who I am, what other choice do I have?"

Dr. Kline tossed his glasses on the desktop. "Try prayer."

"Don't be facetious."

Leveling Tommy with an intense gaze, he said, "I wasn't. I'm very serious."

Tommy stopped in his tracks, considering what the man said. "You know, when I first came to New York I met a priest who told me that my answers were inside me. I figured pulling that out of me was your job."

Dr. Kline took a deep breath. "I'm going to give you some books on meditation and visualization techniques. I want you to try this for a year. Keep up the journal. Write down your dreams. I have to believe you're on the verge of a breakthrough. We could be only days away from it, but if you're resistant to coming here, you're stopping yourself. And that's not what I want for you, Michael. Maybe you should go back to the yoga you learned in 'Nam."

"Yoga? Does this mean I have to give up my running?"

Smiling, Dr. Kline said, "You need both to help you with your stress."

"Hey, my stress is expensive stress. I get paid the big bucks because nobody takes on the kind of lost cases I take."

"Just like me, huh?" Dr. Kline laughed.

"Maybe I am a lost cause," Tommy replied dourly.

"No one is lost forever, Michael. We've done all the tests. You have no brain damage, no disease, nothing medically wrong. I can't give you a pill to give you a life."

"I know," Tommy sighed. "So, I'll give yoga another shot. What have I got to lose?"

"Nothing. And I'll see you next year. Unless, you do have a breakthrough. A big one. Then you call me."

"Deal," Tommy said shaking his hand.

Tommy left the building with a reading list and the phone numbers of four private yoga instructors.

In the hour he'd been with Dr. Kline, snow had covered the city with a thin white veil. Frantic late shoppers scurried along the sidewalks, their shopping bags brushing up against Tommy as he walked back to his office building. In the distance, he heard an ambulance siren. A bus coughed. A child laughed. A young couple argued under the walk sign at the curb where Tommy came to a stop.

He watched the pretty dark haired young girl dressed in a pink fleece jacket and white wool slacks smile at the young man with her. Abruptly, the young man stopped arguing, smiled back then pulled her into his arms and kissed her.

"Dazzling," Tommy said to himself.

She dazzled him.

"You dazzle me."

The memory of his own voice hung frozen like an icicle in his brain. Suspended. But complete. Yet fragile. It was one of a hundred isolated thoughts and memories he'd strung together. Yet they had not formed a complete picture.

What he did know was that Christmas and all its holiday sentimentalities and trappings, had a great deal to do with his past.

The light turned. He crossed the street leaving the kissing/arguing couple behind.

Snowflakes caught in Noelle's dark hair and long eyelashes as she stood at the streetlight kissing Jarod.

"I hate it when we argue," she said, pulling up the hood of her pink fleece jacket.

"So, don't argue with me. Just marry me and be done with it."

"I'm not ready to get married. I'm too young. I have to finish school and I want . . ."

"There's a lot of 'I' this and 'I' that going on here, Noelle," he replied.

"See?" She smiled her thousand mega-watt smile at him. "You shouldn't marry me because I'm selfish."

"Ugh," he groaned. "I hate it when you do that. You are the least selfish person in the world."

"Not true. My mother is the least selfish."

"Actually, that's right." He took her hand. "And we're going to be late for lunch with her if we don't catch this light."

"It's only a few more blocks to the Plaza. I was having so much fun kissing you."

Jarod smiled wickedly. "Then let's kiss at the Plaza."

"Okay," she laughed, skipping behind him.

Snow fell in flakes the size of feathers, obstructing Tommy's view. Traffic began to slow. The ordinary hustle ground to a walk. People smiled at each other.

"Merry Christmas," a middle aged woman said to him as she came out of Bloomingdale's.

"Merry Christmas," he replied, standing aside and letting her walk past him. As he did, he noticed the store windows for the first time that season.

Snow scenes of ice skaters filled the window. Metallic silver paper lined the back walls and blue lights illuminated the silver "lake" and flocked trees. A Christmas tree decorated all in blue lights, silver balls and blue stained glass crosses filled a second window.

"Blue lights remind me of Mom," he said aloud.

Chills slaked his flesh. His eyes flew open as he woodenly walked to the window and placed his hands on the glass.

"Blue lights remind me of Mom," he said again with more knowing. More emotion.

"Blue lights remind me of Mom!" he said, shouting the words aloud.

His heart banged inside his chest. He felt flushed. "Blue lights! Blue lights!"

He grabbed the teenager holding a black boom box to his ear and said, "Blue lights remind me of Mom!"

"Far out, man." The teenager continued on bouncing to a Bob Marley song.

Tommy did a little dance shuffling his feet in the snow and clapping his hands a la Fred Astaire. "Blue lights remind me of, Mom!" He sang the words adding melody.

Tommy wanted to hug every person he saw, but thought better of it. People would think he was crazy. "No they won't!" he yelled flinging his head back, letting the snow fall in his face. "This is New York! Nobody cares about anybody in New York!"

"Blue lights." He stopped himself. "I have to get some blue lights. And a tree. A wreath too. More blue lights."

He dashed into Bloomingdale's.

Noelle clutched Jarod's hand. "Did you see that lunatic? Dancing around and what was that he was screeching?"

"Heck, I don't know, baby. It's New York. It's Christmas. The crazies come out at Christmas."

"Boy, they sure do."

Susie sat in the Oak Room with her hands wrapped around a cup of hot tea.

"Mom, I can't believe I'm saying this," Chris said looking down at his semester grade sheet. "But this is the best Christmas I've ever had."

"Don't tell your sister you got a four point," Susie said.

"And miss all the fun? I want to see her pea green with envy."

"Chris, it's easy for you. As you've always said, you're a musical genius. She's now decided to go into pre-law. Just like her father."

"*Would* have gone into law, Mom." Chris said. He didn't get the chance very often but when he did, Chris felt it was his duty to coerce his mother into moving on with her life. Somehow, he had to convince her that Tommy Magli was never going to return from Vietnam or the dead, which was Chris' opinion of what the military had been trying to explain to his mother for twenty years.

"I get your point," she replied.

"Do you?"

"You think your father is dead."

"Mom, everyone thinks he's dead. I bet if you asked Grandpa, he'd say that."

"Jed believes that Tommy is alive."

"I meant Grandpa Howard."

Draining her tea, she looked around. "Let's not talk about it." She checked her watch. "Where is your sister anyway?"

"So, are you dating anyone?" Chris prodded.

"Don't be ridiculous. Everyone I know is married. Anyway, I'm too busy with the new store. Oak Brook, you know. I got a great deal on a lease at River Oaks, too."

Chris eyed her suspiciously. "Not *everyone* you know is married. Face it, Mom, you're beautiful for an older woman."

"I'm not that old," she quipped.

"You're my mother. To me you're ancient. Not as ancient as Grandma, but old, you know?"

"Thanks a lot."

"All I'm saying is that Noelle and I are grown up now. It's time for you to have a life of your own. You've sacrificed enough for us."

"I know what you're saying."

"And?"

"I'll think about it."

Chris took her hand and squeezed it. His eyes were earnest. "Really, really think about it?"

She took a deep breath and exhaled as if the idea was foul. "I'll try. Anyway, I wouldn't even know how to go about it. And I am just too . . . old."

"Ask Grandma to fix you up. She's always got someone at that Yacht Club she's talking about who just got divorced and . . ."

Susie threw up her palms. "No way! It's taken me a lifetime to get her to stop trying to control my life. We have come a long way."

"Okay, not Grandma then. What about Colleen? She knows lots of people."

"Chris, you're really pushing." She checked her watch again. "Where is Noelle? I'm starved."

Noelle came up from behind Susie, winked at Chris giving him the "shh" sign and put her hands over Susie's eyes. Jarod stood behind Noelle.

"Guess who?"

"Kathryn Hepburn?"

"Noelle," she said leaning down to kiss her mother's cheek.

"Where have you two been?" Susie asked, as Noelle kissed Chris' cheek, then sat next to Jarod.

"Walking," Noelle said, taking off her pink fleece jacket.

"We would have been here sooner but Noelle wanted to watch some crazy guy dancing out in front of Bloomingdale's. She dawdles, you know," he teased.

"I do not."

"What crazy guy?" Chris asked moving his grade sheet closer to Noelle.

She glared at him. "You got a four point, right?"

"Yes," he said gloating.

"Creep." She stuck her tongue out at him playfully.

"Yes," Susie said. "What crazy guy? You know people do bizarre things during the holidays, Noelle. You shouldn't get too close to someone like that. What if he'd grabbed you and stabbed you or took you hostage at gunpoint."

Noelle picked up her menu. "Oh, Mother. He was just saying something about blue lights. His mother loved blue lights. Was all. You know they have that lovely window scene at Bloomingdale's with the blue lights and ice skaters and all."

Susie nodded thoughtfully. "I've seen it. The best they've ever done. You know your first Christmas outfits I ever made were . . ."

"Blue velvet and blue brocade," the twins said in unison.

Susie smiled, and then frowned. "We always have blue lights on our tree because Tommy's mother loved blue lights. They remind him of her."

"Reminded. Past tense, Mom," Chris said.

"Don't start," Noelle warned. "I want to enjoy our trip."

Susie tapped her cheek with her fingertip. "How old was this crazy man."

Noelle's eyes flew open. "You don't think?"

Chris slammed his palms on the table so hard the silver jumped. So did everyone at the next table. "That's it! I'm not doing this anymore. Just stop!"

"Chris. You're making a scene," Noelle said.

Jarod leaned back in his chair, ready for flight to the nearest exit. "Maybe I should go . . ."

"Stay," Noelle said.

Susie swallowed hard. "Yes. Stay, Jarod." She looked directly into Chris' eyes. "We're staying right here. No one is going anywhere. We need to order. Isn't that right, Chris?"

Chris sucked in a breath. "Yes. Then after lunch we're going to the room and call Grandpa and Grandma in Hawaii and see if Grandpa Jed likes Maui as much as they always have."

Susie kept eye contact with her son. "It was very lovely of them to give Jed this trip, wasn't it?"

Chris smiled. The danger had passed. His mother was not going to run out into the streets of New York chasing down a total stranger who was perhaps not half as nuts as his mother. Dance or no dance.

"After Midnight Mass at St. Patrick's, we're all going to Joannie's house for brunch. Right, Mom?" Noelle said.

Smiling warmly, Susie said, "Yes. And tomorrow for Christmas dinner as well. You'll be there, won't you, Jarod?"

"With bells on," he said, noticing the tension easing around the table.

"Then it's all settled," Susie said, giving a piercing look to her son. "For now."

"Settled," Chris replied and looked down at his menu. "Now is just fine."

Tommy bought a live tree at a corner lot where the proprietor had marked the cost down to half. He paid four young boys to carry the tree to his apartment building as he had five Bloomingdale's bags and no taxi would agree to take the tree.

He gave each of the boys five dollars and thanked them.

The tree came with two boards nailed to the trunk so erecting the tree was a simple matter. Tossing his overcoat over the sofa, he instantly threw himself into the task of lighting the tree.

Whisking both tiny all-blue lights and the traditional sized lights out of their new cardboard boxes, he plugged them into the extension cords he'd found in the pantry closet.

The heavy falling snow out the window blocked nearly all the daylight so that when Tommy turned on the blue lights, they instantly cast a magical glow.

"This is right. This is it," he said happily feeling those familiar goosebumps shoot down his spine.

He finished the lights and stood back and stared. They gleamed at him, beckoning him to their world; a magical illuminated world where he could find his own past.

"It needs something more."

He stared.

The tree called to him.

"Popcorn."

The idea came to him naturally. He didn't want to get too excited. He wanted to stay calm. But all kinds of memories were flooding back to him.

He went to the pantry and took out a package of microwave popcorn and put it in the microwave.

Mom strung the popcorn with a berry, then a kernel of corn.

Again, he heard his own voice talking as if he had tapped into that lost plane where he'd said those very words.

He didn't have cranberries in the apartment but one of the paralegals sent him a bouquet of holly with red berries. Finding needle and thread in his junk drawer, he began stringing a holly berry, then a kernel of corn.

When the berries were gone, he placed the single strand on the tree.

He sat on the floor cross-legged like a child and gazed at the tree. Staring at the tree for long moments ran into a half an hour. Then nearly forty-five minutes.

In his vision, the tree lights appeared to expand and waver like a mirage. His mind wandered.

He didn't know it, but he had just accomplished his first meditative state.

Then it happened.

263

He crossed into that other realm. And he heard the voices from the past.

"We always did the popcorn and berries. One kernel. One berry. One kernel. One berry. It's prettier that way, don't you think?"

"I do," a girl's voice answered.

"I like only the blue lights."

"When I was little, Mom told me a tree looked more like the North Pole that way, all icy and blue."

"She was right. It's heavenly," the girl's voice said.

"Yeah, like stars . . ."

Then he leaned down and nuzzled the girl's neck and he smelled her.

"*Shalimar!*" Tommy shouted and jolted himself out of his meditation.

"My God! That's what Amy used to wear."

He bolted to his feet. "So was that it? That was my attraction to Amy? That she smelled like this other girl? And was this other girl my wife?"

Chills again. Confirmation.

"Yes, that's it. She was my wife. The Shalimar girl. And Mom. Is she alive?" he asked himself.

No. The answer came.

Chills again.

"No, Mom is dead. Died," He shook his head, hoping to dislodge more memories." "She died just before I met the Shalimar girl."

"And Dad?" He asked himself.

"I feel he is alive."

Goosebumps again. Tommy checked his arm. "Very interesting. Each time I'm right about my thoughts, I get these goosebumps."

Excitement filled his nerves. "I'm onto something. Really onto something."

Smacking his fist into his palm, he said, "This is good. This is good."

"And Mom is not Mary Kelly?'

No.

He shivered. "Hot dog!" He jumped in the air.

"Breakthrough!"

Dashing to the phone, he punched out Dr. Kline's number.

The voice on the other end said. "This is Dr. Kline. Thank you for calling. I will be on vacation until January 8th. If you have an emergency, call 212-556-9090 for Dr. Schwimmer. Have a Merry Christmas and Happy Hanukkah. Shalom."

"Dr. Kline, this is Michael Kelly. I'm not sure this is a breakthrough, but something is happening to me. I'll call you in a couple weeks. Shalom, my friend. And thank you! Merry Christmas to me!"

The Christmas Star

Chapter Thirty-Two

New York, Christmas Eve, 1991.

Sherry Wilson sat in the pew next to Susie in between Joannie and Noelle. Chris and Joannie's husband, Bob, sat in the pew in front of them as they had been five minutes too late in arriving to claim an entire pew.

"I love St. Patrick's," Joannie whispered to Susie. "And the pink and white poinsettias this year are so much better than that awful red. I'm so sick of red."

"Sherry, what did you find out?"

"Honestly, Susie," Sherry said. "Can't I enjoy the choir for five minutes?"

Susie tugged on Sherry's coat sleeve. "Are you nuts? I've held my breath for three days waiting for you to get back from Washington. What good is a political operative if you can't get me some inside information?"

Sherry looked at her friend. They were both getting older. Forty-three wasn't what it used to be, but it sure hung better on Susie than it did on Sherry. And Susie had had two children, whereas, Sherry never married. She was a "careerist". After Katie Roberts' wedding in 1976, Sherry had taken her Harvard Law degree and moved to Washington to pursue a job in politics. Two years ago, she'd landed a job with a small, but prestigious New York law firm who were enamored of her Washington connections. Over the years, she had tried every avenue she could to dig up information about Tommy Magli for Susie, but the end was always dead.

Just as dead as Sherry was convinced Tommy Magli surely was. The only person who kept up hope was Susie.

Sherry had half a mind to lie to Susie and tell her that she discovered he had indeed died in that helicopter crash.

"What did you find?"

"Okay, but you won't like it. And you can't do anything with it because it's really, really top-secret. I could get nailed for doing this and my friend could get fired."

"And?"

"Tommy was in a helicopter crash all right, but it wasn't the one the Pentagon claims he went down in."

"What? Why?"

"Because, Tommy's helicopter was in Cambodia where the US never sent troops. Laos either, for that matter. He was one of an elite corps of secret agents on a highly classified mission. In fact, other than a half dozen regular flights into the hot zones, he had volunteered to be a spy from the get go."

"You mean he planned all this?"

"As far back as boot camp."

"He kept saying he was the best of the best," Susie replied.

"He was. He had a fake ID. Fake papers and we don't know who's papers he got. They never went back to recover the bodies until a year ago. By that time . . ." She shrugged her shoulders.

"They were already gone or buried."

"Right," Sherry said.

"I'm right back where I started."

Sherry took Susie's hand. "Listen. Someday they may disclose these files, but who knows when that will be. Maybe not even in our lifetime. As your friend, Susie, you can't live your life without living it. Find yourself a nice man and make a life. Do something selfish for yourself."

Susie smiled. "Look who's talking."

"We aren't getting any younger and know what? I have been taking a look around and I don't have half the great life you have." Sadness riddled Sherry's eyes.

"That's not true. All those years in D.C. You made all kinds of headway for business women. Why, the list of legislation that you assisted for the environment by being a lobbyist . . ."

"Susie, you have two kids. Noelle is out of law school now. She and Jarod are getting married. Chris is a published song writer! What I wouldn't give for your life."

"Bite your tongue."

Sherry grinned. "You've had a wonderful life."

Susie looked up as the processional started. She saw children dressed as shepherds leading a girl dressed as Mary and a boy dressed as Joseph to the crèche.

"It was on a night like this at Holy Name Cathedral in Chicago that Tommy and I celebrated Mass. He pinned me with his Sigma Chi pin that night. And we conceived Chris and Noelle. I never dreamed I would have this life. I never dreamed God would take him from me."

"Susie . . . I never heard you say this."

"It's true. I have believed against all odds all these years. And now I realize maybe I was wrong. Maybe God did take him. And I just haven't accepted it is all. Maybe Chris is right. Maybe I should rethink my life. Get a life, as the kids say. Maybe God doesn't want me to waste any more of my time on a dream."

Sherry was stunned over how struck she was by Susie's words. Her heart felt a chill. She clutched Susie's arm. "You listen to me, Susie Howard Magli. I take it all back. Every word of it. I don't know why I'm saying this, but I'm covered with chills from the top of my head to the tip of my toes. Forget what I said. Forget I ever brought up finding another guy. If ever I doubted Tommy's existence, it stops now. Tommy is alive. I can feel it just as you've always said you feel it.

"You have to keep believing, Susie. You have to believe for me and for your kids. Don't you give up. Don't you ever give up! You hear me?"

Susie was crying. "I'm so tired of believing. I just can't do it anymore." She hung her head.

Sherry mustered her courage. "Okay. I'm going back to D.C. On my time and my nickel. And I'm going to keep digging. You hear me? I'm going to find out just where the chopper went down. I'm going to find out whose papers or dog tags they gave him and I'm going to track him down. I have connections and maybe it's because you have needed my connections is the only damn reason I was ever put on this earth."

Susie caught her spirit and felt her own courage born again. "You would do that?"

"I don't have many friends, Susie. I've been too busy building this career of mine. You taught me what being a friend was back in high school. You need me now. And I'm not going to fail no matter how long it takes. No matter what."

Susie flung her arms around Sherry. "I love you."

"I love you, too."

The choir's voice rose in crescendo singing "Adeste Fidelis". The congregation came to their feet as the priest began the mass.

Susie stood taller and more confident about the future than she had for a very long time. She and her friend were going to find Tommy.

Her soul told her so.

Chapter Thirty-Three

Chicago, Christmas Eve, 1994.

Susie hauled an English style doll pram up the stairs of Noelle and Jarod's northside brownstone. Chris was unloading shopping bags of gifts out of the back end of the green Explorer.

"Mom, when I have a daughter, are you going to be this over the top about spoiling her as well?" Chris asked.

"When you finally get over the fact that you are not a starving artist in New York, and an employed Chicago playwright and composer with a smash hit at the Blackstone, I might add, and ask Kara Armstrong, whom I think is the most precious girl, to marry you and produce a grandchild, we will discuss the issue at that point."

He raced up the steps to help her with the door smiling broadly. "Mom, I'm giving Kara the ring tonight. After Midnight Mass at Holy Name Cathedral . . . just like you and Dad."

Susie stared at him in amazement. "No way."

"Way."

Tears began to spring to Susie's eyes. "You aren't doing this for me? Because I've bugged you too much?"

"Mom," he sighed. "I didn't move back to Chicago because of you. Neither did Noelle. She got a great job offer here. She could never do this well in New York. Me, either, it turns out. I'll never regret my time there, but it was time to come home. You know?"

"Yeah, I know," she said.

"Kara will be here any minute. Don't let on about the ring. I want it to be a surprise."

Susie started to go inside, then turned back abruptly. "Chris, she does think you're going to propose doesn't she? I mean, you're pretty sure she'll say yes, aren't you?"

"She subscribed to Bride's Magazine last year," he laughed. "I got the hint."

"Oh, thank God," she sighed.

"Gwamma!" Angela shouted running to the front door. She flung her three year old arms around Susie's thighs. "I missed you so much!"

"I missed you, too, precious. It's been all of what? A week since you stayed all Saturday with me at the store?"

Angela hung back, sticking her index finger in her mouth. She twisted her toe on the wood floor as she stared at the toy pram. "Is that for me?"

"How many other little granddaughters do I have?" Susie asked placing the pram in front of Angela.

"None."

"Then who could this be for?"

Angela looked up at Susie. "Sometimes you bring toys for Mommie."

"Those are collectable Barbie dolls," Susie corrected.

"But I wuv 'em," Angela replied using her coy expression and tucking her chin.

"They're for later," Chris said moving in behind his mother.

"Wow! Unca Chwis! Whose is all those?" Angela shouted jumping up and down in a red and green plaid taffeta dress from Susie's holiday collection.

Noelle came into the foyer wiping pumpkin filling off her hand. "Mother, is Jed on his way over? I swear I will never get the hang of pumpkin pie," she said kissing Susie's cheek and giving Chris a peck on the cheek.

I'll Be Home For Christmas played on the surround sound stereo Jarod had installed two years ago on the main floor. Susie still felt her heart stop when she heard the song.

Tommy come home.

It was just a little prayer. A little thought. It didn't stop her life like it used to. She'd taught herself to go on after the thought riveted across her brain and lodged in her heart. She'd taught her soul not to scream out any more, thinking he'd appear in a dream. Or on the street corner. Or in a movie theatre.

Seldom did she scan a crowd for his face. She didn't stop at the Cubs games to watch every over six foot tall man as they entered the bleachers any more. She didn't listen to sad songs. She didn't jump when the phone rang late at night thinking he was on an overseas call. She didn't check the mail with a catch in her throat and she didn't string popcorn and berries any more.

But she still kept blue lights on her Christmas tree just as did Noelle in her brownstone. Even Chris, skeptic that he was, decorated his tree with solely the blue lights. In their tiniest measure, it was their way of remembering Tommy.

"Gwamma, come see the twee!" Angela said taking Susie's hand and pulling her toward the living room. "It's weawly big."

They walked into the living room with it's turn of the century fourteen foot high ceilings, authentic Victorian furniture reupholstered in soft golds, chocolates and tans. The paneled walls gleamed of fresh wax, the Persian rug had been recently taken out to be cleaned and even with her monstrously busy schedule, Noelle had found the time to hang fat garlands of pine cones, holly and blue velvet bows over the draperied windows. Cut glass rose bowls sat in clusters on the coffee table with blue flickering candles inside.

The tree nearly touched the ceiling.

"See the angel, Gwamma? Her name is Angewa. Wike me!" Angela gazed up at the blue and silver angel with white wings. "Isn't she beautifo?"

"Yes, she is darling, just like you."

"Oh, Gwamma. I wuv you!" Angela said, flinging her arms around Susie again.

Susie picked her up and carried her closer to the tree. "It's the most beautiful tree I've ever seen."

Noelle walked in behind them. "It should be. Two thousand lights."

"What?" Susie asked.

Chris gasped. "You're certifiable, Noelle. You know that?" He teased.

"Shut up!" Noelle shot him a damning look.

"Don't say shut up, Mommie. It's not nice," Angela said.

Noelle tapped her daughter on the nose. "You can always say shut up to a brother. That's legal."

"And you should know," Susie laughed.

Jarod came in the back door carrying an armload of firewood. "Hey, everybody's here," he said kissing Susie on the cheek.

"I'll help you with that, Jarod," Chris said.

The doorbell rang.

"I'll get it," Susie said. "I bet it's Jed."

"Or Kara," Chris said handing the box of fireplace matches to Jarod.

Susie went to the door and opened it. "Jed! Kara! You're both here!"

"Wow! Wook at the pweasants!" Angela said scrambling to get down out of Susie's arms. "I can hep!" She extended her arms.

Kara was all smiles and blonde hair and anticipation. Kara was a mix of Mid-west moxi, Eastern seaboard aristocratic bone structure and just enough dramatic flare that would keep Chris on his toes. She was intelligent and loving. She was a perfect fit in the family. Susie loved her already and she could tell from the breathless glow about her, that Kara was indeed expecting to be proposed to.

"Kara! Welcome home." Susie hugged her.

"Thanks, Mrs. Magli. Chris is here, isn't he?" Kara asked, her eyes scanning the room impatiently.

God, how she reminds me of myself when I knew Tommy would walk in the room at any second.

"Uh, huh. Helping Jarod with the fire in the living room."

"Oh, good." Kara rushed inside.

"Hey, sweets!" Chris hugged her and whirled her around. "Marry me!"

"What?"

Chris turned crimson. "Darn. I blew it!"

The entire family burst into laughter.

Jarod was howling. "So, that's how a romantic comedy playwright pops the question? Just hey ya, baby, marry me?"

Kara was laughing and crying. "Chris, you are just so crazy! I love you."

Chris was laughing in spite of himself. "I had this whole romantic thing I was going to do at Mass tonight. Now, I can't."

"Oh, yes you can and you will." Kara said looking around at the family. "After all, I haven't said yes."

"What?" Chris felt his knees go weak.

She looked down. Then popped her head up. Her very serious expression burst into a huge smile. "Yes!"

"Oh thank God!" Chris picked her up and whirled her around again.

"Where's my ring?" Kara asked.

"Not so fast. You have to wait till tonight. Like I planned."

"Chris Magli!" She popped him playfully on the shoulder. "You are so mean!"

The phone rang.

"I'll get it," Noelle said going to the foyer table where the phone sat. "Hello? Grandma. Where are you? Everyone's here . . . yes. Sure. Just a minute."

Noelle walked up to Susie. "It's your mother. She wants to talk to you."

Susie took the phone. "Mother, wait till you see this tree. Your designer will be green with . . . what's wrong?"

The laugher died.

The candles flickered. Only once.

The room went cold.

"Oh my God," Susie said turning ashen.

Instinctively, Noelle turned on her heel and faced her mother. Dread swept over her as Chris held his breath.

"We'll be right there." Susie's hand was shaking as she tried to depress the 'talk' button. A sob born from the depths of her soul exploded.

"Daddy's had a heart attack."

*　　*　　*　　*　　*

Susie raced through the hospital corridor with Chris, Noelle, Jarod carrying Angela, Kara and Jed running behind her, their coats flapping open like a swooping flock of dark angels.

Mary Elizabeth had just walked out of ICU with the doctor.

"Mother!" Susie shouted too loudly, disrupting the workers and patients, but she didn't care. Her father was dying.

Mary Elizabeth's white face was streaked with tears. She threw her arms around her only child. "He's barely hanging on. He wants to see you as soon as you got here."

Susie glanced at Doctor Tremont. He nodded. "Go. Quickly. There's not much time."

She stared at him. Her mind refused to let the truth enter. *Not much time. What does that mean?*

Susie pushed the door open and held her breath.

How could this be? How could he suddenly be so weak and tiny and white?

"Daddy."

Her legs were suddenly lead. She could barely walk, knowing each step she took to be with him, gave him less reason to hang on.

"Angel," he breathed the word slowly, his lips barely moving. "It hurts."

"Fight it, Daddy. Don't leave me here!" she pleaded.

His eyes were pale floating orbs in a cloudy sea.

When did his eyes grow so milky? When did he get so frail? Why didn't I see?

How could I have saved him?

"I have something to tell you, Susie," he whispered in nearly inaudible sounds. "They told me . . . I have to go. Can't stay here anymore."

"Who told you that?" she asked incredulously.

"The beings of light. They're calling me. I can see them," he said, awe filling his expression as he looked just past Susie towards the wall.

What is he seeing?

Tears flooded her eyes. *I hate death. I hate death.*

She squeezed his hand. "Stay. Don't go. Don't go." She thought that if she clung very hard to him, she could keep him on earth. She could will him back to health. "You're not a quitter. You never were."

"Take care of your mother."

"Daddy, no."

He could barely talk. His breath was shallow, his eyes closed, and somehow, she knew he'd never open them again. He wasn't listening to her. Nothing she said was making a difference.

All she could do was allow God to have His way.

"Daddy. If you have to go, when you get to heaven, tell Tommy I love him."

"He knows, angel." He swallowed hard, forcing himself to speak. "But I'll talk to him for you."

"Promise?"

"Promise," he breathed painfully.

His eyelids dropped, the pressure on her hand eased and Braxton slipped away.

A shrill noise from a machine behind her jolted her.

"Flat line!" Someone shouted.

Rubber soled shoes squeaked against floor tiles as nurses scrambled into the ICU area. Metal rings scratched against a steel rod as a nurse flung a curtain around Braxton's bed. Plastic wheels of a two-tiered stainless steel cart containing clanging instruments rattled against the floor. A cacophony of human fear filled the air.

People have it all wrong. Death is not silent. It's loud and frightening like banshees in a nightmare.

Doctor Tremont rushed into the room. "Get me the paddles!"

"You have to leave, Miss," a female nurse said.

"No!" Susie sobbed.

Doctor Tremont shouted orders. "Get her out of here! Clear!"

Mary Elizabeth rushed to Susie's side.

Susie clung to her father's hand. "He's not dead. He's still warm, Mother. Here, feel his hand."

"Susie," Mary Elizabeth urged through her sobs, "come with me."

"Nurse!" Doctor Tremont shouted. "Prepare the Epinephrine."

"Yes, doctor," a voice answered hurriedly.

"Clear! Clear!"

Above the din, Susie could still hear the heart monitor screaming out it's flat line state. Blinded by a wall of tears, she felt as if she had a blindfold on. She heard Noelle scream for her grandfather outside the door. "No! Not my Grandpa!" she wailed.

Susie heard Chris' despair-filled moan. She remembered reading once that in death hearing was the last of the senses to go.

"Daddy!" *Can you hear me?*

"Susie," Mary Elizabeth said in a calm, disconnected tone, "he's dead."

She looked at her mother. "This is what it feels like?"

Mary Elizabeth nodded and pulled Susie into her arms.

"I couldn't do anything. I couldn't help him. I don't know what to do," Susie sobbed, "except cry."

The funeral was held the day after Christmas. Holy Name Cathedral was nearly full with friends, clients, fellow parishioners, family and the members of the Sheridan Shore Yacht Club. The mechanic who tuned Braxton's cars sat next to the gardener. The floral designer who decorated the gold and white Christmas tree which Susie had never liked, cried incessantly.

Though still in shock, Susie found that suddenly, she was the head of the Howard household.

In the hospital, Mary Elizabeth had appeared to be strong, but once she was home, Doctor Tremont had found it necessary to tranquilize her.

Mary Elizabeth explained they had been loading the car with food and gifts to take to Noelle's house. Braxton had backed the car out of the garage while Mary Elizabeth carried the cake container and the box of Godiva chocolates out the back door.

She had been chattering away, happy to have the whole family back in Chicago even if it wasn't at their house. She hadn't noticed, at first, that Braxton did not respond. Often, he ignored her.

Just as often, she didn't expect him to respond. It wasn't until she'd finished loading the trunk and opened her car door that she noticed he was slumped over the steering wheel. He was still alive when she called 911. He was still alive when the paramedics came in less than six minutes. He was still alive when they put him in the ambulance.

Mary Elizabeth arrived at the hospital behind the ambulance. After parking the car, she walked into the emergency room where Doctor Tremont met her. She took one look at the man's fallen face and she knew Braxton would not live. She barely remembered calling Susie.

Mary Elizabeth hadn't the first idea of how to arrange a funeral and Susie took over. She called the church, the funeral home director, ordered holy cards, chose the casket, the lining and arranged for the burial plot in the Howard family section of the Wilmette Cemetery. She ordered the casket flowers and found a caterer to handle the family meal after the burial. Then she got on the telephone and spent seven hours calling friends, distant cousins and close associates. A friend of Susie's in advertising at the Chicago Tribune heard about Braxton's death and asked Susie to grant a personal interview the day after the funeral.

"Braxton Howard is a Chicago institution. His life meant something to a lot of people," she had said.

"I'll do the interview."

Noelle helped Susie with the Will and legalities, but she herself, found she was nowhere near as strong as Susie.

"How can you make all these calls, Mother, when you haven't slept in forty hours?"

"I have no choice. Besides, I always told Joannie, Grandmother Howard was very strong. We have a lot of strength in our Howard genes."

"Then where is mine?" Noelle asked.

"You'll have it when you really need it," Susie said, but she could tell Noelle didn't believe her.

Chris leaned on Kara to help him deal with death. Because he'd never known his father, he'd never thought about what it was like to know someone, to love them, to expect them to always be in your life, and then to lose them.

Even in the first hours when they'd gone to the hospital from where Mary Elizabeth had called, Chris had literally depended on Kara to hold him up. He slept with her that night, spooned inside her embrace and sobbed for his grandfather. "I promise I'll never die first, Chris. I'll always be here for you," Kara promised.

Noelle was speechless. No matter what Jarod did to bring her out of her catatonic-like state, she didn't respond. Angela cried incessantly more out of fear of what was happening to the living adults around her than to the fact that her Grandfather was dead.

Angela had walked up to the open casket on Christmas Day and asked Susie, "Why is my Gwandpa in a box?"

"Because he's dead," Susie said, though she wasn't quite sure herself. Susie had spent all her life telling herself that Tommy was not dead. That he was alive. Now she wondered if the reason she'd done that was because she'd never seen his body in a box like this.

Angela leaned over touched Braxton's arm and nudged it. "Gwampa! Wate up!"

Susie scooped Angela into her arms. "Gwampa! Pwease wate up!"

Angela realized that Braxton did not move. And then she knew. "My Gwampa's dead," she sobbed and buried her head in the crook of Susie's neck.

"Yes he is, darling. Grampa is in heaven now."

"I want to see him, Gwamma. I want to see him."

Flooded eyes kept Susie from seeing the people around her. Loving people who came to help. Came to offer condolences. People whose hearts were not in so much pain.

Joannie gave the eulogy and when she finished, every person agreed with her that the world would not be quite the same without Braxton Howard in it.

As the priest finished the last prayers of the Mass, Susie lifted her eyes to the stained glass windows where the sun poured into the cathedral showering them all with rainbows of colored light.

"Be well, Daddy, and if you see Tommy up there, don't forget to tell him I love him."

New York. New Year's Eve, 1994.

Tommy slept fitfully on the sofa in the glow of the blue Christmas lights. Dick Clark was counting down to midnight, the Times Square Ball was about to drop, but Tommy wasn't on the earth.

"Hello, Tommy. I thought I'd find you here," Braxton said.

"Who are you?" Tommy asked.

"You know who I am."

"Not really. But you called me Tommy."

"That's your name," Braxton said.

"Tommy what?"

"Three kings. Remember the feast of the Three Kings."

"The Epiphany," Tommy said.

Braxton smiled. "Well, I have to go now. I just came here to tell you that."

"Here? Where is here?"

"I'm on the Other Side. But you're still in the dream."

"What dream?" Tommy asked.

"The earth dream. It's not reality, you know," Braxton explained. "You're living the dream. I'm living reality."

281

Confused, Tommy asked, "Who are you?"

"Take care, son," Braxton said and vanished.

"Son? Am I your son? Are you my father?"

Tommy awoke with a jump. He felt as if he'd fallen from a great height. He clung to the sofa.

Raking his hand through his hair, he bolted off the sofa. "What was that? What the devil was that?"

Hand shaking, he steadied himself against the back of a wing chair. "Something is wrong. Something is wrong in the universe. I can feel it. It's as if someone very close to me has died."

He looked around him. Everything was just as he'd left it. No glass broken. Pictures still hung on the walls in tidy straight lines.

No earthquake.

But he felt as if he'd just lived through an earthquake.

"My journal." He rushed to the bedroom. Grasping his journal off his bedside table, he opened it.

"Write the dream. What did he call me?"

Though fresh, the dream was already fading.

"Tommy!"

Chills shot down his back.

"My name is Tommy and something about the three kings."

"Tommy King. Kingsley. Kingman. King . . ."

On the television, he heard the crowd roar as the ball dropped. Auld Lang Syne played in the background. Then Dick Clark's voice faded.

The dream became clear again.

"My name is Tommy. And someone is trying to contact me. Someone who just died. Someone I used to know."

Goosebumps enveloped him.

For the first time in his life, there was nothing cold about them.

Chapter Thirty-Four

New York, November, 1995.

From the night of his spiritual visitation, Tommy's dreams came in waves, stacked on top of each other so that Tommy would have to wake himself up to write down what he was being told. Though his ghostly visitor never revealed his own name, he guided, prodded and informed Tommy about his past in snippets and clips revealing a life like a film that had been spliced once too often. It was there, but it made no sense.

To get even more focused, Tommy remembered Dr. Kline's suggestion to try formal meditation. The more he relaxed about himself, his work, his life, the more information he received.

By St. Patrick's Day, Tommy dreamed about Susie. He saw her face as a young girl. He knew her name was Susie. He saw their wedding day, but could not pinpoint the city. He knew now that it was her voice he'd been hearing all these years. He saw her riding in a red 1965 Mustang and saying, "And we'll stay at the Plaza. The Plaza is the best."

By Easter, he began a series of dreams with symbols. For a month and a half, he tried to draw the symbols but they meant nothing to him. The first looked like a blue shield. Sometimes he saw a cross. Sometimes he saw the cross on top of the shield. At first, he thought it was a family coat of arms. But searching libraries and the Internet did not bring him any closer to recognition.

By the Fourth of July, his dreams showed him a seal. He saw himself walking over the seal. It was not the United States seal, nor that of a foreign country. He focused on the seals of each and every one of the states of the union.

Nothing.

He made a catalogue of seals and coats of arms, focusing on each for a day. If his memory was not jarred, he put a red cross through the icon and moved on to the next.

In August, he took on a case involving a custody battle between a Manhattan socialite, Charlotte Banning Blake, and her Hollywood producer ex-husband, over their twin daughters. When the woman came to his office complete with a nanny, a personal assistant and the twins in tow, Tommy froze.

"Twins." He looked at her, then at the twins and back to the mother.

"You did read my file, didn't you Mr. Kelly? You look at them as if you hadn't a clue . . ."

"Twins," he held his breath. "I have twins."

"Really? I didn't know you were married," Mrs. Blake said.

Smiling he looked up. "Yes. I am. And I have twins."

"How old are they?"

"They would be twenty-nine now. They were born on . . . on . . ."

"On what, Mr. Kelly?"

"September twenty-fifth," he said proudly, this new information ringing true to the marrow of his bones. "A boy and a girl. Just fraternal twins."

"Well, I'm here to discuss my identical twins, Mr. Kelly," she said.

"Of course," he replied making a note to himself to search databases for all twins born twenty-nine to thirty years ago.

He was finding his life. And nothing was going to stop him until it all fell into place.

Chicago, Illinois - Thanksgiving

Susie and Jed were driving to Mary Elizabeth's house for Thanksgiving dinner when her car phone rang.

"Noelle," Jed said.

"Nah, Kara." She smiled.

"One dollar says it's Noelle," Jed challenged.

"You're on. Hello?"

"Girlfriend, you are not, just not, going to believe where I'm calling you from!" Sherry said.

"I give. Where?"

Jed leaned over. "Noelle?" He mouthed.

"Sherry!" She nodded to Jed.

He snapped his fingers, giving her the 'aw shucks' look.

"Where are you?" Susie asked.

"I have been in Saigon for the past month! It's for a case I'm working on for the firm. But I figured, what the heck. Remember, last year I said I'd find Tommy for you?

"I do."

"Well, I got a lead. I can't promise anything, but I'm going to Cambodia to check out this one helicopter crash site. I'll call you if I dig up anything. But don't throw in the towel yet, okay?"

Susie turned white. "Please don't waste your time."

"Susie, don't you want to really know? If there are remains, don't you want them sent home? Don't you want closure?"

"No. Yes. I guess."

"I'm all the way over here. There are files I can get to these days that I couldn't pry open with a napalm bomb before this, you know?"

"I know."

"I gotta run. But say a prayer. What if, by some fluke, he's still alive?"

"He is," she said suddenly, shocked at herself. Even to this day, no matter what she'd said to anyone to appease them, even to herself, deep down, she'd never given up on Tommy. She was still hoping. Her soul was still praying.

New York, December 3, 1995.

The dream terrified him. He felt a stinging in his heart, but knew he was not shot. The pain went deep inside him where he could harbor it and pretend it didn't exist. Like a menacing dragon who slides into his cavern lair for centuries, biding its time, waiting for his day of reckoning, the evil slept.

Then he heard the voices.

"You'll learn, the less you know the better," the man's voice said.

Even in the dream, Tommy recognized the voice. He heard the sound of the helicopter blades as they flew over the jungle.

"Cambodia," another voice said.

He felt a stabbing pain in his heart. The pain was not physical, but emotional. His innocence had been shot. Adrenaline pounded through his body as he fought for his life.

Who was this man he was fighting? How did he get on board? Why were his hands around his throat, trying to strangle him?

Tommy's head hung out the open doorway. He saw the earth rising up to meet him. They were going to crash.

"I'm no coward!" he shouted in the dream.

Death was coming for him, but not from the gunshot. Not from the Cong. The betrayal was killing him.

The helicopter blades whooped. Gunfire. Bullets whizzed toward them. He fought off his attacker.

He grabbed the gun, ready to fire at the enemy as they flew closer to extinction.

A vision of a girl's face wafted across his mind.

"Susie," he called, thinking she would come to him.

I love you. I'm coming home.

The dream went black.

Tommy bolted awake. "Holy Mother of God!" Sweat slaked his entire body. His muscles were so tensed, he ached all over. He bolted out of bed and began pacing.

That was it. Something happened on that helicopter. Something before we crashed. I was betrayed. But who? Why? No one else knew what was happening. Where was everyone else? Why can't I remember?

He stopped pacing. He gazed out the window; snow was falling, coating the bare tree branches with fluffy icy mounds. "Susie."

He dropped to his knees. "Susie. Susie!"

He saw every facet of her face. Extending his palm he believed he could touch her. He snapped his hand back. "Who are you that you can haunt me so and not tell me where the hell you are?"

The dream held the truth and it settled into the dark lair where the dragon slept.

In that instant, the past awoke.

He jumped to his feet with glee.

The rush of his awakening took his breath away and made his head ache. "I need an aspirin."

He went to the bathroom and closed the medicine chest and peered into his reflection.

"What happened on that chopper, man? What do you know that terrorized you so much you blocked Susie out of your mind and life for three decades."

The reflection was silent.

Hoping to prompt his mind out of oblivion, he repeated. "Susie. Susie."

He saw symbols again and they whirled like a kaleidoscope and finally the colors fell into place.

"Sweetheart of Sigma Chi," he heard inside his head as if the reflection had spoken.

Eyes rounding into globes of awareness, he took a deep breath. "The coat of arms! That was the Sigma Chi coat of arms I've been seeing for years!"

Memories flooded him.

"The blue lights on the Christmas tree. Fraternity house. Making love . . . to Susie. Christmas Eve."

Her voice flooded the room like a tidal wave. *"The Christmas Star, Tommy. It will always be our star."*

A puzzled look flew across his face. "The Christmas Star? What's that about?"

Star. Star. Christmas. Star.

"It comes back every thirty years, Tommy. I read it in the newspaper," she said.

Tommy instantly went to his laptop and logged into the Internet. "If it was in the newspaper once, there has to be a record.

Scrolling through the archives of *The New York Times*, Tommy found an article the week prior regarding the Christmas Star.

"My God! This thing does return every thirty years."

The Christmas Star can be viewed best from one o'clock in the morning of December 24 and December 25 in the southwestern quadrant of the sky.

Tommy rubbed his arms, chasing eerie chills away. "Am I nuts? Or do I get the distinct feeling none of this is by chance?"

Staring at the laptop's screen saver of galaxy's of stars, Tommy found himself free falling back in time to bits of the life he'd forgotten.

He saw himself walking up the steps of a huge mansion. He saw the faces of two older people in their early forties.

Braxton. Mary Elizabeth.

"I know them! I know this house."

As if he was time traveling, he walked through the expensive double doors of a mansion. He saw Mary Elizabeth standing in a formal living room, her jewels glittering in the light from the crackling fire in the fireplace. She wore a threatening look on her face and he could sense she did not like him. Braxton was holding a crystal glass with curiosity creasing his brow.

Elaborate floral decorations the likes of which he'd never seen festooned the double staircase, banister, mantle and reception hall. A twenty-foot plus tall white-flocked tree stood majestically in the living room. Glittering gold balls, gold brocade bows, gold frosted berries, gold birds, and delicate Renaissance gold angels studded the tree.

"A designer did the tree," Susie whispered to him. "I hate it."

Tommy didn't say anything to her at the time, but he knew he loved it. He loved the majesty and triumph of it. To him it looked as if the angels were flying down from the clouds of heaven. In that moment he thought he understood Susie's parents better than she did. They were strong people who believed deeply in all they stood for. He sensed they were proud and though their pride might be currently misguided by ego, they were not vindictive or mean hearted.

They only wanted the best for their daughter. It was their right and he wanted desperately to tell them he understood their misgivings.

Before he had a chance to say a word, Mary Elizabeth fainted.

Seeing her drop to a heap, Tommy came out of the meditation.

"Braxton was the ghost who came to me last year in that dream. He told me my name. *He* is Susie's father!"

The vision and the information began to fade. Slamming his hand on his desk he shouted, "Wait! Come back! What are your last names?"

Inhaling deeply to muster more courage, he stiffened his back and placed his fingers on the keyboard.

"There can't be that many Braxton's in this country," he said to himself as he began his Internet search for a man and name he'd seen in a meditation.

December 20, 1995.

Sherry sat on the plane going over notes, replaying her tape recorder and logging information into her laptop. What had started out for her as a favor to a friend and simple curiosity on her own part, had turned into one of the most bizarre investigations of her life.

Through her days in Washington to her new life in New York defending influential clients, she'd never dreamed that she would be the key to uncovering a case of military intelligence espionage and unearthing counterspies.

Her initial research for her law firm was completed in a week in Cambodia. Once she'd started to track down Tommy Magli, she found clues that had never been checked out. Information about his mission had been purposefully passed over by the military at the time. By the time the United States was pulling out of Vietnam, the military had determined that Tommy Magli was missing in action.

Sherry flew to the site of the helicopter crash and found all debris long gone or grown over. The military had searched the area several times and never found any clues. She went to the nearby village, which was now four times the size it was thirty years ago. While drinking a cup of tea at a local café, she was approached by a man of about thirty-nine or forty.

"The last time I saw an American, he was wearing a uniform."

"When was that?" she asked.

"Ten years. Others . . . like you. Dey come. Look for missing men. Dey look trails to past. You here, same t'ing?"

"Yes. How did you know?"

"Look 'round," he extended his arms. "No'ting here. You waste trip . . . fly across world for no'ting. Only t'ing here is . . ."

"Secrets?" she asked.

His dark eyes pierced her. "Who you look for?"

"Tommy Magli."

"Don't know him."

Sherry's eyes perused his face carefully. "You speak awfully good English for a local."

"I learn in da war. My sister ran away with GI. She marry him. She live in Los Angeles. Now she send me photographs. We e-mail."

"You're kidding."

"No. Life is different now."

Sherry chuckled. "Thank God." She drained her tea, then looked up at him. "What's your name?"

"Nguyen."

"Nice to meet you," she smiled.

He lingered at her table. He moved his foot as if to walk away, yet he remained.

"You have a secret, don't you, Nguyen? One you've never told?"

"I like your face," he said taking a chair from the rickety table behind him and sitting down.

Chills coursed her spine. "Tell me."

"It was in 1966. September."

Sherry sucked in her breath. "Not the twenty-fifth?"

"Yes, twenty-fifth. The helicopter shot down close here."

"I saw the area."

"The GI's all dead. Split apart. In pieces. It was bad. Except one."

"One?"

"Michael Kelly. I drag him to my aunt's hut. He was heavy. Very difficult. He was tall and I was only ten. My aunt box my ears for putting us in danger. He live in hole in ground we cover with a mattress. Tree weeks den he come out. Many wounds. His head, too. We take care him."

"This Michael. You liked him."

"He my friend," Nguyen said sadly. "He try to help us go to United States. But he fail. It grieve him."

"You saved his life."

Nguyen nodded. "I t'ink of him. Last week I have dream 'bout him. He is young in dream. Now he is old. I am old," he chuckled lightly, then stared at the marred tabletop.

"Was he very tall?"

"Yes. Tall even for American."

"Dark hair? Blue eyes? Good looking?"

"Yes," he replied. "But kind eyes. Good man."

"And his name was Michael? That makes no sense to me. The man you are describing sounds like Tommy."

"His papers say Michael Kelly of New York City. He lose his brain. No memory."

Sherry's eyes shot wide open and she slapped her palm on her forehead. "Amnesia?"

Nguyen shrugged his shoulders and shook his head.

"He . . . he not remember his name."

Sherry shivered. Her mind raced a million miles a minute. She could nearly hear the pieces of Tommy's life falling into place. The roar of it was exhilarating.

"He not remember anyt'ing. Not his name. Where he live. He have dreams at night. Very bad. De crash, he say."

She stood and extended her hand. "I want to thank you for sharing this information with me, Nguyen. You have helped me tremendously. I want you to know. I live in New York City. I will look up Michael Kelly and I'll tell him that I met you.

Nguyen smiled. "You tell him I have dream 'bout him. I t'ink 'bout him."

"You were more than friends, Nguyen. You were like brothers. Saving his life was very heroic. I personally want to thank you."

"You welcome."

Once back in Saigon, Sherry poured over military records for both Michael Kelly and Tommy Magli. She discovered that Tommy's commanding officer was Albert Aloysius Brookings the Third. *The Boston Brookings?* Using her laptop, she searched databases for information on Brookings from Boston.

She scanned the Boston Globe archives for any information on the Boston Brookings and found plenty.

Indeed, A.A. Brookings III was from an illustrious family, but he was a thorn in his father's side. A.A. Brookings, III had a police record. On two occasions, he'd been arrested for possession of marijuana in the early sixties when drugs were not widely used. He was accused of two thefts in high school. One of the high school principal's house from which he stole money, alcohol and a gold pocket watch. His father hired an expensive Boston lawyer and the case was dismissed.

The second incident occurred in his senior year when he stole three cases of beer from the loading dock of a local Irish pub. A.A. Brookings did community service time and paid a fine of five hundred dollars.

In his freshman year at Harvard, he was kicked out for cheating. In his sophomore year at Boston University, he was suspended for alcohol possession and disorderly conduct. One account of an on-campus brawl contained the fact that A.A. Brookings had sustained a broken arm and a concussion. He and three other freshmen had created a chapter of a radical Marxist-Leninist group. No disciplinary action was taken. However, he was finally expelled for cheating on a semester exam.

Sherry stopped. "Why would this privileged kid hook up with socialists? Something's not right here."

Instinctively, she back-tracked and found a file dating back to his prep-school days. In sixth grade, A.A. Brookings attended a Jesuit school. His counselor and mentor was Father Pedro Negrin. In the dossier was an article about Pedro Negrin who claimed relationship to Juan Negrin, the famous Socialist doctor who led the Spanish government in 1937 after the rebellion in Barcelona. Pedro Negrin had left Spain and gone to Russia to study to become a Jesuit priest at a time when Marxist ideals were being spread across all of Europe.

Sherry couldn't believe her eyes. A.A. Brookings had Communist leanings since puberty. "No wonder he fought his capitalist father tooth and nail."

She opened another file.

"So if you were Communist, A.A., what the hell were you doing on a chopper headed into Cambodia on a secret mission for the US? Unless it was your intent to make sure all those men never came back."

New York. Friday, December 21, 1995.

Walking out of the New York City Court House, his trial over with a plea bargain that would please his partners into granting huge year-end bonuses to the firm's staff, Tommy hailed a cab.

A college student, dressed in jeans, Nike shoes and a purple and gold Northwestern University jacket got out of the cab and held his hand out to an elderly woman. "C'mon, Grandma. I'll help you."

"Oh, thank you, Jed." She crawled across the bench seat and stood with the aid of her cane and her grandson's arm.

Tommy stared at the Northwestern symbol. His memory came rocketing back. In an instant he saw the University's seal. He saw his own feet walking over the seal. For years he'd thought the seal was a state seal of some kind. It had never occurred to him it was a university seal.

"Chicago," he breathed the word aloud.

"Pardon me, sir?" the young man asked.

"You're from Chicago."

"I go to school there. Northwestern. I'm in pre-law."

"So was I," Tommy smiled as broadly as he could. Suddenly, his face fell again. "Jed. She said your name was Jed?"

"That's right. Say, do I know you?" The young man started backing his grandmother away from Tommy nervously.

"No. It's just that, well. My father's name is Jed," Tommy smiled even wider.

"Cool beans. Well, we gotta go," the young man said, taking the older woman by the arm.

"Sure. Sure." Tommy nodded.

"Hey, buddy," the cabbie said. "I ain't got all day."

"Yeah."

As they rode downtown, Tommy's mind was filled with hundreds of vignettes. His life came swirling back at him like a funnel cloud. He saw his father when he was a child. He played baseball with his dad. He saw his mother in a coffin and this time he felt overwhelming sadness and loss. He saw his father sitting idly in a Lazy Boy chair watching television. He saw a bottle of Jack Daniels and a scrawny Christmas tree. He heard his father's voice. He heard laughter and tears.

He heard everything except a last name.

Back in his office, Tommy called his assistant, Gretchen. "Book me on a flight to Chicago. Tomorrow if you can," he said shuffling through the stack of phone messages on his desk.

"You have Mr. William's attorney here tomorrow. You can't cancel this close to Christmas. Unless you'll be back for Christmas."

"Back?" The thought hadn't struck him. If he went to Chicago looking for a life he lost, would he even want to come back to this life? Would he want to keep that life? And what if Susie, whoever she was, wasn't there? What if she was dead? What if she had another life? Another husband. What if she didn't want him anymore? And what would he tell her?

Sorry I forgot about you for thirty years.

His stomach turned over.

What am I doing?

He had first names of several people in his life, but he still didn't have answers. He had unearthed a half-life. Not a whole one.

He was in no-man's land. It was more frightening than hell.

"Forget it."

Her hand fell to her thigh still grasping her Palm Pilot on which she recorded everything. Even her daily calorie intake. "Forget the ticket or the Williams' appointment?"

"The ticket."

"Good," she said looking down. "Because everything is booked. Solid. It's Christmas. Most people plan for it, you know," she said sarcastically.

Throwing her a teasing smirk, he said, "I got that memo."

"Tomorrow is Saturday. Most people have Saturday off. But not me. No. I'm loyal to my boss. He's a nice guy. He doesn't really need me to work on Saturday before Christmas!" She elevated her voice with each word.

"Huh?" he said fumbling with his cursor. "Tomorrow is great!" He waved to her over the computer screen.

"Clueless," she mumbled to herself and left.

Tommy went back to his laptop. "I've been doing this all wrong. I've been looking for live people. What if Jed is dead? What if Braxton is dead?"

Logging on, he began with obituaries that went back to 1965. He began his search with all males over thirty-five with a first name of Jed.

The list was in the thousands. He narrowed it to those in Chicago and the surrounding suburbs.

Information flew at him at lightening speed.

Night fell. The staff closed down their desks for the day. A knock on his open door jolted him out of his reverie.

It was Mark Carter, a new law school graduate. He was one of the few unattached males in the small firm along with Tommy. Everyone knew Michael Kelly seldom dated and if he did it was a blind date with somebody's sister who was in town. Michael's years with Amy had left him with the reputation for being incapable of commitment.

"You wanna go grab a beer? Scotch maybe?"

Tommy looked up. "Mark?"

In that instant, he didn't see Mark Carter. His memory showed him a scene of himself walking across Northwestern's campus. Mark Conner, not Carter, came up to him.

I'm outta here, man. The voice from the past said.

I screwed up. I bet I don't pull even a 65 on the first course....I'm driving to Toronto with Jesse there. I love this place. My father went here. And his father. This can't be happening to me.

Suddenly, Tommy knew what had happened to him. He'd screwed up, too. He'd flunked out. He'd either been drafted or he enlisted.

That was how he came to be in the Marines.

"Hey, Dude! Snap out of it!" Mark Carter said. "You comin' or not?"

"I c . . . can't."

"I know you don't have a date!"

Tommy stared at him somberly. "I've decided it's time I got a life."

"You? No way! Sorry, old man. No offense. It's never too late they say," Mark hit the doorjamb with his palm. "Well, hey, wish me luck. Maybe I'll find the woman of my dreams tonight."

Woman of my dreams.

"Good luck," Tommy said and gave him a salute.

"Thanks. I'm probably going to need it."

296

Chapter Thirty-Five

New York, Saturday, December 22, 1995.

Tommy found the biggest part of his life in the obituaries. In an article in *The Chicago Tribune,* he found a memorial to Braxton Howard. There was a photograph.

The second Tommy saw it, he slapped his back against his chair wanting as much distance from the shock of the truth as he could find.

The man staring out of the photograph was the face of the man who'd come to him in a dream and told him his name was Tommy. He was the same man who had been standing in the mansion with Susie in his meditation. Braxton Howard had indeed visited him from The Other Side, just as he'd stated. It wasn't a dream after all.

His mouth went dry as adrenaline barreled through his body. His fingers shook as he scrolled the cursor down on the computer screen.

The obituary stated that Braxton Howard left a wife, Mary Elizabeth, a daughter, Susie Howard Magli, and two grandchildren, Christopher Magli and Noelle Magli both twenty-eight years old.

"Twins!" Tommy breathed the word reverently.

Susie Magli.

My name is Tommy Magli.

Without reading the rest of the obituary, he logged on to the Northwestern University web site. Photographs of the campus rang true in his memory. He found the telephone number to the administration office.

"Hello, I'm trying to track down my academic records for a job interview I'm having the first of the year. I wonder if you could help me."

"Of course, sir. And your name?"

"Tommy Magli." It was the first time in thirty years he'd said his name aloud and it felt like resurrection. He wanted to

297

shout his name from the top of the Empire State Building. He wanted to write it one hundred times on a black board. He wanted to sign it on his driver's license.

"That would be Thomas Magli, I assume," the woman said.

"Ah, yes."

"Address?"

"I'm . . . in New York."

"I mean your address at the time of your admission."

"I don't remember exactly, but I was there in 1965."

"That's fine, sir. This will take awhile to locate. I can mail your records to you."

"I need them faster!" he said too anxiously. "I mean, that if you could fax them that would be fine. I don't need an original."

"We close at noon on Saturdays, sir."

"Please? You would make my Christmas if you could do this for me."

"Well . . . okay. What's your fax?"

"212-556-8787," he said. "And you can find it this morning?"

"Hold on. Sir, I found it. Must not be that many people on-line. Okay. I'm sending the file to you via email and by fax."

"This is great!" he said.

After the information came through, Tommy found the web page of the National headquarters of Sigma Chi. He requested a list of the pledges and actives at Northwestern University in 1965 and 1966.

Within fifteen minutes, Tommy was staring at two lists on which the name Thomas J. Magli appeared.

The moment was surreal. Had he been an alien on another planet, he couldn't have felt more out of place.

"I am Thomas Joseph Magli. Of Calumet City, Illinois." He said the words aloud for his senses to absorb their impact. "I was top of my class. I met Susie Howard at a mixer on campus. I fell in love with her at first sight."

Holy Name Cathedral is my favorite church for midnight Mass.

"That's where she'll be!"

He hit his speakerphone. "Gretchen. I don't care how you do it, get me on a plane to Chicago. Today. In the next couple hours if possible."

"Sir, you have never traveled on a Friday at Christmas."

"I know that. What's that got to do with anything?"

"Did you ever see that movie? *Trains, Planes and Automobiles?*"

"No."

"Rent it. Then let's talk," Gretchen quipped.

"I said, I don't care how you do it!"

"Hey, be nice. I gave up my Saturday morning to work with you on this goofy stuff."

"I am eternally grateful. I mean that sincerely."

"Okay. Reservations. Yeech! But it's your life," she snapped and hung up.

Tommy smiled. "Yes. It is."

Tommy grabbed his coat, cell phone and laptop. He flung the door to his office open.

"I'm going home to pack. Call me on my cell when you get me a flight."

Glaring at her boss, Gretchen said, "I take it I'm through for the day?"

"Uh, huh," he said thrusting his arms into his over coat. "Just get me a flight!" he said excitedly.

"Don't hold your breath. So far, I can route you to Atlanta then to Chicago. It'll take nearly a day to get there."

"I don't care!" He replied jubilantly.

"What? You won't stand in line for Starbucks!" she gasped.

"This is different," he beamed. "I'm going home!" He raced out of the office, waving back to Gretchen. "Book those e-tickets then take off. Merry Christmas!"

Rising out of her chair she leaned over the desk to watch him fly down the hall, his overcoat flapping behind him like a cape. He kissed the Fed Ex delivery woman on the cheek and wished her a Merry Christmas. He hugged one of the paralegals who was coming out of the elevator and wished her a Merry Christmas.

The Fed Ex woman walked into the office. "What's up with him?"

Gretchen shook her head. "Too many reruns of Scrooge."

Tommy packed in a flash. His mind racing faster than his hands could fly, most of what he threw in his suitcase he didn't need. He left behind his toiletries, cellular batteries, but he remembered his Daytimer. Finding a cab, he headed for Kennedy airport. As he passed through the city streets for the first time in thirty years, every Christmas light, tree, wreath, child's face and church bell took on a new meaning for him.

He had been robbed of his life all these years. He could wallow in self-pity and blame fate, God and the government for his lost years.

Instead, he chose to thank them all.

Tommy Magli was one human being who knew poignantly, the precariousness of every second one has with their family.

For the rest of his life, he wouldn't waste time again.

Gretchen looked up at the exhausted looking woman standing in front of her.

"I need to see Mr. Kelly. It's urgent," Sherry Wilson said.

"I'm sorry, Miss Wilson, that's impossible," Gretchen said.

Gretchen glanced at the appointment book. "Maybe we could book you for January . . ."

Sherry slammed her palm on the desk. "Look, I've been on a plane for two days and a half. I'm still jet lagged. I have to see him."

"Mr. Kelly isn't here."

"Not here?"

"That's what I've been trying to tell you. He left about an hour ago."

"When will he be back?"

"He didn't say. He's on his way to Chicago."

Sherry gasped. "Chicago? Then he knows?"

"Knows what?"

Sherry calmed herself. "Did he mention a Tommy Magli?"

"Is he a client?" Gretchen asked.

"No."

"I don't understand." Gretchen's eyebrows knitted.

Sherry glanced around the office. "You don't happen to have any photographs of Mr. Kelly, do you?"

Gretchen bristled. "Say, what kind of joke is this?"

"Believe me, it's not a joke. I have information that could be of vital importance to Mr. Kelly. I think. If he is Mr. Kelly." Sherry paused thoughtfully. "Does he have a cellular number where I could reach him?

Gretchen was guarded. "That's a private number. I'm not allowed to give it out to anyone. Even Mr. McHenry doesn't have that number," Gretchen lied.

Sherry forced a smile. "I know you don't know me. I used to be a lobbyist in Washington. Now I work at a law firm in New York. I can get my own secretary and my law partners on the phone if you need convincing." Sherry leaned over the desk again. She was nose to nose with a stunned Gretchen. "I need his cell number. Got it?"

Gretchen swallowed hard. "First, give me your secretary's phone number."

Sherry straightened and folded her arms over her chest. "It's 212-899-4350."

Gretchen dialed the number.

"The Pentagon should hire you," Sherry said.

Without glancing up, Gretchen said, "I worked there for two years."

"Figures."

Gretchen verified Sherry's credentials and gave her Tommy's private cellular number.

Sherry dialed the number on her own cellular phone.

"We're sorry. But all circuits are busy now."

Tommy flew to Atlanta, but the lay over was seven hours until he could catch the flight to Chicago. While he waited, he placed calls to Chicago directory assistance.

He wrote down the address of Mrs. Braxton Howard. And as he did, the scene of the mansion came back to him. Each time he placed the smallest bit of information into his head, his memory banks opened like file drawers.

He went to the airport restaurant and ordered a slice of pizza. Chicago style. Just looking at the pizza, he remembered that his father loved to make his own pizza.

In the next moment, he remembered his old telephone number.

Dialing his father's number, he realized his cellular battery was running low.

He went to the pay phones but had to stand in line for nearly thirty minutes to make a call. The call was never picked up. Not wanting to frighten his father at the shock of hearing his voice, he decided not to leave a recording.

* * * * *

Jed raced into the house when he heard the phone ringing. "I thought you'd get that," he said to Susie who was loaded down with a dollhouse she'd made for Angela.

"The wall fell down and I was regluing it. I figured they'd leave a message."

Jed checked the recorder. "Nope, no message."

"Did you get the pastries yet?"

"Profiteroles. Best I've ever made," he said proudly. "And already in the backseat."

"I put our overnight cases in the back."

"I saw," Jed said. "This is going to be the best Christmas we ever had," Jed said merrily.

"You say that every year," Susie said.

"Well, I have a feeling about this one," he said picking up the newspaper. "Did you see this article? The Christmas Star is back. Thirty years ago tomorrow night," he said. "Some astronomers think it's the Star of Bethlehem, but I guess you already know that."

"Uh, huh."

Susie's eyes swam as she looked at the newspaper. *That was the night Tommy and I . . .*

Her heart ached under the weight of her memories and her hopes never fulfilled.

Jed saw her tears. "There now," he put his arm around her shoulder. "You'll hear from Sherry. Is she back now?"

"She should have been today or yesterday. I left a message at her apartment."

"Well," Jed said taking the doll house from her and carrying it to the front door, " . . . then you will. She's a good girl. She'll do the best she can."

"She can't bring the dead back," Susie replied.

Jed looked away, took a deep breath and put his mind back on loading the Explorer.

Tommy gazed out the massive window at the pelting rain. He overheard passengers as they passed the bad news back and forth throughout the terminal.

"Sleet. Snow. Delays. Cancellations." The words crushed Tommy's hopes of making his connecting flight.

By eleven that night, his flight to Chicago was delayed until morning. There was no hope for it. He was going to have to spend the night in the airport.

Finally finding a vacant seat, he slumped down grasping his hanging bag in his lap.

Weary from excitement and anticipation, his chin fell to his chest.

Sherry dialed Tommy's cellular incessantly. It was early the next morning when she got through.

"Hello," a sleepy male voice answered.

"Is this Michael Kelly?" Sherry asked.

"Yes."

"Thank God. My name is Sherry Wilson. I have been trying to contact you for days."

"Miss Wilson. I'm in Atlanta about to board a plane. Could we talk about this tomorrow?"

"No! It can't wait!"

"I don't understand."

"Frankly, Mr. Kelly, I don't know how to begin. I was hoping to meet you face to face. So that I would know, before I just jumped right into this."

"Know what?" he asked handing his boarding pass to the attendant.

Sherry paused, suddenly unsure of how to begin. What if Michael Kelly was indeed Michael Kelly and not Tommy Magli? How would she explain that? And what if he didn't remember who he was?

Oh, the heck with it.

"Mr. Kelly. Could I ask you a few questions first? Just to make sure I have the right person?"

"Sorry," Tommy said. "But you're breaking up. I'm going down the jet way now and won't be able to talk much longer."

"I think I know who you are."

Tommy entered the plane.

The flight attendant spied his phone. "Sorry, sir, you'll have to turn that off. We are expecting a quick loading time and want to get in the air as quickly as possible."

"So do I!" he replied jubilantly. "You have no idea how long I've waited to make this flight!"

Moving toward his assigned seat, Tommy said to Sherry, "Just a minute. I want to get your number."

"That's not necessary," Sherry said.

"Then I can call you back," he sat down and took a pen out of his inside jacket breast pocket. "Okay, shoot."

"It's 212-899-4350. Now, Mr. Kelly."

"Great! Manhattan. Then we'll have no problem catching up after the holidays. Thanks, Miss Wilson. I'll give you a call." He snapped off his cellular phone.

Sherry listened in stunned silence to the dial tone. "I wish I'd known Tommy better. I don't know if that was his voice or not! I can't call Susie when I'm not certain."

She looked at the clock. "I wonder what time he arrives in Chicago?"

Christmas Eve at O'Hare airport was bedlam. For Tommy, it was eternity just making his way through the terminal to the rental car desk.

"I have a car reserved for Thomas Magli," he said.

The clerk checked the computer. "I'm sorry. Do you have a confirmation number they gave you?"

"Confirmation?" He shook his head. "My assistant forgot to give it to me. Try the name Michael Kelly."

Frowning the clerk cleared his throat. "So which one is it? Kelly or Magli?"

Tommy took out his New York driver's license. "Kelly. Like my license."

"Okay . . . fine. Don't you just love the holidays," the clerk mumbled sarcastically.

Tommy refused to take the man's bait. He was probably as tired as Tommy.

"Sir, I can't find Michael Kelly either. Are you sure you rented with us?"

"I'm a Gold Club member."

"And you made the reservation. For today?"

Tommy cringed. "My flight was delayed in Atlanta. It was for yesterday."

The clerk was surprisingly empathetic. "I don't have a single car. No one does."

"This is not happening," Tommy groaned.

"Sir, there's a shuttle to downtown. My suggestion is to take the bus to Michigan Avenue and either bus or cab from there. It's Christmas Eve, sir. Every cab in the city will be working."

"Good tip," Tommy nodded, picked up his bag and left.

The shuttle bus turned out to be a blessing in disguise. Being a passenger, Tommy was able to view the changes in Chicago since his distant memories of it thirty years ago. Yet many things were the same.

The expressways were wider and the northwestern prairies were overbuilt with housing and strip malls that looked like the rest of homogenized America.

However, the Water Tower still stood proudly on North Michigan Avenue, though it was now surrounded by glittering shopping towers and designer boutique stores. The river sparkled in mid-afternoon sun just the way he remembered. The Tribune Tower and the Wrigley Building struck him with familiar awe.

He got off the bus just as his cellular phone rang.

"Mr. Magli?"

Tommy's heart stopped. "Who is this? And how do you know . . ."

"Who you are?" Sherry finished the thought for him. "Please don't hang up on me this time. I would have called earlier, but I was up all night trying to reach you and then this morning, I fell asleep on the sofa." She sucked in her breath and continued.

"I'm a friend of your wife's."

"Susie?"

"You remember her now?"

"Yes."

"When did you get your memory back?"

"Two days ago. Say, how do you know this?" He asked spying a restaurant. He rushed across the street hoping for a warm corner in which to listen to what Sherry had to say.

"And that's why you are in Chicago? To see Susie?"

"Yes. Is that bad?" He swallowed hard. *Please say no.*

"She's not remarried if that's what you want to know," Sherry said. "She's been waiting for you to come home."

"Impossible." *But wonderful!*

"Not for Susie. That woman's got faith. Buckets of it. It wasn't until after her father died last year that she started to waiver. Doubt herself. She always told the kids and me . . ." she paused. "Did you know about the children?"

"I've had dreams of her telling me about twins. But I don't remember them."

"You shouldn't. You never saw them. Your chopper went down the night she went into labor."

"The same night?"

"Yes. She almost died."

"She died," he gasped. Then he understood. Spiritual events had come together for them both. Perhaps he'd died, too. Perhaps it hadn't been a dream at all. Maybe he and Susie had gone through simultaneous Near-Death-Experiences.

Tommy continued. "I remember the strangest dream. At least I told myself it was a dream. I was in heaven and there was a girl. We promised we'd find each other."

It was Sherry's turn at surprise. "You had the same dream? She told me about that dream. She talks about it all the time. It's one of the reasons she believed you were still alive. It's given her such strength."

"My God."

"Tommy, Susie has moved heaven and earth for thirty years to discover what happened to you. She went to Washington, to the Pentagon. She wrote letters, she joined coalitions, groups, support networks, everything trying to find you. For some bizarre reason, God picked me to be the one to accomplish her goal for her. I had to go to Cambodia on an assignment for my law firm here in New York. Since I was half way around the world and Susie had done me a favor once, I told her I'd dig around and see what I could find out about you. Find your body. I don't know what I thought I'd find."

"You did all this as a favor to Susie?"

"Yes."

"Some favor."

Sherry continued. "She's the only person I know who understands what it takes to be a real friend. She's special."

"I know," he said.

Sherry explained, "I knew I could access files and records a lay person would never be allowed to see. I have several connections in Washington and through them and the fact that many old records are currently being disclosed and made public, I was able to piece together what happened to you."

He wiped his hand over his face, still disbelieving. But still hoping. "There are so many gaps in what I remember."

"I think I can fill in the gaps for you, Tommy. Why your chopper went down. Why it was so traumatic and why you haven't remembered any of this for thirty years."

His voice was somber. "Just recently in the past month, I have finally been able to relive that crash. I saw my Commanding Officer, Lieutenant A.A. Brookings, knife three of the guys on that helicopter. I had my gun trained on the Cong below who were firing on us. He jumped me. We struggled. Instead, our chopper was hit. I jumped out of the doorway just as it blew apart. The blast threw me even further from the wreckage."

"That's when Nguyen found you?"

"You know about him?"

"I met him," she smiled proudly. "What you don't know is that the men on the ground you were supposed to pick up were not wounded or simply missing. They were Green Berets and had been in Cambodia gathering intelligence from the Cong for over six months. The information was so vital, so secret, that had those men gotten back to US intelligence headquarters they could have changed the course of the war. Brookings' job was to see that those men never made it back. As a counter-spy, it was his job to kill them, kill all of you on the chopper and then he had carefully planned to take asylum in Cambodia with the Cong."

"My God! Why would anyone want to do that? I can't fathom that kind of betrayal."

"Exactly. That's why you blocked it out. Brookings hated his decorated, accomplished, war-hero father and grandfather. He felt he could never measure up. His insecurities festered and ate a black hole inside him. I read a psychological profile on him that made me cringe. His father was not only cold and distant, but also abusive. A.A. grew to crave the negative attention his crimes received from his father. In other words, he twisted his life to make his father miserable.

"But to become a traitor to his country . . ."

"It's the same evolution of a serial killer," she explained. "He did it all, as they say, until finally, his recklessness got himself and many others, killed."

Tommy was silent.

"Are you okay? Did I go too far?"

Sucking in a deep breath, Tommy said, "I was just thinking of all the waste. My life. His life. All those lives. Wasted."

Thoughtfully, Sherry asked, "Where are you now?"

Tommy looked out the window. "I don't know. Some café, near Tribune Tower. It's snowing."

"Merry Christmas, Tommy. And welcome home."

"Thanks," he said and hung up.

The Christmas Star

Chapter Thirty-Six

Chicago. Christmas Eve, 1995

Tommy stood in front of the Howard mansion. Though it was only four-thirty, winter night had fallen. Every light in the house was blazing, casting golden puddles of light on the snow covered lawn outside. Each of the windows was decorated with a pine wreath and inside the living room at the window stood a tall Christmas tree lit with blue lights.

"Only blue lights," he inhaled the thought along with the cold December air. "Susie would do that for me. I was right, she must live here now," he said to himself as he walked up the brick walkway.

The trunks of a dozen maple trees that lined the circular drive were wrapped with crystal lights. Beneath the maples, a life-sized manger scene had been erected and was lit by spotlights.

Gone were the flashy designer topiary's and glitzy door decorations he remembered Mary Elizabeth had liked. This house reflected more of the true meaning of Christmas. Knowing Braxton was dead caused him to wonder if his passing had altered Mary Elizabeth's perspective.

Once Sherry had disclosed all of her research into his past, his dreams connected instantly like a follow-the-dot drawing.

He remembered everything now.

Sherry had promised not to telephone Susie ahead of his arrival. He didn't want her shock to come from a phone call.

He knocked on the door.

A man in a tuxedo opened it. "Good evening," he said.

"David?" Tommy asked remembering the name of the butler who had first greeted him in 1965.

"No, sir. Matthew. Is there something I can help you with?"

"I'm here to see Mrs. Magli. Er, and Mrs. Howard. The whole family actually."

"I'm sorry, sir, they've left for Mass."

311

Confused, Tommy checked his watch. "But it's only four-forty. Mass is at Midnight."

"I beg your pardon?" Matthews said. "There is no Midnight service at Holy Name Cathedral. Not since, well, twenty years I know about. It's not good for the children to be up so late on Christmas." He winked.

"Children? I thought they were grown."

"The grandchildren, sir."

Tommy blanched. "Grandchildren."

I'm a grandfather. I've missed so much . . .

"What time does Mass start?"

"Why five o'clock, sir."

"And then they'll be coming back here?"

"Are they expecting you, Mr. . . . ?" Matthews asked cautiously.

Tommy beamed. "I should say they are. And the name is Magli. Tommy Magli."

Clamping his hand over his mouth, Matthew's eyes grew to the size of saucers. "Perhaps you'd like to come in, sir."

"Perhaps you'll call me a cab."

Traffic crawled. The last of the stores were closing and both shoppers and shopclerks emptied out of the Loop buildings.

"Look at the snow coming down now," the cab driver said. "I hate this stuff."

"Christmas isn't Christmas without snow."

"I'm Jewish."

"Hannakah, then."

"Makes me no never mind," the driver said as they crept through the green light.

Tommy drummed his fingers. "Maybe you could go down Lakeshore. I won't make it to Mass on time. It's five forty-five already. It's almost over."

"Hey, it's rush hour."

Tommy sat back. He bit his thumbnail. Where was all his patience? He'd never felt like he was racing against time like this before.

Matthew had told him that after Mass the entire family would go to Noelle's house for supper. Susie, Jed and Mary Elizabeth were not expected back at the mansion until eleven when Mary Elizabeth normally retired.

The cab wove in and out of traffic. Tommy sat on the edge of his seat.

"Pull over here. I can run the rest of the way."

"Are you sure?"

"Yeah. Maybe you can knock off early and see your family, too."

"Bah. My family? A pain in the tush. Who needs 'em?"

Getting out of the cab, Tommy leaned into the window. "You have no idea what it's like to not have a soul in the world to call your own."

The driver stared at Tommy.

"Lonely."

Tommy slapped the side of the door and raced off.

The Cathedral was just as he remembered it. The stained glass windows glittered like jewels. The choir was singing "Hark the Herald Angels Sing". His heart pumped as he ran down the sidewalk.

The congregation had begun to trickle out the doors. Couples huddled together. Children were in awe over the falling snow.

"It's snowing! Now it's really Christmas, Mommie!"

Tommy worked his way around the people. The crowd thickened as he bounded up the front steps. Shoulders pushed against him.

"Hey, watch it," an old man said.

"Sorry," Tommy smiled moving forward.

Standing aside for a trio of teenagers linked arm in arm, Tommy stood on tiptoe making certain Susie had not already left the church.

Dread filled him. *I have to find her.*

"Excuse me, excuse me," he said pushing forward.

More people thronged past him. For every step he took, he seemed to fall back two. Hundreds of parishioners filtered out of the church hindering Tommy's progress.

"Susie!" he shouted to the surrounding crowd. "Susie!

Susie waited for the people in front of them to leave. Then she turned to Noelle who was holding Angela.

"Let's go down to the crèche," she said.

"Gwamma. I want to go home and see if Santa came."

"I know, darling, but I always say a prayer for your Grandpa at the crèche."

"But what if Santa came and I missed him!" Angela started to cry.

Noelle leaned her face to her daughter's ear. "It's tradition, Angela."

"It means a lot to me, Angela," Susie said holding out her arms and smiling.

Angela looked at her. "Okay, Gwamma."

"That's my girl," Susie said while Noelle put Angela on the floor and Susie took her hand.

"I'm coming, too," Chris said taking Kara's hand. "Do you feel up to it, sweetie?"

Kara nestled her infant in the crook of her arm. Looking down at the six week old infant she said, "What do you say, Tom, Junior? Do you want to light a candle for your Grandpa?"

She looked at Chris. "He says 'yes'."

Kissing her cheek, Chris said, "I still think they should have let Junior be the baby Jesus this year. He's the most handsome baby at Holy Name." He slid his finger against the baby's cheek coercing a coo and then a bubble from the baby's lips.

Jed took Mary Elizabeth's arm. "Jed, you don't have to help me. I can make it on my own."

"I wasn't helping you. I was leaning on you," he chuckled.

The family walked away from the congregation toward the front of the church as the organ continued to play the last carol.

Tommy was inside the door but still wasn't making headway. Fearing he'd missed her, he shouted, "Susie!"

A little boy pushed on Tommy's leg. "Move!"

Tommy scanned the crowd. "Susie. Susie!"

Finally into the vestibule, Tommy searched the faces coming toward him. "Susie!" he shouted as loud as he could.

Kneeling at the crèche, Susie felt chills descend her spine. "Susie!"

She stopped praying and looked at Chris. "Did you hear that?"

"Hear what?" Chris asked. "All I hear is the organ."

"Susie!"

Her blood turned cold. She gasped.

"Mom, what is it?" Noelle asked.

"You're as white as a sheet," Chris said.

"Susie!"

"Tommy!" She called back as a radiant smile burst across her face.

"Susie!" his voice came over the tops of the heads of the crowd.

The organ resonated with the final notes to the carol but Susie heard him calling to her.

Is this a dream? A joke? Please God. Let it be him!

Susie stood up. "Tommy!"

"Mom, have you lost your mind?" Chris asked.

"Susie! Susie!" Tommy's joy-filled voice rang through the Cathedral.

Shaking, Jed grabbed Chris's arm. "It's him!" Jed's face beamed with an angelic light.

"What?" Noelle's sharp intake of breath frightened Angela.

The little girl clung to her mother's leg.

"Susie," Tommy stretched around the middle aged man pushing his elderly mother in a wheelchair out of the aisle.

Susie walked away from the crèche then past the altar and to the middle aisle.

"Tommy!" She yelled as loud as she could.

He burst through the last of the crowd.

"Susie!"

Racing toward her, Tommy nearly tripped, but kept going. He felt as if he were racing across a universe.

Blinded by tears and hampered by joy ringing through her body, Susie rushed toward Tommy her arms outstretched. "Tommy, darling!"

He scooped her up into his arms, his mouth coming down over hers in a kiss they'd waited a lifetime to share.

Chris and Noelle stood stunned.

"My boy!" Jed burst into tears as he hobbled quickly toward his long lost son.

Noelle kissed Jarod. "My father! He's come back for us!"

Angela let go of her mother's leg and walked toward the stranger who was kissing her grandmother. "Gwampa? Gwampa?" She turned back to Noelle who had her fist thrust in her mouth, to choke back her sobs. "Mommie! Look! Gwampa Tommy came home. Just like Gwamma always said he would!"

Angela raced down the aisle, overtaking Jed and flinging herself into Susie and Tommy's legs in an embrace.

Kara clung to Chris's arm. "It's a miracle!"

Tommy clutched Susie's face peering into her eyes. "Let me look at you! You haven't changed a bit. Still my sweetheart of Sigma Chi." He kissed her repeatedly.

"Oh, Tommy. Tommy!" She kissed him back crying and laughing with joy. "What happened? Where have you been?"

"Amnesia. I was in New York." He kissed her between words on the lips and eyelids.

"I can't believe it. I thought I saw you in New York." Her eyes flew open. "It was you!!"

"Oh, Susie, it was your faith that saved me," he hugged her tightly.

Angela tugged on his pant leg. "Gwampa!"

Tommy smiled through his own tears. "And who is this?"

"Your granddaughter. Angela. She believed, too."

Chris' tears dropped in globs to his lapel. "I should have believed."

Noelle took his arm. "In your heart you never gave up. None of us did." They walked up the aisle toward the father they'd never met.

Mary Elizabeth stood in the background watching her family. She heard every note the organ played. She saw each and every individual tear being shed by the people she loved. She smelled the pine of the Christmas trees on the altar and scent of the red roses next to her. She witnessed an eerie golden glow around all of them as they moved toward Tommy and Susie. It was God's light that surrounded them. It was the glow of love. That night, her heart grew to a proportion she'd thought only angels could house.

In that moment, she thought she saw her husband's smiling face beaming out at her just past Tommy's shoulder.

He nodded to her.

She smiled and nodded back. She wasn't seeing things. Braxton had appeared to tell her that he was alive in spirit and that he was with her always. He was doing what he could to bring the family back together. She was filled with awe at the miracle love had made.

"Oh, Braxton, we are a holy family after all."

THE END

The Christmas Star